CHRISTMAS FOR THE SHOP GIRLS

RACHEL BRIMBLE

B

Boldwood

First published in 2019 as *Christmas at Pennington's*. This edition published in Great Britain in 2025 by Boldwood Books Ltd.

Copyright © Rachel Brimble, 2019

Cover Design by Colin Thomas

Cover Images: Colin Thomas

The moral right of Rachel Brimble to be identified as the author of this work has been asserted in accordance with the Copyright, Designs and Patents Act 1988.

All rights reserved. No part of this book may be reproduced in any form or by any electronic or mechanical means, including information storage and retrieval systems, without written permission from the author, except for the use of brief quotations in a book review. This book is a work of fiction and, except in the case of historical fact, any resemblance to actual persons, living or dead, is purely coincidental.

Every effort has been made to obtain the necessary permissions with reference to copyright material, both illustrative and quoted. We apologise for any omissions in this respect and will be pleased to make the appropriate acknowledgements in any future edition.

A CIP catalogue record for this book is available from the British Library.

Paperback ISBN 978-1-83703-057-6

Large Print ISBN 978-1-83703-058-3

Hardback ISBN 978-1-83703-056-9

Ebook ISBN 978-1-83703-059-0

Kindle ISBN 978-1-83703-060-6

Audio CD ISBN 978-1-83703-051-4

MP3 CD ISBN 978-1-83703-052-1

Digital audio download ISBN 978-1-83703-055-2

This book is printed on certified sustainable paper. Boldwood Books is dedicated to putting sustainability at the heart of our business. For more information please visit https://www.boldwoodbooks.com/about-us/sustainability/

Boldwood Books Ltd, 23 Bowerdean Street, London, SW6 3TN

www.boldwoodbooks.com

I'd like to dedicate Christmas for the Shop Girls to my husband and amazing daughters who continue to tolerate my somewhat erratic behaviour throughout the writing of every book. You mean the world to me and I couldn't do anything I do without you.
The three of you really are my world... Xx

1

LONDON – NOVEMBER 1911

Stephen Gower clasped his hands behind his back and fought to keep his gaze steady on Inspector King's. 'I appreciate that, sir, but it's for the best that I leave. I've explained—'

'And your explanation does not sit well with me.' The inspector leaned his considerable bulk back in the chair behind his desk and narrowed his grey eyes. 'Those young women and Detective Constable Walker were murdered at someone else's hand, not yours.'

Tension stiffened Stephen's shoulders. 'That may be so, but it was me who chose to not immediately act on those women's fears. I should never have sent Walker to investigate instead of going myself.'

'And who's to say your being there would have stopped what happened? It could just as easily have been you who was killed. The Board's investigation into your accountability that night will be sorted out as quickly as possible. You acted appropriately and I'm confident the Board will echo my sentiments.'

Stephen shook his head. 'Sir, I appreciate your support—'

'But instead of biding your time, you come to me with the

daft idea of working as a security watchman at Pennington's Department Store. What on earth were you thinking by taking yourself off to be interviewed without waiting to hear what the Board have to say?'

'I need to work, you know that. I can't sit around doing nothing while I wait for the decision to be made about whether or not I can continue to work for the constabulary. My mind is filled with those murders constantly. I can't eat or sleep. I need some time away from London. Some time to get my head around everything that happened.'

King rose to his feet, his cheeks mottled. 'How will a detective of your calibre ever be happy wandering back and forth around a damn department store? You'll be bored out of your mind within a week.'

Stephen stood a little straighter. He didn't doubt the inspector's summary was wholly accurate, but he had to get out of the Yard. Out of London. To stay in the capital, to continue working for the police, where memories and images haunted him, was impossible.

He held the inspector's gaze. 'I submitted my resignation over a month ago, sir. Today I leave. There's nothing more to discuss.'

The clock on the office's grey wall ticked away each second, and when the raucous cheer of his fellow officers rang in the distance, Stephen hardened his resolve. Undoubtedly, a criminal of some description had been apprehended. Most probably someone who'd avoided capture for a considerable time, judging by the continuing cheers and laughter.

Yet the inspector did not so much as glance towards the door. Stephen kept himself still. He would not – could not – falter in his decision to leave. No matter what the inspector said or did next, for Stephen's sanity, he had to go.

Today.

'Fine.' Inspector King raised his hands in surrender. 'Go. But there is no chance I'll be accepting this' – he lifted Stephen's letter of resignation from his desk – 'until we hear from the Board.'

'But you'll keep it?'

'Yes, but I won't be opening it. Not yet. If there's nothing I can do to change your mind, you'd better get going.' He slowly walked around the desk and stood in front of Stephen, surprising him when he clasped his shoulders. 'You're a fine officer and an even better man. One case will not finish your time here.'

A knot of shame and frustration pulled tight in Stephen's gut. 'I don't see Walker's, Fay Morris's and Hettie Brown's deaths as a *case* and never will.'

The inspector's wily gaze burned into Stephen's. 'Whether it was their deaths, the manner of their killing or the fact we didn't get to them before that bastard Thorne did, I only want what's best for you. And...' He inhaled a long breath. 'If you can't stand more than a day in that bloody shop, you come back here and I'll find you a place to work. It might not be at the Yard, but I'll find you something.'

Stephen gave a curt nod, every nerve in his body urging him towards the door. 'Duly appreciated.'

'Good.' The inspector released Stephen's shoulders. 'Then you'd better get going and leave me to break the news to the team. Damn shame you don't want them to know until you're gone. The least they'd want to do is give you a proper send-off.'

'It's better this way, sir.' The coward's way. But how could he stand his colleagues adulation or pity?

'For you maybe, not the rest of us. Go on, get out of here.'

'Sir.'

Stephen picked up his suitcase and left the office. As he walked, he glanced at the men he'd worked with for several years, pleased by their triumphant expressions and mile-wide grins. Once upon a time, the thrill of a capture had been all Stephen needed to sustain him. Not any more. Even as he passed his colleagues' desks and out to the reception area, none of the previous satisfaction he'd found in his work returned. Instead, only a deep, dark sense of failure lingered. Would *always* linger.

Pushing open the building's double doors, he hurried down the concrete steps and into the street. The noise, smog and oppression of London pressed down on him from every direction, making him quicken his steps and bow his guilty head. The sooner he got to Bath, the better.

The blood of two prostitutes and a fellow officer smeared not only Stephen's hands but his soul, too. Culpability writhed deep inside him like a debilitating poison, seeping into his veins and tainting all he was as a policeman and a man. Discovering their bodies, bloodied and beaten, had been the end for Stephen as a public protector and the end of him as a man anyone should rely upon.

Those young, innocent women had come to the police for help. Had petitioned Stephen and Detective Constable Walker as they'd approached the Yard's entrance, insistent that someone was out to get them. Out to kill them. Having smelled the alcohol on their breath and noted their ragged dress and dirty hair, Stephen hadn't been as invested in their claims as he should have been. Instead, with a nod of his head, he'd told Walker to take their names and addresses as a cursory measure, wrongly assuming them either drunk or deranged – a supercilious assumption he'd pay for until his dying day. Later, when he'd ordered Walker to follow up the women's complaint, it had been a command that had cost a young constable – a good and potentially excellent detective – his life.

Which was why Stephen should not be at the Yard making decisions, giving orders. He should be dead, buried six feet under, where he couldn't put anyone else's life at risk.

Damn near jogging along the Victoria Embankment, Stephen clasped his suitcase tighter and lifted his arm to hail an approaching cab. Slowly falling snowflakes wetted the tip of his nose and cheeks and he raised his eyes to the ominous late afternoon sky.

The fact he and his team had eventually tracked down the killer and ensured Thorne hanged from the neck as he deserved served no penance. Stephen doubted it ever would.

So he would return home. Return to Bath, work at Pennington's and spend some overdue time with his mother. His need to flee bordered on cowardice, but a liveable alternative continued to evade him.

He pulled open the door of the cab and stepped back as the driver leaned forward in the light from the lamp beside him. 'Where can I take you?'

'Paddington.'

'Right you are.'

The cab soon drew up outside Paddington, its huge structure rising like an armoured phantom through the snowflakes, and Stephen stepped out onto cobbled stones. He reached into his pocket and handed the driver a cash note. 'Keep the change.'

'Very grateful to you, sir. Safe journey.'

Stephen stared after the cab as it pulled away. *Safe journey.* God only knew what awaited him in Bath, but, with Inspector King's warnings of guaranteed boredom ringing in his ears, he entered the station.

2

CITY OF BATH – NOVEMBER 1911

Cornelia Culford strode into her brother's dining room, hurriedly pulling on a pair of kid leather gloves, her hat ever so slightly askew. 'Why on earth did you allow me to sleep for so long? Did Esther take the children to school again? Oh, Lawrence, really. I am perfectly capable of tending to my children, working and ensuring I help around the house. Esther is looking ever more tired. She should be—'

'She thinks you are marve—'

'Esther is with child. How do you think it makes me feel when—'

'If you'll let me say something...' Her brother arched an eyebrow above the edges of his broadsheet newspaper.

Cornelia slumped, her nerves stretched and her heart racing from having to dress and prepare herself for work at Pennington's Department Store in half the usual time. Damn her soon-to-be ex-husband and his latest letter that had kept her tossing and turning through the night.

He thinks to take the children? Over my dead body. All I was he killed, and now I am reborn. He will never again put me down with his razor-sharp tongue. Never slap or curse me. And he will never, ever have the children.

'Cornelia? Are you even listening to me?'

She blinked from her thoughts and fought to keep the distress from her face. 'Sorry. What did you say?'

'I said, Esther asked that I let you sleep and commandeered the task of taking the children to school. All before I'd barely opened my eyes this morning. You know how she is around Alfred and Francis.' He smiled. 'How she is around *all* children.'

Cornelia sighed. 'She's been a wonder ever since the boys and I came to live with you. I've no idea how or when I'll be able to return your generosity. A newly married couple with a soon-to-be divorced sister and her abandoned sons living with them is hardly recipe for a lustful honeymoon period.'

'Lustful? Do you mind?' He laughed. 'It's barely past eight-thirty in the morning.'

'Eight-thirty?' Cornelia gasped. 'I must go.' She glanced at the table and pinched a slice of buttered toast from Lawrence's plate. 'Life feels such a struggle at the moment. To lose my job as well...' She bit into the toast and then, realising she'd smeared butter on the thumb of her glove, groaned and tossed the toast onto his plate. 'Now look what I've done.'

'Cornelia...' Lawrence put his paper to the side and gently curled his fingers around her arm. 'Just listen to me for one minute, will you?'

'Lawrence, please, I need to go.' Her carefully erected facade of strength and positivity wavered under her brother's love. She had to be stronger than this.

'Not before I've said what I have to say.'

The concern in his tone pushed at her conscience and Cornelia nodded.

'Esther and I are worried about this ideal life you think you need to create for Alfred and Francis. You're tired, quite possibly play-acting and most certainly afraid. You do not need—'

'Afraid?' Humiliation burned hot at Cornelia's cheeks. 'Don't be absurd. I'm determined, strong and wholly more capable than either you or David give me credit for.'

'Do not compare me to that waste-of-space, cheating husband of yours. I may be a lot of things, but I am not a philanderer, a deceiver or a man who will ever walk out on his children.'

She closed her eyes. 'I'm sorry. Of course, you're nothing like David. You are the antithesis of him, in fact.' She glanced at the clock above the dining-room mantel. 'Let us talk about this later. I really must go.'

'Pennington's are unlikely to sack you if you are a few minutes late. Your divorce hearing is coming up. I want to be sure you're ready for it.'

Cornelia swallowed at the reality of having to face David in court. The fear of what he might say, to what the lawyers might subject her, made her ever so slightly sick. 'Of course I'm ready,' she lied. 'The sooner David is out of my life, the better.'

'That's just it. I'm worried you think once – *if* – your divorce is granted, you will be able to begin making your own plans. Whereas the truth is David might want to stay in contact with the children. Which means he'll be in contact with you. You must prepare yourself for that. For the boys' sake, if not for your own.'

Cornelia looked towards the window, away from her brother's penetrating gaze. How was she to tell Lawrence that David intended to fight for full custody of the children? He would retaliate in anger and, for all her brother's love for her, one wrong step and he could unwittingly ruin her chances of keeping them. 'David's interest in the children is little more than a way to hurt me. It wouldn't surprise me, when we are at the hearing, if he wants nothing to do with them.'

'Don't you think his solicitor would have advised him to show willing regarding paternal contact in front of the judge?'

Angered, Cornelia faced him. 'Why are you saying these things to me? Can't you just be supportive?'

'I *am* being supportive.' His jaw tightened. 'And I'll do everything I can to keep David from making your lives any more miserable than he already has. But that doesn't mean I'll let you believe it won't be incredibly tough in that courtroom.'

Denial caught like barbed wire in Cornelia's throat, preventing a sharp retort. 'I need to go. We will speak more this evening.'

She swept from the room and into the hallway, quickly buttoning her coat before she made for the door.

As she hurried along the street, Cornelia's mind filled with David and his soon-to-be fiancée, Sophie Hughes. His long-term fancy woman might well be the daughter of Baron Hughes of Middleton Park, but as she'd been conducting an affair with Cornelia's very much married husband for over three years, *Miss* Hughes was nothing short of a harlot rather than an heiress.

Cornelia sucked in a breath against the cold November air. Rain had fallen for most of the previous day, and with dawn came a cold frost and a decline in temperature. With five weeks until Christmas, she hoped the bitter morning wasn't setting the scene for the rest of winter.

So far, she'd hidden the stigma of her divorce from her colleagues at Pennington's, keeping any potential friendships at bay. No matter her loneliness, her usual trust in people had been shaken, but Cornelia would not allow her distance to last forever. She had nothing to be ashamed of.

Situated on Bath's premier shopping street, Pennington's

Department Store had become her focus the moment she'd discovered Esther, Lawrence's lovely wife, worked there. Having made the decision to petition for divorce, Cornelia's main concern had become building a new life for herself and her children. The famous department store was now her answer to making that happen.

Pennington's had given her hope of a better future, provided an opportunity to become her own person, away from the constraints of her failed marriage and preventing the horrible prospect of returning to Culford Manor. Although her ancestral home was magnificent and the envy of half the county, the house was filled with ghosts of past hurts and trials that neither she nor Lawrence had any care to revisit.

If she was to return, begging for room and board, Harriet, their younger sister and current lady of the house, would positively gloat over Cornelia's need. The woman wanted little more than to become a living embodiment of their tyrannical, social-climbing monster of a mother.

As the memory of her mother's passing pressed down on her, Cornelia lifted her chin. Living and working in Bath was her way of orchestrating a new and happier life. Her sons were surrounded by more love and care than they'd ever been with their often-absent father. Not to mention witnessing the physical violence she endured at David's hands.

Their relocation from Oxfordshire to Bath had been paramount in providing the time she needed to get them on their feet.

She would not fail in her endeavours for new-found freedom.

Pennington's rose above the adjacent stores either side of it on Milsom Street and Cornelia buried her worries, forcing her mind to her work. She rushed through the doors held open by two uniformed attendants, quickly flashing a smile of thanks at the handsomely dressed men before hurrying to her post in the jewellery department.

3

Cornelia drew a feather duster from beneath Pennington's jewellery counter and flicked it over one tray and then another, her mind barely at work, instead lingering over her upcoming court hearing. The letter she'd received from David burned like a smouldering ember in her pocket. Despite her anger, she kept her smile firmly in place and quietly hummed as though all was right in her fragile world.

She'd never told anyone, including Lawrence, about the physical assaults David had inflicted upon her during their worst confrontations. Her pride and shame had been enough to prevent her sharing her sufferings, but, more importantly, she had absolutely no wish to deepen her brother's anguish. David's infidelity and betrayal had been more than enough to provoke Lawrence's protective temper without drawing him to remember their father's cruelty towards him.

Her secrecy had been all well and good when David hadn't contested the divorce, but now he'd mentioned custody of the children, she wondered whether revealing his mistreatment towards her might thwart his intentions. Divorces were more likely to be granted on grounds more suited to the husband than the wife, but maybe David's violence could come to serve her rather than shame her.

He had written that he had every intention of marrying Sophie Hughes as soon as legally possible. They planned for the wedding to take place on 6 April next year and would then take their honeymoon on the maiden voyage of RMS *Titanic* bound for America. The gaiety and spite in his words were almost certainly Sophie's embellishment.

Cornelia snatched a cleaning cloth from beneath the counter and attacked the countertop with gusto. She had no need to know their plans when David hadn't so much as asked how Alfred and Francis were. Why should she wish him well when her bitterness was still so raw, so all-encompassing?

'Ah, Cornelia.' Her supervisor, Mrs Hampton, strode towards her. 'I need you to check on an order for me. It seems the loading department has a discrepancy and, as you put the order through, you're the best person to resolve the issue.'

Worry immediately struck Cornelia. Pennington's had been a huge avenue to buoying her confidence, and fear of losing her position sharply rose. She'd only been working here a couple of months, which made her position precarious. Especially considering all her other skills lay in the running of an estate. Who else would employ her if she left Pennington's without a decent reference? She straightened her shoulders. 'Of course. Can I ask who the order was for and when it was placed?'

Mrs Hampton lifted a ledger onto the counter. 'It was a bracelet you boxed a couple of days ago. The delivery was to be made the same day, but somehow it was noted that it was to go out tomorrow. Do you remember which day Mrs Bainsbridge requested?'

Cornelia frowned. She remembered the bossy, toffee-nosed

Mrs Bainsbridge only too well. 'I do. In fact, I remember following her every word as she chopped and changed her mind about products and delivery times. I am one hundred per cent certain I placed the order as she instructed.'

Mrs Hampton nodded, her gaze on the ledger. 'Hmm, I don't doubt you are right. Mrs Bainsbridge is a loyal Pennington's customer, but she can be most trying at times.' She smiled. 'Speak to Mr Marshall in the loading bay and ask that the delivery is made a priority. I will forewarn Mr Carter and Miss Pennington, in the event Mrs Bainsbridge finds it necessary to complain.'

Dread knotted Cornelia's stomach. 'You think Mrs Bainsbridge would go to the store managers about this?'

'Anything is possible, unfortunately. We must prepare ourselves for all things. Customer service and satisfaction are Pennington's priority. Always.'

Cornelia swallowed. 'Absolutely. I'll be as quick as I can.'

She hurried onto the shop floor, heading for the loading bay situated at the back of the building. She smiled and nodded at the hatted men and women customers as she walked, her shoulders high with a dignity that came from being dressed in Pennington's distinct winter uniform... even if her stomach wouldn't cease churning with uncertainty.

David's letter crackled against her thigh as her long skirt swished around her ankles and her heeled boots tip-tapped against the marble floor. She was determined to look only to the future. David could do as he pleased. He would not win custody of the children. Nothing he did or said would affect her. Not any more.

She gasped and drew to an abrupt stop as a man walked backwards into her path, seemingly oblivious to her presence or anyone else's.

Not wanting the broad and exceptionally tall gentleman to step on her toes, she shot out her hand and pressed it firmly against his back. 'Excuse me, sir.' The man turned, and Cornelia smiled. 'Did you not see me?'

He immediately stepped back. 'I beg your pardon, ma'am. I was watching the door and didn't see you there.'

'And nor will you see anybody if you continue to walk backwards.'

He dipped his head. 'Indeed. I apologise.'

'Apology accepted.' She ran her gaze over his uniform. 'Oh, do you work here?'

'I do.' The man offered her his hand. 'Stephen Gower. Nice to meet you.'

Cornelia slid her hand into his and the breadth of his fingers covered hers completely. 'Cornelia Park... Culford. Miss.'

'Park-Culford? That's an unusual—'

'A slip of the tongue. My surname is Culford.'

His deep, dark brown eyes travelled over her face before he nodded. 'Culford.'

'Yes.' Cornelia looked to the main entrance. 'I must go. I have an errand in the loading bay.'

'Very well. It was nice meeting you.'

She stepped forward and then stopped again, her curiosity sparked by the quiet study in his eyes. She turned. 'You're new here, are you not?'

'I am. I started as a security watchman just this morning. I hope you'll forgive my nearly trampling you. I'm still familiarising myself with the store, its staff and customers, and breaking a lady's toes is hardly the best way to go about it.'

Cornelia smiled, consoled that she wasn't the only one overawed by Pennington's size and reputation. 'Well, good luck, because I've been here a little over two months, and some days I find myself as unfamiliar with the workings of the store as I was on my very first day.'

'That's good to know, although as security I need to make sure I get a handle on things quicker than most.'

Cornelia studied him as he surveyed the bustling area around them. His dark hair was almost the same shade of brown as his eyes, his jaw as finely shaped as his mouth.

Once again, he offered her his hand. 'Well, I should get on. It was nice meeting you.'

She forced herself to hold his gaze. David always hated her conversing with other men, and his long-reaching dominance continued to linger no matter how much she might hate it. It was rousing to fight back. 'You have a natural authority about you, Mr Gower. I don't doubt you will excel in your role here. Welcome to the Pennington's team. I wish you every happiness in your work.'

He slowly drew his hand from hers as his gaze darkened with unease. Cornelia frowned. 'Did I say something wrong?'

He shook his head. 'Not at all. Goodbye, Miss Culford.'

She opened her mouth to halt him, but, with four strides of his long legs, Stephen Gower was swallowed up in Pennington's crowds.

'Well,' Cornelia murmured. 'What a strange man.'

Shaking her head, she walked beneath a Christmas garland of holly, ivy and tiny sparkling sequins arched over the store's double doors and tried to embrace a little of the season's joy, but even with a light snow falling outside, nothing helped.

4

Elizabeth Pennington, co-owner of Pennington's, walked across her office on the store's executive floor towards her husband, where he stood staring out of the window.

'The poor man has only been working here a week, Joseph.' She gently placed her hand on his rigid back. 'You cannot raise the subject of Lillian's murder with him yet. We must bide our time.'

His jaw tightened. 'Time – *wasted* time – is all I think about.' The low growl of his voice wound a knot in Elizabeth's stomach.

He sharply turned, his beautiful blue eyes blazing with frustration. 'Another woman is dead. Another woman murdered while trying to help the poor. Beaten and stabbed in an alleyway. Possibly dragged there. How can the police not see this is almost identical to what happened to Lillian?'

Pain seared Elizabeth's heart to see such anguish in his eyes as she stood before him unable to soothe him. Unable to help him. 'I'm just asking that you wait a little longer before approaching Mr Gower. He was under no obligation to disclose his previous position at Scotland Yard, but he did, and now we must respect his honesty by allowing him to work freely for us. At least, for a while.'

'I wouldn't have to ask him at all if the damn police would open their eyes and ears and take what I have to say seriously.'

'I know, but—'

'Mr Gower could help us, Elizabeth. He'll have contacts, strategies and skills that could find her killer once and for all. He wasn't just any ordinary policeman, for crying out loud. Stephen Gower worked for Scotland Yard. Bath's crimes will be a drop in the ocean to him when he has dealt with the violence prevalent in London.' He stepped away from her, swiping his hand over his face. 'I am tired. Tired and angry. It's been nearly four years and still the man who killed my wife roams free. I won't stand by any longer when our own investigations are getting us nowhere.'

Tears pricked Elizabeth's eyes and she blinked them back, hating herself for the jolt in her heart that Joseph had lately begun to refer to Lillian as his wife over and over again when it was now Elizabeth who wore his wedding ring. Yet, how could she not forgive him his pain when she felt it so deeply too? Until Joseph accepted he had no fault in Lillian's murder, that he wasn't to blame for not accompanying her on her rounds that night, Elizabeth feared he would suffer for the rest of his life.

'You need to calm down.' She took his hand. 'I am hurting for you so much, but with each week that passes I fear what you will do next. We have to be sensible. Methodical and careful. The last thing we want is for Mr Gower to leave Pennington's because of the pressure we are putting on him with something that has nothing to do with his employment.'

'That won't happen.'

'How can you be so certain?' She tightened her grip on his fingers, desperate to find the words to placate a little of the dangerous frustration bubbling inside the man she loved with all her heart. 'Stephen Gower must have left Scotland Yard for a reason, or why else would he be here? Who's to say it isn't police work he has tired of? To present him with an unsolved murder on his first week at the store will serve no positive purpose. You must trust me, Joseph.'

He ran his gaze over her face. 'I do trust you.'

'Then leave Mr Gower be. At least for a little while. Please.'

He closed his eyes and tipped his head back, his pulse visible in his neck.

With each passing day, Joseph's behaviour became more and more unpredictable. His once soft and happy gaze angrier and more frustrated. They had known each other – loved each other – for almost two years and the longer his first wife's killer remained undetected, the more Joseph became enveloped in a dark and dangerous shadow, despite all Elizabeth's efforts to offer escape from his misery.

Helplessness pressed down on her as she cupped his tense jaw. 'I understand that Mr Gower could be the key we have been waiting for, but let's ensure he stays at the store for as long as possible. That's all I'm asking. We will ask for his help when the time is right.'

'There's that word again. Time. I'm sick to death of it.'

Shooting her a glare, he strode to the door and left her office. Elizabeth watched him storm past her secretary's desk and along the wood-panelled corridor to his own office.

What was she supposed to do to make him listen? To harangue a member of staff in such a manner wasn't just unfair, it felt morally wrong. Mr Gower was perfectly in his rights to go about his work unmolested, but Joseph continued to hang renewed hope of bringing Lillian's killer to justice on a complete stranger. Elizabeth crossed her arms. It gave her an incredibly bad feeling.

She slowly walked to the door and softly closed it, but her hand remained tight around the handle as a lone tear slipped down her cheek. What else could she do but try to keep Joseph calm? To prove she understood his vexation. Yet, she knew in her heart that if he approached Mr Gower prematurely and too vehemently, everything they hoped to gain would be lost.

Pushing away from the door, she walked to her desk and pulled some papers towards her. For the twentieth time in as many days, she scanned Mr Gower's application for a job as a Pennington's security watchman. There was no clue as to why he had left Scotland Yard, only that his superior had given him temporary leave for an undetermined amount of time. Which had been perfectly acceptable to Joseph... considering the assistance Mr Gower could possibly provide him.

Elizabeth frowned. Stephen Gower hadn't entirely left the police force. Could he be on some sort of a sabbatical? In Bath for another reason? A personal reason? Why would a man, a sergeant no less, leave such a position unless he needed to distance himself from detection and crime solving?

The pressure of finding Lillian's elusive killer was bringing strain on Joseph, but it was also perpetuating a threat to his and Elizabeth's newly married life. She wanted a baby. A family. To show their love through the birth of their children. Joseph would not even consider that happening until Lillian's murder was resolved. Which was exactly why Elizabeth had agreed, at least in principle, with the notion of involving Mr Gower.

It could no longer just be her and Joseph doing what they could to find this faceless animal. Too much time had passed, and they had got no further in the hunt. The Bath police had failed to turn up a single lead and the press were no longer interested. Or at least they weren't until this most recent killing. Joseph was right, the similarities were too many to ignore. The poor woman's body had been found in an alleyway near the city's slums. A good woman doing her best to provide a little food and comfort to the poor, just like Lillian. Stabbed and left for dead, her basket of offerings strewn.

Surely the police would have to step up their investigations once more? Charitable women helping the needy should not be at risk of being murdered. The whole situation was repulsive. There had to be a way to make the police listen to Joseph. But, once again, having taken his statement, Joseph was turned away. Accused of hysterical miscalculation, of imagining links that did not exist. Hence the escalation in his volatile behaviour, his deepened anguish and liability to do something – anything – he hadn't done before.

And it was that risk, that possibility, that made Elizabeth's hands tremble as Stephen Gower's application slipped onto her desk.

5
___

Stephen sat alone in Pennington's staff dining hall, the day's newspaper open in front of him as he read the latest articles about King-Emperor George V's upcoming visit to India. It was reported that the much-anticipated coronation, or *Durbar*, as it was called in India, would take place two weeks from now, on 12 December. The procession and celebrations were expected to be of a magnificence never seen before by the British public. It would be interesting to see what images filtered through over the coming days and weeks.

He leaned back in his chair as his mind filled with the comings and goings at Pennington's. The over-the-top glitz of the place, with its chandeliers, displays of fresh flowers and alabaster columns, Pennington's decor was a far cry from the surroundings he was used to in his police work, but he'd conceded that the contrast could possibly do him some good. Lord knew, he wanted to embrace anything that provided distance from his life in London.

Men and women chattered and laughed all around him. An air of companionship that wasn't too unlike the camaraderie he'd enjoyed at the Yard. The staff appeared happy. As though their working lives satisfied them as much as their personal lives. Not that he would know about such things considering he'd always spent more enjoyable hours at work than alone in his lodgings.

Sara, his ex-fiancée, had been gone from his life for two years and the pain he'd felt at her walking away no longer hurt as it once did, but that didn't mean he didn't still feel the void she'd left. She could hardly be blamed for her honesty. For the integrity she had shown by admitting the prospect of life as a detective sergeant's wife wasn't for her. His often-missed meals, the forgotten planned days out and visits with their families had eventually taken their toll and Sara had told him she was too young, too hopeful of a happy future, to marry someone entrenched in the lives of London's worst kinds of people.

He hoped she was happy with her life. After all, considering everything that had happened, Sara had been right in her thinking and her wish to be away from him.

Picking up his tea, Stephen glanced at the wall clock and quickly drained his cup.

'Ah, Mr Gower.'

A male voice sounded across the room and Stephen turned. Joseph Carter. One half of Pennington's management team.

'Mr Carter, sir.'

Stephen half-rose in his seat and Carter stilled him with a raised hand. 'No need to stand on ceremony. I'm glad I've caught you when you've finished your lunch.'

Resuming his seat, Stephen nodded. 'Is there something I can help you with, sir?'

'On the contrary. I thought you might appreciate a closer tour of the store. I've meant to catch up with you ever since you arrived, but it's been one thing after another and I have only just found myself with a free half an hour or so.' Carter smiled, his blue eyes bright and friendly. 'So, what do you say? Shall we take a walk?'

Stephen glanced around him and caught the curious gazes of a few of his colleagues, while others seemed impervious to Joseph's presence. Did upper management make a habit of visiting the staff quarters?

He faced Carter. 'I don't see why not, considering you're the man in charge.'

'Then it will be a pleasure for us to get better acquainted.'

Stephen placed his cup, plate and cutlery on his tray and carried it to the clearing station before joining Carter at the dining-room entrance.

Carter smiled. 'Why don't we start on the third floor and work our way down?'

Following him from the dining room, they strode along the corridor towards the lift and Carter pressed the call button. 'The fifth floor is the executive floor. As you probably know by now, the fourth floor houses the Butterfly restaurant as well as a few private offices, and the shopping departments are spread out on the ground, second and third floors. It's on those three floors that you'll be spending most of your time. Petty theft is a problem in every city, as I'm sure you know. But here at Pennington's, we intend to keep any such activity to a bare minimum, if not eradicate it altogether. Having said that' – Carter watched the dial above the lift as it slowly moved down the floors – 'I appreciate it will be a tough task to ask of you or any of the security watchmen. Even someone with your exemplary skills.'

Immediately uneasy, Stephen stared at Carter's turned cheek. 'My skills, sir?'

His employer turned, his genial smile dissolving as his gaze sobered for the first time since he'd walked into the staff dining quarters. 'You were forthcoming in your interview about your former position at Scotland Yard, Mr Gower, and that experience can only be advantageous to Pennington's.'

Stephen carefully studied him, annoyed that his police work should be raised so soon. 'Maybe, but I hope I made it clear that my days at the Yard are to be forgotten for the time being.'

'Of course, but that's to Pennington's benefit and the constabulary's loss, I'm sure.'

The lift shuddered to a stop before the attendant stepped out and dipped his head. 'Mr Carter, sir.'

'Good afternoon, Henry. I trust all is well today?'

'Yes, sir.'

'Glad to hear it. The third floor, please.'

Stephen took a free spot a little away from Carter and the five other people in the lift, as Carter shared a few moments' conversation with them. A horrible suspicion niggled that his new employer had orchestrated this impromptu tour as a way to discuss Stephen's career in London, rather than his work at Pennington's. Well, if that was the case, Carter would soon learn he was on a fool's errand.

They arrived at the third floor and stepped onto the elegantly decorated landing. The carpet flowed in a full circle around the grand staircase, which spiralled down the centre from the fourth floor to the store's atrium. The bright and inviting departments were each marked by white alabaster columns, the wares displayed in such a way as to entice eager customers deeper inside. Pennington's was, in short, pretty spectacular.

'So...' Carter walked to the mahogany balustrade and opened his arms, pride showing in his slightly flushed cheeks. 'This is Pennington's, Bath's finest department store. But, in many ways, it's more than that. My wife and I want people to come here not just to shop but to socialise, spend enjoyable time and make friends. To return again and again with more and more friends and family. Our entire mission is to make Pennington's a place accessible to people from all walks of life – male, female, young or old, rich and not so rich.'

'It seems you are well on your way to achieving your goal, sir. The place is packed to the rafters and has been all morning.'

'Yes, but still Elizabeth, my wife, and I remain unsatisfied. We want Pennington's to be a place people feel safe, free of crime and judgement. That's where you and all the staff come in, Mr Gower. Everyone who works here is an integral part of the machine. One that I do my best to keep running smoothly, but I can't always do that when other matters weigh me down.'

Carter's lower, more urgent tone drew Stephen's focus from the bustling atrium, unwelcome concern rippling through him.

The man's jaw was tight, indecision clear in his eyes, before his smile reappeared, and he patted Stephen's shoulder. 'Come, let us tour the third floor. You have much to learn and get acquainted with.'

Stephen stepped forward, surreptitiously glancing at Carter again. His demeanour was changeable, on edge. Something serious bothered his new employer and Stephen had a horrible feeling that same thing would soon be bothering him too.

6

Cornelia emerged from Pennington's staff exit onto the street and immediately ducked for cover under one of the store's window awnings. The rain fell in huge, fat drops, careening diagonally on a fresh wind. Without an umbrella, she would be soaked to the skin by the time she reached Lawrence's house. She shivered and pulled her coat belt tighter around her waist. She'd been on her feet for five hours since lunch and was entirely exhausted. It was just as well she had nothing planned this evening other than eating dinner with her family, bathing the boys and putting them to bed. She didn't doubt she would tumble into her own bed shortly afterwards.

Looking up at the dark sky, she grimaced. How long was she to wait here? Or should she make as graceful an attempt at hurrying home as she could?

'Maybe you'd like to share my umbrella, Miss Culford?'

Cornelia started. 'Mr Gower.'

He smiled, his dark brown gaze amused under the light spilling from Pennington's window. 'I don't think this rain is going to let up any time soon.'

Cornelia hesitated as thoughts of David's reaction to her going anywhere with another man surfaced. 'I thank you, Mr Gower, but I'm most likely going in a different direction.'

'I can't possibly stand by and let you go anywhere unprotected in this weather.' He offered her his arm. 'Let me walk you home. Or were you hoping to catch the tram?'

Cornelia stared into his eyes, looking for any sign that his offer was anything less than gallant, and saw only kindness. 'I am walking, but... well, if you're quite sure.'

'I am.'

Steadfastly burying her reservations, she slowly took his elbow and they started along the street.

'So.' Mr Gower cleared his throat. 'Where is home?'

'The Circus. I live with my brother, his wife and their children. Well, Rose and Nathaniel are actually Lawrence's children rather than Esther's, but...' *What are you doing? Stop babbling.* 'Anyway, yes, I live on The Circus.'

'Well, that's not too far at all and I am currently staying with my mother, who has a house on Gay Street. We are almost neighbours.'

His friendly tone eased a little of her tension and Cornelia released the breath she hadn't been aware she'd been holding. 'Currently staying? You have a house outside of Bath?'

The silence that followed immediately told Cornelia she'd said something, or rather asked something, that Mr Gower had not welcomed.

Her cheeks heated. 'I'm sorry, I was just making conversation. If you don't want to—'

'London.' He stared ahead, his jaw decidedly tighter. 'I live in London, for the majority of the time.'

'Oh, I see.'

They continued along the street, the atmosphere growing

increasingly strained with every step. What on earth was she doing walking along a dark street with a strange man? If Lawrence were to look out of the window on their approach, his questions would know no bounds.

'Can I ask you something, Miss Culford?'

She glanced at him. 'By all means.'

'How well do you know Joseph Carter?'

'Not very well at all. My sister-in-law, Esther Stanbury – she's the head window dresser at the store – is very good friends with Miss Pennington and Mr Carter, but I barely know them at all. At least, at the moment I don't.'

'But that could change?'

'Maybe, in time. I've only been in Bath a short while. If I stay here longer, I assume I will get to know them socially because Esther and Lawrence regularly dine with them.'

'Right.'

The quiet contemplation in his tone piqued Cornelia's curiosity and she glanced at him again. 'Why do you ask?'

'No reason.'

Their eyes met and his gaze roamed over her face. When her cheeks warmed a second time, she quickly looked away. 'There's always a reason behind every question, don't you think? You must have wanted to know *something* about Mr Carter.'

'Not all questions. After all, what might my reason for asking you to share my umbrella have been, other than a want to keep you dry?'

She detected a teasing in his tone, and she laughed. 'You really are quite the conundrum, Mr Gower. One minute so very serious, the next you seem to be almost laughing at me.'

'Not at all.' He dipped the umbrella as the wind and rain changed direction. 'I am just trying to find out as much as I can about my new employers. You, on the other hand, I believe I owe an apology.'

Cornelia frowned. 'For?'

'Almost breaking your toes on our first meeting.'

'Oh, that.' She waved dismissively. 'It's forgotten and forgiven.'

'Good. Clean slate, then.'

'Absolutely.'

The tension dissipated and Cornelia's steps turned lighter as they ascended the steep gradient of the cobbled street that led to The Circus. As they drew close to Lawrence's house, she eased Mr Gower to a stop. 'I think it for the best that I say goodbye here.' She glanced along the circular street. 'I prefer my brother didn't see us, if you don't mind. He's rather protective of me these days and I don't want what has been a pleasant walk home ending in altercation.'

'Of course.' He released her arm. 'Why don't you take my umbrella? You can return it to me tomorrow at the store.'

'Oh, I couldn't possibly—'

'I insist.' He gently pushed the umbrella into her hand, their fingers brushing, before he winked and turned, slowly retracing their steps out of The Circus.

Cornelia watched him until he disappeared out of sight. She had thought Mr Gower quite strange at their first meeting, but now he had caught her attention in the most unexpected way. He seemed mysterious and she had no idea why that should make her any keener to get to know him, but it did.

His height, glossy dark brown hair and eyes made him attractive in an understated way that was mildly appealing. After living with David's egotistical manner for ten trying years, Stephen Gower seemed – at least, on the surface – a most pleasing breath of fresh air.

As she strolled towards Lawrence's house, her smile slowly dissolved as, once again, thoughts of the upcoming court hearing loomed in her mind. As much as she might want to instigate some friendships at Pennington's, her impending divorce continued to hold her captive under the fear of how she would be received by her peers.

She lifted her chin. She had to believe her worries unfounded or she would crumble... and that could not happen. For the sake of her children, if not herself.

Upon reaching the house, Cornelia let herself in and was taking off her wet coat when Charles, Lawrence's butler, emerged from the direction of the kitchen.

'Good evening, Miss Cornelia.' He took her coat and hat. 'The mistress is in the drawing room if you'd like to join her. Can I bring you some tea?'

'That would be most welcome. Thank you.'

Cornelia walked upstairs into the drawing room and smiled. Esther lay on the sofa, her hand gently touching her stomach, her eyes glazed in thought. Cornelia's heart kicked with pleasure. She was so happy for her brother and Esther's upcoming arrival. Lawrence was already a remarkable father and Esther loved his children, Rose and Nathaniel, like her own. This new baby would be a welcome addition for all of them.

'Good evening, Esther.'

'Oh, Cornelia. I was miles away.' Esther snatched her hand from her stomach and blushed as she moved to swing her legs to the floor. 'How was your day?'

'Absolutely fine, and don't you even think of getting up.' Cornelia nodded towards Esther's neat bump. 'Is my future niece or nephew making their presence known, by any chance?'

Esther laughed and immediately relaxed back against the cushions, her hand returning to her stomach, her pretty hazel eyes shining. 'Yes, as he or she has for most of the afternoon. Lawrence likes to think we have a cricketeer on the way. Whereas I think he or she might be an overzealous cello player if the sharp direction of his or her elbows is anything to hold measure by.'

'I remember those days well enough. Alfred was so much quieter when I carried him than Francis. It seems to me they are unborn as they are in life. So be warned.' Concerned by the fatigue lines around her sister-in-law's eyes, Cornelia sat beside Esther and gently lifted her stockinged feet into her lap. 'Here, let me rub your feet for a moment before the children descend from the nursery for dinner.'

Esther closed her eyes as Cornelia began. 'Oh, goodness, that is heavenly.'

Cornelia smiled. Esther had been looking more and more strained over the last few days. Even before Cornelia had come to Pennington's, she'd thought Esther the hardest working woman she'd ever known. Now she believed her to be almost beyond human. Not only did Esther have her work at the store, she was a staunch campaigner for the women's vote, had co-founded a new Bath branch of suffragists, loved and cared for Lawrence's children – not to mention satisfying the whims of her rather demanding Aunt Mary.

Would she find Esther's strength within herself one day? Grab the world with both hands and shake it until her views were heard too? Would she live with confidence and happiness? Right now, she felt little more than a shadow to Esther's brightness.

She turned from looking at her hands to find Esther carefully watching her. 'Is everything all right, Cornelia? You were miles away.'

Cornelia sighed. 'I was just thinking how much I admire you.

You work so hard at Pennington's, come home and see to the children, spend time with your friends at the Society...'

Esther laughed. 'Admire me when I manage to deliver this baby safely as you have Alfred and Francis. Or when I've helped to secure the women's vote or learned to cook as well as Mrs Jackson. Those are things to admire, too, you know.'

'You have no idea how much it means to me that you esteem me in any way. I... feel such a failure. A failure to my marriage. To the boys. To Lawrence.'

'You are a failure to no one, and how on earth could you be to Lawrence?' Esther frowned. 'Your brother is in complete awe of you. He's proud you are going through with the divorce. Proud you are trying to make a new start for yourself and the children. Didn't he do the same thing when he left home? You are a Culford through and through, Cornelia, and I refuse to listen to another word of self-doubt from you. Now, I have a favour to ask.'

Cornelia relaxed her tense shoulders, encouraged by her sister-in-law's confidence in her. 'Anything. You know that.'

'Lawrence is helping with plans for another demonstration in Laura Place this coming Saturday. It's truly wonderful how many members of the Men's League he's persuaded to attend.' Esther grimaced. 'Of course, we can only both be there if you don't mind looking after the children while we're gone. I promised Helen the afternoon off to be with her beau and, as much as I love Charles and Mrs Jackson, neither of them has Helen's patience to tend to four children for the entire afternoon.'

'Of course I'll look after the children,' Cornelia said, as she continued to massage Esther's feet. 'It's the least I can do.'

'Only, I don't want you to feel you have to do anything as a way of thanking us. You are an important part of our family. Our house is yours.'

'I know, but I like to help if I can. But are you sure you're not too tired for the demonstration? You seem so completely exhausted this week. You have been working with the suffragists almost every night and the campaigning on Saturday is bound to take its toll. You must take extra care of yourself. For the baby's sake, if not your own.'

'It's been a tougher few days than usual, I must admit, but most of the organisation is in place now. Plus, I've had to take into account that Elizabeth wants something from every department to be displayed in Pennington's windows before Christmas, which hasn't been an easy task. I'm sure I'll be fine. I'm tired, but loving my work, as always. The new windows will certainly be my biggest project before I leave to have the baby.'

'When will you leave?' Cornelia asked, secretly hoping her sister-in-law had changed her mind about working for the next few weeks. 'Have you spoken to Miss Pennington about it?'

'Yes, and she's been wonderful. I know it's far from usual for an expectant mother to work so long through her pregnancy, but I so want to stay until Christmas.' Esther put her hand on her stomach. 'Of course, asking Elizabeth if she would be godmother to the little one might have helped in persuading her.'

Cornelia smiled. 'I'm sure it did. You're going to be a marvellous mother, Esther. You will take a new baby in your stride, just as you did Rose and Nathaniel. When Abigail died, I feared Lawrence would never find another wife. Their marriage was arranged and lacked love, but he was loyal and committed.' She squeezed Esther's foot. 'Neither he nor I could have expected you to come along and fill his heart like no woman has before.'

Esther blushed. 'Oh, stop it. And, for your information, I

didn't take Rose and Nathaniel in my stride. I was downright terrified of them in the beginning.'

'This baby is going to be the luckiest child. Lord knows, if I'd had half your strength, I would've left David years ago and then, maybe, the boys would be happier than they are now.' Tears clogged Cornelia's throat, and she swallowed, quickly looking towards the drawn drapes at the window. 'You've taught me that life for women might not be the same as it is for men, but that doesn't mean we can't do all we can to narrow the gap.'

'Hear, hear.'

7

Stephen leaned back in his mother's dining-room chair as she laid a dinner plate in front of him laden with beef, roast potatoes, carrots, parsnips and cabbage. Despite his tiredness, he inhaled deeply, the aromas making his mouth water.

'I've only been home two weeks and I'm already putting on weight.' He smiled. 'Are you trying to fatten me up for Christmas?'

Her brown eyes glinted with mischief. 'You'll go a long way to feeding a lot of people once I've cut you up into bite-sized pieces.'

'Is that so?' Stephen picked up his knife and fork as she lifted a white porcelain jug and smothered his meal with rich brown gravy. 'Well, I'm not running around as I was, so I'm going to have to keep an eye on you and your cooking. Don't want to start piling on the pounds.'

She took her seat opposite him and tucked a stray curl behind her ear. 'What's the harm in putting on a little weight? As you said, it's not as though you're chasing down criminals at the moment.'

Stephen inwardly grimaced. They'd spoken briefly about the Board's investigation when he'd arrived, and his mother had immediately jumped to his defence, dismissing the whole thing as if it was no matter to her or in any way affected her faith in him. Yet the tone of her voice illustrated her hidden concern and fretfulness. Just another reason to dislike himself.

'So, how are things at Pennington's? You've barely mentioned the place since you've been working there.' She cut into her potatoes. 'It must be interesting. Seeing all those different people from all walks of life. Pennington's has changed. Everyone seems welcome there these days, not just the uppity lot we used to see coming in and out of its doors. Pennington's still isn't for me, though.'

Stephen watched her. 'Why not?'

She lifted her shoulders. 'I like to shop at the market, where I can see and touch things without feeling I'm being watched.'

Stephen smiled, amused by her disgruntled expression. 'You'll hardly be watched. It's a friendly place. You'd like it there, I'm sure.'

'How can you say I won't be watched when you're working there as a watchman?'

He chewed his food and swallowed. 'Mr Carter is adamant that customers never feel ill at ease. If there is an attempted theft, then we step in only if we are certain of the offence and perpetrator. The last thing Pennington's wants is a reputation for wrongful intervention or customers feeling spied on.'

'Hmm. I'm not convinced.' She popped a forkful of food into her mouth, her eyes glazed in thought. 'So, you like it there, then? You trust your new employers?'

'Of course. Plus, I've only heard people saying good things about Pennington's. Do you know something heinous I should be aware of?' He wiggled his eyebrows in an effort to lighten the mood.

She visibly bristled, sending her grey curls juddering. 'There's no need to mock my concern. You can't trust anyone these days. Look at that poor woman killed down by the river just the other day.'

Stephen hovered his fork by his mouth, his instincts immediately leaping to life. 'Killed?'

'Didn't you read about it in the papers? Some poor dear was ambushed or suchlike. Her body found in an alleyway near the river. They think she was delivering food to those less fortunate.' His mother shook her head. 'I have no idea what the world is coming to. Used to be a time I felt safe in my bed. Not any more.'

Despising his instantaneous professional interest, but unable to resist it, Stephen cleared his throat. 'How was she killed?'

'Stabbed, they say.'

Stephen stared at her bowed head and fought the sudden urge to leave the table and seek out the newspapers his mother left stacked in the parlour. He was suspended from the Yard. A civilian and not a constable, yet murder was murder. How was he supposed to ignore that?

His mother lifted her eyes to his, her expression sombre. 'Such things make me happier than ever you are home. At least for a while.'

He put down his fork and covered her hand with his own. 'Don't let this killing spook you, Ma. Things like this don't happen very often in Bath.'

'You say that, but there have been others. Admittedly, a long time ago, but still.'

Stephen studied her as she ate, his heart swelling with love for the one person who had always loved and cared for him no matter what.

'I'll be staying for the next few weeks, at least.' He raised his eyebrows and looked into her eyes. 'Promise me you won't go dwelling on this murder. I don't want you fretting over it.'

Her cutlery lightly clattered against her plate as she put down her knife and fork and reached for her water. 'Do you think you could ever be more content here than you were in London?'

'You think that I was unhappy in London?'

'Not unhappy, exactly, but you can hardly blame me for being a little concerned how the murder of your poor colleague and those women must be affecting you. There's a lot a child can try to hide from their mother, Stephen, but we always know when our children are suffering.'

'I'm hardly suff—'

'And we know when they are withholding things from us too.' She put down her glass. 'There's no shame in wanting a fresh start. There's only so much a man can take living a life filled with crime and punishment, after all. I had hoped you might consider coming home permanently.'

Words stuck in his throat. He had no idea how long he'd be in Bath. How long before he heard from Inspector King. All he wanted for the time being was to keep his head low and use his time at Pennington's to stave off inevitable feelings of boredom and helplessness.

He put down his knife and fork, stood and lifted his plate. 'I'm getting along well enough at Pennington's. Let's just wait and see, shall we?' He fought to soften the tone of his voice. 'I'm sorry, Ma, but I am absolutely done in and can't even find the energy to eat this delicious food you've prepared for me. Do you mind if I box it up for my lunch tomorrow? Make a sandwich or something? I have another ten-hour shift ahead of me and could do with a few hours' shut-eye.'

She studied him before pushing her plate away. 'Here. Could you see to mine, too? I think I'll have a read in front of the fire while it dies down and then go to bed myself.'

Avoiding her gaze, Stephen took her plate and walked along the narrow hallway to the kitchen. His childhood home was a small but comfortable town house, an easy twenty-minute walk to the town centre and Pennington's. With three bedrooms, a sizeable kitchen and parlour, indoor plumbing and water, it was all his mother wanted or needed. He hoped he could remain here while the Board carried out their investigation, but, if his mother's concerns about him escalated, he'd have no qualms about leaving and finding somewhere else to stay. No doubt by answering her unwanted questions, he'd only add pain to her life. After all, he already had to others.

Once he'd washed the dishes and put everything clean and dry into the cupboards, he made himself and his mother a cup of tea, bid her goodnight and walked upstairs into his old bedroom. He firmly closed the door and wandered to the window.

The night sky was pitch-black, the stars few and rain streamed diagonally in the light of the street lamps. Tomorrow the pavements would glisten with puddles, the air cold and damp… not unlike his mood.

He pondered his time so far at the store. It was fair to say the job was easy, if not altogether boring. If he didn't think about Joseph Carter and their brief half an hour together, he could say his time at Pennington's had been as good, if not better, than he'd expected. He'd had visions of old ladies wanting directions, upper-class toffs looking down their noses at him or women dressed to the nines striding around the place. Yet, on the whole, he'd found nothing but pleasant colleagues and customers too intent on shopping to pay him any attention.

And that suited him just fine. Remaining inconspicuous was all he wanted while he was here.

Plus, he couldn't deny Cornelia Culford was also a reason behind his growing relaxation at Pennington's. Her stunning face filled his mind's eye. It had been a long while since he'd been so struck by a woman's beauty, but with her dark chestnut hair and startling blue eyes, Miss Culford was hard to ignore. He guessed her to be around his age and he couldn't help but wonder why she wasn't married. Not that it was any of his business. He certainly didn't want anyone prying into his life, after all.

He turned his mind back to Joseph Carter. His employer had not shared what bothered him, but Stephen had caught Carter staring at him time and time again, day after day. He didn't doubt it wouldn't be long before Carter approached him again. And, when that time came, he'd have no choice but to listen to what he had to say. Whatever it was, Stephen would pass on his advice, but, if the problem was of a criminal nature, he refused to get involved.

If the Board found him guilty of irresponsibility or worse, God only knew how he'd face his mother, let alone Inspector King. If that happened, Carter should feel grateful that Stephen refused to help him, whatever his problem. As far as Stephen was concerned he was culpable for three deaths and he had no right to involve himself in anyone else's life. A guilty verdict would be welcome. Justice well and truly served.

He closed his eyes and the gruesome sight of three beaten and bloodied bodies showed behind his closed lids. Tears burned, and he squeezed his eyes tighter, despising his weakness. There would never be a day he'd forget Hettie, Fay or Detective Constable Walker. Never a day Stephen would tell himself he had done the best he could. All he could hope for was that, at some point in his pathetic life, he'd be able to meet his own gaze in the mirror.

8
———

Satisfaction swept through Elizabeth as she slowly walked around Pennington's second floor. It was the first day of December and the store had never looked more beautiful, thanks to the talented efforts of her friend and head window dresser, Esther Culford, and her team. The entrance columns to every department donned bright red ribbon and climbing ivy, the newel posts of the grand staircase decorated with silver and gold bunting. Everything was spectacular and wholly Pennington's.

How she would miss Esther when she left in three short weeks to await the birth of her babe. Guilt that she hadn't done more to encourage her friend's early departure niggled at Elizabeth's conscience. Considering Joseph's increasingly worrying behaviour, it was no surprise she had succumbed to her own selfish need for Esther to stay longer at the store. Lord knew it helped to know she only had to venture to the design or ladies' department to have a good chance of finding her friend.

And it was Esther she sought out now.

Entering the ladies' department, Elizabeth was pleased by its busyness and the underlying sense of heady excitement prevalent amongst the female clientele as they perused the merchandise, dutifully attended to by her staff.

'Miss Pennington, good afternoon.'

Elizabeth smiled as she turned to the head of the department. 'And the same to you, Mrs Woolden. I trust all is well?'

'Very well, indeed.' The older woman beamed, her gaze full of pride. 'Was there something you needed from me?'

'I was actually looking for Mrs Culford.'

'She is busy measuring up some dresses in the back room. Would you like me to summon her?'

'No, that's quite all right. I'll go through and talk to her.' Elizabeth glanced around the department again. 'Keep up the good work.'

She left Mrs Woolden and strode behind the serving counter towards the back room. Pulling aside the curtained partition, she found Esther scrutinising several dresses hung on a rack, her brow furrowed in concentration.

'Isn't our winter clothes collection cooperating with whatever it is you have in mind, Esther?'

Esther visibly started. 'Elizabeth! I didn't hear you. Are you looking for me?'

'Yes, but please, finish whatever it is you're contemplating. Your expression was not of someone particularly happy with what they are seeing. Is something wrong?'

'Not at all. I just want every single window to be perfect before I leave and, for once, I can't find exactly what I need.' She shook her head. 'Maybe it's the baby affecting me, I don't know.'

'What do you mean?' Concerned, Elizabeth stepped closer and cupped her friend's elbow. 'Are you feeling all right?'

'I'm feeling marvellous but finding it harder and harder to concentrate as the baby grows.'

Elizabeth's guilt intensified as she steered Esther towards a long sofa at the side of the room. 'Then take a minute or two to talk to me. Come and sit down.'

Esther exhaled heavily. 'It does feel welcome to sit awhile. Was there something in particular you wanted to speak to me about?' She looked into Elizabeth's eyes, her gaze concerned. 'You don't look yourself, even though I can tell you're trying your best to hide it.'

Elizabeth briefly closed her eyes. 'There's not a lot I can conceal from you, is there? I wanted to talk to you about Joseph.'

'Joseph? What's the matter?'

Elizabeth studied her friend, fighting a horrible sense of betrayal towards her husband. What happened in their marriage should stay between them, but the more his anxieties grew, the more Elizabeth struggled to help him. If she didn't share her worries with someone soon, she would explode.

With no mother, a father she couldn't abide for the majority of the time, and very few friends outside of the store, it was Esther who she grew closer and closer to the longer they worked together. Esther could be trusted. She loved Elizabeth as Elizabeth loved her. They were friends. Good friends.

'Elizabeth?'

She blinked and released her held breath. 'I really shouldn't be burdening you with this, but I don't feel I can cope with things on my own any more.'

'Whatever it is, let me help you.'

Elizabeth took Esther's hand in hers and stared at their joined fingers. 'Have you read about the recent murder here in the city?'

'Of the woman offering charity to the poor? Well, yes, it's awful. Why?' Esther's cheeks paled. 'It wasn't someone you knew, was it? Not someone who worked at Pennington's?'

'No, but her death has sent Joseph into a worse state of mind than ever. It's Lillian, you see. He's convinced the same man who murdered her murdered this woman too. He's... he's not thinking straight, Esther, and I'm scared.'

'Scared? But surely Joseph won't do anything silly. He's a sensible, straight-down-the-line sort of a man. You know that better than anyone.'

'Which is why I am so afraid about the change in him. And now he knows we have an ex-Scotland Yard sergeant working here, he's determined Stephen Gower is the answer we've been waiting for.'

'The security watchman?'

'Yes. He's relocated here from London. I have no idea why, but he has made it clear he is here for a while and Joseph sees that as a sign he was sent here for him. For Lillian.'

'And he intends to ask Mr Gower to help find a killer? But that's madness. He can't just blurt something like that to a relative stranger.'

'I know.' Elizabeth slipped her hand from Esther's and collapsed back. 'I don't know how to calm him. How to make Joseph see that we must bide our time. What can I do? It's killing me to see him acting so out of character. He's so on edge and I feel powerless to do anything to help.'

Esther's brow furrowed as she stared across the room. 'You know, it's not impossible that Mr Gower will help him.'

Surprise that Esther would agree with Joseph, rather than her, made Elizabeth sit up straight. 'You think I'm wrong in delaying Joseph talking to him?'

'No, but I do agree with Joseph that he must at least try to take advantage of anything, or anyone, who might be able to help lay his demons to rest. Life is too short not to grab every opportunity of living with a peaceful heart and mind. We both know that.' Esther stood and paced in front of the sofa, her arms crossed above her expanding stomach. 'Maybe we could act as intermediaries with Mr Gower. We would be a lot calmer and a lot less of a threat to him than Joseph. Especially if he's acting so unpredictably.'

Elizabeth shook her head, unsure if any of them approaching Mr Gower was a good idea so soon. 'I really think we need to give the poor man enough time to at least settle at Pennington's before we mention anything to do with his policing and the murders. Whatever will he think of me and Joseph as employers? Asking anything of him outside of his role here is highly unorthodox. Not to mention unprofessional.'

'Hmm. I see what you mean.'

Elizabeth stood. 'Let me think what to do. I feel better just sharing this with you. Every time I'm with Joseph, I am as jumpy as a cat. I had to tell you what is happening. I am so going to miss you when you leave.'

'Well, it's not for a few weeks yet.'

'I know, it's just...'

'What?'

'I also recently received a letter from my father, and it has not helped with my anxieties. He's in Paris and had much to say about the department stores there.'

'Ah. You're worried his interest in the store might re-emerge from its relative silence?'

Dread knotted Elizabeth's stomach and she pressed her hand there as she paced. 'I couldn't bear it if he came back here. With everything happening with Joseph, to have my father reappear and cause us trouble might be the last straw.' Resentment bubbled inside of her and she halted, crossing her arms to stop the trembling in her hands. 'He gave the store to Joseph and me without condition. He has no right.'

'And did you tell him as much?'

'Of course, and he said he was merely *informing* me of the goings-on in France. Nothing more.'

'But you don't believe him.'

'Or trust him. I never will.'

Esther sighed and tucked her arm into Elizabeth's. 'Why don't you come with me to the design department and see how the windows are coming along? I'm sure that will cheer you up.'

Elizabeth forced a smile and tried her hardest to bury the worries hounding her. 'I'm sure that will be the perfect antidote.'

They walked from the back room of the ladies' department and out into the main corridor. But Elizabeth's mind still remained troubled with the best thing to do as far as Joseph and Mr Gower were concerned. It felt right that she did all she could to protect Joseph's heart from further distress, further disappointment, and if that meant she had to be firmer with him than she ever had before, so be it.

It had taken a life of struggle, pain and humiliation to get to where she was as the mistress of Pennington's; it had taken even more to give her heart to a man and believe true love really existed. She could not risk anything, or anyone, endangering the happiness she and Joseph had now that they had found each other.

9

Cornelia stood alone in the small playground area in front of Alfred and Francis's new school waiting for them to finish for the day. Mothers, nursemaids and nannies waited in groups of four or five. Others huddled in trios, sharing umbrellas as the drizzle dampened the shoulders of their capes and jackets. She curled her gloved fingers tighter around her purse, the icy wind biting at her temples.

The women's attention to her had gradually changed over the weeks. Gone were the curious yet warm glances, the odd soft smile and nod from mothers tentatively offering gestures of intended kindness or friendship. Now their stares lacked the welcome of before, their smiles and nods practically non-existent. Clearly, somehow, they had learned of her impending divorce and judged her accordingly. Quite possibly the knowledge had come from something Alfred or Francis had said in the classroom and she could hardly reprimand them for speaking the truth.

She gently stamped her feet, pretending it was for warmth rather than her discomfort at the scorn of the women around her. She pulled back her shoulders, determined to brave the snide or judgemental looks that came her way.

Holding the gaze of one particularly hardened ringleader, Cornelia's heart beat out every one of the five seconds it took for the woman to look away before she turned to her cronies, said something and they burst into an unladylike barrage of spiteful laughter. Cornelia drew on Esther's strength, tenacity and resilience. It was impossible that her ostracisation would go on forever.

The pealing of the school bell rang across the playground, and Cornelia breathed a sigh of relief. The school's dark blue door opened and Miss Barclay, the boys' teacher, came out first, wrapped in a black woollen coat and matching gloves, her young students lined up behind her. A woman who had devoted her life to children, first as a governess and now as a school teacher, Miss Barclay's commitment, attentiveness and care had played a huge part in Cornelia's decision to send her boys to this particular school.

One by one the pupils ran onto the playground and into the waiting arms of their mothers or nannies. Cornelia lifted onto her toes, but she couldn't see Alfred or Francis anywhere as the area around her filled with childish chatter and laughter.

Her heart picked up speed as her panic grew and she pushed her way through the barrier of bodies.

'Excuse me. Sorry, excuse me.' She kept her gaze resolutely on Miss Barclay, fear for her children overriding any concern for anything these women might think or feel. At last, she reached Miss Barclay. 'Miss Barclay? Where are Alf—'

'Ah, good afternoon, Mrs Parker.' The teacher nodded, her dark brown eyes tinged with kindness as she assessed Cornelia over the edges of her spectacles. 'Alfred and Francis are in the classroom. I'm afraid I must ask for a few minutes of your time.'

'Oh.' Cornelia's relief that the boys were safe was quickly quashed by concern about what they had been up to. 'Of course.'

'Just this way, please.'

Miss Barclay turned on her heel and stepped back through the school door, leaving Cornelia to follow. She sneaked a peek behind her. Two or three groups of women still loitered in the playground, their malicious gazes studying her. Shooting them a glare, Cornelia quickly followed her sons' teacher inside.

The smell of beeswax and chalk surrounded her as she entered the school and followed Miss Barclay along a corridor decorated with pictures of holly-and-ivy-strewn fireplaces and candled fir trees drawn in sweet, clumsy, carefree crayon and pencil. The drawings and brightly coloured classroom doors, along with Miss Barclay's amiability, had left her in no fear of Alfred and Francis settling well at St Barnard's Primary School.

Not that she'd had any experience of a real school herself. Her mother had not allowed Cornelia or her younger sister to linger in education any longer than the law demanded. The great Ophelia Culford was everything her daughters needed in a teacher. After all, couldn't everything be learned within the four walls of a nursery with regards to decorum, dressmaking, jewellery and the skill of catching a wealthy husband?

To her mother, things like arithmetic, grammar and book-keeping were for boys' futures, not girls'. Why would she ever consider her daughters' desire for independence, to work and discover the world in their own way?

The notion was laughable.

Alfred and Francis sat at a double wooden desk at the front of the classroom and Cornelia carefully studied them. Any hope her children were about to be praised quickly vanished under the ferocity of Francis's scowl.

'Are Alfred and Francis in trouble, by chance?'

'I'm afraid Francis is, Mrs Parker.' Miss Barclay held her hand out to the desk beside Alfred and Francis. 'Please, won't you sit down?'

Cornelia glanced at Alfred. Her elder child stared straight back, his dark blue eyes clear of any guilt, his mouth relaxed and semi-smiling. She sat and shifted her gaze to Francis. He glared back at her, his arms crossed high on his chest, lips pursed and his chin firmly jutted.

Suppressing a sigh as exhaustion bore down on her, Cornelia faced their teacher. 'Can I ask what Francis has done?'

Miss Barclay stared at Francis, her face expressing concern rather than admonishment. 'Francis has been caught flicking rolled-up paper at students when my back is turned. He put chalk on three boys' chairs twice this week and, finally, he deemed it funny to draw a bottom on my chalkboard when I left the classroom for less than five minutes. Your son, Mrs Parker, seems to be struggling with some discontent either at school or home and it's my wish to get to the bottom—'

Francis sniggered, and Cornelia shot him a glare.

'Needless to say,' Miss Barclay continued, 'Francis does not seem to appreciate the gravity of these misdemeanours. I, on the other hand, most certainly do.' She stood and splayed her fingers on her hips. 'Now, this is your last chance to tell both myself and your mother what is causing this behaviour, Francis, or I will have no other option than to inform the headmaster.'

Cornelia raised her eyebrows in warning at her younger son. She did not want either of her children to have a reputation as a troublemaker and having one of them expelled would hardly be an appropriate thank-you to Lawrence and Esther after all they had done for her.

'Well, Francis? What do you have to say for yourself?'

The anger and resistance in his eyes did not waver. 'It's not my fault.'

'What isn't?' Cornelia snapped, annoyed and more than a little shocked at his insolence and temper. 'The drawing? The chalk?'

'All of it.'

'Then whose fault is it?'

'Yours!'

Cornelia flinched. 'Mine?'

'Yes. If you hadn't left Papa and moved us to stupid Bath, I would still be a good boy. If you weren't getting divorced, me and Alfred wouldn't be teased, pinched and prodded by our classmates. It's your fault. Yours!'

Silence fell on the room with the violence of a slamming door. Harsh. Sharp. Angry.

Cornelia's heart raced as warmth infused her from face to foot. *My God, what have I done to my children? I had no idea Francis was harbouring such resentment.* She looked at Alfred, who stared down at the desk. Did he blame her for their life now too? She turned to Francis. *Where is my shy little boy of a year ago? The son who stood behind my skirts, afraid to say so much as boo to a goose.*

'I want Papa back,' Francis grumbled.

Before Cornelia could respond, Alfred reached across the desk. He clasped his brother's hand and looked at his mother. 'Francis is just muddled, Mama. He doesn't mean it.' He turned to his brother. 'Do you? Once Mama finds it in her heart to forgive Papa things will be better, I promise.'

Francis stared sullenly back, his cheeks bright red and his lips tightly closed.

Alfred's maturity was shaming, and Cornelia's heart sank. How had everything become so complicated? How had she not realised just how badly the boys had been affected by the separation? By everything they had seen and heard when she and David lived as husband and wife? She had been so determined to blame David's actions for hurting their children that she hadn't considered for a moment the boys might blame her.

Guilt twisted her heart. From now on, she would ensure they were entirely protected.

She drew in a strengthening breath. 'Your father gave me no choice but to leave, Francis. You know this.' Hating the crack in her voice, Cornelia kept firm. She didn't feel weak. Only guilty and at a loss for what to do except to take her hurting son into her arms. 'Everything will be all right. You will soon see your father once everything has quieted down and we are more settled.' She glanced at Miss Barclay, who watched Francis, her gaze filled with concern. 'You like living with Uncle Lawrence, don't you?'

Her son continued to glare, his silence deafening with the depth of his hurt and confusion. Miss Barclay cleared her throat and, when she spoke, her tone was significantly softer.

'Mrs Parker, I think it might be best that you take Alfred and Francis home and discuss things privately. Under the circumstances, I will not speak to the headmaster, in the hope that Francis accepts that when we are angry, we need to find another, more productive way to vent that anger, rather than upsetting other pupils.' She stared pointedly at Francis. 'Do you understand, Francis?'

He stared at his knee as he bounced his foot up and down.

Cornelia curled her hands tighter around her purse. How could she have not noticed these changes in her precious little boy? Had Lawrence or Esther?

Guilt dried her throat, and she coughed. 'Answer Miss Barclay, Francis.'

He hitched his crossed arms higher. 'I want to go home now.'

'Oh, we are, but first you will apologise to Miss Barclay and, if she wishes, tomorrow you will apologise to anyone else you have troubled. Do you understand?' Cornelia held his sullen stare until he dropped his gaze to the floor and nodded. 'Good. Then look at Miss Barclay and start as you mean to go on.'

Slowly, Francis lifted his head, his eyes gleaming a little under the lights. 'I'm sorry, Miss Barclay.'

She softly smiled. 'Apology accepted. Now, I suggest you go home and think what you want to say tomorrow to the boys concerned.'

'Yes, Miss.'

Cornelia stood and offered her hand to the boy's teacher as they got to their feet. 'I'm sorry for the trouble, and you have my word I will speak to Francis and there will not be any recurrence.'

Miss Barclay offered a brief smile. 'Then I'll see the children bright and early on Monday morning.'

Cornelia nodded, turned and held her hand towards the door. 'Come along, boys. We will talk further at home.'

Her children walked ahead of her, and Cornelia followed, straight-backed and full of resolve. Alfred had been right in stating she needed to forgive David if they were to move forward. But how was she to do that when she could barely think about him, let alone talk to him? It was a week until the court hearing. How was she to forgive him when all her shame and humiliation would be laid bare for the judge to hear?

She'd never forgive David. Not ever. How could he have sabotaged their marriage and risked hurting the boys? Destroying their family? Well, his affair had blossomed into an upcoming marriage and there was no chance Cornelia would stand by and let her children become embroiled in David's treacherous new beginning.

10

Stephen tugged at his tie knot as he stood in Pennington's lobby, carefully eyeing the crowds. Despite knowing Elizabeth Pennington took immense pride in the store's uniforms, he couldn't get used to quite how rigidly he was expected to wear his tie. When he'd worked the Yard, his tie, although properly knotted in the morning, would invariably end up loosened.

Apparently, Miss Pennington and Mr Carter were responsible for some sort of overhaul of the grand department store and were doing everything in their power to ensure her father's stern, upper-class methods of doing business were never resurrected. Although Stephen had no idea how a pristine uniform symbolised such a rebirth.

He continued his stroll around the atrium, scanning the area with a practised amiability even as he scoured the masses for any sign of wrongdoing. Just the same as he would have in London. He almost laughed at the ludicrousness of such a comparison. He was surrounded by myriad sparkling, shining merchandise. Perfume, flowers and hair cream stormed his senses and classical music constantly drifted to his ears.

Pennington's was so far from his usual habitat he wondered if he'd ever become accustomed to life here, should he choose to stay. Of course, Bath had its seedier side; the murder his mother had told him about was ultimate proof.

He'd avoided reading the papers for fear he would be unable to resist digging a little deeper. He had neither authority nor jurisdiction. Or competence, come to that.

Pennington's was a far cry from anything other than glamorous opulence, whereas most of London's streets were dark, filled with smoke and fog. The stench of urine, waste and days-old food scattered about the streets and gutters.

Yet he had thrived there. Until the murders.

Without a doubt, the store was a whole new world that would take some getting used to. Dotted around the huge space were mannequins of both male and female forms sporting all the latest fashions, from suits and dresses to hats, shoes and jewellery. Amid these waxed humans were marble plinths with great flowing flower displays tumbling from circular bowls rather than vases, the bouquets were so huge.

And lights. Lots and lots of lights. From enormous chandeliers suspended above the sea of shoppers to lamps on counters and, of course, the awesome glass dome than shone multi-coloured prisms in every direction, over every product.

Gone were the days of old-style dry goods stores. The consumer wanted and expected more. Clearly, Pennington's had people in charge who were on the front foot, innovative and eager to expand goods and services, ensuring anything and everything was as aesthetically pleasing as possible. Every product was meticulously designed to play on customer senses. Almost the entirety of merchandise on the ground floor could be touched, smelled or tasted. In short, Pennington's was the epitome of shopping genius.

A group of excitedly chattering, smartly dressed women gazed upwards towards a display of amassed open fans and umbrellas. The creation was by one of Pennington's dressers: Amelia Wakefield, Stephen thought her name was, but couldn't be certain.

He walked past the women and his gaze was drawn to the jewellery counter. Cornelia Culford stood behind the glass cabinets, serving a gentleman dressed in a dark suit and matching top hat. She carried herself with calm authority, her hands slim and delicate, the subtle shine of her nails glinting against the pieces displayed in front of her. She shifted her attention from the jewellery to the customer, who seemed as entirely entranced by Miss Culford as he was his potential purchases.

Stephen understood the sentiment. The gentleman could hardly be blamed if he offered to buy the entirety of the velvet-covered tray Miss Culford had laid before him, faced with her dark hair piled high on her head and styled in thick waves, her pink lips and dazzling smile.

'Mr Gower, isn't it?'

Stephen blinked and faced Miss Pennington as she came to stand in front of him, her green eyes bright as she smiled.

'Yes, it is.' Stephen nodded. 'It's a pleasure to finally meet you, Miss Pennington.'

'And you. Mr Carter has been full of praise for you.' She cleared her throat and glanced around them. 'I understand you've moved here from London?'

He sensed a hesitation in her question. Had her husband sent her to speak to him? Stephen straightened his shoulders, regretting how close he'd come to Cornelia Culford's counter. He glanced in her direction. She stared at them, her brow furrowed as the gentleman customer peered at a bracelet through his monocle.

He turned to Miss Pennington and tried to ignore the strength of Miss Culford's stare. 'I have.'

'Do you have family here? Friends?' Miss Pennington's smile was still in place, but curiosity, as opposed to congeniality, now burned in her eyes. 'I imagine Bath seems positively sedate compared to the bright lights of London.'

'I wouldn't say that.' Stephen looked past her towards the crowds of people walking back and forth. Something told him Elizabeth Pennington was a woman who liked answers. He needed to respond with the utmost caution. He carried far too much shame that he didn't want becoming public knowledge. 'Bath is a city just like any other.'

'Is it?' She raised her eyebrows. 'I beg to differ. I have travelled to London for both business and pleasure many times and feel it has none of the old-world charm found in Bath.'

Surprised she would like anything 'old-world', Stephen asked, 'And you like that?'

'Of course, why wouldn't I? Bath is a beautiful city.'

'It is, but a city is a city, Miss Pennington, and it holds the same unsavoury sorts as London. The same crimes and the same poverty.'

Her smile dissolved. 'Indeed, and it continually bothers me how and when that will ever be resolved. Mr Carter mentioned you have worked for the police. I can only surmise once a policeman, always a policeman, judging from your, might I say, rather cynical view of city life.'

Stephen's defences slipped into place. 'Maybe, but that's not to say I continue to linger in my previous role. There are reasons I left London and I have no intention of resurrecting them in a different place. If you'll excuse me?'

Without waiting for her answer, Stephen walked in the opposite direction, his pulse thumping. Damn. Why had he reacted so vehemently? And to one half of Pennington's management, for crying out loud. If she didn't report his discourtesy back to her husband, it would be a miracle.

Onwards he walked, not really seeing or hearing anything around him. Once again, his fingers pulled at his collar and tie. Inside Pennington's walls, the constraint felt like a noose... and maybe that feeling was exactly what he deserved.

'Mr Gower? Sir? I say, Mr Gower?'

He turned to the feminine voice behind him, already knowing who hailed him and entirely discomfited that Cornelia Culford had chosen to follow him. 'Miss Culford. What can I do for you?'

She faltered in her steps but continued forward, a light flush on her cheeks. 'I was a little concerned by your changing expression when you were talking with Miss Pennington. I wanted to make sure you are all right.'

'I'm quite all right, thank you.' Stephen looked away, hating that he had to speak to her in such an abrupt manner, but having her show him concern would only lead to more questions and deeper curiosity. 'I'm a grown man, Miss Culford, and more than capable of speaking to my employer.'

'Oh, I know, I wasn't implying...' She exhaled and dropped her shoulders, a smile creeping onto her pretty lips. 'I just have a wish to make you welcome, Mr Gower. As we're both new here, it might be good for both of us if we could get along. Be friends.'

'Friends?'

'Yes.' Her eyes were kind. 'You do have friends, don't you?'

'Well, yes, I suppose. Colleagues.'

'There you go, then. From this point forward, we are friendly colleagues. How will that be?'

Before he could answer, she hurried back through the crowds, presumably towards her station at the jewellery counter.

Stephen stared after her. What in God's name had just happened? She considered them friends now? Well, she'd better think again if she thought they'd start having lunch and so forth together. Cornelia Culford might need a friend or two to get through her working day, but Stephen certainly didn't, and the next time he spoke to her, he'd make sure she understood that.

Next time.

11

Cornelia walked slowly towards her brother's home as the conversation between Stephen Gower and Elizabeth Pennington replayed over and over in her mind.

There had been something in Mr Gower's changing expression that had pulled at her. Made her further extend her hand in friendship. He'd looked so defensive and angry with Elizabeth, and then when Cornelia had spoken with him, he'd looked vulnerable and confused. She understood that mix of emotions only too well. Maybe they could find their feet together. Goodness knows, she'd appreciate seeing a friendly face whenever she came to work.

She'd overheard Elizabeth say he'd worked for the constabulary in London. This new information had struck Cornelia's interest immediately. Could it mean Mr Gower was familiar with the goings-on of court cases? Maybe he could help her prepare for her hearing at the end of the week?

Fear over the potential loss of her children haunted her every thought and a horrible premonition that David and his lawyer would succeed in tying her in knots had kept Cornelia tossing and turning night after night.

Her heart lay heavy in her chest as she walked, her fingers slowly turning numb in the steadily decreasing temperatures. A young family passed her and Cornelia lingered over their two small children as a treacherous tear slipped down her cheek. Were they going to dinner somewhere fancy? Maybe a show? She had once thought she and David would be happy, living their lives and becoming closer over time, spending time together as every family should.

She had been a fool.

Although their eventual marriage had been assumed since they were children by her parents and David's, both she and David had entered into it willingly. Having known each other for years, their parents' lands touching one another's, Cornelia had been confident that their fondness would blossom into love.

When the boys were born, she and David had been delighted, both feeling their family complete.

Until David realised the commitment expected of a father. That his and Cornelia's days of hosting dinners, going on holiday on a whim or seeing shows and plays were no longer what she wanted. Once that was clear, he'd found amusement elsewhere.

For a long time, she'd assumed he was frequenting a gentleman's club, meeting up with other landowners once his father started passing more and more responsibility for the Parker estates onto him.

But no, he had undoubtedly been unfaithful to Cornelia for years before he supposedly had his heart taken by Sophie Hughes.

Discovery of his betrayals had been a strain from the beginning.

Cornelia believed in loyalty, care and commitment. His philandering had been a knife in her chest that had only dug deeper as time wore on, until there was nothing between them but resentment and distrust.

The marriage was over long before it had come to divorce.

The front door of the house beside her opened and a laughing couple burst onto the pavement, the tinkling of piano keys and laughter echoing from the within as they embraced. Cornelia swallowed the lump in her throat. Would she ever find such happiness in a man's arms?

She looked ahead and quickened her pace, drawing forth every ounce of her inner strength.

She had to find a way to arm herself. To build a fortress around her weaknesses and stand firm and confident in front of the judge. David had not been a husband to her for many years, a father even less so in many ways. She would not lose the children to him. She couldn't.

With his experience in the police, Stephen Gower would know about court procedures and there was every possibility he could help her. She liked him and was quite certain they would get along famously given half a chance. She would do all she could to deepen their burgeoning friendship in the next day or two, bury her shame and tell him her situation.

He would help her, wouldn't he? Of course he would.

Reaching the house, she put the key in the lock and stepped inside. Today was one of the two days each week that she worked a ten-hour shift at Pennington's, and she was exhausted.

It was almost eight o'clock in the evening, but childish screeches and giggles emanated from the drawing room upstairs. Instead of the sounds making her want to run and hide under her blankets and sink into blissful oblivion, she absorbed her children's happiness like oxygen. As long as they remained in her care, everything would be fine. She unpinned her hat, somewhat dampened by the rain, and set it on the side table in the hallway.

Francis's antics at school had been troubling, and she'd immediately written to David, asking that he visit the boys or at least telephone, praying some connection with his father might ease Francis's clearly unsettled state.

Not that she expected David to respond.

A dark and ugly cloud of resentment came over her and Cornelia immediately fought against it. She would not allow David to infiltrate the boys' happiness this evening. David was responsible for his relationship with their sons and, even though she did not want him winning full custody, she hoped he had a genuine wish to remain a part of their lives. If he proved to her he did, then she would be open to visitation and the boys staying with him over the holidays... albeit the mere thought of Sophie Hughes playing a part in their family irked Cornelia to the bone.

Charles emerged from the direction of the kitchen and strode along the hallway, his face unusually grave. 'Miss Cornelia. Welcome home. Can I help you with your coat?'

'Good evening, Charles. Please.' She sighed. 'It's still drizzling out there. I'm yearning for a white Christmas, as I do every year, but I'm sure I'll be disappointed once again.' She frowned as he took her coat. He seemed to be avoiding her gaze, hesitant, as though he had something difficult to say. 'Is everything all right?'

Finally, he looked at her. 'I think it best you go into the parlour, Miss. There has been an... incident.'

Cornelia glanced along the hallway. 'An incident? What has happened?'

'Please...' He extended his hand in the direction of the parlour. 'It will best for your brother to explain.'

She nodded and quickly walked away, her heart thundering. Charles had looked so sombre, but it couldn't be anything to do with the children, whose laughter still filtered downstairs. Was it Esther?

Opening the parlour door, she entered and stopped.

Esther trembled where she sat on the sofa, Lawrence holding a cup and saucer towards her and staring at his wife with concern, his jaw tight. The atmosphere was strained with something Cornelia couldn't put her finger on, but whatever it was had raised every hair on her body.

Stepping further into the room, she gently cleared her throat. 'Lawrence?'

He started and turned, his face pale with an anger she hadn't seen in him since they'd lived at Culford Manor.

Cornelia swallowed and glanced at Esther, who continued to stare at a spot on the carpet, her shoulders shaking. She looked to Lawrence. 'What has happened?'

'Esther was manhandled by some ruffian as she walked home from Pennington's.'

'What?' Cornelia rushed to Esther and knelt down in front of her. She placed her hand on Esther's cheek. 'My darling, are you all right?'

Esther merely nodded and Cornelia turned to Lawrence. 'What happened?'

'He tried to grab her, but she screamed and fought him off.' He glanced at Esther, his face mottled red with suppressed rage. 'And now she has pains.'

'The baby? Have you telephoned for the doctor? The constabulary?'

'Absolutely no police.'

The low, firm tone of Esther's words sent a jolt of shock through Cornelia. Esther's eyes were rimmed red but wide and lit with a fire that broached little argument. Her ashen cheeks and trembling body belied the firmness in her tone.

'Esther...' Cornelia took her sister-in-law's hand, and as Lawrence vacated his seat, heading for the drinks cabinet, Cornelia sat beside her. 'This man is clearly dangerous. We have to tell the—'

'He was not dangerous. He was inebriated and thought himself extremely amusing.' Esther grimaced and pressed her hand to her stomach, her breaths a little harder. 'The doctor is on his way. I will be perfectly all right.' She closed her eyes and Cornelia held tight to her hand as she glanced across the room at Lawrence.

His knuckles were white around his filled glass. 'I can't let him get away with this, Esther. I won't.'

'You will. I don't want this pursued any further.' She resolutely held her husband's gaze. 'That is my decision. All that matters now is the baby and what the doctor says. I will not have you waste another moment thinking of the man who nudged me.'

'Nudged you?' Lawrence's voice was incredulous. 'The man grabbed your arms, pushed you against a wall, for crying out loud. If I ever find him, I'll string him up by his damn ba—'

'Lawrence, enough.' Cornelia stared at Esther's turned cheek, wondering what on earth could be going through her mind in that moment. Esther wanted this baby so much. If anything should happen as a result... 'Esther, what happens next is entirely up to you.' She shot a glare at Lawrence before facing Esther once more. 'The most important thing is you remain calm and only think of the baby.'

'Then tell that to your brother.'

Cornelia stood and walked to Lawrence, gently gripping his arm. 'This isn't about you. It's about Esther. Right now, you have to do as she asks.'

'How in God's name do you expect me to stand by and let this hooligan get away with touching my wife? Frightening and molesting her?'

Cornelia tightened her grip. 'Because that is what Esther wants. He's gone, but the baby is here, Lawrence. That's it. At least, for now.'

Their gazes locked as Cornelia's pulse raced. What if Esther had been assaulted? Or killed? The recent murder of the poor woman by the slums rose in her mind and she squeezed her eyes shut. It didn't bear thinking about, but it was clear that all Lawrence could do for the time being was exactly as Esther asked.

The doctor was on his way. All would be well.

Slowly, Lawrence's arm slackened under her fingers and he nodded. 'So be it. For now.'

He drew away and resumed his seat beside Esther, sliding his arm around her shoulders and pulling her close.

Thinking it for the best to leave them alone, Cornelia quietly left the room and pulled the door shut.

The noise from the nursery had quieted somewhat, but the sounds of the children's voices soothed her shaken nerves. She stepped towards the stairs, suddenly desperate to embrace Alfred and Francis. They had all come together as a family: she, Lawrence, Rose, Nathaniel, Alfred, Francis... and Esther, who, Cornelia believed, was becoming a solid lynchpin who would keep them all together, come what may. So, when Esther was weakened, Cornelia would be strong.

Once upstairs, she pushed open the drawing-room door. The children, except for Francis, immediately abandoned their play with the army of toy soldiers and horses strewn across the carpet and enveloped her in a tangle of arms around her legs and waist. Their soft innocent smell and chattering greetings instantly warmed her.

She hugged them back, her relief wavering as she stared at Francis over the other children's heads. 'Well, that's the sort of welcome a mother and aunt should receive every time she returns from work.' Her younger son sat alone on the carpet, his gaze intent on a toy carriage. Cornelia straightened, the children's embraces easing away as they returned to their play. 'Francis? Have you a hug for me?'

Francis pushed to his feet and, with his gaze on the carpet, approached Cornelia and tentatively put his arms around her. 'Welcome home, Mama.'

Tears pricked her eyes as she pulled him close. 'I hope you've had a good evening, my love?'

He merely nodded before extracting himself and returning to the carpet. Her heart sank. Was her younger son's unhappiness her fault? Should she have continued to accept David's affair with Sophie Hughes forever?

She swallowed and drew forth her determination. No, she should not. What kind of lesson would she be teaching her children if they grew up to think it acceptable to treat their wives in the same way? She had discovered the affair a long time ago and, somehow, she'd allowed David to convince her his adulterous liaison with Sophie Hughes was over.

So many lies. So much betrayal and heartbreak.

Actions spoke louder than words and her boys would understand that David's behaviour should never be tolerated in a marriage.

She took a seat next to Helen. 'Esther and Lawrence are waiting for the doctor to arrive.'

'It's so terrible.' Helen lowered her voice. 'I have been trying my best to keep the children amused and out of the way, but they know something's wrong. Is the mistress still having pains?'

'Yes, but I'm sure she'll be perfectly all right.'

'All Mrs Culford was fretting over earlier was the upcoming ball she and the master are arranging at The Phoenix. She shouldn't be worrying over such things now. Is there anything I can do to help with that, do you think?'

Cornelia watched the children. 'You already do more than enough. I will see what I can do to help.' She faced Helen again. 'Raising funds for the suffragists is so important to Esther, and she's even involving the suffragettes to unify the Cause. No matter the women's chosen methods of campaigning, their goal of securing the vote is the same. Do you know the date Esther and Lawrence are planning to hold the ball? I'm afraid I haven't asked as many questions about it as I should have.'

'The sixteenth, Miss.'

'I see. Then once Esther has rested for the night, I will speak to her in the morning. Lawrence is an active member of the Men's League fighting for the vote and his owning the hotel makes him a solid and influential figure around town. I'm sure, between us, we can ensure the ball goes ahead as planned.' She smiled encouragingly at Helen even as Stephen Gower – *Detective Sergeant* Stephen Gower – filled her thoughts once more. With Esther's attack, she had more reason than ever to befriend him. 'Do you happen to know if Esther has invited any of the staff from Pennington's to the ball?'

'Yes, I believe so. Elizabeth Pennington and her husband will most certainly be there. I think Mrs Culford's colleague, Amelia Wakefield, was mentioned and a number of others. There will be plenty of people there you're acquainted with.'

'Good. The most important thing is we ensure the ball is a success. We cannot let Esther down.'

'I completely agree.'

Cornelia stared towards the children again. Despite tonight's assault on Esther, too many people had been invited to the ball for it to be cancelled and surely one more person attending wouldn't affect any plans already in place? She would extend an invitation to Mr Gower herself. Although it was probably for the best that she kept her intentions from Lawrence for the time being. Mr Gower had come in and out of her mind all day, but it would be a mistake to evoke Lawrence's and Esther's suspicions about her interest in him.

12

In the staff quarters at Pennington's, Stephen shrugged into his overcoat before reaching for his scarf. All day, customers had been ducking inside the store to seek refuge from the unexpected rain and sleet. Money and Pennington's black and white shopping bags had exchanged hands at a mind-boggling speed. Christmas 1911 was fast approaching, and it seemed the drop in temperatures had not dissuaded people from picking up last-minute gifts, decorations and table dressings.

Reaching into his locker, he retrieved his umbrella and hat before relocking the door. Walking to the row of seats in the centre of the room, Stephen sat heavily, blindly placing his belongings on the chair beside him as dejection settled in his stomach.

Although he was beginning to find his feet at Pennington's, he hadn't entirely put himself forward with regards to building a rapport with his colleagues. His old life at Scotland Yard was proving a difficult obstacle to overcome in order to be a more relaxed individual who woke, went to work and finished with a pint or two in the local pub.

The Board's investigation into his part in the deaths of Constable Walker, Hettie and Fay continually harangued him. The days passed and, still, he received no further word from Inspector King or anyone else. The distance between Bath and London had been what Stephen had needed, but as time wore on, it felt as though he was on the moon. The lack of communication was harder to bear than he'd first envisaged. Although his torment was just. Deserved. And he'd damn well carry it for the rest of his life.

He uncurled his fisted hands and flexed his fingers, trying to push some of the tension from his body. Although he fought to deny it, he already missed policing, missed the chase, the net closing in. Even the damn paperwork had given him a deeper sense of worth than his work at the store. In his time here, he'd stopped one elderly lady at Pennington's doors, duly escorting her to a corner of the department and asking that she return the scarf and brooch she'd lifted. Her innocent gaze had enlarged behind thick spectacles, but the paste diamonds at her throat and ears and the subtle scent of expensive perfume had done little to conceal her crimes. Joseph Carter had let her go with a warning, but the twinkle in her eyes indicated her career of shoplifting and masquerade was far from over, even if she wasn't welcome in Pennington's again.

Standing, Stephen put on his hat and picked up his umbrella before walking from the quarters and along a corridor to the stairs that led to the staff exit.

In addition to the elderly woman, there had been two other persons he'd apprehended. One a young boy of thirteen or fourteen caught slipping several ties from a display at the entrance to the men's department, and a middle-aged housewife who could clearly afford the lifted shawl and set of embroidered handkerchiefs found in her handbag but had evidently felt inclined to prove something to herself and Pennington's.

Three culprits and three warnings.

These people weren't the criminals he was used to detaining. Surely the monotony would get to him sooner rather than later? What then? He couldn't make a decision about anything until he knew the state of his police career.

He continued up the stairs before pulling open the door to a narrow corridor, nodding to the colleagues who accompanied him along the way before he reached the exit and stepped outside.

He sucked in the blast of cold wind that hurtled through the alleyway, the main street shining like a beacon up ahead. Christmas decorations glistened beneath the rain, amber light reflected in the puddles from the street lamps. People rushed back and forth, their heads ducked beneath sodden hats or umbrellas, their overcoats pulled tight across their bodies. The shop windows on either side of him glittered and winked with brightly decorated displays of clothes, toys and trinkets. All manner of gifts carefully and artfully swathed in great swirls of white, green and red satin, reminding everyone of the festive season.

The one thing Bath had over his sleazier patch in London was the excitement and anticipation of Christmas. Victoria and its surrounding area faded beneath the bright lights of Oxford Street and Piccadilly, and so Christmas had not been entirely felt at Scotland Yard.

At least not the gaiety.

More, the drunken brawls, domestic violence and child beatings perpetuated by the overindulgence of drink, laudanum or opium.

A person could certainly visit Harrods and Selfridge & Co

for the pomp and decoration in London, but what of those living amidst the squalor and filth? Holidays were inevitably short-lived, if they knew of them at all. In Bath, people seemed to revel in events. Everyone apparently having one memory or another of the Coronation, which took place earlier in the year, and nobody appeared any less eager to celebrate Christmas.

Except him.

He lifted his gaze to the banners and streamers hung across Milsom Street and tried to drum up some enthusiasm for the twenty-fifth. Nothing but the weight of his solitude echoed back to him.

Pushing his scarf deeper into the neck of his overcoat, he started his walk past Pennington's brightly lit windows. Maybe he could pick up a fish supper for him and Ma. She deserved a treat after looking after him as she had for the last couple of weeks.

As he neared Pennington's gilded double doors, Stephen slowed. Joseph Carter stood on the store's steps, staring ahead, his arms crossed and seemingly oblivious to the last shoppers exiting behind him. The two doormen standing to the side of him brusquely rubbed their gloved hands together as they waited for their employer to depart so they could lock the doors and get themselves home for the night.

The expression on Carter's face once more indicated a troubled man. No matter how many times Stephen told himself to turn away from his employer's interest in him, Carter's countenance made it incredibly hard to do so when it was clear he suffered.

Inhaling, Stephen stepped forward. 'Good evening, sir.'

Carter started, his charismatic smile slipping into place, his eyes clear and alert once more. 'Gower. Good evening. Off home, are you?'

'Yes, sir. Thought I'd pick up some hot food along the way. It's a good evening for fish and chips.'

'You sound like my father. Fish and chips eaten out of the newspaper is the only way to enjoy them, according to Robert Carter.'

'He sounds a fine man to me, sir.'

'Oh, he is.' Carter's voice grew wistful. 'One thoroughly enjoying his retirement.'

Stephen studied the thinning crowds as people hurried back and forth, a passing tram fit to bursting with commuters as they returned home after a day's work. 'I would've thought you'd be keen to get home and into the warm.'

'Oh, I will. In a while.'

The ensuing silence and Carter's stiffened tone prodded at Stephen's conscience. How was he supposed to ignore a troubled civilian after what had happened last time? Could he really live with the risk of missing something that might help Carter? If Stephen turned away again…

He fought the harried beat of his heart, the way coldness swept along the length of his spine. Helping people was what he'd been trained for – what he'd spent twelve years concentrating on since he was eighteen years old. Joseph Carter was a decent man. Highly regarded by staff and customers alike. Word around the store denoted he'd quickly risen from humble beginnings as a glove maker in a small shop on Pulteney Bridge, owned by his father, to becoming one of Pennington's executives. A skilled master of his vocation, Joseph Carter had burst into Pennington's armed with an array of exemplary gloves and designs, going on to prove himself one half of a formidable team alongside Elizabeth Pennington. They had then fallen in love and later married.

On paper, Joseph Carter should be the cat who'd got the

cream, but in these woebegone moments, he wore the expression of a man who'd lost a fortune by betting on the wrong horse.

What choice did Stephen have but to step into the lion's den?

He cleared his throat. 'When I first came here, you implied something was preying on your mind.'

Carter turned, his blue eyes darkening. 'Yes, I remember.'

'Do you mind if I ask if whatever bothered you has been resolved?'

Carter drew his concentrated gaze over Stephen's face, a muscle leaping in his tightened jaw. He quickly turned away and stared straight ahead.

'Far from it. In fact, the problem becomes infinitely worse every day.' Carter spoke the cold, stilted words from between gritted teeth, his shoulders high and his entire body rigid.

Damnation. Stephen briefly closed his eyes before opening them again. 'You inferred there's a possibility my previous work with the police might be of some help to you.'

Carter turned again, the same dark preoccupation in his eyes. 'I did. Do you think you could wait awhile for your fish and chips?'

Stephen nodded. What sort of trouble he'd just stepped into he had no idea, but whatever it was, he instinctively knew his quiet role at Pennington's was endangered. Well, whether for better or for worse, it was clear there would be no going back. Of that much he was certain. 'Yes, sir. I think I could.'

'Then come with me.'

Carter walked back through Pennington's main entrance, leaving Stephen to follow. He nodded at the doormen, flinching slightly when the doors were pulled closed behind him with a loud thud, the bolts thrown into place with ominous finality.

Carter led the way through Pennington's semi-darkness

towards the grand staircase. 'We'll have to take the stairs to the fifth floor,' Carter said over his shoulder. 'The lifts would have been locked down for the night.'

Stephen stared at his employer's back. The fifth floor was the executive floor. Whatever he was about to be privy to was clearly serious.

Further trepidation pressed down on him when they emerged into the thickly carpeted corridor, the walls covered with highly polished wood panelling. Stephen glanced at the closed office doors on either side of him. Various heads of departments' names were etched into the opaque glass windows, unlit wall sconces lining the long corridor until they entered a smaller office housing a chair and desk, wall shelving full of folders, sample books and other paraphernalia. Everything looked meticulously organised. The antithesis of his haphazard filing system at Scotland Yard, although there had never been a file, report or statement Stephen couldn't put his hand on at any given time.

Carter glanced over his shoulder. 'This is Mrs Chadwick's office, my wife's secretary. Let's go in and see Elizabeth.'

Stephen nodded, made all too aware of the depth of Carter's distraction by his use of Miss Pennington's Christian name to an employee. He now knew that whatever Carter had to tell him was personal, and his wife had knowledge of whatever it might be. Experience had taught him it was always better when spouses knew of one another's troubles. Secrets could become the biggest threat to any relationship and, most certainly, a hindrance to any investigation.

Relaxing his shoulders a little, Stephen followed as Carter knocked and entered a back office situated past Mrs Chadwick's desk.

'Elizabeth. I've brought Mr Gower to talk to us. It's time we asked for help.'

She lifted her gaze from the papers on her desk and stared wide-eyed at her husband. Slowly, the shock was replaced with what looked to be unconcealed obligation. She stood, walked around her desk and stared hard into Carter's eyes before turning to Stephen.

She smiled as she slipped her hand onto her husband's arm as though to hold him still. 'Mr Gower, thank you so much for agreeing to speak to us.'

Struck by the sudden and unmistakable tension that shrouded the room, unease rippled along Stephen's spine. Before now, he'd only witnessed a relaxed closeness between the young couple in front of him. He nodded. 'You're welcome.'

Carter's gaze lingered on his wife's turned cheek before he eased his arm from her grasp and waved towards a small seating area by the window. 'Why don't we take a seat?'

Stephen took a deep breath and walked across the room to sit on one of the two velvet-covered armchairs. Miss Pennington and Carter sat side by side on the settee beside him. The swish of traffic passing along the rain-soaked streets and the chatter and laughter of the passing pedestrians filtered through the windows, only enhancing the tense silence inside.

'I think it best if I start at the beginning.' Carter exchanged another glance with his wife, before focusing on Stephen. 'Did you hear about the murder committed recently? A woman was killed, and her body found in an alleyway close to the river.'

Stephen's unease escalated. 'I did, sir. Yes.'

'There has been pitifully brief coverage in the newspapers and, it seems to me, detectives and the police are failing to uncover any clues or information leading to an arrest. The whole thing is a farce.'

Stephen stared at Carter's wretched expression, his eyes blazing with anger and disgust. 'Did you know the victim, sir?'

'No.' Carter looked again at his wife, before closing his eyes and dipping his head. He seemed to fight to gather himself before he stared directly at Stephen. 'But from the newspaper coverage, the similarities hit a little too close to home.'

'Joseph...' Elizabeth Pennington gripped her husband's tense arm, her gaze pleading as she looked at his downturned face. 'Maybe we should speak with Mr Gower another time. It's been a long day. You would be better to go home and—'

'We are speaking to Mr Gower now,' Carter snapped. 'I have no wish to go home or anywhere else.'

Elizabeth Pennington's jaw tightened before she looked away towards the windows. Stephen slowly uncrossed his legs and leaned forward, disquiet whispering through him.

'If you did not know this woman, can I ask why you are so clearly distressed by her death? Was she an employee of Pennington's?'

'No.'

'Then—'

'My first wife was murdered, Gower. Killed and left in an alleyway close to the river.'

Stephen stared at Carter, then Elizabeth Pennington, a prickle of trepidation passing through him. Miss Pennington, again, carefully watched her husband, her green eyes glistening with what looked to be unshed tears.

He clasped his hands tighter in his lap, sickness heavy in his stomach for Carter's devastating loss. 'I'm sorry to hear that, sir. I assume your wife's killer was never found? That you think what happened to her might in some way be linked with this new murder?'

'Yes.' Carter's eyes darkened with anger. 'The similarities in this new killing and my first wife's are too many to ignore. The woman's body was found very close to where Lillian was found. She was stabbed and the food she was carrying stolen. My wife was a charitable woman, Gower. Some might say too charitable, but there was nothing, or no one, who could've stopped her from helping those less fortunate.' His hand trembled as he ran it over his face, his skin pale. 'The dangers were many when she delivered food and clothes to the slum's poor and, most evenings, I would accompany her for fear of her coming under attack in the exact way she was, come the end.'

Understanding dawned as Stephen stared into the sad eyes of a man who still held himself responsible for his wife's death. 'But you didn't accompany her on this particular night?'

'No.' Carter shook his head, his hand clasping Miss Pennington's so hard she winced, but she didn't remove her fingers. 'And that's something that will never cease to haunt me.'

Elizabeth Pennington's gaze was full of anguish. 'Joseph—Mr Carter has done everything he can think of, for many years, to find the man who murdered Lillian. Not only has he undertaken his own investigations, he has repeatedly appealed to the police for help, to no avail. As an ex-policeman you will understand how these random killings quickly become cold when they take place in areas where anger, theft and violence are commonplace.' She glanced at Carter again, her gaze pleading and her tone soft. 'We would really like your help, Mr Gower.'

Nausea rose bitter in Stephen's throat as he looked between Carter and his wife, the beaten and bloodied bodies of Walker, Hettie Brown and Fay Morris rising in his mind's eye. He swallowed. 'I'm no longer with Scotland Yard. You know this.'

'We do...' Elizabeth glanced at her husband, who continued to stare at Stephen, torture etched on his face. 'But isn't there something you can do? Anything that might help us uncover a lead, a possibility of where or how to start looking for this man?' She shook her head. 'My husband cannot go on not knowing who is responsible for murdering his wife. Not seeing justice served for the woman he once loved with every part of him. This is murder. How are we to turn away from such a thing or even begin to move on with our lives without someone paying for the pain and loss of life they've caused?'

Claustrophobia closed in and Stephen curled his hands into fists, his pulse thumping. If the Board discovered he was embroiled in a murder investigation while on suspension, the chances of him being reinstated were close to impossible. His choice of whether to return obliterated before he'd had the opportunity to even consider the remote possibility. How in God's name had this happened? But what the hell was he supposed to do? If he failed Carter as he had Constable Walker, Hettie and Fay, he would most likely face criminal charges, let alone losing his damn badge. But to walk away and do nothing…

He stood and held Carter's gaze. 'I'm sorry, sir, but—'

'Please, Gower. At least think about it. You have family in Bath, do you not? You know the area, know how to speak to people. Please.'

Helplessness and responsibility as a public servant pressed down on him and Stephen closed his eyes to Carter's pain. What did it matter that he eventually found the killer in London? It had done nothing to assuage Stephen's guilt for three people being murdered on his watch. His mind was warped by blame, his skills damaged. If Carter looked to him to seek redemption for his wife and Stephen dashed the man's remaining hopes, what then?

He turned away from Carter's and Elizabeth Pennington's wretched faces. The pleading in their eyes was excruciating.

Pacing a circle, Stephen pushed his hand into his hair and tightly clenched the strands.

Stopping, he turned and looked deep into Carter's eyes. 'Whereabouts did this recent murder take place?'

'In an alleyway by the Rising Sun public house. The name of which is an irony in itself considering its location.' Carter stood, eagerness filling his expression. 'I could take you there now. It would help you to see where Lillian was attacked, wouldn't it?'

Elizabeth Pennington stepped forward and grasped her husband's arm again, her green eyes flashing with clear impatience. 'Joseph, let Mr Gower think.'

Stephen took a deep breath. 'You need to speak to the Bath police. Tell them how you fear the details of this latest murder bear similarities to your wife's. They will listen to you and undoubtedly take your claims seriously, if you press them.'

'I have tried that several times. They don't listen. They think they know best.' Carter's eyes bulged with rage. 'How many times have you dismissed a civilian's claims in the past, Mr Gower? Are you telling me when you worked for the Yard you heeded all information as it was given to you? Did you not occasionally consider people's insight and observation as little more than overwrought hysteria?'

Stephen's heart raced. Carter could not possibly have known how quickly, how brutally, he'd stabbed a knife into his conscience... into his culpability. He swallowed. 'I shouldn't be investigating anything right now.'

'I understand but, please, at least look into what has been reported. I'm begging you. I...' He looked into his wife's eyes, covered her hand where it lay on his arm. 'We need this agony to end. It has to.'

Stephen looked at this young, inspiring couple and his heart sank. How was he to refuse them at least a preliminary enquiry?

The chances were, anything Stephen attempted would come to nothing, considering how little he now knew of Bath, its districts and people. But shouldn't he do something – anything – to try to help?

He drew in a long breath, slowly released it. 'Gather everything you've already tried, any clippings of this latest murder and the similarities with your wife's killing. I'll take a look, but I'm not making any promises I'll uncover any more than you have.'

Carter slumped as his gaze filled with undisguised relief. 'Thank you. Thank you so much.'

Stephen put on his hat and dipped his head. 'Goodnight, sir. Miss Pennington.'

With heavy steps, Stephen walked to the door and out into the corridor, wincing when he heard a strangled sob and Miss Pennington's soft murmurings as she comforted her husband.

Stephen closed his eyes. What in God's name had he got himself into?

13

Cornelia carefully watched Esther where she sat up in bed with her breakfast tray across her knees. Her brow seemed to be permanently furrowed since her assault and when she'd picked up her teacup, Cornelia noticed her sister-in-law's hand trembled. The tension in the house was so strained, and no matter how Cornelia tried to reassure Lawrence all would be well, he wore a constant scowl.

She laid down the morning paper in her lap. 'Is there anything I can do for you? You look so tired.'

Esther's eyes were wide and uneasy above the rim of her cup. She sipped her tea. 'No, I'm fine.'

'You are far from fine. What is it?'

Esther briefly closed her eyes, and when she opened them again, tears shone on her lashes. 'I feel as though I'm losing myself, Cornelia. Which is something I feared happening over and over again when I began to fall in love with Lawrence. Now, it seems, everything I wanted to avoid has come to fruition.'

'Like what?'

'Oh, I don't know.' Esther glanced nervously towards the closed bedroom door. 'I just feel so utterly useless. How am I supposed to support Lawrence and the others at the hotel with regards to the ball? How am I to discuss and make plans with Elizabeth and Amelia when I am away from Pennington's? I am little more than a burden to everyone the longer I remain confined to bed.'

'You are not a burden and never will be. You must rest. You had a bleed yesterday and the doctor said bed rest was imperative. We have to be extra vigilant for the sake of the baby. I know, as does Lawrence, how hard it is for you to be confined to bed like this, but it won't be forever.'

'But I need to do something. I have worked ever since I left home, and I cannot stand being so unoccupied.'

Since Esther's bleeding, the entire household had been consumed with fear for the baby and, as much as Cornelia understood her sister-in-law's frustration, she could not allow Esther to take any risks. 'Why don't I go to The Phoenix after work and ask Lawrence for one or two tasks that you could do for the ball? There must be something that needs organising or ordering that you can do from your bed.'

'He would never agree.'

Cornelia lifted her eyebrows and stared hard at Esther. 'Since when have you bowed down to that brother of mine? We will insist. If I am side by side with you in your need to work, then Lawrence will have little chance of dissuading us. Wouldn't you agree?'

A tentative smile lifted Esther's lips, her eyes shining a little brighter. 'Well, when you put it like that...'

'Leave everything to me. Now, what could you do in the way of helping Elizabeth? Doctor Rubinstein hasn't said you will be well enough to return to work anytime soon, but I'm sure Elizabeth can be persuaded it will be a good idea for me to bring some light work home for you. How about I bring your sketchpad and pencils? You can easily work on your designs.'

'Oh, Cornelia. You're a marvel. I barely slept last night fretting over this and that, instead of concentrating on what I can do, rather than what I can't. If I can work in some small way, it will hasten the time and my confinement considerably.'

'Good. Then I will come home this evening armed with tasks for you to do.' She stood and leaned over the bed to kiss Esther's cheek. 'Now, I must go before I'm late. I'll take your tray downstairs and tell Helen you are resting. Please, close your eyes and try to get some sleep.'

Esther's brow creased again. 'There is one more thing.'

Cornelia lifted the breakfast tray. 'Yes?'

'How are things at the store in general?'

'What do you mean?'

'I'm worried about Elizabeth and Joseph and hate that I can't be there to support them. She sent me word that things will go along just fine without me, but I very much doubt it. She and Joseph are not getting along as they usually do.'

Cornelia frowned. 'Is there anything I can do to help?'

'Maybe, but not yet. I just want you to keep an eye on Elizabeth. If you think she is in any way unhappy, you must tell me.'

'Of course.' Cornelia nodded, curious. 'But you're aware of what it is that is causing them problems?'

'Yes, and if I feel I must tell you in order to help them, I will. I promise. Joseph and Elizabeth are very dear friends of mine and I hate to see them this way.'

'Well, I am always here, you know that. I will see you later.' She turned towards the door and stopped, her mind on her employers and the oddness in Stephen Gower's expression during his conversation with Elizabeth. 'You know, I thought about mentioning your attack to Mr Gower. He worked for Scotland Yard before he came to Pennington's. I overheard Elizabeth mention his work as a detective. There might be something he could do to help us find the man who hurt you.'

'Yes, she told me, but don't bother the poor man with what happened to me. It's not something I want him to be concerned with.'

'But he might be able to—'

'The man is at Pennington's to do his work and leave at the end of the day. It's not fair to unnecessarily burden him... unless we have to.'

Something in Esther's tone suggested that she might have to ask for Stephen's help at some time, but not right now.

Cornelia lowered the breakfast tray to the bed. 'I also thought to speak to him about the divorce hearing. If he's an experienced police officer, he might have some idea of what could occur in court. Any advice he can give me could help in my defence against David.'

'Hmm, that's true.' Esther collapsed back against the pillows. 'Maybe it would be beneficial to speak to him about that, but not about me. It also wouldn't hurt for you to get to know him a little better.' Her tone turned pensive. 'It would certainly be far easier for you to do that than Elizabeth.'

'Elizabeth wants to know Mr Gower better? But why?'

Esther's cheeks reddened. 'I will share with you what I can in good time. You should go or you will be late. Have a good day, won't you?'

Cornelia picked up the tray, her mind full of the implications of why Elizabeth Pennington would have an interest in Mr

Gower. 'I'll see you this evening, then.' She feigned a glare. 'And, in the meantime, behave.'

Cornelia left the room and quietly closed the door. Some way or other, she would speak with Stephen Gower. Today.

Because there was definitely something going on...

14

Cornelia lifted two empty boxes from the floor behind Pennington's jewellery counter and added them to the pile waiting to be collected by someone from the loading bay. She put her hands to the base of her spine and stretched her knotted muscles with as much decorum as possible, surreptitiously watching Mrs Hampton as she served two customers who'd been dallying over the merits of bracelets versus necklaces for half an hour.

Dropping her hands from her back, Cornelia tidied the area. Time and again, Mrs Hampton managed to retain absolute patience and amiability, no matter how fussy the customer. Her manner was impeccable, a trait Cornelia was determined to master.

It had been a busy morning, with customers intent on buying the perfect pieces of jewellery for their loved ones. As Christmas neared, the packaging service Pennington's offered had gathered momentum, the duration spent with each customer lasting longer and longer. Her time had been limited by unpacking and refilling the velvet trays beneath the glass counters, but her pride swelled in a job well done.

Stephen Gower strolled towards the counter, his hands laced behind his back and his eyes slightly narrowed as he surveyed the area around them. Cornelia's stomach knotted with a sudden nervousness. Her desperation to keep Alfred and Francis safe – Esther and the baby safe – meant she had to at least try for Stephen's help. But how would he react to her bothering him with something so personal? A divorce was never considered a positive thing and the last thing she wanted was Stephen's judgement.

He so often displayed a deep seriousness. A gravity she now suspected stemmed from his police work. Although a good-looking man, it was more than his tall stature and broad shoulders that drew her to confide in him. His entire being emanated a calm reassurance that all would be well when he was around.

But how was she to approach such a delicate subject?

She glanced at Mrs Hampton, pleased to see her still occupied with customers.

Making a snap decision, Cornelia abandoned her unpacking and quickly stepped to the counter. 'Mr Gower. Good afternoon. How are you today?'

He turned, a flicker of surprise passing through his dark brown gaze. 'Miss Culford. Quite well. How are you?'

'I'm well, thank you. Can I interest you in anything for your wife, maybe?'

He slowed to a stop, a small smile lifting the corners of his mouth. 'My wife? I am a single man, and one who doesn't very often indulge in jewellery shopping.'

'Well, that is a shame,' Cornelia said, perturbed by the unexpected pleasure it gave her to discover him unmarried. 'Buying jewellery for someone special can be equally as satisfying for the buyer as it is for the receiver.'

His gaze lingered on hers before he turned to scan the busy atrium once more. 'Is that so? Well, right now, I'm working but—'

'You'll come back later?'

He faced her, his eyebrows lifted. 'I was going to thank you for your courtesy towards my non-existent wife.'

She laughed, her heart lifting at the teasing in his eyes, her confidence bolstered. Goodness only knew what tragedies, violence and criminal activity he'd seen over the years, but it seemed Stephen Gower had kept his sense of humour.

'Are you due for a tea break shortly? Only I'd like to speak to you, if I may.'

Wariness immediately darkened his eyes. 'Oh?'

'It's nothing serious, I just wanted to speak to you about the upcoming ball at The Phoenix Hotel. Have you heard about it? It's in aid of women's suffrage. Many Pennington's staff will be attending, and I wanted to give you the details in the hope you're free that evening. It's on Saturday the 16th.' Her garbled words tumbled from her mouth, leaving her slightly breathless, her heart thumping.

He studied her, his focus slipping to her lips for a moment before he met her eyes once more. 'Balls are not exactly my kind of thing, Miss Culford, but thank you for thinking of me all the same.'

Her heart sank with disappointment at his easy dismissal. Whether or not it was wise to like him so much, or so hastily, she would have welcomed the opportunity to spend some time getting to know him away from Pennington's.

When he moved to walk away, she took a deep breath and leaned across the counter, not entirely prepared to accept defeat just yet. 'Why don't we meet for tea in the staff quarters in half an hour? We could still have a little chat.'

His gaze once again turned amused. 'You really are quite the determined lady, aren't you?'

Pleased by his summary, she nodded. 'Yes, Mr Gower. I am.'

Shaking his head, he continued on his way.

Cornelia watched him go with no idea whether or not he would meet her, but, either way, she'd be waiting. She sensed that he was a kind and caring man. A man who would be willing to speak with her. If she could find out more about him, about his previous work, then their conversation might turn naturally to her life, too.

'Cornelia? Do you think you could spare some time to do some more work this afternoon?'

She started. 'Of course, Mrs Hampton. I apologise.'

'Apologies only go so far. Will you please see to the customers waiting over there while I help Mr and Mrs Luton?'

'Yes, Mrs Hampton.'

'You can take your break in half an hour if you wish, but I'd like you back here in twenty minutes. No excuses. We will undoubtedly be run off our feet until closing.'

Cornelia hurried to help the waiting customers. A smartly dressed man and woman who had more than enough money to spend, judging by the pearls around the lady's neck and ears and the gentleman's gold pocket watch and cufflinks. 'Good afternoon, how might I help you?'

The following thirty minutes passed in a blur and Cornelia was soon heading to the staff quarters. She quickly walked downstairs and entered the communal room, looking for Stephen. Spotting him sitting alone and reading a newspaper at a table in the far corner, Cornelia exhaled as relief swept through her. Yet he seemed entirely engrossed in his reading and she hesitated, suddenly feeling it an inopportune moment to disturb him.

No, she had to speak to him while she had the chance.

She strode forward, her buoyancy more than a little enforced, but, after years of practised happiness when she'd lived with David, she was confident in her charade.

She stopped at the table. 'Can I get you a cup of tea, Mr Gower?'

He lifted his study from the open newspaper, his eyes momentarily glazed before he blinked and his focus cleared. 'Tea? Yes, of course. Allow me. Take a seat and I'll get us a cup each.'

Enjoying his easy gallantry, albeit mixed with a curiosity as to what he'd been reading to cause such seriousness in his expression, Cornelia sat. 'Thank you. That's very kind.'

'Not at all.'

He walked towards the serving counter at the side of the room and Cornelia surreptitiously pulled the newspaper closer. She quickly scanned the articles, noticing a small piece about the recent murder in the slums. Was this what he'd been reading? Her quick scan of the page didn't provide anything else that might have caused his perturbed expression.

'Here we are.'

She quickly sat back in her seat, her smile in place. 'Oh, lovely. Thank you.'

Gratefully accepting the cup of tea, she cautiously sipped before lowering the cup to its saucer. 'So, how are you finding Pennington's? I hope you've settled in?'

'I have. The staff seem friendly enough. There are a few characters who are a little curious, but I'll just give them a wide berth, I think.'

'And do I fall on the side of friendly or curious?'

'Oh, definitely curious.'

'Really?' She smiled. 'Yet, you're still sitting with me.'

'Only because I found you difficult to refuse earlier. The question, Miss Culford, is *why* you wanted to speak to me. I've the distinct impression something far more pressing than a Christmas ball is bothering you.'

A faint heat warmed her cheeks. It should come as no surprise he should suspect her motives. A police sergeant did not rise to such a position by accident. He must have been an exemplary officer and, as shameful as it was, her natural inquisitiveness meant she suddenly held a deep wish to know why Mr Gower now worked at Pennington's.

Or if he wasn't really a watchman at all and here under a different guise. She picked up her cup. 'Your accent is London-based, isn't it?'

He nodded and their eyes locked for a moment.

Awareness skittered over the surface of her skin, causing her to quickly feign interest in his abandoned newspaper. 'I'm originally from Oxfordshire.'

'Not too far from London, then.'

'No.'

Silence fell and Cornelia scrambled to think of something, anything, to say. 'So, how are you finding Miss Pennington and Mr Carter?'

She lifted her eyes to his, but he turned away to study the area around them, a muscle flexing in his jaw. 'Why do you ask?'

Cornelia swallowed, his immediate distance was palpable. What on earth had she said? How was she to bother him with her own miseries if the mere mention of their employers annoyed him? The last thing she wanted to do was risk his further detachment.

'Well, I...' She struggled to find the right words and slumped.

Honesty was always the best policy. 'I've heard it said about the store that you once worked for the police.'

He faced her, his expression inscrutable. 'You've heard it said?'

'Oh, fine.' She leaned back a little from the intensity of his stare. 'I overheard Miss Pennington mention you once worked for the police.'

He studied her before he picked up his cup. 'I worked for Scotland Yard, but that part of my life is neither here nor there right now.'

She battled for something else to say. Could he be at Pennington's under subterfuge? His true identity confidential and possibly dangerous?

She lifted her gaze to find him watching her, caution clear in his dark eyes.

'I shouldn't have reacted so animatedly to learning of your previous position, Mr Gower. I apologise. I imagine police work can be extremely dangerous.'

'Indeed, it can. So, if there's no other reason for this tea and chat, Miss Culford...' He slowly stood. 'I'll return to the shop floor. Good afternoon.'

Words failed her as she helplessly watched him walk through the throng of workers towards the exit. She closed her eyes, shame pressing down on her. He had every right to keep his life private. Hadn't she wanted the same thing when she started working here? Now that she wanted his help and had no choice but to share her life, she somehow expected the same from him? She had no right.

She opened her eyes and stared towards the door. When she'd been a child, she'd relied on her own devices and behaviour to save her from her father's cruel attentions. Then she'd been forced to do the same again with David, once he began to look at her with derision and loathing. It came as no surprise that the whole idea of being honest about her weaknesses and fears with yet another man was mortifying and terrifying.

But what choice did she have if she was to keep her children safe beside her?

Mr Gower could not have been a policeman without care for the public's sufferings. Such a thing was impossible. If she could enlist his help, she would be doing something towards fighting to get her life back. Her children's lives. Such steps would make her feel worthy again. To prove herself more than the reason behind her children's sadness.

Cornelia pushed to her feet. She had to be strong and assured for her boys, Esther and Lawrence.

Never stop fighting. Never give up.

And, as God was her witness, she never would.

15

Elizabeth stared at Joseph as he happily cut into fish and potatoes, his shoulders more relaxed than they had been in days. Although it was inevitable she was about to upset his positive mood, she had to say something. He had to know just how angry she'd been that he'd approached Mr Gower, despite her reservations and specifically asking him to wait a while.

She looked about the busy restaurant, hoping the noise and bustle would be enough to cover her voice should it accidentally rise. Diners surrounded them and all appeared far too interested in their companions to be concerned with her and Joseph. The Pump Room wasn't really the type of place to tolerate arguing couples, but she hoped that propriety would be to her advantage. She and Joseph would have to retain a modicum of self-control and keep their tempers intact.

She studied him again and her stomach pulled with treacherous desire. The constant fire and passion in their relationship meant that, as heated as their quarrels might become, the bedroom reconciliation was equally as fervent.

He looked up and his smile dissolved. 'Is everything all right, my love?'

She hesitated for a fleeting second before putting down her cutlery and reaching for her wine. 'No, Joseph, it's not.'

Concern immediately clouded his gaze. 'What has happened?'

'You.'

Two spots of colour leapt into his cheeks and he slowly lowered his knife and fork. 'Ah, so, we are about to speak of Mr Gower, I presume.'

She took a fortifying sip of wine and lowered her voice. 'You should not have spoken to him without us further discussing it. It was too soon.'

'I beg to differ. The man has agreed to look into things, has he not?'

'So he said, but who knows how Mr Gower felt about being hoodwinked into such a task? I half expected to come in this morning and one of us find his resignation on our desk. It was wrong to ask so much of him without either of us really knowing him. We have no idea who he is, or how he might react to what he now knows about Lillian.'

'And still you don't understand.' Anger flashed in his brilliant blue eyes, his mouth a thin line.

'I do understand.'

'No, Elizabeth, you don't. I have to do something. Why is that so difficult for you to comprehend? It's been years, and still a man with my wife's blood on his hands walks free. Now a second woman has been unlawfully killed. Why on earth should I keep my silence? Mr Gower worked for Scotland Yard. He can help us.'

Frustrated, Elizabeth glanced about them, guilt niggling at

her that she'd caused her beloved husband so much upset. 'I love you, Joseph. So much.'

'I know.' He reached across the table and squeezed her fingers, his gaze softening. 'As I love you, but I can't let Lillian's murder stay in the background of our lives any more. I won't. I want her killer found and brought to justice.' He shook his head, his eyes unblinking. 'I have to do this. The time is now. She deserves to rest in peace.'

Tears pricked Elizabeth's eyes as unwelcome selfishness pressed down on her. 'And what about us, Joseph? What about our lives? Our future?'

'What of it?' He slipped his hand from hers, his jaw hardening. 'We have years ahead of us. We have plenty of time.'

Pain slashed her heart. 'How can you say that? You, of all people, know how quickly life can change. How things can be taken from us in a single day.'

His cheeks reddened and he glared for a long moment before slowly closing his eyes. His shoulders slumped. 'You're right. I'm sorry.' He opened his eyes, his gaze sad. 'I know I'm not the man you married right now, but give me time and he will return. I promise.'

'Oh, Joseph.' She forced a smile. 'I know he will.'

'Then, please, just show me a little more patience. I can't go through this search without you beside me, Elizabeth. You're my heart and my strength. I need you to believe we will bring this nightmare to an end.'

'I do, Joseph. Really. My hopes are on Mr Gower's shoulders as much as yours, but we must work together. I can't stand by and let you run off with any idea that comes into your mind. We are the figureheads of Pennington's. The people our staff and customers trust to keep the Pennington's name as revered as it is across the county.' Her heart beat a little faster as she reached again for her wine. 'My father is still very much alive, Joseph. He could return from his travelling and pull the rug from beneath our feet without warning. I can't take my eyes off Pennington's or our marriage for a moment. I refuse to give him any excuse to take back what he gave us.'

His eyes darkened. 'He won't. I will never allow that to happen.'

'Then we must remain in the here and now as much as we can, while still doing everything to find Lillian's killer. But, please, can we also make our own plans? Doing so will not mean we are sacrificing anything of the investigation.'

He frowned and reached for his wine. 'What plans are you referring to?'

She swallowed as the familiar pull low in her abdomen gave another untimely tug. 'Children, Joseph. I want us to try for a baby.'

His cheeks immediately paled, and Elizabeth held her breath, her heart breaking.

She held his gaze. 'Do you not want us to have children? To be parents to a little boy or girl?'

He picked up his wine. 'Of course I do. In time.'

'But not now? Then when?' She curled her fingers around the stem of her wine glass to hide their sudden trembling. 'You once told me it was my strength and determination that made you fall in love with me. I haven't changed. I am still the woman you married, and I still want to build a life with you. To love you for the rest of my life.'

He lowered his gaze to his plate before pushing it away. He lifted his eyes to hers. 'And I want you. We will have children, Elizabeth. There is nothing I want more, but for now I must ask you to wait. Once Lillian's killer is behind bars, the rest of my life will be yours. I promise. But... this *has* to be done first.'

A small spark of hope ignited in Elizabeth's chest and she relaxed her tense shoulders. 'Then I will wait.'

He looked into her eyes as though seeking evidence she spoke sincerely. Whatever he saw in her gaze must have pleased him for his face broke with a wide smile. 'It won't be long, my love. Mr Gower will be the man, the key, we have been waiting for. I am so certain of that. Just a little while longer and our lives together can truly begin.'

She took his hand and held it tightly. 'I hope so, darling. I really do.'

16

Later that evening, Stephen walked through the centre of town and along Bath's sloping cobbled streets, heading towards the river. With each step, the aromas of roasted meats, cooked vegetables and spices wafting from open restaurant windows, and the high-pitched gaiety of the richly dressed men and women, lessened. Instead, the stench of rotten food, human waste and the murky smells of the River Avon increased.

A strange sense of familiarity enveloped him as he continued ever closer to the slums and shacks of poverty and away from the sand-coloured town houses of wealth and prosperity.

Any sense that Bath was far removed from the deep, dank streets of London faded as the cries of hungry babes blended with the cursing and swearing of painted prostitutes and stumbling drunkards. His instincts were on high alert as people pitched back and forth along the street, their glazed eyes and their ruddy cheeks personifying their misfortune.

The name of the street he searched for was stamped on his memory, the map he studied earlier in the evening clearly drawn in his mind. If his mother had wondered at his slovenly state of dress, the purposely applied streaks of charcoal on his face and hands, she hadn't questioned him. Instead, she'd merely assessed him from head to toe as he'd passed her in the hallway to the front door, nodded and continued on her way to the kitchen.

His old life hadn't remained a secret for long inside Pennington's, but he'd worry what to do about that in good time. For tonight, he wanted to see the location of the murder that had further inflamed Joseph Carter's need to seek retribution for his dead wife.

He reached the railed embankment edging the River Avon and hitched up the collar of his overcoat, bending his head away from the stagnant smells that whipped along the walkway on a steadily rising wind. He passed darkened forms squatting in corners, some with earthenware jugs clutched in their hands, others with their eyes closed in slumber or distress.

Stephen's stomach lurched at their plight, but he pushed onwards until he came to the area he'd circled on his map, determined by the clippings Carter had given him and through his own research. He stared along the narrow street, with shacks and run-down houses either side, pleased to find the street empty of any humanity, merely inhabited by a couple of stray mongrels as they rooted through discarded trash.

The deeper he walked into the foetid space, the more memories assaulted him. Once again, Constable Walker, Hettie and Fay invaded his thoughts and deepened his guilt. This street bore a horrible resemblance to the place where their bodies had been discovered. The same brown moisture glistened on the mossy walls to pool in dirty puddles at his feet. The same smells of filth and refuse infused his nostrils. The only source of light came from an overhead window and the street lamp at the far end.

He pulled a rag from his pocket and pressed it to his nose and mouth.

The woman had been stabbed and her basket of offerings thrown to the ground, her killer pocketing all he wanted before fleeing. Stephen could hardly blame Carter for clinging to the similarities between this recent attack and that of his wife. Yet, for Stephen, the similarities held little meaning when stabbing and bludgeoning happened all the time throughout England's capital city.

But did they happen with the same frequency in Bath? After scouring the newspapers, past and present, he thought not. Assault on women trying to help the people unfortunate enough to find themselves trying to survive here was abhorrent and surely unusual enough to raise concern, even amongst the slums' downtrodden residents.

Why would someone attack the very people trying to help them and their neighbours? Unfortunately, logic rarely existed amid desperation and depravity. When a person was starving, sleep-deprived and desperate, they lashed out and took what they could without preamble. When a father repeatedly failed to keep his family fed and warm, he could turn vicious and violent. But what sort of person plunged a knife deep into a women's belly, withdrew the blade and struck a second and third time? That was the similarity that bothered him. It didn't speak of a hungry man, it spoke of an angry man. A man intent on settling a score. Of taking revenge.

But why against these particular women? Were they targeted? Or was it their charity that awoke the beast? Either way, if the perpetrator came from the lowlier side of Bath, it was probable he was still in town. The odds of getting out of the slums were stacked against children born into squalor to a nearly impossible height. Years of resentment, struggle and death seeped deep into their blood and marred their souls. Meaning they remained here to adulthood and eventually death.

Footsteps a distance away, followed by the crash and bang of something metal hitting the cobbles spun Stephen around as his muscles tensed. He slid his hand into his pocket and curled his fingers around his cudgel, the blunt weapon his only defence. He wasn't foolish enough to venture into an area such as this without protection.

A man in a dark overcoat and tattered top hat lumbered towards him.

Stephen braced for whatever might come next. 'You there. What are you doing?'

Still, the man came forward. As he stepped closer, Stephen took in the tears and patches on the stranger's overcoat, his laceless boots and the bottle gripped in his hand. A modicum of tension left Stephen's shoulders. If the man was drunk it would be to Stephen's advantage, but if he was play-acting...

'Stay back,' he growled. 'I want no trouble.'

The man stopped a few feet away and swayed back and forth. He lifted his head and his dark eyes glinted in the half-light. 'Who the bloody hell are you? I saw you come in here and waited for your return. Thought a gentleman masquerading as a dropout might be needing some help from someone who knows this stinking place.'

Not taking his gaze from the man, Stephen glared. 'You live around here?'

'Live?' The man tipped his head back and laughed, revealing a few blackened teeth and a puff of breath so rancid, it practically scorched Stephen's eyelashes despite the distance between them. 'A man don't *live* here, sir. He bloody survives, is what he does.'

The man fell against the wall beside him, his shoulder acting as an anchor and Stephen risked a few steps closer. 'Do you know about the murder of a young woman down this way recently?'

The vagrant took a swig from his bottle and swiped the back of his hand across his mouth. 'Yeah, what about it?'

Barely two feet separated them as Stephen tightened his grip around the cudgel. 'Did you know her? The woman who was murdered?'

''Course not. She was hardly the type to give the likes of me her name, was she? She was a good sort, though. Kind. Pretty.' He took another tug on his bottle. 'Came here to do good and got killed for her efforts.'

Surmising from the conversational tone of the man's speech and his relaxed demeanour he was unlikely to stage an attack, Stephen withdrew his hand from his pocket. 'Did you see anything that night?'

'Nothing. They reckon she was dragged into this street from down by the river, so someone must've seen something. Not that anyone would admit to it. Who wants the law on your back when you can barely remember your own name?'

Stephen considered what use this man could be to him. A possible ally or informant was better kept close. He extracted a few pennies from the inside pocket of his jacket and held the coins out in his palm. 'Here. Take this.'

The man eyed the money, his body a little more upright than before. 'What's that for? I ain't one of those nancy boys, you know.'

'I'm sure you're not, but I'd appreciate you asking a few questions about the murder to some of the people who live, drink or sleep around here. What do you think?'

The man reached out and slowly took the money, staring at it before slipping the coins into his shoe. 'You'll be coming back then?'

'Yes.' Stephen nodded and walked past the man towards the light at the end of the street. 'I'll be back.'

17

Cornelia had just put her hand on the gate to Lawrence's house when his front door swung open. Helen emerged wrapped in a coat and scarf, her hat pulled so firmly onto her head the brim almost touched her eyebrows.

'Good evening, Helen.' Cornelia closed the gate. 'Are you finished for the day?'

'Oh, no. I'll be straight back once I've picked up this prescription. Poor Mr Culford is beside himself, but I insisted he stay with Mrs Culford.' Helen's eyes were wide and her lips trembled as though she tried to stop herself from crying.

Concerned, Cornelia glanced towards the house. 'How is she?'

'Not very good at all, Miss. Her colour is awful, but the doctor is pleased that her second bleeding seems to be slowing. The biggest challenge for poor Mr Culford is keeping Mrs Culford resting. She's not one for sitting still, as you know.'

'Indeed, I do.' She squeezed Helen's arm. 'Which is precisely why we'll do all we can to prove to her that the world is still turning and nothing will go wrong at home, in Mrs Culford's work at the store or with the children. Agreed?'

Helen smiled and her tense shoulders slightly relaxed. 'Agreed.'

'Good, now off you go. I'll see you in a while.'

Cornelia stepped back to let Helen pass and then quickly entered the house. Discarding her coat and hat, she hung them on the stand by the door before peeling off her gloves.

The only sounds were the murmurs of male voices on the top landing. Where were her sons, niece and nephew?

She strained her ears towards the kitchen, relieved to hear Mrs Jackson's voice occasionally interrupted by one of the children's. Charles' absence was significant when he was so very rarely away from the hallway or nearby vicinity. Cornelia quickly mounted the stairs and hurried towards her brother and Esther's bedroom.

She slowed to a stop when she reached the top floor.

Lawrence spoke quietly on the landing with an older gentleman with salt-and-pepper hair and a neatly trimmed beard.

She had not seen Lawrence wearing such a terrified, ravaged expression for years and her heart broke for the anguish he must be suffering. Esther and the children were his entire life.

'Lawrence?' She gently touched his arm. 'What can I do?'

Her brother met her eyes. 'It looks as though Esther and the baby will be all right. Given time. This is Doctor Rubinstein.'

Cornelia nodded. 'Hello.'

The doctor offered a small smile, his gaze solemn. 'Good evening.'

'This is my sister, Cornelia, Doctor.'

'Nice to meet you.' Doctor Rubinstein glanced towards Lawrence's slightly ajar bedroom door. 'Mrs Culford is sleeping now. I've given her a draught that should keep her sedated and peaceful until morning. Your maid has gone to get a small supply of sedative should it be needed tomorrow.' He looked at Lawrence. 'There is no need for panic or overt concern, Mr Culford, but it's important your wife takes complete bed rest for at least another week. As for her returning to work before the baby is born, that, unfortunately, is no longer an option. You must see to it that Pennington's are informed first thing in the morning. To carry on as she has will almost certainly mean tragedy, if not for Mrs Culford, then the baby. Do you understand?'

'I do.'

Lawrence's jaw was so tight Cornelia couldn't help but think she could bounce a penny from it. He looked at her and the anguish in his eyes cut to her core.

She tightly gripped his arm and faced the doctor. 'Miss Pennington and Mrs Culford are very good friends. I'm sure Miss Pennington will ensure her immediate departure, regardless of what Mrs Culford might try to insist.' She looked at Lawrence and softly smiled. 'I assume Esther has argued she's quite all right to continue working?'

Lawrence nodded, seemingly unable or not trusting himself to speak.

'Very good.' The doctor nodded at each of them. 'Then I will bid you good afternoon and I'll come by again the day after tomorrow to see how Mrs Culford is progressing.'

Cornelia released Lawrence's tense arm. 'I'll see you out, Doctor.'

'No, no. You stay with Mr Culford. He needs a stiff drink, I think.'

The doctor lifted his hand in a farewell and headed downstairs, carrying his hat and black bag.

Cornelia slid her hand into Lawrence's elbow and pulled him close. 'She'll be all right. You must believe that.'

'I know.' He pushed some fallen hair back from his face, his hand trembling. 'But I must do something about the man who caused this.'

'There is nothing you *can* do. He's out there somewhere amid thousands of people. Just concentrate on what you can do. Take care of Esther.'

'She was asking for you earlier. I think she might want to speak with you about Elizabeth.'

'Cornelia?' Esther's weak call filtered through the open door. 'Is that you?'

Cornelia squeezed Lawrence's arm and hurried into the bedroom. 'It's me, my darling. How are you feeling?'

She walked to the bed and sat on the edge. Esther's skin was pale, her eyes deeply shadowed above grey circles and her lips almost white.

Esther weakly smiled and moved her hand across the bedspread to Lawrence's as he sat on the other side. 'I'm sorry for frightening you, my love.'

'None of this is your fault.' He raised her hand to his lips and pressed a kiss to her knuckles, his eyes tightly closed. 'But no more work, Esther.' He opened his eyes. 'Please.'

'I know. The doctor...' She swallowed. 'He's made it clear that I need to rest and then slow down. I will send a message to Elizabeth in the morning and ask that she comes by with Amelia. There is much to be done, but I know Amelia is more than capable. I won't risk myself or our baby, Lawrence. I love my life now too much to squander it.'

'Good.' He pressed another kiss to her knuckles. 'I couldn't bear it if anything—'

'None of that.' Esther smiled. 'Now, how about you ask Mrs

Jackson to prepare some tea and you leave Cornelia and me to talk? There are some things she can help me with, too, if I am to be housebound.'

He left the room and Cornelia inched a little closer to her sister-in-law.

Tears immediately sprang into Esther's eyes as she shook her head. 'I'm scared, Cornelia. Really, really scared.'

'Oh, my love.' Cornelia leaned forward and gently embraced her. 'Everything will be just fine as long as you do as the doctor says. Babies are stronger than we think. You'll see.'

'I know, but I'm still so worried about Elizabeth. Now we know I won't be returning to Pennington's, I have no choice but to burden you, I'm afraid.'

'Nothing is a burden if it means you will look after yourself and the baby.'

'Elizabeth and Joseph are struggling with a personal issue. One I fear will never be resolved unless someone from the authorities is willing to help them. I now believe Mr Gower came to Pennington's for just that reason.' She gripped Cornelia's hand. 'And I know you are more than capable of supporting Elizabeth and Joseph in my absence.'

'What are they struggling with?' Cornelia frowned. 'And how does Mr Gower fit into it?'

Esther sighed. 'Elizabeth visited this morning, before my scare, and told me that she and Joseph have spoken to Mr Gower and he has agreed to make some preliminary enquiries.'

'Into what, exactly?'

'The murder of Joseph's first wife, Lillian.'

'Murder? My God.'

'Exactly. It happened several years ago, but her killer remains undetected. A recent murder took place under very similar circumstances and now Joseph is convinced the killer of

Lillian and the new killing were carried out by the same person.'

Cornelia stared into Esther's frightened eyes. 'This is awful. I had no idea. Poor Mr Carter.'

'He has struggled with his loss for years, but the murder of a second woman has deepened his anger and determination to see justice done.'

Disbelief wound through Cornelia as she tried to imagine what it must be like for her employers to live with such a thing. Stephen had to help them, if he could. Surely, he would not turn his back on them?

Of course, if he did agree to give his aid with regards to an unsolved murder, there was every chance he'd find helping Cornelia with a domestic court case laughable.

And she could hardly blame him.

She closed her eyes, ashamed for thinking such selfish things after learning of Mr Carter's suffering.

'So,' Esther continued, 'You must do all you can to support Elizabeth and Joseph through this terrible time. I can't be at the store and Elizabeth will only be able to come and visit me when she can. Are you becoming friendlier with Mr Gower?'

'I wouldn't exactly say friendly.' Cornelia grimaced as she thought of the way he'd left her sitting alone in Pennington's staff quarters. 'But that doesn't mean I won't keep trying.'

A little light came into Esther's eyes. 'That's just what I need to hear. I want you to do all you can to ensure he helps Elizabeth and Joseph. This is important to me, Cornelia. You have no idea how much Elizabeth and Joseph have done for me by giving me a start at Pennington's and their friendship since. They won't get through this alone.'

Cornelia firmly squeezed Esther's hand. 'I will befriend Mr

Gower, don't worry. And I'll do everything in my power to help with his investigations and support Elizabeth.'

'It may be that Mr Gower is their only hope. The police are doing nothing to help and—'

'I'll be there for them. Do not distress yourself. If Lawrence were to see you this way...'

'I know and that's why I can only entrust this to you. He cares for me and the children more than anything. If he thought Elizabeth was taking over my thoughts, I worry he'd come to resent her.'

'He won't. I'll ensure it. I will speak to Mr Gower about the court hearing and press him to help Miss Pennington, too. He appears so serious, maybe even a little detached at the store, but whenever I've spoken to him, I've sensed a deep compassion there. I have offered the hand of friendship and I hope, if I tread carefully, he will come to welcome it.'

'But it's not long until the hearing. How will you convince him to help you?'

'I must, for Alfred and Francis. Nothing and no one will stand in my way and leave it open for David to take them away from me.'

'Good.' Esther collapsed back against her pillows and closed her eyes. 'Now you are in charge, I can rest.'

18

Stephen paused on the steps of Pennington's grand staircase and surveyed the scene ahead of him. It was a bright, crisp day and the rainbow of light from the glass dome cascaded over the shoppers and merchandise. Smiling faces and good cheer abounded as customers wove from one counter to another, intent on buying gifts, food and decorations.

The string quartet set up on a dais in the very centre of the vast space played carols, the soft music serenading consumers and adding a touch of the exceptional that was wholly Pennington's. Everywhere Stephen looked, garlands of ivy, entwined with flashes of red holly and pearlescent mistletoe, hung from counters, balustrades and lights. Golden bells and angels dotted arrangements of scarlet poinsettia and jewel-coloured ribbons over department entrances and the lift doors.

Unexpected pride rose inside him. It would take a very hardened individual not to be affected by such a special department store. He descended the stairs, keeping his eyes peeled for anything untoward.

Just as he stepped onto the atrium's marble tiles, a

cacophony of discord broke out. People gasped and hurried away from the entrance, swaying and jostling one another, their faces filled with fear or disgust.

What on earth was going on?

Stephen shouldered his way through the crowd. 'Excuse me, sir. Madam, might I get through? Thank you.'

Two doormen tussled with a shabbily dressed man, whose greying hair was matted and dirty.

Stephen gripped one of the doorman's shoulders. 'What seems to be the problem here?'

'This' – the doorman lost his hold on the man and reached out again to grab the unwelcome guest's arm – '*tramp* thinks he's perfectly entitled to walk in here and talk to whomever he pleases, that's what.'

Stephen looked closer at the man's reddened face as the two doormen continued to manhandle him towards the door. It was the vagrant he'd met in the alleyway. *For the love of God...*

He stepped forward and once again touched the doorman's shoulder. 'Let him be. I'll wager it's me he's here to see.'

'What?'

'Let the man go.' Stephen kept his voice purposely low, but firm, as he glanced around the sea of curious or repelled faces surrounding them. 'I'll ensure he's taken outside.'

Judging by the set of the doorman's shoulders and scowl, he was reluctant to release the man but eventually loosened his hold and stepped back. 'Let him go,' he ordered the second doorman. 'Mr Gower claims to be familiar with this... *gentleman*.'

The vagrant was shoved towards him and Stephen sucked in a breath at the overwhelming stench. He glared at the doorman, his hand firmly on the vagrant's arm. 'Thank you.'

'For Christ's sake, who the bloody hell—'

'Enough of that,' Stephen cut off the vagrant's words over the gasps and huffs of the watching crowd. 'Let's get you outside where we can talk.'

Ignoring the people around them, Stephen frogmarched the man to Pennington's double doors, pushing one open and escorting his 'friend' onto the street.

He walked him away from the entrance and released him. 'How in God's name did you know I worked here?'

The man tugged at the lapels of his sorry-looking overcoat, theatrically brushing at the soot- and grime-covered material as though it was a new purchase from Pennington's men's department. 'I have ways and means of finding out about anyone unusual who comes down by the river.'

'Is that so?'

'Yeah, it is.' The man straightened his top hat and rubbed his finger under his nose, his fingerless gloves revealing his chapped knuckles and dirty nails. 'And you know what I say is true, or how else would I be standing in front of you as I am right now?'

Stephen could hardly argue with the man's logic. He glanced along the street. 'Fair enough.' He faced the vagrant. 'And as you are here, I assume you have some information for me?'

The man grinned and puffed out his chest. 'I do.'

Stephen raised his eyebrows. 'Which is?'

'If we're going to be conducting business, don't you think it would show a bit of etiquette if I knew your name?'

Stephen carefully assessed him. Despite his dress and general unkemptness, the man carried an aura of self-assurance. There was a quiet intelligence and perceptiveness in his silvery-blue eyes, indicating a man who had not always lived – or survived – on the streets.

Stephen cleared his throat. 'My name is Stephen Gower. And you are?'

'Herman Angel, sir. At your service.'

Stephen's curiosity increased as the man took off his hat and swept it in an arc, executing a bow. Clearly, he had once known social manners.

'Well, it's good to see you again, Herman.' Stephen nodded. 'Your visit will be even more welcome if you have something worthwhile to tell me.'

Herman straightened and arched an eyebrow before extending his open palm.

Understanding the universal gesture, Stephen reached inside the trouser pocket of his uniform and extracted some coins. He dropped them into Herman's outstretched hand. 'Well?'

Herman counted the coins and slid them inside his jacket, his eyes lighting up with satisfaction. 'I asked around as you instructed. About the woman.'

'And?'

'And I've been told about a bloke bragging that it was him who killed her.'

'This man...' Stephen's heart picked up speed. He hardly dared to believe such a thing could be true. 'Admitted it was him? Who is he?'

'Not as much admitted, but, to my friend's mind, he seemed to know a whole lot more than he would have if he hadn't been there that night.'

'And who was this man? Your friend knew him?'

'Knew *of* him. There's a difference.'

Stephen carefully assessed Herman's expression, looking for any sign he lied or exaggerated. The other man stared back, his gaze not in any way furtive or disingenuous.

Stephen frowned. 'So, all you can tell me is that you know of someone bragging about this poor woman's demise, but you don't know his name or where I can start to look for him?'

Herman's eyes glinted with amusement. 'Did I say that?'

Stephen tensed, his previous fondness towards Herman threatening to dissolve as quickly as it had emerged. 'Don't play games with me, Herman. You'll lose.'

Their gazes locked before the other man dropped his shoulders and flapped his hand dismissively. 'Ah, and I thought you was a bloke who could take a joke.'

'I don't joke. Not about murder.'

Two spots of colour stained the vagrant's cheeks as his gaze darkened. 'Neither do I. You might assume I walk these streets without care or dignity, but you're wrong, Mr Gower. I have plenty of respect for my fellow man… and woman.'

'I'm glad to hear it. Now, what else can you tell me?'

Herman took a long breath as he looked past Stephen's shoulder along the street. 'I don't know the individual's name, but he's rumoured to be residing near the river, amongst the trees beneath Pulteney Bridge. If you're thinking to look for this arsehole, I suggest you start your search there.'

Adrenaline sparked treacherously in Stephen's blood at the prospect of chasing a potential lead. 'Good. That's information I can use.'

He looked towards Pennington's doors and paused. Cornelia Culford stood on the store steps, slightly shivering, her arms tightly crossed as she watched them. What was going on with the woman that she seemed to be near him at every turn?

He quickly faced Herman. 'Thank you. If you hear anything else, keep it under your hat and don't come back here looking for me. I'll come and find you. Understand?'

Herman's eyes shadowed with consideration before he gave a slow nod. 'No doubt I'll see you soon then.'

Touching his hat, Stephen's new friend meandered along the street, shoulders hunched against a bitter wind that had been rising since first thing that morning.

Turning, Stephen met Cornelia's gaze. It was clear from her expression he had absolutely no way of avoiding talking to her.

He slowly ascended Pennington's steps and looked into her wide, blue eyes. 'Miss Culford.'

She nodded, her gaze sombre. 'Mr Gower.'

'What can I do for you?' Stephen was struck anew by her eyes and the caramel curls that framed her temples. 'Only, I think it would benefit both of us to get back inside.'

'I witnessed the commotion a while ago, and when someone said you took control of the situation, I wanted to make sure you were all right.'

'As you can see, I'm fine.' He gently took her elbow. 'Now, might I escort you back inside?'

'Not yet. I...' Unfamiliar hesitation flashed in her eyes before she cleared her throat and stared at him with complete resolve. 'I need your advice.'

Unease rippled through him. 'My advice?'

'Yes.' She dipped her head towards the side of the steps, indicating they should move away from the stream of customers walking back and forth around them. 'It's about something quite sensitive.'

He studied her. No doubt she intended to ask for a favour of some sort, but he couldn't stand the way she trembled in the cold. If he listened, then maybe he could get her back inside sooner rather than later. Stephen guided her to the side of the entrance. 'How can I help?'

She looked into his eyes, searching for God knew what, before blinking and taking a deep breath. 'I will soon be facing a judge, Mr Gower. In court.'

'Court?' Shock reverberated through him. 'For what?'

'A divorce. *My* divorce.' Her cheeks reddened. 'My husband – soon-to-be ex-husband – is threatening to take my children.' She lifted her chin. 'But I won't allow that to happen and I hope you can help me.'

Stephen briefly closed his eyes. What in God's name had he done to be dragged into not one but *two* cases of people wanting his help because of his police experience?

He met her gaze and found it softly laced with pleading… any refusal he might have momentarily harboured dissolved. Why would she come to him for help unless she had absolutely no one else to ask? Was she alone and fighting to draw a line through her past just as he was?

Rubbing his hand back and forth over his jaw, he sighed. 'Then I'd better hear the whole story. How about meeting for coffee after work?'

Relief lit her eyes, turning them such a brilliant, mesmerising blue, Stephen's heart stumbled a second time.

She grasped his arm. 'Oh, thank you. Could we possibly meet at lunchtime? Only, I work half a day on Wednesdays. Could you get away around one o'clock, do you think? There's a wonderful teashop not far from here.'

'Of course.' He smiled yet was scared senseless by the unexpected lift in his chest. This woman was beginning to affect his judgement and that was not good. Not good at all. 'Now, let's get inside.'

19

Elizabeth stood from her chair beside Esther's bed and walked to the window. 'Let's open this window, shall we? It's awfully stuffy in here.'

'You can blame Lawrence for that. He's told Helen to ensure the windows are kept shut as though a breeze might pass across me and send my blood pressure spiralling.'

Elizabeth smiled through her concern for Esther's current state. 'Well, be that as it may, I'm a firm believer in fresh air, regardless of the time of year. We'll keep it open for just a few minutes.'

Esther sighed as she pulled herself a little higher against the pillows. 'Shall we discuss some of the plans I've drawn up for you?' She reached for the sketchpad that lay open on the bedspread. 'I'm confident Amelia will understand everything I've drawn and my written instructions.'

Elizabeth nodded, her obsession with the window displays had lessened more and more, when they should have been growing in Esther's absence. 'I'm sure she will. I've seen a huge improvement in Amelia's confidence and assertiveness the longer she continues to work with you. You've produced quite the apprentice.'

'She is most certainly an evolving advantage. In fact,' Esther lifted her study from the sketchpad and met Elizabeth's gaze, 'I think you shouldn't hesitate in giving her more responsibility. I could quite possibly be away from the store for months once the baby is born. Amelia is more than capable of voicing her own ideas and, once she believes you'll listen to her, I think she will surprise you.'

'No surprises needed. I've been watching her and am very pleased with what I've seen. She's excelled at every task each of us has set her, and now it's just a case of encouraging her own self-belief. Something we could all do with at times.'

'Indeed. Well, I'm very glad to hear you are happy with Amelia's work, it settles a little of my guilt for having to leave earlier than planned. So, here's what I have in mind for the east window…'

Elizabeth's mind drifted to Joseph as Esther spoke and, no matter how hard she tried to focus on her friend's words, Esther's voice faded. Sickness rolled through Elizabeth's stomach whenever she considered what Stephen Gower might, or might not, uncover. Now that Joseph had promised her they would begin to think about starting their own family once Lillian's killer had been found, she worried more than ever that the arrest might never happen.

'Elizabeth?'

She started, a smile automatically curving her lips as she looked at Esther. 'Yes?'

'I'm entirely convinced you haven't heard a word I've said. What's the matter? Is it something at the store bothering you? Joseph?'

Elizabeth sighed. Esther was so mature, astute and wise,

there was little point in Elizabeth even trying to hide her stresses and strains. Her dear friend would be more upset should Elizabeth not confide in her than about any problem she might present her with.

She sat down. 'After Joseph practically accosted Mr Gower at the store and frogmarched him into my office, he's been on worse tenterhooks than ever.

'I have no idea how he'll react should Mr Gower say he can't do anything to help. I'm feeling less and less of a wife to him, Esther. I should be able to allay his fears or provoke his confidence, but I am at a complete loss over how to help him.'

Esther stared for a long moment before dropping her gaze to the sketchpad, her lips pulled into a straight line. Slowly, she raised her head, a soft apology in her hazel eyes. 'I've asked my sister-in-law to support you and Joseph through this during my absence.'

'Oh, no. You've told Cornelia about our troubles? But that was unnecessary. The poor woman has enough on her plate, from what you've told me.'

'Yes, but she's also strong, Elizabeth.' Determination darkened Esther's gaze. 'Strong, passionate and knows when wrong is wrong. She will be a support to you. I also think you need to lean a little more on Amelia too. Together, the four of us could help one another through all that we are struggling with at the moment.'

'You cannot expect me to lean on Amelia as I would you.' Elizabeth was incredulous. 'Do you really think me so weak that I need an army around me in order to stand side by side with my husband?'

'Don't we all?'

Surprised that Esther would admit such a thing, Elizabeth dropped her arms and turned away from her, a rare nervousness twisting her stomach. How could it be possible that the awful murder of Joseph's first wife threatened to harm her and Joseph's marriage today? She had stood up to her tyrannical father for years, had learned to live without the love of her mother and, eventually, brought her dream of running Pennington's to fruition.

All done alone.

Now it seemed she needed a circle of support around her to help Joseph and keep their marriage strong.

'There's no shame in asking for help, you know,' Esther said softly. 'It took me a while to accept that, but it's true. Leaning on other women, family, friends, even work colleagues. It's only dented pride that gets in the way of us having a way to ease some of the pressure of our problems. Won't you at least think about letting Cornelia help you? Even if it's a step too far to involve Amelia?'

Elizabeth resumed her seat beside the bed, a flicker of hope lighting inside her. 'It would certainly help to have someone to talk to about this while you're away. Of course, I know I can visit you anytime, but it feels so different without you at the store.' She smiled wryly. 'I fear we've become faster friends than I intended when we first met.'

Esther grinned. 'And I, for one, am glad. We *are* friends, Elizabeth. *Good* friends. What is the harm in both of us making new ones? Women need to support one another in this world. Men don't have the same cares and concerns we do. They don't react to problems in the same way either. Women talk and discuss, more often than not, with candid honesty. Plus' – Esther's eyes twinkled with mischief – 'it seems Cornelia is striking up quite the friendship with Mr Gower. Who knows if he might one day be a part of our lives on a more intimate footing?'

Curious, Elizabeth leaned a little closer. 'What are you saying?'

'I think there is something there between them. A spark of attraction, maybe. Cornelia intends to ask him for some advice regarding her divorce hearing. She wouldn't do that after David's betrayal unless she sensed something good and true in Mr Gower. Don't you agree?'

Hope rose once more, and Elizabeth smiled. 'Yes, I think I do.'

'Good. Then you'll share something of your troubles with Cornelia? Let her help you speak to Mr Gower. Maybe it would be beneficial for her to act as a medium between you. That way, she can tell you what Mr Gower has uncovered, and you can tell Joseph in the hope that he doesn't put too much pressure on Mr Gower directly.'

'Yes. That could definitely work. I don't want Joseph to be under any false hope. It will be the undoing of him if his ambitions of finding this man are quashed too soon. He needs the time to deal with the outcome, whatever that might be. I love him so much, Esther. I'm his wife and he will always have me to lean on. Of that much, I can promise him.'

'Of course.'

Feeling better than she had for days, Elizabeth picked up Esther's sketchpad and purposefully pushed worries about the investigation to the back of her mind. 'So, tell me more about these designs.'

20

Smiling to herself, Cornelia walked along one of Bath's many parades and through a darkened passageway that opened onto a small courtyard. When she'd suggested Mrs Margate's tea shop for her meeting with Stephen, she'd delighted in telling him that some of the houses surrounding the small shop dated back to the 1500s, one being home to a famous baker and his family. Although Stephen had appeared slightly bemused, his willingness to help her lessened her embarrassment. He must like her at least a little if he was willing to listen to her woes about her divorce.

She took a moment to appreciate her surroundings. As well as the homes, bakery and Mrs Margate's tea shop, two archways stood on either side of the courtyard, the passages leading to opposite ends of the city. Some young trees and shrubbery adorned the centre of the space, with three benches around its circumference, where people sat talking, reading or watching the world go by.

Approaching the small, cottage-style tea shop, Cornelia studied the bay window framed with checked drapes, the painted metal sign swinging to and fro in the light wind and the closed door with an 'open' sign hanging behind the glass. A safe, welcoming place where she hoped she'd be able to speak frankly without sending Stephen running for the hills.

Taking a strengthening breath, she pushed open the door and a bell tinkled her arrival.

Easing the door closed, she scanned the interior. Every table was occupied, including those close to a gently burning fire in a large open hearth.

'Miss Culford?'

Stephen had risen from a table at the back of the room, his smile warm and, judging by the way he waved, he was happy to see her.

Her confidence buoyed, Cornelia returned his smile. 'Mr Gower.' She weaved between the tables and stopped at his table. 'Thank you for coming.'

He pulled out her seat. 'Of course.'

'Thank you. After' – she glanced around them and sat – 'what I told you about myself and how you so kindly listened this morning, I think we've earned the right to rid ourselves of formalities, don't you? Please, call me Cornelia.'

He sat. 'Cornelia it is. And Stephen, from now on. However, you should know your situation neither alarms nor shocks me.'

A blush warmed her cheeks as his soft gaze lingered on hers before she abruptly picked up the menu. Tall and broad, with dark hair and neatly trimmed moustache, he really was most handsome. As for his deep brown eyes… Well, they were just dangerous.

She slowly raised her eyes. 'Have you chosen what you'd like? I insist you allow me to treat you.'

He carefully studied her before dipping his head and taking

the menu. He perused the offerings. 'Coffee and a slice of lemon sponge, I think.'

She smiled. 'Lovely, and I'll have tea and some jam sponge.'

A young girl came to their table, smartly attired in a black dress with a ruffled white collar and cuffs and a clean apron tied at her waist. 'Good afternoon. What would you like today?'

Cornelia tried and failed to drag her gaze from Stephen as he reiterated her order and placed his own. He finished with a kind smile. 'Thank you.'

'You're welcome. I'll be right back with your tea and coffee.'

As the waitress retreated, Cornelia inhaled. 'I felt prepared for the court hearing until David, that's my husband, said he wanted the children. Now I feel woefully unprepared and, quite frankly, terrified he'll triumph.' The words tumbled from her mouth, as if she'd carefully rehearsed what she would say when she and Stephen met.

He leaned his elbows on the table, linking his fingers and laying them barely inches from hers on the lace tablecloth. 'Cornelia, before you go any further, I'm afraid I must first ask you a difficult question..'

Dread coiled in her stomach. 'Yes?'

His gaze remained steady on hers. 'Does your husband have reason, any reason at all, to believe his counsel has inarguable justification he should be sole guardian to your children?'

Pride swelled inside her, evoking her need to blurt every sin David had committed and how she'd done nothing to provoke his treatment of her. She stifled a protest as anger rose that she had to answer such a question, that she had to prove herself a fit parent when David was so profoundly unfit. If she reacted emotionally instead of rationally, she knew it would only make her ill-equipped for the hearing. Lawrence had counselled the need to remain calm and composed at all times, and that was exactly how she would be now.

She lifted her chin. 'No. He has no reason whatsoever. I was a good wife to him and remain a good mother to my children.'

'Then why does he look to take them away from you?' His gaze softened. 'What are their names, by the way?'

Her strength faltered under his gentle tone. 'Alfred and Francis. They are eight and six.'

He smiled. 'A handful, no doubt?'

'Sometimes, yes, but also the loves of my life.'

The waitress returned and placed tea and coffee pots on the table, turning over the cups already laid in their saucers. 'Here you go, sir, madam. I'll be straight back with your cakes.'

She walked away, and Stephen cleared his throat. 'I assumed when you approached me for advice that your husband had a basis for his claim to your sons.'

'I have no idea what David has planned, which is the reason I am so terrified. Our marriage went from amicable, to tolerated, to downright resented. By both of us.' Her hands trembled as she lifted the coffee pot and filled his cup. 'Milk? Sugar?'

He shook his head. 'No, thank you.'

She willed him to ask another question, but the ensuing silence made it clear he wouldn't until she spoke further. How could she have expected he'd be any different? He was an ex-police sergeant. A man used to exercising patience, listening and making people talk, persuading them into confessing things they would prefer to keep buried. Her vulnerability threatened to sabotage her courage, but she had to push on for Alfred and Francis. She could not lose them.

After she'd poured her tea, added milk and sugar, she forced herself to meet Stephen's gaze. 'David has been having an affair for several years. An affair I discovered, and which he told me was over. I believed him but soon uncovered it had neither ended nor lapsed at any time. I told him I wanted a divorce and he laughed but did not contest it. I thought everything would be done and over with cleanly and quickly. Until he told me he wanted the children.'

Deep concern burned in Stephen's dark brown eyes. 'So, you want my advice on the best chance to swing the judge's decision in your favour?' He exhaled heavily. 'I'm sorry.'

'Sorry?' Disappointment dropped like a stone into her stomach. 'You think the judge will rule for David? He'll take the children?'

The urge to stand and shout at Stephen that he was wrong swept through her. David would *not* take the children. Would not ruin her life when she'd finally found the courage and strength to leave him, to move them to a new city so she could raise Alfred and Francis with standards and morals that surpassed her husband's in every way.

'Cornelia.' He gently covered her hand on the table. 'I said sorry because if you want your children, you're going to have to fight for them. With everything you have in your arsenal. Affairs happen. Husbands and wives cheat as though they are the only people their behaviour affects. That is neither true nor acceptable. As a policeman, I have seen...' His jaw tightened. 'So much hurt, spite and anger thrown between two people who are meant to love one another. Marriages that were arranged. Marriages that were forsaken and abused. Marriages...'

A shadow fell across the table, and he abruptly pulled his hand from hers. His expression transformed when he smiled at the waitress.

'Your cakes, sir and madam. Is there anything else I can get for you?'

'No, thank you.'

'No, thank you.'

They answered in unison and tension filled the air. Cornelia had no idea how to dispel it. For months she'd known the gravity of the situation she faced, but to hear Stephen speak with such passion – such truth – had thrown her into a whole new sphere of panic.

The waitress retreated, and Cornelia fought to calm her racing heart. If she wanted Stephen's help and experience, she had to be entirely honest with him. Reveal every skeleton in her closet. Did she really think she wouldn't have to make the abuse she'd suffered public? Her divorce was a fight to the bitter end and she had to use everything she had to keep Alfred and Francis safe and happy.

She swallowed. 'Past indignities make me reluctant to share what needs to be made public. To have my brother and his wife hear of what I endured…' Tears pricked her eyes. 'I really want there to be another way, but I know, deep inside, telling the judge everything is exactly what I have to do.'

Stephen's gaze grew intense on hers. 'Which is?'

'David hit me. He hit me many, many times.'

21

A deep, dark fury ignited inside Stephen as he saw the shame in Cornelia's eyes. The thought that a man – *any* man – might raise his hand to her. To hurt her in even the slightest way...

He knew all too well how spousal abuse could go from bad to worse. He'd seen cases of it over and over again. Violence permeated cities, towns and villages. Assault. Battery. Murder. Images of Detective Constable Walker, Hettie and Fay surged his mind, their bloodied and battered bodies like blurred tattoos on his brain. Sometimes, the entire world felt like a vile and uninhabitable place. The notion that Cornelia had suffered such viciousness behind closed doors, in the supposed sanctity of marriage, infuriated him.

He lowered his coffee and slowly slid his hands from the table to clench them in his lap. 'When did this first start?'

Her throat moved as she swallowed, her beautiful blue eyes fretful. 'Quite a long time into our marriage.'

'When he started seeing this woman?'

She swallowed again and nodded. 'I think so. Yes.'

'I see.' He briefly closed his eyes and took a long, calming breath before opening them again. 'And he took his frustrations out on you?'

She picked up her tea and sipped, the china clattering lightly as she returned the cup to its saucer. 'That's the conclusion I came to a while ago. The more he saw of his lover, the more he resented me. We had another... scuffle one afternoon while the children were at school. That's when he told me, shouted at me, that he'd taken a lover.'

'And your reaction?'

A flush stained her cheeks as she looked to the table. 'I demanded he stopped seeing whoever she was immediately. He laughed, and I insisted a second time.'

'And?'

She lifted her eyes. 'And he stormed off, came back later, assuring me it was over with no further explanation or elaboration.'

'Did he apologise?'

She shook her head.

Bastard. Stephen clenched his jaw as a strong urge made him burn to take her in his arms, comfort her, while all the time plotting a way to find her son-of-a-bitch husband. He couldn't afford to care this deeply, or so quickly. What did it say about his feelings for her? What did it say about how badly he was failing in his mission to live a quiet life away from crime and punishment until he heard more from Inspector King and the Board's investigations?

Yet the idea of having a woman like Cornelia – beautiful, strong and loving – and a man squandering her devotion made him sick to his stomach.

A dangerous desire for retribution swelled inside him. Every time he saw a case of domestic abuse, he found himself wanting to string up the husband, brother or son involved.

He forced his focus back to the here and now. He could not turn away from her. Was she not in need of his help even more than Joseph Carter? Her pain was being played out now, whereas Carter's was already years old, with no promise of a conclusion. Cornelia's court case was a different situation entirely. She must win both her divorce and her children.

He sipped his coffee. 'Did he ever hit your children?'

Her eyes widened with defensiveness. 'Never. If he had, I can't tell you what I would have been capable of. But just because he controlled himself with the children doesn't mean I'll risk him gaining full custody and having them live with him and his wife-to-be. All too soon, Alfred and Francis will encroach on David's desire to do what he loves.'

'Which is?'

'Courting. Spending money. Showing off. Anything and everything that feeds his ego and in some way elevates his position in society.'

Stephen considered her as his temper cooled to a low thrum deep in his stomach.

He leaned forward and slid his cake to one side, his appetite gone. 'Have you told your lawyer about your husband's physical treatment of you?'

She shook her head.

Stephen frowned but kept his voice purposefully gentle. He blamed her for nothing. 'Why not?'

Tears glazed her eyes. 'Shame. Fear. So many things have prevented me from sharing what was happening with anyone, let alone a lawyer.'

He drew in a long breath and released it, hating that anyone – especially a man meant to love her – should make her feel so afraid. 'Then you must tell him. It will be difficult to have your personal life made public, but it's imperative any threatening behaviour, any violent or mental anguish you've suffered as a result of your husband's actions, is heard in court. The judge needs to know you asked your husband to end his affair and he lied when he said that he had. That will be pivotal in the decision of whether or not to grant the divorce. Probably even more so when deciding who has custody over Alfred and Francis. If you can show you were repeatedly betrayed and that he raised his hand many times to you, it will be to your advantage.'

Her face had paled, and her eyes were sadder than ever. His heart twisted with sympathy. She lowered her gaze. 'This will hurt Lawrence so much.'

'Lawrence?'

'My brother.' She lifted her eyes. 'He's married to Esther, Pennington's head window dresser. She's good friends with Elizabeth Pennington. I'm sure she'd never divulge details of my personal life, but I'd die of shame if Miss Pennington were to discover how weak I've been.'

'Hey.' He gently grasped her hand. 'You aren't weak. You left him, did you not? You took your children to a safe place and filed for divorce. You are strong, Cornelia, and you'll need to be even stronger in the next few days.'

Tears glinted in her eyes. 'The hearing is on Friday.'

Stephen gave a curt nod. 'And you'll be ready. I advise you to telephone or visit your lawyer this afternoon and insist he speak with you. Tell him everything you've told me and, I think, something else.'

'Something else?' Her brow creased. 'But I don't have anything else.'

'Yes, you do.'

'Such as?'

'You were forced to leave the familial home.' Adrenaline swept through him. 'The fact you live with your brother now and haven't taken your children somewhere where they might be at risk will be considered. Instead, you live with a respected and wealthy hotel owner and his family. Your children are safe and, I assume, attend a good school. On top of that, you are not demanding ludicrous amounts of money from your husband but have sought employment and are earning money of your own. I think the judge will look favourably on your actions and decisions.'

Hope sparked in her eyes and a small smile curved her pretty lips. 'Do you really think so?'

'I *know* so. The points your lawyer must press are: one, you gave your husband the chance to mend his ways; two, you were physically attacked and verbally slandered; and, three, you were forced to leave the family home with your children because his conduct continued, despite his assertion the affair was over.'

'Well, all three of those points are entirely true.' Her smile widened, but the worry in her eyes remained. 'Stephen, thank you.'

'There's nothing to thank me for. You have already done right by yourself and your children in every way. A judge will see that, I'm sure.'

She picked up her tea and drank. Stephen stared at her bowed head. Despite his confidence in everything he had said to her, he remained worried. Time after time, he'd seen judges rule in favour of abusive and neglectful husbands. Rule that men alone held the knowledge of how a household ought to be governed. Consideration was rarely given to the children's wishes, or their mother's love for them.

An unexpected longing to kiss her rose inside him. He quickly looked down at his coffee. He had no right to desire her. His ex-fiancée had broken off their engagement after realising she could not live as a constable's wife. He'd taken a few lovers since, but they too had concluded his work was either too time-consuming or dangerous. He was damaged. Afraid and angry. And in no way suitable as a romantic partner. Cornelia needed a decent man. A man she could be proud of after everything she'd been through. Maybe one day he would be different, but he was loath to believe it quite yet.

Responsibility pressed down on him.

He'd already trodden the path of no return by agreeing to investigate the murder of Joseph Carter's wife. The last thing he wanted was to hurt Cornelia, if she should ever come to return the stirrings of fondness that swirled inside him.

Building a new life with her children was her priority. As it should be. She was as scarred as he was. But whereas he'd failed in his decision-making, every choice she'd made had been brave and conscientious. She was a woman who deserved so much more than a man like him.

Her cup clattered against its saucer, and he raised his eyes to hers. She smiled. 'Now, there's something else I need to ask you.'

'Oh?'

'Are you helping Joseph Carter and Elizabeth Pennington with something?'

Disappointment dropped like lead into his stomach and his defences slammed into place. Had Carter shared that knowledge with her? Or was it Elizabeth Pennington? 'Why would you ask?'

Her smile dissolved as she blushed. 'As I said, Esther is my sister-in-law and very good friends with Elizabeth. Esther is expecting a child and on strict bed rest. She will not be returning to Pennington's and is deeply concerned by something Joseph and Elizabeth are struggling with. She's aware you worked for Scotland Yard and that Elizabeth and Mr Carter have spoken to you. If you've agreed to help them, I'd like to assist in any way I can. I've promised Esther I will support her friends in her confinement. Please, Stephen, let me help you.'

'Cornelia...' He clenched his jaw. 'You cannot get involved.'

'I know the gravity of what Mr Carter and Elizabeth are dealing with and the situation is just as pressing as my divorce. They deserve peace the same as anyone else, don't they?'

A horrible self-loathing pressed down on him. Not everyone in this world deserved peace. 'And how, exactly, do you think you could help?'

'I'm not entirely sure, but with your instruction, I would willingly do—'

'Stop.' He lowered his voice. 'Investigating a crime is not a pastime. It's dangerous. Potentially fatal. Don't you think you have enough to deal with right now without getting involved in something that could land you in new trouble?'

Her cheeks darkened and the excited fervour faded from her eyes, making Stephen want to stand and leave, lest he spoke the apology and words of comfort battling with his conscience.

She glanced about her. 'I just thought—'

'What Joseph Carter and his wife are struggling with is dangerous. I want you to stay well away. All they think I am doing at the moment is looking at the avenues they've already pursued. I won't tell either of them anything unless it is solid evidence that will lead to finding his first wife's killer. It's imperative Carter's hopes aren't raised without just cause. Do you understand?'

She stared at him, as a slow, fiery passion darkened her eyes. 'Yes.'

'Good.'

'But I am not afraid, nor am I someone to shrink away from anything life might throw at me. I'm without a husband whose care and protection I once thought I could rely on. If I can help you, Esther, Elizabeth or Mr Carter as they've helped me, I will. Because of your advice there's every chance I will keep Alfred and Francis. Because of Esther, Elizabeth and Mr Carter, there is every chance I'll have a future where I can provide for my children and be independent and free to pursue the life I want. I owe you all. Do you not see that?'

He shook his head. She could not get involved with his investigation. How would he ever recover if she was hurt or worse? 'The nature of Mr Carter and Miss Pennington's troubles is criminal. I've not even promised I will help.'

'So, they assume you are merely *thinking* about helping them?'

'Yes.'

Finding it difficult to look at her and not weaken, Stephen stared across the shop.

'But you've already done far more than they think, have you not?'

He snapped his gaze to hers. 'For the love of God, Cornelia. Leave it be.'

'Stephen, please. I can speak in confidence to Elizabeth and reassure Esther her friend is supported. If you'd prefer Joseph not to know you are investigating his first wife's murder, then I will honour that.'

Stephen withdrew his wallet and tossed a note onto the table. 'Here. Now, enough of this. You need to stay away from anything concerning Joseph Carter. I mean it.' He stormed from the tea shop, leaving her alone and hating himself.

22

The anger in Stephen's eyes and the passion in his words continued to nag at Cornelia an hour after she'd left the tea shop. She tightened her fingers around her purse and stared around the outer office of Bloom & Hartford Associates. Her lawyer, Mr Hartford, had agreed to see her without an appointment if she was willing to wait for him to finish with the client currently in his office.

With Stephen's advice at the forefront of her mind and her courage strengthened by being brave enough to confess her treatment at David's hands, she had walked straight to her lawyer's office, afraid her renewed courage might ebb away if she didn't speak to her lawyer immediately.

She also feared her bravery might evaporate if she couldn't make Stephen understand how important it was that she felt useful, that by acting as an intermediary between him and Elizabeth, she was doing something to avenge the unlawful killing of a good and innocent woman. As selfish as it might seem, she needed something new to focus on.

Since leaving the tea shop, she'd repeatedly wondered why

Stephen had left Scotland Yard to work at Pennington's. He'd been so assured in his advice about the divorce hearing that his reasons must surely be personal, rather than professional; problems that had led to his resignation. *If* he'd resigned, of course. There had to be something more to it. Something he held close. And something he most definitely wouldn't share with her. At least, not yet.

The door to the inner office opened and Cornelia sat up, nerves taking flight in her stomach.

Mr Hartford was rotund and red-cheeked, in his early sixties, with a shock of snow-white hair and matching whiskers. He invited a tall, well-dressed gentleman to walk out of the office ahead of him, his hand outstretched. 'I will see you again soon, Mr Battersby. Try not to over fret. The situation is all in hand.'

'Thank you, sir.'

Mr Hartford smiled. 'Won't you come through, Mrs Parker? Would you like tea? Coffee?'

Bitterness coated Cornelia's throat at his use of her married name, but she forced a smile and rose. 'No, thank you.'

'Then come right this way.' He paused beside his secretary, a pretty young woman with blonde hair and bright blue eyes. 'Would you mind bringing me a cup of coffee when you have a moment, Miss Anderson?'

'Of course, sir.'

Once in his office, Cornelia sat across from his desk and laid her purse on the floor, crossing her legs at the ankle. She inhaled a long breath before meeting Mr Hartford's soft and steady gaze.

'So, how can I help?' he asked. 'From your tone on the telephone, I gather it's most urgent.'

'It is. I have something of importance to share with you

before the hearing on Friday. Something I think might tip the judge's decision in our favour.'

'Oh?' Mr Hartford leaned back and laced his fingers across the considerable bulge beneath his waistcoat. 'And what would this something be, exactly?'

Shame and embarrassment threatened, but Cornelia straightened her spine against any weakness. 'I didn't tell you everything about David's treatment of me before because I'd clung to the hope I wouldn't have to make such a thing public. However, now he's filing for custody of our children, he's left me no choice.'

Mr Hartford sat forward and frowned. 'Go on.'

She swallowed. 'He hit me over a period of several years, Mr Hartford. Not enough to bruise me, but enough to dampen my spirit and strength. Pushing, shoving, the occasional slap. Nothing that would be visible, because he wouldn't have wanted anyone to know.' She took a breath. 'However, he has underestimated the love I bear for my children and I'm prepared to fight him with everything I have. Why should a wife who is assaulted have to wait until the beating becomes life-threatening before she can file for divorce? I was forced to leave our home because of David's affair and continuing lies. I'd hoped that, alone, would grant me a divorce. However, I'm now afraid of losing my children.'

The door opened behind her, and Cornelia turned to see Miss Anderson walking into the room, her footsteps muted by the thick green carpet.

Cornelia's cheeks heated at the thought of what the woman might have heard, and she silently admonished herself. It was too late for such nonsensical egotism. The court hearing was mere days away and then many more people would know, including Lawrence.

'Thank you, Miss Anderson.'

As soon as the door closed, Mr Hartford gave a firm nod, his eyes slightly glazed in concentration.

'Well, you were right to give me this information, Mrs Parker. I have no doubt it will prove vital during the hearing. However, I have concerns.'

'Which are?'

'I need an assurance that you are strong enough to fight whatever your husband might chose to accuse you of. He may well already have forewarned his own lawyers about these potential allegations. If he has, there is every possibility they would have concocted a plausible defence. Are you prepared for cross-examination, Mrs Parker?'

The memory of Stephen's determination and passion in the tea shop surged into Cornelia's mind, strengthening her resolve. 'I'm prepared for that and anything else David might claim or counterclaim. I want my divorce, Mr Hartford, and I want my children.'

He studied her, and she forced herself to remain still under his scrutiny. Her life and those of her children hung in the balance. One wrong move on her part and David would take everything she loved in one fell swoop.

She lifted her chin. 'So, does this new information reinforce my case or weaken it?'

A smile played on Mr Hartford's lips as satisfaction lit his canny, grey eyes. 'I do believe it reinforces everything.'

She exhaled a relieved breath. 'Excellent.' Her shoulders relaxed, and she stood. 'Then I will be on my way. I've already imposed on your time. Thank you so much.'

'Not at all.' He stood and offered his hand across the desk. 'I will see you at the courthouse on Friday, Mrs Parker. Eleven-thirty sharp.'

'Indeed, you will. Goodbye for now.'

Holding her head high, Cornelia walked through the outer office, down a flight of stairs and onto the street. Power washed through her. Her time was now, and she would lead her life as she saw fit. Alfred and Francis were her babies. Her entire reason for living. And, all too soon, David would feel her wrath, which he alone had provoked.

Cornelia passed the stalls, flower-sellers and a young boy sweeping the streets. She sidestepped the rubbish and manure that littered the cobbled roads, her mind and heart happier now she was set on a new and exciting direction.

She arrived at Lawrence's house and entered the hallway. Meeting her gaze in the mirror, she removed her hat, pleased to see her eyes shining with renewed happiness. All would be well.

Cornelia climbed the stairs, determined to tell her brother and Esther about her discussions with Stephen that afternoon. Or, at least, the discussions about Joseph and Elizabeth. She wouldn't tell Lawrence about David's abuse, lest her brother erupt with rage prior to the hearing. If he learned of it in court, at the same time as everyone else, then he'd be prevented from acting on impulse. It would be better that way. Much better.

She gently knocked on their bedroom door.

'Come in.'

Cornelia plastered on a wide smile and entered the room, relieved to find Esther in bed, as she was supposed to be.

'Good afternoon, you two.' She came to a stop at the side of the bed and carefully studied Esther's tired eyes. 'How are you feeling?'

'A little better.' Determination showed her sister-in-law's gaze. 'I am quite sure if I rest for another day and night, I'll be perfectly all right to attend the hearing.'

'You need to stop worrying about that and concentrate on

you and the baby,' Cornelia admonished. 'That's the most important thing right now.'

'Well, that and the fact I can't stop worrying about Elizabeth and Joseph.' Cornelia glanced uneasily at Lawrence.

'Don't look so surprised, Cornelia. I know Esther well enough to suspect something was bothering her in addition to the baby.' He looked fondly at his wife. 'There are no secrets between us. She's told me about Joseph's first wife and the state the man is in at the moment. A perfectly understandable state, in my opinion.'

Relieved that she would not have to keep another revelation from Lawrence, Cornelia exhaled. 'Well, I'm glad you know. Three heads have to be better than two. So, I have some news.'

Esther and Lawrence looked at her expectantly.

Cornelia took a deep breath. 'I took tea this afternoon with Mr Gower and we had a marvellous time...' she coughed lightly. 'For the most part.'

Esther frowned. 'Meaning?'

'Meaning, he became rather upset when I asked if I could help if he takes up Mr Carter's case.'

Lawrence frowned. 'Esther's told me she's asked you to do what you can for the Carters, but are you sure you want to get involved?'

'Absolutely.' She held his gaze, determined he would not sway her. 'If I can help, I will.'

He studied her before raising his hands in surrender. 'As you wish. You are your own woman now.'

'I am.' Cornelia looked at Esther. 'I haven't given up persuading Mr Gower to accept my help.'

Disappointment clouded Esther's eyes. 'I suspected he wouldn't be happy about your involvement. It might have been better for me to share the conversation I've had with Elizabeth first.'

'You've spoken to her about my helping?'

'Yes. She was reluctant too, at first, but, after I convinced her it was not a sign of weakness to accept help, she seemed encouraged by the prospect of your support.'

Cornelia smiled. 'I'm glad and, despite Mr Gower's irritation, I'm convinced I did the right thing speaking to him.'

'Why would you think that, if the man became annoyed?' Lawrence frowned. 'How on earth could that be good?'

'Because Mr Carter and Elizabeth have no idea Mr Gower has already taken it upon himself to investigate further. They think he is still considering what they have told him. However, it was quite clear from what he said that he's already gone much further than he's admitted. Give me a little time and I'm sure he'll allow me to act as a go-between with Elizabeth. He's adamant he doesn't want Mr Carter's hopes raised prematurely, and I can help to ensure that doesn't happen. He is most certainly the right man to help them. I have no doubt he would've been remarkable in his role at Scotland Yard.' She frowned. 'I still haven't discovered why he came to leave, but I will. In time.'

Esther smiled, her gaze happier than it had been for days. 'I think, between us, everything will work out for the best. Elizabeth and Joseph deserve peace and happiness. We will do everything in our power to ensure that happens.'

Cornelia nodded, the passion she felt about her own troubles merging with a determination that Elizabeth, too, would be triumphant and able to make plans for the future without the past holding her hostage.

23

Elizabeth entered Pennington's design department, Esther's latest sketches and instructions in her hands. She scanned the moderately sized room, pleased that the team had grown from four workers to ten since her father had passed Pennington's reins to her eighteen months before. It showed the progression and success she'd brought to the store despite his disparagement and scorn over the years.

She was all she had known herself to be and had proven it accordingly... much to her father's undoubted chagrin. Edward Pennington still felt no immediate need for innovation. Instead, he held fast for a continued class divide. Would prefer that Pennington's only served the upper class and gentry. If the store were to have a visit from royalty at some point in the future, Lord only knew what it would do to his heart.

Elizabeth approached Amelia, where she worked at a sewing machine. In her early twenties, quiet and unassuming, Amelia could be mistaken for a young woman who wished to work her days at Pennington's, do as good a job as possible, and then return home to her family for the evening. However, Elizabeth had an eye – an instinct – for ambition. Especially in women.

And Amelia had a recognisable spark in her eyes when she worked. A discreet, yet tangible desire to impress not only Elizabeth, but Esther too. If Amelia wanted to prove herself valuable to the store, Elizabeth would make sure she had every opportunity to do so.

She smiled. 'Amelia. Good afternoon.'

The young woman turned from her work, her pretty brown eyes dazed with concentration before she blinked and immediately moved to stand. 'Oh, Miss Pennington. Good afternoon.'

'Please, don't get up. I just came to give you these. I had every intention of leaving them on your table with a note. You were at work early this morning.'

Amelia blushed. 'Yes, I am most mornings. Especially with Esther being away.'

Elizabeth held out Esther's papers. 'I spent some time with her yesterday and she gave me these for you. They are some additions and adjustments she's made to the window designs she knows you're familiar with. She is still working despite her confinement, but I doubt you are any more surprised by that than I am.'

Amelia flashed a rare grin, her gaze softening. 'No, I'm not. Esther is remarkable. She's taught me so much.'

'And it's because she's taught you so well that I have an opportunity for you that I hope you'll accept.'

'Oh?'

'How would you like to become the temporary head of the design department?'

Her eyes widened. 'I couldn't possibly—'

'You can and, if you'd like the position, it's yours until Esther returns. *If* she returns.'

'But—'

'Amelia, you must start to believe in yourself as I do. Here, take a look at these sketches.' Elizabeth sat on a stool next to her and spread out Esther's designs. 'Now, tell me you don't know exactly what Esther would like to be done and how she envisions the windows will look.'

Amelia hesitated, her slightly panicked gaze lingering on Elizabeth for a moment, before she slid her focus to the papers. Her brow furrowed as she reached out her fingers to slide them over the designs. Elizabeth bit back a smile as Amelia's gaze darted back and forth, bottom lip pulled between her teeth, her gathering excitement clear to see.

She lifted her eyebrows. 'Well?'

Amelia nodded, her gaze still on the papers as she flipped between them. 'These alterations are perfect. They will make all the difference. Esther has such an amazing ability to immediately see where we can merge departments. I have no idea how she does it so seamlessly.'

'Which is exactly why I made her the head of the department, and you're well on your way to following in her footsteps. Permanently. I want you to begin having more confidence in yourself. There is every possibility of you becoming equally as talented as Esther. You are under her tutelage, after all.' She touched Amelia's hand and the young woman faced her. 'Esther is prematurely confined, the baby is not due until March, but she wants to continue to work as much as possible, which means you and I, possibly you alone occasionally, will visit her at home. That way, you can ask her all the questions you want as you work.'

Amelia slowly exhaled, relief clear in her eyes. 'Oh, in that case...'

'You'll take the position as head of the department?'

Amelia glanced at the papers again before pulling back her shoulders and giving Elizabeth a firm nod. 'I will.'

'Excellent.' Elizabeth smiled. 'That's settled, then.'

Abruptly standing, Elizabeth walked to the wall of windows that gave in enough daylight in the summer to light the room, but in December, the newly installed electric lights were entirely relied upon.

'It must get gloomy working down here in the winter months. I hope you don't find it too hard.'

'Oh, not at all. In fact, I would rather be at Pennington's than at home twenty-four hours a day.'

Immediately concerned, Elizabeth turned. 'Is something not as it should be at home... if you don't mind my asking?'

Amelia cheeks reddened a second time and she shook her head. 'I shouldn't have said anything, I'm sorry.'

'Don't be.' Elizabeth resumed her seat beside the younger woman and gently touched her arm. 'I like my staff to be happy, Amelia. In and out of the store. It's my mission that Pennington's is a place where people aspire to work and, once they secure a position, they have no desire to leave. For that to happen, myself and Mr Carter will do all we can to ensure our staff lead the best lives possible. Professionally *and* personally.'

Amelia stared into Elizabeth's eyes, her hesitation clear. She swallowed. 'I often feel I have so much to be ashamed of.'

'Ashamed? Whatever do you mean? Your work is exemplary, your colleagues like you and Esther couldn't be prouder of your progress.'

'I don't mean at the store. Pennington's is everything to me. My saving grace. I am so happy when I'm here. You must believe that.'

Elizabeth's concern deepened and she made a silent vow to spend more time with Amelia until she got to the bottom of whatever it was bothering her at home. 'I do believe it, which is why I am concerned for anything marring that happiness. Now, know that I am here, my office door always open, should you wish to speak to me. About anything. You have so much to be proud of and, in my experience, shame is a wasted emotion. Life is for the taking, Amelia. Let past mistakes and abuses go. It's the only way to survive.'

Amelia's gaze swept over Elizabeth's face before her eyes darkened with a spark of determination. She gave a firm nod. 'I understand.'

'Do you really?'

'Yes.'

'Good.' Elizabeth stood. 'Then I will leave you to work. I have some exciting plans for the New Year. Plans that will most definitely include you and could, quite possibly, change your life forever.'

24

Cornelia tucked Francis's bed sheet and blanket more securely under his chin as Alfred climbed into the bed next to his brother. She studied her younger son as she sat alongside him, a copy of Robert Louis Stevenson's *Treasure Island* open in her lap. 'How are you feeling, darling?'

He blinked, his bright blue eyes indicating that, for now, he was content. 'Fine.'

'Just fine?' Cornelia gently laid her hand on his cheek. 'Not happy?'

He shrugged his slender shoulders, carefully watching her.

As her love for her sons caused a hopeless ache in her heart, she looked across at Alfred. 'And you, my love? How are you?'

'Well, Mama.'

She smiled. 'Well, that's good. One out of two isn't bad.' She turned to Francis. 'What can I do to make you happy?' she asked gently. 'Is there something special you'd like for Christmas?'

His eyes darkened with the stubborn determination she was becoming all too familiar with. 'Papa. I want Papa for Christmas.'

The ache in her heart deepened as Cornelia battled to keep her smile in place. 'Papa has other plans for Christmas, but I'm sure he'll want to spend some time with you in the New Year.' She looked to Alfred again. Her elder son stared back, his expression unreadable. 'And what about you? What would you like for Christmas?'

'I keep thinking about the nice time we had with Rose and Nathaniel at Grandmama's house in the summer.'

Dread unfurled inside her. Alfred couldn't possibly want to go back to Culford Manor, could he? Back to the childhood home that held such horrific memories of her parents' mistreatment and abuse towards their children... Lawrence, especially. Her mind reeled as she struggled for an excuse, a reason, why they could not go back. There was not a chance on earth that Lawrence would agree.

She swallowed. 'Grandmama's?'

'Yes. It would be fun to spend Christmas there. We could see Aunt Harriet, go riding, and the pond might be frozen and we can skate.' His eyes lit with excitement as he scrambled into a sitting position beneath his covers. 'Wouldn't that cheer you up, Francis? We could have adventures like they do in *Treasure Island*. Me, you, Rose and Nathaniel can pretend we're pirates.'

Cornelia watched Francis as he carefully considered his brother's suggestion. The wilfulness faded from his eyes, to be replaced by animation. 'That would be fun.' He turned to Cornelia, his smile wide. 'Could we, Mama? Could we go to see Aunt Harriet and the horses?'

Words stuck in Cornelia's throat at the dire prospect of suggesting to Lawrence that they return to their childhood home for Christmas. He would never agree to spend what should be the happiest, most joyous time of the year in the one place he hated more than any other. Not to mention that the doctor was unlikely to allow Esther to travel to Oxfordshire in her current state of health.

She closed the book in her lap. 'Well, I could certainly ask Uncle Lawrence and Aunt Esther what they think.' She walked to a small bookshelf under the bedroom window and placed the book on top. 'But I can't make any promises, or that Aunt Esther will be well enough to make the journey. This is the first Christmas since they married. I'm not sure Uncle Lawrence and Aunt Esther will want to spend it in such a big house. They might want a quieter Christmas.'

Alfred's eyes widened with expectation. 'But you'll ask him?'

Cornelia smiled at her sons, her heart heavy. 'I will, but no promises.'

Alfred grinned.

'Thank you, Mama.' Francis clapped, his gaze happy.

She laughed, before taking a deep breath. When Lawrence realised that returning to Culford Manor for Christmas would cheer the boys, he might relent, especially if the doctor agreed Esther was well enough. As for her apprehensions about the house, she would bury them. Lawrence's feelings and happiness were her bigger concern.

'Goodnight, my darlings. Sleep tight.'

'Goodnight, Mama.'

Cornelia walked to the door and blew them a kiss before leaving the door slightly ajar. With slow and heavy footsteps, she headed across the landing to Lawrence and Esther's room.

She and Lawrence owed it to Harriet to see how she fared. The house now belonged to all three of them, after all. It was wrong that Harriet had been left to her own devices these past few months. When their mother passed and left everything to Lawrence, he had not wanted any part of the estate but, with

Cornelia's gentle persuasion, he had eventually agreed to splitting the lands between their parents' three children equally.

Harriet had no wish to leave the manor, claiming she knew their mother better than anyone and would continue to run the estate accordingly. Lawrence had broached no argument and Cornelia had willingly left Harriet to her domain, too.

But that didn't mean she and Lawrence shouldn't be visiting every now and then to reassure themselves that Harriet was well and the estate thriving.

She knocked on the bedroom door, aware of how being bedridden would be stretching Esther's patience. It was imperative Cornelia tread carefully. The last thing she wanted was for Lawrence to lose his temper and further upset Esther.

'Come in.'

Cornelia found her brother and Esther in bed, the sheets pulled up around them, as they read in companionable silence. The scene was one of loving peace and she was loath to break it, but asking Lawrence about Culford was like ripping a bandage from a wound. Quicker was always better.

'Well, the boys are abed for the night. I think I might have some hot chocolate. Would either of you like to join me?'

'That sounds wonderful.' Esther smiled. 'Thank you, Cornelia.'

She looked to her brother as he turned the page of his book. 'Lawrence?'

'Hmm?'

Cornelia raised her eyebrows, her hands tightly clasped in front of her. 'Chocolate?'

'No, thank you.' He glanced at her, flashed a smile and returned to his reading.

Taking a deep breath, she approached the armchair beside him. 'I've just been talking to the boys about Christmas.'

'Oh?' Esther lowered her book, her gaze happy. 'Are they excited?'

'They weren't. Not at first.'

Surprise sparked in Lawrence's eyes. 'Why ever not? I would've thought they would be as full of excitement as Rose and Nathaniel are.'

'I'm afraid not.' Cornelia sighed and slumped her shoulders. 'They are thinking of David. Of his absence.'

'Oh, Cornelia.' Esther's gaze softened with sympathy. 'I'm so sorry.'

'It's all right. I will get them through this first Christmas without him, but...' She glanced at Lawrence. 'They did tell me about something that might cheer them up.'

Lawrence frowned. 'And? What was it?'

'They mentioned spending Christmas at the manor.'

His jaw immediately tightened, his eyes darkening. 'You know how I feel about that house.'

'Of course I do, but isn't going there for Christmas something you'd at least consider? It would make them so happy.'

'Why on earth do they think that godforsaken place will make their Christmas happier? The thought of setting foot on that estate again sickens me. I hope you gave them a flat no?'

'I couldn't.' Cornelia swallowed, hating she'd provoked her brother's rare irritation. 'They seemed so sad, but once Alfred suggested it, they lit up like candles. How can I refuse them? Would it be so bad? We owe it to Harriet to go there, if nothing else.'

He studied her a moment, his eyes losing a little of their anger. 'I intended inviting her here for Christmas. Esther and I don't want Harriet alone in that house, with only the staff for company, any more than you do.'

'But you know how Harriet feels about the manor. I'd wager

a hundred pounds she'd rather spend Christmas there than here. She'll no doubt have plans to entertain her friends and the local gentry. If Esther would like to, and the doctor says she is safe to travel, couldn't we lend ourselves to the possibility we might enjoy ourselves too? It would only be for a few days. A week at the most.'

Lawrence's gaze lingered on hers before he looked to the fire crackling in the hearth, his lips tightly pressed together. Cornelia turned to Esther, praying her sister-in-law sensed her desperate need to cheer her children. Damn David and his selfish decision to spend Christmas at Middleton Park, Sophie Hughes' ancestral home in Colerne, a small village not far from Bath, rather than see his children. Although, on reflection, that scenario might well have caused her impossible grief and anxiety.

Esther gave a discreet nod and turned to Lawrence. 'Cornelia's right, my love. If it would make Alfred and Francis happy, and the doctor says I am fit enough to travel, could we not go? The house belongs to all three of you. Harriet has been alone for some time now. Don't you want to see her? Ensure she is happy?'

A muscle flexed in Lawrence's jaw as he faced Esther, his eyes devoid of emotion. 'I telephone her regularly. She is quite all right.' He slowly closed his book and placed it on the small table beside him before tossing back the covers and striding to a small mahogany cabinet at the side of the room. 'Harriet has made it perfectly clear she has no need for me or Cornelia to visit. She's in her element as lady of the manor.'

Esther glanced at Cornelia. 'All the same, I'm sure she'd welcome her brother, sister, niece and nephews at this special time of year.'

Cornelia mouthed a thank-you to Esther as her brother opened the cupboard door and extracted a decanter and glass.

The sound of liquid being poured broke through the tense silence and Cornelia swiped her slightly clammy hands over her skirt.

Lawrence walked to the fireplace and looked into the flickering flames, his knuckles white around his glass. 'The abuse I suffered at our parents' hands almost escapes me these days.' He lifted his eyes to his wife. 'Because, at last, I am happy. At peace.' His gaze hardened as it drifted to Cornelia. 'If I go back, I have no doubt my peace would once again be shattered.'

'Not if you don't allow it.' Cornelia stood and approached him, gently placing her hand on his arm. 'Lawrence, please. I've nothing else to offer my children but my love and this one wish. No present, song or game will fill the hole David has left in their lives. This is their very first Christmas without him. Please. Let me do this one thing for them.' He ran his gaze over her face before looking past her to Esther.

Cornelia held her breath.

Seconds passed and then he faced her. 'I'll think about it.'

She released her held breath and smiled, her fingers tightening on his arm. 'That's all I ask. Thank you.'

'This is not a yes.'

'I know, and I won't press you.'

'I need a few days to think. No matter how much Esther might try to persuade me of Harriet's amiability, I'm quite certain she won't welcome our descent on her. I'll need to speak with her first, not to mention the doctor. Going to Culford will be a flat refusal if Rubinstein thinks there's even the tiniest risk to Esther and the baby.'

'Of course. I'm happy to telephone Harriet for you, if you think it will help.'

'Not yet. Leave things with me for the time being.'

'As you wish.' Cornelia slipped her hand from his arm and

flashed a grin at Esther, who smiled back, even though her concerned gaze continued to return to her husband. 'Thank you, Esther. Now, shall I see about that chocolate?'

Cornelia hurried from the room with every confidence Lawrence would come to see how important it was that Alfred and Francis enjoyed Christmas. The changes in her life meant it was her responsibility to explore new ways to make her children and herself happy. Although she might fail to provide them with the perfect family home she dreamed of, she would certainly try with everything she had.

25

Stephen strolled past the entrance to Pennington's men's department, his mind filled with what Herman Angel had told him about a possible suspect squatting near Pulteney Bridge. The need to pursue Herman's lead continued to nag at him, no matter how much he wished to quash it. However, as for Cornelia becoming embroiled in this tangled mess... that was another thing entirely.

God only knew how he would persuade her to leave the situation in his hands. He had dealt with a hundred and one women who had her fighting spirit, but he'd yet to encounter one who touched his buried feelings. The woman had reawakened something inside him. Something deeper than he'd even felt for his ex-fiancée. Their relationship now felt as though it had been a cordial romance. A joining of two people who liked one another's company. Whereas a mysterious tension crackled between him and Cornelia. *Good* tension. A connection with the possibility of real, in-depth passion that might lead them to trouble of the emotional kind.

As Stephen walked, the sensation he was being watched stole over him and he turned.

Damnation.

Joseph Carter strode towards him, his determined gaze steadfastly focused on Stephen despite the crowds of people who walked back and forth excitedly chattering and calling to one another. The second floor of the mammoth store buzzed with its usual, endless activity.

'Mr Gower. A word, if I may?'

Stephen blew a heavy breath. As if he had any choice in the matter. 'Yes, sir.'

'Walk with me.' Carter stared ahead, lines of fatigue showing around his eyes and the corners of his mouth. 'I understand there was some trouble at the store entrance a couple of days ago. A vagrant wanted access. A man I'm told you are acquainted with.'

'Hardly acquainted, sir.' They descended the grand staircase and Carter led them around the first-floor landing. 'I claimed to know him, so the matter was settled as quickly and as quietly as possible.'

Carter abruptly stopped, his gaze annoyed. 'Is that so? Well, I'm sorry, Gower, I'm not entirely sure I believe you. It's one thing if you don't want to do what I ask of you, quite another if you willingly lie to me.'

Stephen paused, mildly disturbed by the vehemence in Carter's tone and the anger in his eyes. This was not the charismatic and charming man who spoke with one customer after another, the staff more than willing to delay their work if it meant sharing a few minutes with an employer they held in such high esteem.

Yet he completely understood the hopelessness and despair so clearly etched on Carter's face.

Stephen gazed out over the crowds. 'Fine. He was a man I bumped into near the slums. I've also read the clippings and your thoughts about the similarities between this latest murder and your wife's.'

'You met this man while pursuing a lead?'

Stephen faced Joseph. 'Not a lead. Rather, I felt compelled to see where your wife's body was found.'

Carter's eyes were shadowed by deep pain. 'And the man who came into the store, he was there? Is he... do you think he could be—'

'No. Absolutely not.'

'How can you be so sure?'

Despite the sympathy that rose inside him, Stephen drew himself up straighter. If he was to pursue the exploration into Lillian Carter's demise, he had to exert his authority. Carter's emotional reaction was understandable, but Stephen would do all he could to manage it. 'You want me to look into your wife's killing, Mr Carter. Correct?'

He nodded. 'Yes.'

'Then you must believe my instincts for what is true are as strong as they are for what is false. I sense the vagrant who came into the store, whatever his circumstances might be now, was once doing all right in the world. He is fundamentally a good and honest man, to whom something happened, as it does to us all at some time.'

Carter's gaze bored into Stephen's. 'What do you mean?'

'Hopelessness, sir. The fear that what life has handed you is all there is and there is nothing anyone can do to change it. Having such a fear doesn't make us bad people, but it does make it damn hard to look at yourself in the mirror.'

The cacophony around them increased in volume as Stephen lapsed into silence, hating that he might have shown too much of his personal feelings. Slowly, Carter walked forward and clasped his hands to the balustrade that ran around the circumference of the landing.

Stephen gave him a moment alone. Carter's shoulders were high and stiff, his back straight. His wife had died almost four years ago, but Carter had somehow managed to go on to make a success of his life. Had been moved to take a second wife, not to mention maintaining a good relationship with his father. The problem was, the most recent murder had ignited a deep-seated passion in Carter to reopen old wounds.

In his desperation to find Walker, Hettie and Fay's killer, Stephen had turned from a good, capable officer of the law to a man obsessed. It had consumed him. Ruined him as a man and a detective. He could not stand by and allow the same to happen to Carter when the man had so much to lose.

Walking forward, he curled his hands around the balustrade next to Carter's. 'I will do what I can to help you, sir, but...'

Carter turned, a flicker of hope mixing with the sadness in his eyes. 'But what?'

Stephen inhaled a long breath, determined Carter understood the ramifications of what he was asking. 'You have to leave me to my investigation. I am a man, not God. I can't make you any promises. The cases I've worked on have not always been solved or resulted in justice. Finding a killer can take time. Finding the evidence to convict a suspect, even longer. If I'm to pursue this search to the best of my ability, you have to promise to give me the space and time to do that. If I were to fail you—'

'You won't.' Carter's impassioned gaze hardened. 'You came to work in this store for a reason. I have to believe that reason has everything to do with me. With Lillian. I promise to believe in you as one man to another. I will neither pursue nor bother you again, but I ask that you do not leave me to linger in ignorance. You will keep me abreast of what you discover. Agreed?'

Stephen held his gaze. To give Carter premature or false hope would be fatal, but he would tell him what he could. He dipped his head. 'Agreed.'

'Good. Then I will leave you to your work.'

Carter moved away from the balustrade and marched along the landing, somehow adopting an expression of smiling affability as though his anxieties had miraculously dissipated.

Leave me to my work.

Stephen clenched his jaw. His work was supposed to be walking around a department store, ensuring nothing was stolen or any trouble made. Now he'd landed himself in a whole lot of complication, so much worse than he could ever have imagined when he'd first come here.

He strode along the landing, not giving a damn that customers hurriedly glanced at him apprehensively. It was Carter's job to be the man at Pennington's helm, maintaining the pretence that all was well within the store. Not Stephen's.

Goddamn it.

Pressure squeezed around him like tentacles. He would have to visit Pulteney Bridge sooner rather than later, but he couldn't until after Cornelia's divorce hearing. His dreams the previous night had been riddled with visions of her weeping, hands reaching for her children, as they were tumbled into a carriage, the phantom-like face of her husband leering through the window.

He'd awoken bathed in sweat and his heart pounding, failure taunting him as the nightmare dissolved with the emerging daybreak.

How was he to leave Cornelia to her own devices tomorrow? How was he to stay away while she publicly revealed her husband's torment and abuse? Would her brother be after David Parker's blood? Lord knew, Stephen understood the potential for that completely.

His choice to go to the hearing was already made. He had to be there. Had to find a way to get an hour or two away from his duties at Pennington's in order to support Cornelia.

Thoroughly agitated, Stephen strode down the final stairs and into the bustling atrium. If he allowed Cornelia to help him find Lillian's killer, would that provide some relief from her fears for her young family? She had said her sister-in-law was close to Elizabeth Pennington, which meant she could possibly come to trust Cornelia too. A murder investigation always started with the victim. This meant if he was to uncover more about the motive behind Lillian Carter's killing, he needed to learn more about the woman herself.

Cornelia could be the best person to speak to Elizabeth Pennington about Carter's first wife. Conversing with Elizabeth had to be easier than it would talking with Carter. He was a man on the edge. A man consumed by torment and tragedy. To use Cornelia and Elizabeth Pennington was a roundabout way of investigating, but it *was* a way.

Carter's wife would be able to provide a more distinct picture of Carter, the man he once was and the man he was today. Information that was vital if Stephen was to develop a picture of his marriage to Lillian. Of the type of person she was, what compelled her to venture into the lowest parts of poverty and desperation. If there was a link between her and the latest victim, maybe it lay in the type of women they were... or who they knew.

Either way, Stephen knew he was tangled up in the case now. Whether he liked it or not.

26

The day of the court hearing broke clear and cold, the sun low in a cloudless sky. As the children walked with Helen around the circular pavement of The Circus, towards school, Cornelia turned away from her bedroom window.

She approached her open wardrobe, flutters of nervous trepidation swirling in her stomach. Today she'd learn if she was to lose her children to their father, but she could not falter or doubt. She must be stronger than she'd ever been before, or else risk falling apart completely.

If the hearing brought the result she wanted, nothing would stop her from returning briefly to their home in Oxfordshire and bringing everything she and the children wanted back to Bath. The day she'd left David, she'd escaped with as few things as possible.

Once she was at liberty to act, she would build a new future for Alfred and Francis. Every decision would be made for their benefit, safe in the knowledge David could no longer sabotage her endeavours. He was free to build a life with the *honourable*

Sophie Hughes and Cornelia would be free to build a life with her boys.

She scrutinised her few clothes and extracted a grey tweed jacket and skirt. She wandered to the tall, free-standing mirror at the side of the room and held the garments in front of her, studying her selection.

Professional, yet demure.

If she teamed it with her favourite black hat, adorned with grey feathers and white berries, black shoes and purse, the ensemble would present a woman taking control of her life. A mother and a wronged, but formidable, wife.

She quickly dressed.

When she'd woken that morning, the quietness of the house had hung over her like an ominous shadow. Now her first layers of armour would soon be in place. Her lawyer presenting David's catalogue of misdeeds would be her artillery and, with Lawrence at the courthouse, Cornelia would have all the army she needed.

She sat at the dressing table in front of one of the windows and carefully arranged her hair, then put on a light covering of make-up. With a curt nod at her reflection, Cornelia picked up her hat and purse and left the bedroom.

As she passed Lawrence and Esther's bedroom door, the urgency in Esther's tone caused Cornelia to stop. She pressed her back against the wall and strained to hear the hushed conversation within.

Late yesterday evening, the doctor had refused Esther's plea to attend the hearing. Now, it seemed, her brother and Esther squabbled... over Cornelia.

'If David wins custody, Lawrence, we have to be prepared for Cornelia's despair. Can you imagine how you would feel to be separated from Rose and Nathaniel? I am yet to give birth to this little one, but I already love your children enough to know I would hate to be away from them for even a day or two, let alone weeks.'

'I know, and I will care for Cornelia, if the worst should happen.' Lawrence's tone was resolute. 'But David will not win custody of the boys today. He's done too much wrong for a judge not to rule in Cornelia's favour.'

'And if he does?'

'He won't.'

'Neither of us can guarantee that. How can we?'

The concern in Esther's voice caused Cornelia to feel fresh guilt at what she was putting her brother and his wife through.

She hesitated and then knocked on the door. Esther's and Lawrence's voices immediately fell silent as Cornelia entered.

Her brother glanced at his wife before facing Cornelia, his cheeks mottled and his jaw tight. 'How are you faring, sister?'

'Very well.' She walked farther into the room, her fingers tight on the brim of her hat. 'I couldn't help overhearing your conversation.' She looked at them. 'Please, neither of you must worry. After all, I've sought advice from a lawyer and a former sergeant of Scotland Yard.' She forced a smile. 'I couldn't be more prepared for whatever might happen this morning.'

Cornelia stood firm, despite the awful fear pulsing through her that the next time she returned to the house, she might be packing the children's belongings for transportation to wherever David might wish to take her beloved boys.

Admiration gleamed in Lawrence's eyes. 'Exactly.' He turned to Esther and slipped his arm around her shoulders, pulling her close. 'See? You must trust that all will be well. Cornelia is a Culford. She's made of strong stuff. Isn't that right, Cornelia?'

'Absolutely.'

Esther bristled and gently shook Lawrence's arm from her

shoulders. 'I didn't doubt that for a moment. Of course you're strong, Cornelia. You're a woman, after all.' She shot Lawrence a pointed look. 'But I can't help worrying that justice won't be done today, and David's lawyer will find a way to undermine all that yours might say.'

'Mr Hartford was encouraged by everything I've told him.' Cornelia gave a dismissive wave, praying Lawrence or Esther hadn't notice the way her fingers shook. She quickly lowered her hand. 'I honestly believe he will win the divorce and the boys for me and then, at last, we can all move forward.'

Lawrence picked up his tie from the bed. 'All the same, I wish there was something more we could add, to ensure David has no case.'

Cornelia pursed her lips. She dreaded to think what Lawrence's response would be once he learned of the deeper abuse she'd suffered at David's hands. Lord only knew how he would react, but today was not about Lawrence, Esther or even David. It was all about Alfred and Francis.

Cornelia cleared her throat and purposefully changed the subject. 'Now, how is Elizabeth? Did you speak to her again yesterday?'

'Yes, she stopped by the house.' Esther sighed, her hand slowly circling her bump. 'She is looking so tired and strained. I fear my leaving Pennington's for the time being hasn't helped.'

Cornelia sat beside her. 'Maybe not, but you are dear friends and none of this is your fault.'

'I know, and Elizabeth is happy to talk to you. She longs for Joseph's complete happiness and fears such a thing impossible until Lillian's killer is found, but she asks that you tread carefully with Mr Gower. The last thing she wants is for him to turn away from the investigation now that Joseph is pinning every hope on him.'

'Every hope?'

Unease crept through Cornelia.

Esther stood, pressed a hand to her back and gently stretched. 'Yes, but I'm sure Elizabeth will explain everything to you.'

'Right. Well...' Cornelia rose and walked towards the door. 'I'm going downstairs and we will leave shortly, Lawrence. I'm not afraid of what might happen today, and neither should either of you be. Everything will be just fine.'

She left the room and walked downstairs, her mind reeling. Just as she reached the hallway, someone knocked at the front door.

Charles quickly appeared and Cornelia raised her hand to halt him. 'I'll answer it, Charles. I know you're always in the middle of something or other.' She smiled. 'Let me deal with whoever this might be.'

'As you wish, Miss Culford.'

Charles retreated and Cornelia walked to the door. Pulling it open, surprise made her step back. 'Miss Pennington! Whatever are you doing here?' Surely Elizabeth's ears must have been burning? She quickly looked past Elizabeth to Esther's assistant window dresser. 'Amelia, isn't it?'

The younger woman nodded, slightly blushing. 'Yes.'

Elizabeth thrust a bouquet of yellow roses towards Cornelia. 'We've come to offer our support. Here. For luck.'

'Oh, they're beautiful.' Cornelia took the flowers, warmth spreading through her. 'Thank you. We still have some time before we leave. Would you like to come in?'

The women entered the house and Cornelia closed the door.

'Go upstairs to the drawing room. I'm sure Esther will be as pleased to see you as I am. Would you like some tea?'

'No, thank you, I'm quite all right.' Elizabeth looked at Amelia. 'Would you like a cup of tea?'

Amelia shook her head, her concerned gaze focused entirely on Cornelia. 'No, thank you.'

Cornelia smiled at the younger woman. 'I'm perfectly fine, you know. There's no need to look so worried.' She placed the flowers on a side table. 'Let's go upstairs.'

Cornelia led the way up the stairs and they entered the drawing room. 'Make yourselves comfortable. I'll tell Esther you're here.'

Knocking on Lawrence and Esther's bedroom door, Cornelia poked her head into the room.

'Esther? Elizabeth and Amelia have called in. Would you be able to join us in the drawing room?'

Esther smiled. 'I'm not surprised Elizabeth's here again. She always shows support to a member of staff having difficulties. I suspect she's brought Amelia so we can talk some more about plans for the store. Elizabeth rarely stops working, regardless of the other troubles in her life.' She turned to Lawrence who stood in front of the window, looking at something in the street. 'Lawrence? Will you be joining us?'

'No.' He glanced at his wife. 'I'll leave you ladies to talk.'

Cornelia helped Esther from the bed and into her robe before leading the way into the drawing room.

As soon as they stepped into the room, Elizabeth patted the seat next to her on the settee. 'Come and sit here, Cornelia. Oh, you are looking a little better than yesterday, Esther. I'm so pleased.'

The kindness in her employer's invitation to sit beside her scattered Cornelia's concerns as a rush of unity came over her. Could these women become more than her colleagues? She'd not heard a word from the women she'd thought of as friends in

Oxfordshire. No doubt David had painted her in the worst light possible, making out she'd abandoned him and taken his children against their will.

She sat beside Elizabeth. 'It's very kind of you both to call.'

'Well, from what Esther has told me about your cad of a husband, no luck will be needed in that courtroom today.' Fiery determination burned in Elizabeth's green gaze. She shot Esther a sly smile and faced Cornelia again. 'The man appears to be unworthy of you *and* your children. The judge will see that as soon as look at... what is his name?'

'David.' Cornelia smiled at Elizabeth. 'And I'm glad you think so.'

'Don't you?' Elizabeth raised her eyebrows, challenge burning in her eyes and, in that moment, Cornelia understood she had one choice. Either rise to the challenge or sink. She had no intention of sinking.

She gave a curt nod. 'Of course.'

'Good.' Elizabeth slid a second look of triumph at Esther, who merely shook her head and rolled her eyes, a smile pulling at her lips. 'So...' Elizabeth faced Cornelia again. 'As no luck is needed, we're here to support you this morning, just as you are willing to support me and Joseph in finding the man who killed Lillian.'

Cornelia studied her employer. Her expression and tone could have been described as confident, even a little blasé. But Cornelia recognised an underlying uncertainty in Elizabeth. She saw that she was forcing herself not to falter, not even for a moment. Something Cornelia found herself practising more and more.

She shook her head. 'Your troubles are different to mine, but by no means less distressing. I want to help you just as Esther would, were she able. I will do everything I can to work side by side with Mr Gower. Of course, I'm not sure he'll want my help, but I will do my best to be your eyes and ears, leaving you to comfort your husband and run Pennington's.'

'Excellent. I'm pleased to have your help, especially if it means my friend does as she's told and rests until her precious babe is born.' Elizabeth smiled at Esther. 'As Amelia and I will be working more closely than ever now, I have also confided my problems to her. The way I see it, if Joseph is on a one-man mission to bring this killer to justice, I am on a four-woman mission to do the same.'

Amelia straightened in her seat, her brown eyes darkening. 'Absolutely. You see, Miss Culford—'

'Cornelia, please.'

The younger woman smiled. 'Cornelia... Elizabeth and Esther have done so much for me – and I don't just mean elevating my position at Pennington's or my involvement with the suffragists. They've taught me about care and kindness, love and commitment to others.'

'You didn't know those things before you came to Pennington's?' Cornelia asked, softly. Amelia was most certainly a quieter member of staff at the store, but she was also one of the most pleasant and amiable, too. 'You are one of the loveliest people I've come to know.'

'That's very nice of you to say, but I also feel a lot of distrust.' She glanced at Elizabeth and then Esther, who nodded encouragingly. 'But I'm sure the longer I work at Pennington's, the more I'll believe there really are many good people in the world.'

Elizabeth squeezed Amelia's hand. 'You will and, considering the plans I have in mind for you, you will soon meet a lot more people than you'll ever find in Pennington's.'

Amelia frowned, but Elizabeth tightened her lips, as though she'd said too much.

Cornelia looked at the trio of women around her. She had never felt such accord. Such strong, unshakeable unity between four women who were once strangers but had joined to become an unbending force.

'So, that's decided then.' Elizabeth suddenly lit up with a happiness that was tangible. 'The four of us will be the strength behind Joseph and Stephen Gower. We'll do everything and anything to find happiness again for my husband.'

A deep sense of camaraderie settled over Cornelia's heart. Nothing and no one would stop her from winning her divorce *and* her children. Nothing and no one would stop her doing all she could to bring Lillian Carter's killer to justice either.

It seemed that in Bath – in Pennington's – she'd found all she needed to push through to the bitter end… in everything.

27

Cornelia's knees ever so slightly trembled as the judge took the bench, the courtroom's dimness and dark wall-to-wall wooden panelling unsettling. The tension was palpable, and she clenched her hands a little tighter in her lap. Tipping her gaze to the ivory ceiling, she focused on the ornate cornices of entwined vines and fruit. Anything to avoid looking at David, where he sat with not one but two lawyers on the table across the aisle which separated them.

Her heart pulsed so loudly in her ears, Mr Hartford's voice sounded far, far away even though he stood right beside her. She blinked and forced herself to concentrate on what was being said.

'Mrs Parker is a law-abiding, moral and attentive mother to Mr and Mrs Parker's children and, until their relationship could no longer be salvaged, a good and devoted wife to her husband. The first and foremost reason she petitioned for these proceedings was to end a marriage that had become increasingly difficult to bear. A marriage that she had done her best over and over again to protect. Unfortunately, Mr Parker's actions and behaviour have made her best efforts unsuccessful.'

The judge peered at Mr Hartford over the rim of his half-spectacles, before he briefly glanced at David. Cornelia followed his gaze and barely resisted flinching. David stared directly at her, his eyes cold and full of malice. His mouth twisted into an ugly sneer. She quickly turned to the judge, anger bubbling inside of her, only inflamed by Sophie Hughes sitting primly upright in one of the seats behind her husband-to-be.

Almost certainly, her presence was just another knife with which David sought to hurt Cornelia. Well, he had failed. Today would be her biggest triumph.

The judge cleared his throat and addressed David's lawyer. 'Does Mr Parker seek to contest the divorce, Mr Hamilton?'

'No, Your Honour. Mr Parker is more than happy to give Mrs Parker a divorce.' The tall, skinny lawyer pushed his fallen blond hair from his eyes and glanced at Cornelia. 'It is their sons, Alfred and Francis Parker, that Mr Parker is unwilling to abandon as his wife would like. He has been a good father to his children, despite the alleged failures as a husband claimed by Mrs Parker.'

Cornelia barely resisted laughing. A good father? Was his absence from the family home in favour of gentlemen's clubs representative of a good father? Were raising his hand, shouting and calling his sons' mother abusive names the acts of a good father? Was—

'Mr Hartford, would you like to respond on behalf of Mrs Parker to her husband's claims of his paternal record? I wish to have all the information from both sides so that I can make a decision about the divorce before we proceed to the custody of the children.'

Cornelia clenched her hands in her lap, her hands clammy

as Mr Hartford came out from behind their table to pace a few steps in front of the judge's high seat.

'I agree with Mr Parker's counsel...'

Cornelia froze, her eyes wide as she stared at Mr Hartford in horror. What on God's earth was he saying? Had he not believed her words about David? Had he sat in his office and allowed her to talk when all the while—

'...that their client has been a good father in as far as being able to gain enough self-control to not inflict on his sons what he has his wife. Your Honour...' Mr Hartford clasped his hands behind his back as he continued to pace, his wily gaze moving from the judge to David and back again. 'Mr Parker has hit his wife several times over many months. Has been conducting an illicit affair for a number of years. An extramarital liaison he promised Mrs Parker was over, and for which she forgave him, on the understanding it was over.

'Mr Parker lied, Your Honour. He lied and continued to see this woman – a woman who sits in this courtroom today – and betrayed Mrs Parker time and time again. He reacted to her request for a divorce with violence and deplorable language. He waited until the children were away from his home before physically assaulting his wife, I admit, but I am not sure any man should be given credit for such premeditated abuse.'

Sickness coated Cornelia's throat and her hands trembled. She could feel Lawrence's stare boring into the back of her head, his anger almost tangible. There wasn't a need to turn in her seat to see the rage that would be on his face, or the shock on Elizabeth's and Amelia's. Shame writhed inside Cornelia until every part of her wanted to flee from the room, but she held fast. She had to hold on...

Mr Hamilton leapt to his feet. 'Your Honour, Mr Parker unequivocally denies these unsubstantiated charges. He confesses to heated arguments between himself and Mrs Parker, but those altercations never once turned physical.'

Cornelia slowly raised her head and turned to David, a fury like she'd never known heating her entire body. Words battled on her tongue. Her heart raced. How dare he deny what he had done to her? How dare he sit there, his face impervious and his shoulders pulled back, as though affronted by the very notion.

She moved to stand when Mr Hartford shot her a clear look of warning and she lowered to her seat.

Her lawyer faced the judge, his cheeks mottled. 'These allegations were not given to me lightly, Your Honour. Mrs Parker withheld the personal details of her and Mr Parker's relationship until the bitter end. I believe she would have taken her husband's mistreatment of her to the grave had he not sought to remove their sons from her care. These are the desperate actions of a mother. A woman so besieged by grief and pain that she might be separated from the boys she holds as her very reason for living.

'I implore you, sir, to take Mr Parker's continued denial and deceit into account when making your decision about custody of Mr and Mrs Parker's children. Added to what we have already heard here today, I would like you also to consider that Mr Parker became engaged to the woman he was conducting an affair with without this divorce even being finalised. His clear desire for a hasty second marriage does not speak of a family man, sir. At least, not in my opinion.'

Cornelia dragged her gaze from Mr Hartford as he resumed his seat beside her and turned to the judge. His gaze bored into hers before he turned to David. 'Mr Parker...'

She closed her eyes and waited for the judge's verdict.

28

Stephen shifted from one foot to the other as he stared at the closed double doors of the courthouse. A light rain had started to fall, causing a cold dampness to the air, but he couldn't leave until Cornelia emerged from within the white stone building. Time and again, he'd considered waiting inside, but to do so felt too much like an invasion of her privacy.

After the way things had been left between them at the tea shop, he'd carefully and steadfastly avoided her at Pennington's, still unsure about her help with the murder investigation. Yet a small part of him wanted her involved as much for himself as Joseph Carter. He liked Cornelia. Admired her, even. She had a strength that appealed to him. Maybe her stubbornness did a little, too. He had always liked a woman with backbone and direction. A woman who knew her own mind.

So, he decided, if she won her divorce but lost custody of her children, she could join the investigation as a way of providing proof he believed in her, cared about her and wanted her – maybe even needed her – beside him.

Her strength was inspiring and strengthening during his

weakest moments, and if the investigation could serve as a distraction from her pain, then he wanted to be the one who enabled it. He might even accept her invitation to attend the ball at The Phoenix.

But if she won her divorce *and* the children... no investigation and no ball. What need would she have to be with him then?

Time passed slowly as he waited for the people just inside the courtroom doors to emerge.

Was it Cornelia and her family? Someone else?

At last, the doors opened, and Elizabeth Pennington and Amelia Wakefield stepped outside, their smiles wide and their expressions happy. They had to be here for Cornelia. She must have triumphed.

Yet he couldn't leave without being certain.

He stretched his neck, trying to see her as more people spilled outside. Then she appeared through the crowds...

If he'd thought her beautiful before, now she looked nothing short of magnificent. Her blue eyes were alight and her cheeks flushed as she accepted embraces from Elizabeth Pennington and Amelia, before they stood back and allowed a tall, dark-haired man to step closer. He pulled Cornelia into his arms and tightly squeezed her, as though he would never let her go. Ignoring a jolt of unexpected jealousy, Stephen studied the man and his trained eye immediately spotted the family resemblance. Her brother, maybe? A cousin?

Satisfied she had both her divorce *and* the children, Stephen turned to make his way back to Pennington's. Joseph Carter had only allowed him an hour away.

'This isn't over, Cornelia.'

Stephen stopped.

'Do you understand?' the man spat between gritted teeth. 'This. Isn't. Over.'

He had to be Cornelia's husband. *Ex*-husband. David Parker. He was of medium height and build, with dark blond hair poking out from beneath his top hat; his face was mottled with anger as he jabbed his finger at Cornelia.

Stephen stepped forward to intervene, when the man he had assumed to be Cornelia's relation strode forward, grabbed Parker's arm and shoved him backwards. 'Get out of here, David, before I damn well throttle you. You're neither wanted nor needed. You've got the freedom you wanted, so leave. Now.'

'You're nothing, Cornelia,' Parker shouted, taking slow steps backwards. 'Nothing.'

Whirling around, he gripped the hand of the younger woman beside him and marched down the courthouse steps. As he passed, Stephen fought the urge to stick out his foot to send the bastard tumbling face first onto the pavement.

He glared at Parker's retreating back, so full of anger that he didn't notice Cornelia approaching until she'd flung her arms around him.

He stumbled backwards and she laughed.

'You're here. Oh, Stephen, I won. The divorce and the children. I have so much to thank you for. If it wasn't for your advice and encouragement, I am certain David would have walked away with my boys.'

His heart beat fast as care for her swept through him. All it would take was a slight dip of his head and his lips could be on hers.

He forced himself to look over her shoulder. Cornelia's friends studied him with mixed expressions of curiosity, delight... and, from her suspected relation, annoyance.

Gently grasping her wrists, Stephen eased her away from his

body. 'You have nothing to thank me for. Everything you've done before and today is to your credit, not mine. Was that him? Your husband?'

Her smile dissolved. 'Yes. *Ex*-husband.'

'Does his threat frighten you? If it does—'

'My days of being afraid of anything David might say or do are over. From now on, everything I do, every decision I make, will be for the benefit of my children or me. No exceptions.'

'I'm glad to hear it.' He glanced over her shoulder again. 'And is that man currently glowering at me your brother?'

She turned and smiled. 'Lawrence, yes. Don't worry, he's a pussycat. He's been so good to the children and me. He and Esther mean the world to us.' She faced him, her blue eyes happy. 'Do you have to return to the store? Only, Elizabeth and Amelia are joining us for tea at the house to celebrate. You are more than welcome to—'

'Ah, no. I have to get back, but thank you.'

'Another time, then.'

Stephen bit back a smile. It was a statement rather than a question. 'Maybe.'

Her gaze sparkled with mischief. 'Definitely.'

Their eyes locked and Stephen's heart stuttered. He quickly looked away. 'I've been thinking...'

'Yes?'

He studied her. 'We should talk about the investigation. I thought if you won custody of the children, you would lose your desire to help with the investigation. I hope I'm right?'

'Not at all. Why would you think so?'

'Because this is dangerous, Cornelia. I don't want to risk you or your children being hurt.'

'And you think I do?' Her eyes darkened with a determination he was becoming all too familiar with. 'I want to help

Esther with this, Stephen. I have to. I don't want her feeling she has to do something to help Elizabeth and risk the baby.'

He looked away from her into the distance, his mind and heart racing with indecision and fear.

Finally, he faced her. 'You will do exactly what I ask of you. No taking matters into your own hands or wandering off to do Lord knows what.'

She gave a curt nod. 'Absolutely.'

Uncertainty warred with longing inside him. It was bad enough that he'd become embroiled in the details of his employers' lives. To involve Cornelia further was a stupidly risky thing to do. Yet she could undoubtedly help. They could work together... Spend time together. That desire was partially embedded in his own wish to see more of her, but also in answer to the deep protectiveness that had consumed him during and after Parker's threats. The closer Stephen remained to Cornelia, the less likely he'd be absent should her ex-husband decide to make a reappearance.

He inhaled a long breath and slowly released it. 'Then, I'd like your help.' Her bright smile stole the air from his lungs.

'Oh, Stephen. Thank you.' She clutched his arm. 'I promise I will only act on your instructions. Only do as you command.'

He smiled before glancing towards her friends again.

Elizabeth Pennington looked at him as though she was itching to speak to him.

Stephen quickly said, 'You are not to divulge anything to Mr Carter of what we do. Not yet.'

She nodded, her intelligent gaze sombre. 'I understand.'

'I want you to find out as much as you can from Elizabeth Pennington about Carter's first wife. How long they were a couple, the state of their relationship and more details about her work. Murder invariably starts with the victim, so it's imperative we know as much as we can about Lillian Carter.'

'I'll speak to Elizabeth as soon as possible.'

'Ensuring her husband knows nothing?'

'Yes, I'm not sure she'll like keeping anything from Joseph, but I'll insist on it for the time being.'

'Good, it's important we get this right.' He drew in a long breath against his growing anxiety of doing something wrong. This time, any errors he made could affect his employers or... Cornelia. He could not allow that to happen. 'My experiences in the police do not make me invincible. I've made mistakes in the past and could again.'

'You don't need to teach me what it is to fail someone, Stephen.'

He lowered his voice, hating the sudden sadness in her eyes 'If you are thinking about your children, you have not failed them. You left your husband because you were doing right by them, protecting them, and now they will stay with their mother, where they belong. Where they will want to be, once they are old enough to understand their father's actions.'

Tears glazed her eyes even as she softly smiled. 'You're sweet.'

He smiled and shook his head. 'Well, that's the first time a person has called me sweet.'

'I find that hard to believe.' She raised onto her toes and pressed a light kiss to his cheek. 'I'll see you at the store on Monday and we'll talk further.'

He nodded, stunned into silence.

Her lips had been soft and warm. Gentle, yet filled with purpose.

Damnation.

He was in deeper trouble than ever.

29

The discreet knock on his office door diverted Joseph's attention from the mass of glove designs spread out on his desk. 'Come in.'

'Mr Carter?' His secretary, Mrs Green smiled. 'I have your father here to see you.'

'My father?' Surprised and pleased, Joseph immediately stood and walked around his desk. 'Then show him in. Thank you, Mrs Green. Could you arrange for some coffee, please?'

'Of course, sir.'

She stood back and Robert Carter ambled into the room, his smile broad and his blue eyes shining. 'Son. How are we this fine day?'

Joseph laughed. 'All the better for seeing you, Pa. What are you doing here? It's been weeks since you dropped into the store.'

'Which is exactly why I'm here.' He embraced Joseph and held him at arm's length. 'Nothing wrong with an unexpected visit from your father, is there?'

'Not at all. Come and have a seat.' He led the way to the

seating area in the far corner of his office and they sank into two overstuffed leather armchairs. 'You're looking well. I assume your trip to the capital wasn't as bad as you feared?'

'No, but that brother of mine has a lot to answer for. He thinks, now we're both retired, we should be kicking up our heels like we're men in our twenties. He's got more energy than is good for him.'

Joseph laughed. 'Well, I'm glad for it. You look happy, Pa.'

Slowly, his father's smile dissolved and concern immediately dropped into Joseph's stomach. With everything else he was dealing with, he wasn't sure he'd have the mental strength needed if anything was upsetting his beloved father.

'Pa? What is it?'

Robert Carter opened his mouth to speak when Mrs Green entered bearing a tray with coffee and a plate of biscuits.

'Thank you, Mrs Green. There's no need for you to pour, I'll take care of it.'

'Yes, sir.'

The moment the door closed behind her, Joseph faced his father and raised his eyebrows, waiting.

His father studied Joseph before leaning back in his chair and placing his hat in his lap. 'I spoke to Elizabeth when I was downstairs.'

Dread unfurled in Joseph's stomach, tension immediately inching across his shoulders. 'And?'

'And she's worried, son. Worried about you.'

Annoyance simmered deep inside Joseph. He felt more than a little betrayed that Elizabeth should discuss him with his father behind his back.

He picked up the coffee pot and began filling their cups. 'She has no need to be worried.'

'Don't lie to me.' His father's tone was clipped and firm.

'She's a strong woman, Joseph. She can handle pretty much anything life throws at her, but when it comes to you, I'm not so sure. The woman loves the bones of you, which is wonderful, until that love becomes a person's weakness. Their vulnerability.'

Swallowing hard, Joseph passed his father a cup. 'She'll be fine. I'll ensure it.'

His father cautiously sipped his coffee. 'And how are you going to do that when it is you that is causing her pain?'

'Me?' Angry, Joseph glared. 'It isn't me causing her pain. It's the bastard who is here, in Bath, and killing again. How do you expect me to ignore that another woman, not acting in any way dissimilar to Lillian, has been murdered? I'm convinced the man who killed the woman by the slum a couple of weeks ago is the same man who killed Lillian. This time he will be caught. I don't care what I have to do, or how I have to do it, I will ensure he is found.'

'And you won't get any argument on that score from me.'

'So, what is this all about if not to warn me off?'

'Because I fear you'll miss seeing that you have a wife who needs you too. A wife who is alive and well and trying her best to be there for you.'

'I know that. I love Elizabeth. She's everything to me.' His father arched his eyebrow. 'Everything?'

Joseph clenched his jaw, his anger slipping away as guilt about how he'd been speaking to Elizabeth recently took over. He swiped his hand over his face and forced himself to hold his father's wily gaze. 'Yes.'

'Then calm yourself down when you're around her. Show her that you see her. Hear her. She wants to feel she is helping you. Supporting you. She's not going to believe she is doing that if you ignore her and go off gung-ho on a one-man mission.'

Joseph stared, before lifting his coffee cup and sitting back in his chair. He exhaled. 'She told you about Gower, didn't she?'

'Yes. And, for what it's worth, I think involving him is the right thing to do. There can't be any more time wasted. Lillian deserves to rest in peace.' His father's cheeks reddened, his eyes cold. 'Her killer needs the rope. It's as simple as that. And if this Gower character can facilitate that happening, then you had no choice but to employ his help.'

Relief loosened a little of the tension in Joseph's shoulders. 'So, if you're not mad about that, you really are just concerned about Elizabeth?'

'I'm just giving you some advice. Take care of her, Joseph. I don't want to see her walk away from you.'

'She'd never—'

'She would.' His father glared. 'Don't ever underestimate what her arse of a father did to her. His treatment of her, his refusal to acknowledge her intelligence and capabilities, will run deep in her for the rest of her life. If Elizabeth thinks you are treating her in any way similar to Edward Pennington, you risk losing her. Mark my words.'

Joseph briefly closed his eyes and bore the jolt of pain that slashed across his heart. His father was right. Elizabeth had been dismissed and ignored for the majority of her adult life by a man who was supposed to love her more than any other.

Now Joseph was that man in her life.

He swallowed hard, his foolishness washing over him, making him want to flee from his office to find Elizabeth. He needed her forgiveness. Her belief that he would never, ever do anything to consciously wound her.

'Damnation. I'm hurting her, aren't I? She wants me for life, Pa. She wants my children.'

Robert Carter grinned, his eyes lighting up. 'Then give yourself to her, Joseph. Yourself, and some little ones.'

'But Lillian—'

'Will always be a part of your life. But she is also now part of Elizabeth's. Don't ignore that. Let her know how much you love her for pursuing Lillian's justice right beside you. Show her you couldn't do this without her. Just *love* the woman.'

Joseph put his cup on the low table in front of them and stood. 'There's somewhere I need to be, Pa.'

'Aye, I think there is.' Robert Carter put his cup beside his son's and stood, pulling Joseph into his embrace. 'Take care of her, Joe. Elizabeth's not as strong as she likes to think she is. None of us are.'

Tears shamefully pricked the back of Joseph's eyes as culpability pressed down on him. He blinked them back and nodded, easing out of his father's arms. 'I understand, Pa. Trust me.'

'Good. Then off you go.'

With another nod, Joseph headed for his office door.

30

Cornelia sat in the passenger seat of Lawrence's sleek, gunmetal grey motor car, speeding away from Bath towards Oxfordshire. Even though Christmas Day drew ever closer, all Lawrence and Esther could think of or discuss was the fundraiser ball at The Phoenix this coming Saturday. Not that Cornelia blamed them. It was a huge coup for women's suffrage, a campaign so close to Esther's heart and she was incredibly disappointed she wouldn't be able to attend.

She looked across at her brother. 'How is Esther? I know she's thrilled by the response to the ball but upset that she won't be there.'

'She is, but relieved that her friend and fellow suffragist Louise will manage things.' Lawrence steered the car passed a horse and cart carrying some milk churns. 'There will be suffragettes at the ball, too, but I trust they'll not think a ball an ideal opportunity for militant action.'

Cornelia grimaced as apprehension rippled through her. Now that her divorce had been granted, her own mortality had preyed on her mind. She was, in effect, her children's only parent now. 'Surely nothing of a violent nature will occur?'

'We can only hope. The Cause remains a huge issue while Parliament stubbornly refuses to even discuss a bill, let alone make steps towards giving women the vote. I fear the campaigning could go on for years, which means more militant action.'

Cornelia stared ahead as Stephen came into her mind. She couldn't help but wonder if he had been present during any of the suffragette demonstrations in London. The newspapers had shown a lot of photographs depicting the violence and police intervention, but she wasn't sure Scotland Yard dealt with that sort of thing.

'It might be beneficial to have a police officer at the ball,' she mused. 'Just in case.' When Lawrence didn't answer, Cornelia glanced at him. 'Lawrence?'

He raised an eyebrow. 'You are really quite taken by Mr Gower, aren't you?'

Warmth seeped into her cheeks even as she lifted her chin. 'Yes. As a matter of fact, I am. He's interesting. Intelligent. Even a little mysterious. All things that appeal to me.'

'You find mystery appealing? Isn't it better for friends to show openness and integrity?'

'He does. I just mean I'm convinced there's more to him. More I'd like to learn. I sense he carries things that have hurt him deeply. Maybe those things are why he left the force.' A desire to defend Stephen rose inside her. 'Maybe even made him seek a different life. A quieter life. Lord knows, I understand that more than most.'

Lawrence glanced at her. 'Do you have a romantic interest in him, by any chance? Don't you think it's a little soon after David to be thinking of stepping out with someone else?'

Cornelia laughed, although secretly delighted her brother should even contemplate her stepping out. 'Too soon? My goodness, you really have no idea how long I've endured a loveless marriage, have you? But, actually, romance is not on my mind.' She shrugged, hoping she was being convincing. 'It is Mr Gower's intellect and company I enjoy. Nothing more.'

'For the moment.'

She shot him a mock glare, relieved that they were approaching the home she and the children had once shared with David. A beautiful, yet modest, house that would have suited her for the rest of her life. Unfortunately, the house would now forever remind her of arguments, accusations and violence.

When they had returned to The Circus after the court hearing, she had been braced for Lawrence's fury at the sufferings she'd concealed during her marriage, but he'd surprised her. His rage was clear in his tense shoulders and pale face, but he hadn't admonished or blamed her. Instead, he'd taken Cornelia in his arms, kissed her hair and promised to be there for the rest of her and the children's lives.

Now tears pricked her eyes as she studied his turned cheek, her heart swelling with love for a man who had known violence at his father's hands throughout childhood and adolescence.

As though Lawrence sensed her watching him, he turned and smiled, his eyes happy.

Cornelia returned his smile. Reassured by his insistence that he accompany her today but praying David had kept his promise to stay away.

Lawrence pulled the car up outside the house and Cornelia stepped out, staring up at the house. Even the wisteria climbing around the door and the small fountain in the garden did nothing to raise her wavering spirits. Her strength faltered as realisation of her uncertain future set in. Who knew what road she and the children would take now? There had been a time when she'd thought herself building a family home, a sense of security and peace for Albert and Francis.

Now she had no idea what she could give them.

Sadness threatened, and Cornelia squared her shoulders, purposefully burying her melancholy. 'Right, let's get started, shall we? The sooner I pick up the things the boys and I want, the sooner we can return to Bath.'

She walked ahead of Lawrence and unlocked the front door. Stepping inside, she strode through the hallway towards the kitchen, resolutely refusing to linger over the sentimental pictures and knick-knacks scattered around the small space.

'Put the boxes from the car by the stairs, Lawrence. I'll put the kettle on. I'm sure we'll welcome a cup of tea before the journey home.'

Cornelia walked into the kitchen that had once felt so homely but now echoed with a cold and sombre emptiness. When tears burned behind her eyes she quickly lifted the kettle, before taking some matches from the shelf above the stove. She lit the burner, fighting the feelings of failure that pressed down on her.

Turning, she found Lawrence carefully watching her, his brow furrowed. She forced a smile. 'What?'

'You have tears in your eyes.'

She blew out the match with a firm puff. 'Don't be silly. I'm fine. Now, why don't you take a seat while I go upstairs and collect our things? I won't be long.'

'Do you need any help?' He glanced around him. 'I am more than happy to—'

'Not at all. Take the weight off your feet. I'll be as quick as a flash.'

Cornelia left the kitchen and headed upstairs. Running her

hands over the wallpaper, she slowly walked along the narrow landing and entered her and David's bedroom. The floral wallpaper and soft pink curtains reminded her of her excitement when she had chosen the room's decoration. She and David had been so happy then, newly married and looking forward to an unknown future.

Or had it just been her full of romantic anticipation? Had David known, deep in his heart, he would never truly love her... never remain true?

Swallowing against the bitterness that rose in her throat, Cornelia quickly retrieved three dresses from the wardrobe and draped them over her arm before grabbing a pair of black shoes.

Keeping her eyes forward, so as not to be tempted to pick up any trinkets that once meant something to her, she left the room and firmly closed the door on her old life.

She quickly walked into the boys' rooms, her heart aching as memories of them as infants and toddlers assaulted her, painfully poking and prodding at her emotions and conscience. How had it all come to this?

As sadness gripped her harder, she angrily swiped at her tears.

David had, at first, wanted the house for himself, but the moment Sophie Hughes's father bestowed a fine property in Colerne on them, David had registered the Oxfordshire house for sale.

Although initially shocked and upset by his announcement the house was to be sold, Cornelia now welcomed the decision. She did not want to even envisage trying to start again in this house with the boys. How on earth would they ever be happy with David's ghost lingering in every room?

She walked from her sons' bedrooms, clutching some toys

and a spare set of shoes for each of them, silently vowing that one day she would have a house of her own.

When Cornelia returned to the kitchen, Lawrence had laid out a teapot, cups and saucers on the table.

'Ah, there you are.' He smiled. 'Tea?'

Cornelia nodded. 'Lovely.'

But he didn't move to lift the teapot and, instead, rubbed absently at a spot on the table.

'Is everything all right?' she asked quietly, as she sat. 'You seem preoccupied.'

He lifted his gaze to hers. 'Esther spoke to Elizabeth this morning. She learned a little about Joseph Carter's first wife.'

'Oh? I had every intention of speaking to Elizabeth tomorrow.' She poured the tea and pushed a cup in front of him. 'What did she say?'

'Well, even though Elizabeth continues to be very distressed by the situation, I think it's a good sign that she's opening up to Esther. I hope that you and Mr Gower can act on the information now that Esther is unable to. No harm must come to her or the baby, Cornelia. I couldn't stand it. Or anything happening to you, for that matter.'

She squeezed his hand. 'I'll be fine, and so will Esther and the baby. I will ensure Mr Gower shares everything he learns with me, but I won't put myself in any physical danger. He's already insisted on as much. I just want to be able put Elizabeth *and* Esther's minds at rest.'

'Do you really think he will be willing to share everything with you?'

'I do. We've struck up a friendship and I know he understands what finding Lillian's killer means. Stephen is a good man. He'll not want Elizabeth and Joseph to suffer any longer than necessary.'

'But, if you're wrong and—'

'I'm not.' She touched gently touched his face. 'I know how much you love your family. I want to do this for you and Esther more than anything. I'm confident I can help.'

'Fine. Then let me share with you what Elizabeth told Esther.' He took a sip of his tea, the cup slightly rattling when he lowered it to its saucer. 'Lillian Carter had been the love of Joseph's life. He adored her just as she did him. After a short courtship, they were married and Lillian moved in with Joseph above the Carters' small milliners he ran with his father on Pulteney Bridge.

'They were deeply in love and running a business that both Joseph and his father cared about deeply. It wasn't until the business began to struggle that Joseph came to Pennington's, looking for his designs to be sold there.' He waved his hand. 'Sorry, I'm digressing. Anyway, Lillian and Joseph often took baskets of food, blankets and knitted hats, gloves and socks to the poor by the river. One night, when Joseph was unable to accompany her, Lillian was attacked and killed there.' Anger shadowed his gaze. 'Joseph has never forgiven himself and vowed not to rest until her killer is brought to justice. That was four years ago and still this animal hasn't been found.'

Cornelia shook her head. 'It's just too awful that such despair continues to shroud Joseph. Clearly, the latest murder was what pushed him to ask Mr Gower for help.'

'Joseph's convinced the killer is the same person who murdered Lillian and refuses to move forward with Elizabeth until he is found. He won't even think about starting a family until justice has been done.'

'Poor Elizabeth, but I understand Joseph, too. How can he even begin to think about bringing a child into the world when he's living with such horrible guilt?'

'Exactly.'

Fear about what she would soon become embroiled in began to grip Cornelia, making her wonder if she had the strength to see through her promise to Esther. Maybe Stephen's and Lawrence's fears for her were warranted. Maybe she shouldn't be getting mixed up in something she wasn't equipped to deal with. Murder. A killer. Darkened alleyways and streets. She had to think of her children. But how could she fail Esther?

She had to tell Stephen everything Lawrence had told her and hope the information led him to uncovering something – anything.

Draining her cup, she held Lawrence's stare. 'Leave this with me. I'll speak to Mr Gower first thing in the morning.' She squeezed her brother's fingers. 'Nothing and no one will stop us from bringing this faceless murderer to justice.'

31

Stephen wandered closer to Pennington's jewellery counter, his focus on Cornelia as she finished serving a customer.

He'd seen her twice during his walkabouts that day and, although there were always customers waiting to be served, her eyes lacked their usual welcoming light. That worried him. She had been so happy after the divorce hearing and that he'd agreed she could help him try to find Lillian Carter's killer. So what had happened between then and now?

Seeing her momentarily alone, he approached her. She was carefully rearranging the jewellery she had been showing the departed customer.

'Afternoon, Miss Culford.'

She started and looked up, a pretty flush colouring her cheeks, her smile just a little too quick and wide to be natural.

'Mr Gower. Good afternoon. Is there something I can help you with?'

He laid his hand on the glass countertop so he did not act on the insane urge to touch her. 'I wanted to make sure you are all right. You haven't looked as happy as I would've hoped since I last saw you.'

'I'm quite all right.' Her smile wavered as she lowered her voice. 'I... wanted to speak to you, actually.'

'Oh?'

'Elizabeth Pennington has shared some information about Mr Carter's first wife.'

'And whatever she said has worried you? Because if it has, maybe you should step back from—'

'No.' She touched his hand before quickly snatching her fingers back and looking over her shoulder. Her superior was watching them while pretending to survey the department. 'I *have* to help. To let my sister-in-law down after all she's done for me...' She shook her head. 'Esther adores Elizabeth. I want to do this.'

Stephen sensed there was more to it. 'Why don't we take a walk on our break? We can talk better away from the store.'

She glanced at her wristwatch. 'Could you take your break now? I was due mine half an hour ago.'

He looked towards Pennington's double doors. Two watchmen stood there and there was another walking the floor. 'I can't see it being a problem. I'll talk to the other watchmen when we leave.'

Her eyes lit with eagerness, even a semblance of happiness. 'Marvellous. I'll just speak to Mrs Hampton.'

She hurried away and quietly spoke to her superior. The older woman peered over her glasses at Stephen, her brow furrowed, before she nodded.

Cornelia quickly walked back to him. 'She's allowed me thirty minutes because I came in early this morning. Do you think you could get away for the same amount of time? I need to tell you everything I know.'

The scent of her hair and the subtle perfume she wore played havoc with his senses, but Stephen gently cupped her elbow and led her towards the staff quarters, where they put on their hats and coats.

Outside, they both gasped as the cold air enveloped them in its icy grip. Cornelia hugged herself and, before he could think about the consequences, Stephen wrapped his arm firmly around her waist.

Her widened eyes met his and, for a brief moment, time stood still. He was aware of nothing but her. Her eyes. Her hair. Her skin.

Her throat moved as she swallowed. 'Stephen...' She whispered his name and his heart raced as he lowered his gaze to her mouth. Her lips softly parted and he could have sworn he saw longing in her eyes. A signal – a hope – that she might feel what was growing between them.

He blinked and glanced along the street. 'Come. There's a small tea shop a short walk away.'

'But—'

Taking her hand, he wrapped his cold fingers around hers and gently pulled her forward. What was the matter with him? They were chasing a killer and he was waiting for the Board's decision about his future, yet here he was, lusting after his accomplice in an investigation, one who, by rights, should never have become involved in the first place. Yet he wanted Cornelia there. He wanted her beside him, which possibly made her more dangerous to him than anything else.

He had to stop this. He could not afford to get entangled with a woman who was hurting. A woman reeling from her ex-husband's betrayal. A woman trying her best to earn her own living, raise and support two children whose cheating father might well want to remain part of their lives.

Complicated. Dangerous... and fraught with the potential to lead to further heartache. He needed to step back, but how was he to do that when he knew it was too late for him to escape unscathed, whether he enforced distance or not? Cornelia Culford had broken down a barrier around his heart. Made him anticipate a possible future where he didn't hate himself.

She'd shown him kindness, trust and belief. Three things he'd had no idea he'd been seeking until this wonderful, beautiful woman came along.

Pushing open the door of the tea shop, Stephen reluctantly released her hand and stood aside to allow Cornelia to enter ahead of him. He exhaled, relishing the heat of the busy shop as he scanned the space for an empty table, but each one was occupied. In the window, there was a long refectory table with stools tucked beneath.

He glanced at Cornelia. 'Is a seat at the window all right?'

She nodded, a puzzled line between her brows. 'Stephen—'

'Take a seat. I won't be a minute.'

He weaved through the tables and ordered their tea at the counter. So many things were happening that he hadn't expected when he came to Bath. It was as though there was some kind of conspiracy to keep him in police work... to stop him believing that he would spend the rest of his days alone.

Both things he didn't deserve. Both things God had no right to dangle in front of him, just out of reach.

He'd failed Constable Walker, Hettie and Fay. He'd failed his fiancée. He'd failed. He was nothing more than a man under investigation for a bad decision that, he still believed, had led to the killing of three people. If he had acted on Hettie and Fay's alarm and investigated their claims himself, who knew if the outcome would have been different?

'There you go, sir.'

Blinking from his thoughts, Stephen paid the woman behind the counter and carried the tea to where Cornelia sat staring out at the bustling street. It was barely three-thirty, but dusk already loomed. Yet when he looked at her, all he saw was brightness and beauty.

'Here you are.' He laid a cup in front of her and slid onto an adjacent stool. 'That might go some way to warming you before we head back.'

'We don't have long.' She picked up her tea and tentatively sipped.

He was pretty sure she'd noticed his hesitation earlier. Had she read the desire in his eyes? The need to kiss and touch her? Somehow, he hoped she had. Hoped the signal he'd inadvertently sent had been received and that she might begin to wonder about him romantically too.

Foolishness on his part, but since when did anyone have control over the heart?

She exhaled heavily. 'Let me tell you what I've learned about Lillian.'

He nodded and picked up his tea. 'Go ahead.'

'Joseph and Lillian married in their early twenties and had a loving and happy union cut prematurely short by violence.' She looked out of the window, her jaw tightening. She faced him again, anger burning in her eyes. 'They worked and lived side by side with Joseph's father at the family milliners on Pulteney Bridge. It seems to me their lives were happy, their future planned. It's terrible, Stephen. How can Joseph ever move forward with such a heinous crime haunting him?'

Stephen picked up his cup. It was a question he'd asked about himself a hundred times. 'I don't know, but we'll do everything we can to help him to do just that.'

She nodded, her eyes full of compassion.

He lowered his cup. 'It seems that everything comes back to Pulteney Bridge. It's where the Carters lived and worked, it's where the man I'm seeking is believed to spend his nights and it's where Lillian would've undoubtedly have been seen the most often.'

'You're looking for someone?' Her eyes widened.

'I visited the slums where Lillian was killed and got talking to a vagrant. That was the man that you saw me escorting out of Pennington's.'

'He's your informant?'

'Yes, but I've yet to go to Pulteney Bridge.'

'But you plan to?'

'Yes. Tonight.'

'Then, I'll join—'

'No, Cornelia, you won't.' He held her gaze, even as her eyes darkened with familiar stubbornness. 'You can help me gather information, but I will not expose you to risk. I have no idea what I'll find – or who. I want you to do as I ask and stay away from anything remotely dangerous or we cannot work together.'

She opened her mouth as if to protest, but the longer she looked into his eyes, the more the wilfulness left hers. Turning to the window, she nodded. 'Fine.'

'I'm asking you to trust me. I know all too well how quickly investigations like this can turn violent. People do not appreciate being followed or pursued. This man by the bridge will be no different. I don't want you mixed up in something where I can't protect you.'

She continued to stare at the street. 'I understand.' The quiet tone of her voice said differently.

He gently touched her hand. 'Do you?'

She faced him, her gaze lingering on his mouth, her blue eyes burning with a determination... a desire... he hadn't seen before. A jolt of attraction shot through him and settled uncomfortably in his chest.

'Yes.' She sighed, the hunger in her gaze vanishing, only to be replaced by acceptance. 'You're right. I must think of the boys.'

Sympathy welled inside him. She suddenly looked so unsure of herself. So unlike the strong woman he was coming to know. Yet her vulnerability made him warm to her even more. Made him want to care for her even more.

He shook off his thoughts and focused on the most important thing right now. Keeping Cornelia and her children safe. 'Good, then I'll go to the bridge tonight and see if I can uncover anything useful. But, for now, we should head back to Pennington's.'

She left her half-finished drink on the table and stood, an underlying challenge simmering in her eyes. 'I won't come to the bridge, but I have to be side by side with you in this. It's important to me and it's important to Esther.'

He studied her, recognising her need to do something worthwhile. Fear for her tip-tapped along his spine. 'You're not a woman to be put off, are you?'

'No.' She smiled. 'Especially when it comes to handsome police sergeants with the most wonderful eyes and a tendency to bossiness.'

The laughter that bubbled in his throat felt good and he shook his head, rare embarrassment warming his cheeks. 'Come along, Miss Culford. We have work to do.'

32

As Cornelia was walking through Pennington's atrium on her way home, Elizabeth Pennington came down the grand mahogany staircase and strode towards her.

Cornelia's stomach dropped. She had nothing new to tell her and the resolve in Elizabeth's expression could not be mistaken.

'Cornelia. Might I have a word before you head home?' Elizabeth stopped in front of her, blocking her path to the door. 'It's about Esther.'

'Esther?' Cornelia relaxed her tense shoulders. Talking about her sister-in-law was much safer ground. 'Is everything all right?'

'As far as I know, but...' Elizabeth glanced around them. 'I spoke to her a couple of days ago and she asked me a lot of questions about Lillian. Did she pass the information on to you, as she said she would?'

Cornelia tensed again. 'Yes, yes she did.'

'And you passed it onto Mr Gower?'

Hopelessness swept through Cornelia. Esther had mentioned on several occasions just how determined Elizabeth could be. How immovable. The longer Cornelia acted as a go-between, the more likely it was that Elizabeth, or indeed Joseph, would lose patience and press Stephen directly. He wanted to avoid that at all costs, for the time being, and Cornelia would do all she could do respect his wishes.

'I did, but...' She gently touched Elizabeth's arm. 'Mr Gower is adamant that if expectations become too high, he'll have no choice but to end his enquiries into Lillian's death.'

'But why? Doesn't he see that Joseph needs to do something?' Two spots of colour darkened Elizabeth's cheeks, her expression annoyed. 'Joseph is hardly the type of man to collapse under the strain of it all. He's already carried this burden for many years. If he could do anything to help find—'

'I hate to say this, but this isn't just about Mr Carter and Lillian. It's also about Mr Gower.'

Elizabeth frowned. 'What do you mean?'

Cornelia sighed, hating to speak about Stephen behind his back but needing Elizabeth to understand that Stephen had to be free to work as he saw fit. 'Do you know why Mr Gower is here? In Pennington's?'

'All I know he is left Scotland Yard and came here. Why?'

'That's the issue. *Why* did he leave London?' Cornelia dropped her hand from Elizabeth's arm and stood a little straighter, determined to match Elizabeth's fervour for answers. 'There must have been a reason. A reason that deeply affects him still. Why else would a promising sergeant of barely thirty years old leave such a prestigious job where every opportunity would be open to him?'

'There could be any number of reasons.'

'Such as?' Cornelia raised her eyebrows as the fear she occasionally saw flash in Stephen's eyes filled her mind. The man grappled with something. Something he fought with whenever his police work came into play. Which it had now, whether he wanted it to or not.

'Well, I...' Elizabeth slumped her shoulders, her gaze softening. 'I don't really know, and I'm not sure Joseph does either. Do you? Is that why you're defending him so ardently?'

Cornelia turned away, lest her growing care for Stephen showed in her eyes. Every instinct screamed at her to protect him, to ensure he was kept from both physical and emotional harm. It was in her nature to protect those she cared for and, somehow, Stephen had been added to her list.

She faced Elizabeth. 'I have no more idea why he left the police than you, but he has the right to keep his reasons to himself if he chooses. All I know is that if you want Mr Gower to help you, you must let him speak to Mr Carter himself. Whenever that might be.'

Elizabeth's gaze hardened once more. 'Otherwise, you'll tell Mr Gower to stop investigating?'

'Yes.' Cornelia lifted her chin, her hands turning clammy around her purse. Could she be risking her job by being so forthright? 'I will.'

Their eyes locked.

Elizabeth Pennington might be her employer and Esther's friend, but for the time being Cornelia's loyalty would remain staunchly with Stephen. When he'd asked her to trust him, it had touched her more than she'd believed possible. He clearly had no idea how difficult it would be for her fully to trust a man again after David, but the fact Stephen thought her capable of it gave her hope that he saw the woman she had once been.

'Fine.' Elizabeth nodded. 'I will do all I can to ensure Joseph leaves Mr Gower in peace... for now.'

Cornelia released the breath she hadn't realised she'd been holding. 'Thank you.'

'But Mr Gower is pursuing lines of enquiry at the moment?'

'Yes.'

Elizabeth stared for a moment longer before she stepped to the side and waved towards the door. 'Then I'll bid you good evening and wait to hear more from you or Mr Gower.'

'Wonderful. Goodnight, Miss Pennington.'

'Cornelia?'

She stopped and turned. 'Yes?'

'Anyone Esther cares for, I do too. When we speak about things not related to the store, I'd like you to look at me as a friend.'

Cornelia smiled. 'I'd like that. Very much.'

'Good, then I will see you tomorrow.'

Cornelia headed for the doors and walked outside. She breathed in the cold evening air and hurried towards The Circus, her mind filled with thoughts of Elizabeth, Mr Carter and, most of all, of Stephen and his plan to visit Pulteney Bridge that night.

A shiver ran along her spine, and she stepped up her pace.

She'd defended him and kept his intentions secret, but that hadn't done anything to calm her fears for his safety. If he was attacked or hurt in any way, how would she know, until he failed to turn up at the store tomorrow? Sickness rolled through her, and she blinked back the tears that sprang into her eyes.

By the time she reached Lawrence's house, she'd managed to settle her stretched nerves and when she pushed her key into the front door, the comfort of home enveloped her. At least she knew the children were safe.

'Good evening, Miss.' Charles emerged from the direction of the kitchen. 'Mr Culford has asked that you visit his bedroom as soon as you arrive home.'

'Is everything all right?' She glanced towards the stairs. It was only seven o'clock, but the house was ominously quiet. 'Are the children in bed already?'

'Um, yes, I believe so.'

The way Charles couldn't quite meet her gaze and quickly turned to hang her coat on the stand by the door deepened Cornelia's concern. 'I see. Then I'll go straight up.'

She walked upstairs and heard Lawrence and Esther's murmured voices behind their closed bedroom door. She knocked.

'Come in.'

Esther was in bed and Lawrence sitting in his robe in an armchair. A newspaper lay open in his lap, his usual glass of evening cognac beside him. They both looked relaxed and happy and some of Cornelia's anxiety dissipated.

At least, it did until they both turned from one another to look at her.

Their smiles instantly vanished.

She forced a soft laugh, her worry rising once more. 'Do I really look so bad? It's been a tiring day, but I hope my appearance doesn't merit the horrified way you're both staring at me.'

Lawrence was the first to regain his composure and he stood, his arms outstretched. 'Sister, come and give your brother a hug.'

A hug? She and Lawrence were close, but his invitation did not feel at all natural. The room now simmered with tension. His proffered embrace was either to comfort or commiserate. Neither of which she welcomed.

Hesitating, she slowly stepped into his arms and let Lawrence hold her, while watching Esther over his shoulder. She seemed intensely interested in the embroidery on their eiderdown all of a sudden.

Cornelia eased back from Lawrence and looked him in the eye. 'What's going on?'

His dark blue gaze travelled over her face before he pulled her by the hand towards a second chair alongside the bed. 'Have a seat. Would you like a drink?'

Annoyance simmered deep in the pit of her stomach. If she had become a protector, so had Lawrence. Their turbulent childhood had brought the tendency out in them both as the elder siblings. Harriet, on the other hand, had adopted willpower and ambition as a means to survive. Maybe all three of them possessed the same traits. Only time would tell.

Slowly, she sat, keeping her back braced for whatever came next. 'I asked you a question, Lawrence,' she said, ignoring his offer of a drink. 'What has happened?'

He glanced at Esther before facing Cornelia again. 'It's David.'

Dread dropped like lead into her stomach. 'What about him?'

'He brought the children here from school this afternoon.'

Cornelia shot to her feet, her heart racing. 'What?'

'Cornelia,' Esther said quietly. 'Please don't upset yourself.'

'Upset myself? What is likely to upset me more than David taking the children from school without my permission?' She faced her brother. 'Why was he here? Tell me.'

Lawrence took her trembling hand. 'The school tried to get a message to you at the store, but when they received no return message or call, they tried David.'

'I've been run off my feet all day, but no one came to me with a message.' She glanced from her brother to Esther, sickness coating her throat. 'Are the boys all right?'

'Yes, but Francis had such an outburst that they are threatening expulsion.'

'What?' Cornelia's chest grew tight. 'Expulsion? Oh, my God.' She sank back onto her seat. 'How could this happen? He was such a happy boy.'

'I know, and that boy is still there, I'm sure,' Esther said softly. 'This will pass. Once he understands about the divorce and sees that David will spend some time with him, Francis will come around.'

'But what did David say? Because there was more, wasn't there?' She looked at Lawrence, anger unfurling inside her. 'Well?'

He passed his hand over his face and straightened his shoulders. 'He threatened to take the children to Middleton Park for the holidays.'

'What?' Cornelia's temper snapped and she shot to her feet a second time. 'Over my dead body.'

'And mine, too.' Lawrence's jaw tightened. 'It will not happen.'

'But if he pursues this—'

'He won't. You have been granted custody of the boys. I can't see that he, or his lover, will want another day in court.'

'Did you say as much to him?'

'I did.'

'And?'

'And he left without as much as a comforting kiss or embrace for his sons. The man sickens me.' Lawrence walked to the bed and picked up his glass, took a hefty gulp of cognac. 'So, if he plans to take the boys for Christmas, we'll take them elsewhere.'

Cornelia stilled. 'The manor house?'

'Yes.' A slow smile curved her brother's lips, a twinkle lighting his eyes.

Love swelled in her chest as relief washed through her.

David would never dare to set foot in her ancestral home. 'You'll really go?'

'For the boys, yes. For you, yes.' He shook his head. 'Believe me, there is no other reason on earth I would do so.'

'Oh, Lawrence, thank you. It's all Alfred and Francis have asked of me.' She rushed to him and embraced him. 'But what of Harriet? I can't imagine she'll—'

'I gave her little choice. We will get through the ball this weekend and then leave a few days before Christmas. Esther tells me you are due to finish at Pennington's for the holidays on the 22nd. Correct?'

'Yes. Elizabeth has been incredibly generous with my time off. I suspect her kindness has a lot to do with the divorce and the children.' Her thoughts shamefully darted to Stephen. How could she disappear when she'd been so insistent she wanted to help him, to be with him?

'Good, then I'll tell Harriet to expect us the day before Christmas Eve.' He smiled and brushed past her to the drinks cabinet. 'Now, sit down and have a drink with us. You've had a nasty shock.'

Cornelia stared towards the night sky through the open drapes. How would Stephen react? Would he miss her? She was woman enough to admit she would miss him. She liked him. Had a sneaking, wholly hopeful notion that they might come to know each other better, grow closer.

Was she behaving like a fool? She had so many responsibilities that must take priority over romantic love.

Damn David.

Would there ever be a time she was not dictated to by him? Would he forever remain in her life, through their children?

Well, whether he did or not, she wouldn't allow him to

control her this way. She had to show him just how strong a woman she'd become.

33

Stephen tried to shake off a feeling of irony as he passed shops and houses with sparkling decorations and streamers, reminding everyone Christmas would soon be upon them. Happiness. Celebration. A New Year promise of fresh beginnings just a hand's reach away. The festivities were a cruel joke.

Working at Pennington's, he didn't need reminding that Christmas lay just around the corner. That he would be alone once again this year. Instead, the rich red, gold and green trimmings and ornaments that adorned every surface and wound around the mammoth banister of the grand staircase only served to emphasise his solitude.

He walked closer to Pulteney Bridge.

His mother had been invited to Bristol to spend Christmas with her best friend and her family and Stephen had urged her to go, saying he had a friend coming to town with whom he'd spend Christmas Day.

The lie still stuck in his throat an hour later.

But he needed the time alone to think. The wait on the investigation into his part in the failings on that horrible, fateful day in London grew worse every day. How was he to make a decision about anything until he knew the outcome?

Burying his jumbled thoughts, Stephen quickened his pace along Bridge Street.

Pulteney Bridge had been one of Bath's attractions since the late eighteenth century and now, with every latticed shop window that lined the bridge either side lit for Christmas, it looked more spectacular than ever. Yet the bridge's exquisite architecture was little more than an illusion, masking what lay beneath.

He slowly walked along the pavement to the far end of the bridge and a small opening that led to some steep stone steps. Furtively, he looked around, before peering into a darkness made even more macabre by the Christmas brightness above.

The damp stones glistened with grime, mud and moss, the walls dripping with moisture. Only a fool would descend these steps at this hour of the night. Only a fool would expose themselves to the drunkards who loitered beneath the shelter of the bridge.

Well, tonight he was that fool.

Holding his breath, Stephen carefully descended, feeling the slip-slide of his boots as he crossed each step worn smooth by time. Emerging beside one of the bridge's stone arches, he stopped, straining to listen to the noises around him.

The odd raspy cough broke the murky air, along with a cacophony of snorting, spitting and cursing. He studied the hunched shadows beneath the arch closest to him and farther along the iron railings to his side. No one seemed to be paying him attention. He was pretty certain most of them didn't care whether it was day or night, who was or wasn't present, or what they were doing.

Slowly, he made his way along the river's edge, looking for

God only knew what. His first job was to act on the scant information Herman Angel had provided and see if he could find anyone else willing to talk. If – and it was a big if – Lillian Carter's killer remained close to the former home of his victim, the man had more nerve than a gambler playing with counterfeit notes.

The paved walkway was empty of people, which came as no surprise, but the air crackled with sounds of humanity, scrapes and scuffles, whispered voices and hacking coughs.

'Well, Mr Gower, you took your time.'

The hairs at the back of Stephen's neck rose and he curled his hand a little tighter around the cudgel in his pocket.

He swung around. Herman.

Immediately relaxing his grip, Stephen fought the urge to smile. The man must have got lucky since Stephen had last seen him. For one thing, Herman had obviously found a place to wash his face and clean his teeth. Both positively shone in the moonlight, while his grubby coat flapped open to reveal what looked to be a barely worn and rather dandyish waistcoat.

Stephen walked closer to where Herman leaned against the railing, casually smoking a rolled cigarette and looking relaxed enough that they could've been meeting in a gentlemen's club.

Shaking his head, Stephen smiled. 'What are you doing here, Herman?'

'Waiting for you, of course.'

'Waiting for me?' Stephen raised his eyebrows. 'Now, why would you think I'd be here tonight, I wonder.'

'I didn't know if you'd be here tonight.' Herman flicked the butt of his cigarette into the river. 'But if not tonight, then tomorrow, or the night after that.'

'Is that so?'

'Yep, whether or not you're really working in Pennington's as a watchman, or whether you're there as a constable, I can smell one of your lot a mile off. As soon as you started asking questions about the dead woman, I knew you wouldn't let things lie. So, I'm here to watch your back, that's all.'

'I see.' Christ, Stephen ground his back teeth. Did he wear his previous occupation like a damn tattoo across his face? 'When did you know I was in the force? More to the point, *how* did you know?'

Herman stepped closer, his newly cleaned face shining brighter, the wider he smiled. He tapped the side of his nose. 'Don't you worry about that. We've got more important things to think about.'

Stephen cast a furtive glance left and right. 'Such as?'

'Such as finding a killer.' Herman tilted his head, inviting Stephen to follow. 'Come with me. I'm guessing you'll want to see where you're most likely to find the man I told you about. He isn't here tonight, but I'll show you his spot, shall I?'

Without waiting for an answer, Herman brushed past Stephen and led him further along the river until they came to a thicket. Ducking his head, Stephen followed his informant through the trees, squinting into the blackness. Once more, he tightened his grip around the galvanised handle of the cudgel.

He had no idea what or who Herman Angel had been before he'd found himself on the streets, but now he'd put himself forward as an ally, Stephen would ensure the man came to no harm.

The area was quiet, compared with the entrance by the steps, only the crunch of their boots on the grass and twigs beneath their feet breaking the silence.

Herman stopped abruptly and stooped to pull a curtain of leaves and foliage to one side. 'There you go.'

Although damp and squalid, the area had been inhabited.

Through the semi-darkness, Stephen saw a couple of blankets were bundled in one corner, the remains of a burnt-out fire in the other. In the centre, discarded tankards, brown paper bags and other debris were haphazardly scattered around.

Stephen frowned. 'This is where he lives?'

'Occasionally. With others. You're unlikely to find him alone. He has protection.'

'Protection?'

'Of course. If he's bragging about murder, he clearly thinks himself safe. You'd be best advised to watch your back, while you're poking about in the man's business, Constable. Or is it Sergeant?'

There was something about Herman's voice that was at odds with the lowliness of their surroundings. Stephen's suspicions that the man wasn't always on the streets intensified.

'What's your story? Why are you living on the streets?'

'You tell me yours, I'll tell you mine.'

Stephen shook his head. 'I don't think so.'

Herman laughed and lifted a nonchalant shoulder. 'Oh, well, it was worth a shot. I have an interest in the law. As an ex-Member of Parliament, I find it as difficult as you do to allow the perpetrators of violent crime to thrive.'

Stephen fought to keep his face impassive. 'You were an MP?'

'Yes, sir.' Herman kicked a blanket. 'Up north.'

So that explained his accent. 'What happened?'

'To bring me here? To be living like this?' Herman smiled again. 'The drink, sir. It can capture a man and hold him tight within its iron claws before he even has the chance to look back and ask what the hell happened.'

Sympathy stirred in Stephen's chest. He'd seen enough good

people in the force brought down by alcohol to know how quickly drink could ruin a person's life. 'Right.'

Herman lifted his eyebrows. 'That's all you have to say? No judgement? No worldly advice?' He sniffed. 'And you call yourself a policeman.'

'No. *You* called me a policeman.'

'Are you denying it?'

'I'm many things, but I'm not a liar, so let me just keep my peace. All right?'

The vagrant studied him before shrugging. 'Fair enough. I'm not one for poking around in people's business.' He flashed a smile. 'At least, I'm not any more.'

'So, this person you heard talking about Lillian Carter. He's been seen here?'

'Every week or so, yes. I'm not saying he's the one that killed her, but it might do to have a word with him.' He drew a breath. 'Although, I have no idea how you'll manage that.'

'You leave that little problem to me. Knowing where I can find him is a good start. I'm grateful for the intelligence. Truly.'

'There were others, you know.'

'Others?'

'Women. Murdered. Not by the slums, like Mrs Carter, but further up the streets. Closer to the bridge. If you look back far enough.' Herman swiped his hand over his face. 'Lillian Carter was liked. She was spoken about with care and respect in one of the worst places in the city. She cared about people. Children, especially. She deserves justice and if you can deliver it, then I'll do all I can to help.'

A spark of adrenaline swept through Stephen. He would have preferred to think the man was lying about multiple murders, but the sincerity in his words spoke of truth. Was Stephen seeking one man who'd killed multiple times? A gang? Or could it be that the killings weren't linked and were entirely random? If what Herman said was true, Stephen had no choice but to dig deeper. There was no way in hell he could walk away from this enquiry now.

It was madness to have Cornelia and Herman anywhere near something so monstrous.

Yet he hadn't listened to Fay and Hettie and they'd died.

What the hell was he supposed to do?

He needed Cornelia and Herman's help. Maybe he could ask Inspector King back at Scotland Yard for help too. There was every chance he would be willing to make some enquiries on Stephen's behalf. King was more than Stephen's superior, he was a friend... of sorts. A man who wanted him to remain in the force, feeling he was too good a detective to lose.

However he looked at it, King would be pleased he'd been right to say that walking Pennington's floors would not be enough for Stephen. If he gave the man credit where credit was due, stroked his ego a little, then perhaps the inspector might be open to digging around.

Drawing a few coins from his pocket, Stephen held them towards Herman. 'Here. Take this for your trouble.'

Hesitation showed in the vagrant's eyes, maybe even a flash of humiliation, before he pulled himself up straight and touched the brim of his worn top hat. He took the money and dropped the coins into his inside coat pocket. 'Thank you kindly, Mr Gower.'

'Stephen.'

Herman nodded, a ghost of a smile curving his lips. 'Stephen.'

Stephen slowly walked to the covered entrance and stopped. 'Are you looking for a place to stay? If I can find you somewhere, would you welcome it?'

For the first time since he'd met him, Herman's expression turned suspicious, his grey eyes wary. 'Why would you do such a thing?'

Yes, why would you? Stephen held the other man's gaze. 'You don't belong here, that's why.'

Herman nodded, a barely discernible dip of his head.

'I might be able to persuade someone to give you a roof over your head for a few weeks. Maybe help you out with some new clothes. You could look for work. Start again.'

Herman smiled, but the suspicion didn't fade from his eyes. 'You fancy yourself my guardian angel?'

'No, but I'm lucky enough to not have lost everything after my own misguided choices. I was supported by friends and colleagues until I could think and walk straight again. Maybe a helping hand is all you need.' Knowing when to walk away and take the pressure off, Stephen pushed back the heavy foliage and moonlight speared the dank ground. 'Where and when can I next find you?'

'Find me?'

'You want to help find this killer?'

Herman nodded.

'Then I'll need to find you, and it's no good you coming into Pennington's until you're cleaned up.'

'Right you are. I'll be around and about here most nights. Come and look for me at this hour.'

'Good. Then I'll be in touch.'

With a final nod, Stephen ducked beneath the foliage and out into the wooded area, heading for his lodgings, his mind filled with Lillian Carter and the possibility of other ghosts.

34

Cornelia entered the magnificent lobby of The Phoenix on the night of the ball and stared around in wonder. Lawrence had been here most of the day and, even though she'd arrived alone, the happy, smiling faces boosted her confidence.

The lobby shone with festivity. Garlands of holly and ivy were strewn around the reception desk and along the mantelpiece of the enormous fireplace, giving a sparkling glamour to the prestigious hotel. Cornelia lifted her gaze to the chandeliers, the lights glinting and illuminating every bauble and bell hanging on the branches of a huge Christmas tree in the centre of the lobby.

'What do you think?'

The smile in her brother's voice as he spoke close to her ear enhanced her happiness. His blue eyes were bright with an excitement she hadn't seen since before Esther had taken to her bed.

She laughed. 'Well, don't you look pleased with yourself?'

'Pleased with myself and my staff.' He surveyed the chattering and laughing patrons around them. 'I'm convinced we have more people here than the number of invitations we issued. The entry fee has been increased at the door, but it seems that hasn't deterred anyone.'

'There are always last-minute arrivals, once people begin to think they might be missing out on something.'

'Which is why we prepared for just that. Although, if the rumour I heard earlier is anything to go by, some people could be here for other reasons.'

Cornelia frowned. 'Oh?'

Lawrence sighed. 'Apparently, a member of parliament was assaulted today, while leaving a meeting of suffrage supporters. An incident like that will only provoke further interest in the Cause amongst the gossipmongers.'

'A member of parliament? But what happened?'

'I've no idea. At least not yet. I'm sure it will be in tomorrow's papers. Anyway, the last thing I want is to turn people away when we're hoping to raise plenty of money for Esther's suffrage group as well as Bath's suffragettes. Tonight means everything to her and I want to be able to take good news home.'

Cornelia gently touched his arm. 'She's going to be just fine, you know. Once tonight is over, we can concentrate on enjoying Christmas as a family. Doctor Rubinstein has given her permission to travel to the manor house, hasn't he?'

'Only if she rests as much as possible between now and then.'

'Which she will. Esther is too devoted to you and the children to risk anything happening to her *or* the baby.'

His brow furrowed as he surveyed the crowded lobby. 'Yes, but she's also devoted to Elizabeth Pennington.'

'Maybe so, but I wouldn't have thought Elizabeth would take

precedence over the baby. I know what she and her husband are dealing with is awful, but Esther knows there's only so much any of us can do to help.'

'Exactly. Which is why she insisted I invite Elizabeth and Joseph to Culford for Christmas.' He faced her, concern still clear in his eyes. 'She said it will help take their minds off things for a few days.'

Cornelia struggled to keep her smile in place. 'They've accepted?'

'Yes.' Lawrence frowned. 'Do you think it's a bad idea?'

'No, not at all.'

Relief showed in his eyes and his shoulders lowered. 'I'm glad you think so because, if having the Carters spend Christmas with us pleases Esther, that's what I want too.'

She tucked her hand into his elbow. 'Come on. I think it's time you found me a glass of champagne and escorted me to the ballroom.'

The dancing was in full swing as they entered the ballroom, and Cornelia gasped. If she'd thought the lobby breathtaking, it dulled against the vivid decoration of the ballroom.

'My goodness, Lawrence, you've excelled yourself.'

His blue eyes crinkled at the corners as he smiled. 'Not me. I have three young women in my employ who took the ball on as a challenge and surpassed my expectations in everything.'

'Ah, yes. Esther told me about them. You gave them this project to keep them out of trouble, if I remember correctly.'

'Something like that.' He squeezed her fingers and lifted a glass of champagne from a passing waiter's tray. 'Here. Now, come with me. I believe there's somebody who has been impatiently awaiting your arrival.'

The teasing tone of his voice and his self-satisfied expression told Cornelia that the person was a man. A man Lawrence clearly approved of.

Her heart sank. Did Lawrence mean to introduce her to someone he hoped she might become romantically interested in? She sent up a silent prayer that her suspicions were wrong. The only man who had been on her mind for the past few days was Stephen. There was no room for anyone else.

Lawrence led her forward, pausing for introductions and greetings, or to talk with people to whom he wanted to extend a personal welcome. Pride cooled a little of her trepidation as Lawrence circulated the vast room with a host's expertise she would have once thought impossible, considering the abuse he'd suffered at their father's hands.

James Culford seeped unwanted into her mind.

Time and again, their father had raised his belt to Lawrence, or pushed him into a downstairs cupboard in one of the many dark recesses of their manor house, sometimes leaving him there for hours. Threats had rained down on Cornelia every time she'd ran to Lawrence's aid, before she'd retreated, fearful for her body... her own fragile soul.

She'd once been weak. Had once feared her father's wrath. Yet, these days, courage and strength burned in her blood.

She pulled back her shoulders. Never would she weaken again.

The music from the quartet on the stage at the back of the room grew in volume. Where on earth was Lawrence taking her?

She looked around the room and froze.

Stephen stood refined and handsome in black tailcoat and trousers, a silver and black striped waistcoat and a pristine wing-tipped shirt complete with bow tie.

A rush of self-consciousness shot through her. She had no

idea how she'd expected Stephen to be dressed tonight... or even if he would come at all. The closer she walked, the more she recognised the desire in his dark eyes as he inspected her from head to toe.

She'd chosen to wear a cream Grecian-inspired dress, with a crossover bodice and long, flowing skirt. Suddenly, she was all too aware of the luxurious crepe de chine petticoat and silk chemise covering her nakedness beneath.

Sensuality washed through her as Stephen continued to study her, as though he might ease the dress from her person without touching her at all.

Lawrence bowed. 'Mr Gower. A pleasure to see you, sir.'

Stephen's eyes never left hers. 'Miss Culford. Mr Culford.'

Lawrence's gaze burned into her, yet she couldn't drag her focus away from Stephen. Somehow, this man – this ex-sergeant – had her ensnared in an invisible trap. A trap she didn't want to be free of.

Stephen finally blinked and turned to Lawrence. 'Congratulations on this evening, Mr Culford. The cause is one I wholeheartedly support, and I was pleased to accept the invitation Miss Pennington extended to a number of Pennington's staff, myself included.'

'Well, I'm glad you're here. My sister speaks most highly of you, sir.' He eased his arm from Cornelia's grasp. 'And, on that note, I'll leave you in her company. I have much to do, as you can imagine. Please, help yourself to champagne and enjoy the dancing.' He turned to Cornelia. 'Cornelia.'

Heat infused her cheeks. What on earth was Lawrence doing? Was Stephen the man he'd said impatiently awaited her arrival? It made no sense. Lawrence had seemed so against her talking with Stephen in the beginning, had not been best pleased by his presence at the courthouse.

Undoubtedly, she had Esther to thank for his change of feeling. Her sister-in-law was one of the most insightful people Cornelia had ever known.

She met Stephen's eyes. He really did look unnervingly handsome. 'I'm so glad you came. I wasn't entirely convinced you would.'

'You look beautiful.'

Her heart kicked, and she dipped her head, delighted by the almost hungry way in which he appraised her. 'Thank you.' She swallowed, the deep pull low in her stomach reminding her of a sexual longing she hadn't felt in years.

'Would you like to dance?'

Surprise rippled through her. Stephen was such a serious man. Yet he was asking her to dance. She really didn't know him at all, and a frisson of excitement burned, knowing she still might have many layers of him to uncover.

'I'd love to.' She put her glass on a small table beside her and took his arm. He led her to the dance floor just as the band struck up a waltz.

Cornelia's heart beat faster, knowing the dance would mean intimate contact. That Stephen would take her into his arms and hold her close. It had been so long since she and David danced. Her legs slightly trembled, fearful she might have forgotten how to execute the steps.

If Stephen sensed her hesitation, his relaxed expression as he eased her body closer to the hardness of his chased away her concerns. As he held her, his chest pressed against her breasts, Cornelia looked into his eyes and any residual insecurity vanished.

He gazed at her with a gentleness that took her breath away, yet deep in the dark brown depths of his eyes, she saw wanting. Desire and admiration.

Neither of them spoke as they dutifully followed the steps of the dance, Stephen effortlessly leading her around the floor, light and confident on his feet. Cornelia relaxed in his arms, feeling as though she'd be safe, wherever he might lead her from now on.

'I've missed seeing you at the store,' he said gently against her hair. 'Are you all right?'

His care for her softened something inside her. 'Mrs Hampton asked that I work in the orders room this week, so I haven't been at the counter very often. Also...' she grimaced. 'I've asked permission to leave earlier for a while so I can collect the boys from school.'

'Oh?'

'Francis... is walking a rather fine line. I didn't want Lawrence's maid to collect him as she has been and be faced with any awkwardness.'

'I see.'

She looked into his kind eyes. 'But let's not talk about me. How are you? It's been so hard not to speak with you about... you know.'

'Pulteney Bridge?'

'Yes.'

His gaze lingered over her face and lips. 'Let us not talk about such things tonight. I will tell you all another time.'

Although desperate to know how his visit to Pulteney Bridge had played out, she also didn't want this romantic moment to end. His fingers tightened at her waist and he pulled her closer. The warmth of his breath teased her, igniting an overwhelming urge to kiss him.

They danced for a few moments longer before he spoke again. 'Shall we go for a walk?'

She nodded as he led her from the dance floor. Cornelia

stared straight ahead, her chin lifted, afraid that people, Lawrence included, might witness her leaving the ballroom to seek a quiet corner with a man no one knew.

Stephen had admitted he wasn't acquainted with anyone in the city, but he'd chosen to come here tonight. Chosen to be with her rather than anywhere else. The notion filled her with a happiness she hadn't felt for years. Of course, there was every chance he was here purely for the Cause, but, deep inside, she sensed he'd come because he'd known how much she wanted him there.

She stood a little taller, confident she could walk beside him unjudged. Allow him to hold her. Allow him to kiss her...

He led her through the lobby and into another room that opened to a huge glasshouse. Lit and decorated in beautiful festive green and sparkling gold, the space was empty but for two or three couples who also appeared to be in search of privacy.

They walked to the windows at the back. The black sky, spangled with stars and a full, round moon, peered in on them, shrouding them like lovers at midnight.

Trying to get control of her silly, romantic heart, Cornelia took a deep breath and faced him. 'Did you change your mind about telling me what happened at the bridge?'

He shook his head, his gaze gentle. 'No. For all the foolishness of it, I just... wanted a moment alone with you. Cornelia...' He exhaled. 'When I saw you emerge through the crowds tonight...'

Her heart picked up speed, a dangerous hope burning inside her. 'Yes?'

'I wanted to kiss you. No matter how reckless that might turn out to be.'

Happiness and raw desire swept over her, provoking an

arousal she wanted to cling onto lest she lose her confidence and courage. Dragging her eyes from his, she turned to look around them.

They were alone. She hadn't even noticed the other couples leave. 'Then kiss me.' She faced him. 'Here. Now.'

35

The moment Stephen's lips touched Cornelia's, a rush of possessiveness came over him. Her lips were hot and inviting, her sexual allure potent. Somehow, he managed to keep his feet on the ground and his hands on her waist. Never in his life had he felt such an instant, intoxicating power. He pulled her closer and she tilted her head to deepen their kiss.

Did she feel it, too? The strength that rippled between them? The understanding? Christ, was he losing his mind?

He abruptly pulled back and her eyes were wide with worry as she stared at him.

'What is it?' She looked left and right. 'Did someone come in?'

Trying and failing to turn away from her wonderful blue eyes, Stephen stepped back and pushed his hand into his hair. 'I have no idea what just happened.'

She smiled. 'If there's a need to explain, then you have no business kissing a woman that way.'

His heart slowed. 'You know what I mean. I didn't think... I presumed...' He shook his head, feeling like an inarticulate fool. 'I'm not sure kissing you was such a good idea.'

The light in her eyes dimmed as her smile dissolved. 'Oh, I see.'

The soft disappointment in her voice hit him like a punch to the gut and he quickly took her hand. 'Cornelia—'

'It's fine. You need not explain yourself.' She pulled her hand from his, fire sparking once more in her eyes. 'But I'm glad you kissed me. If nothing else, it's proved what I've thought true for a while.'

He swallowed, itching to touch her, caress her, feel her. 'Which is?'

'That you came to Pennington's for a reason. I *met* you for a reason.'

That was it exactly. And now his life had been turned on its axis.

He was a man of commitment, loyalty and integrity. Cornelia mattered to him. To her family. And now to Elizabeth and Joseph Carter.

Stepping closer, he brushed a fallen curl from her cheek, moved his thumb across her soft, bottom lip. 'I don't regret kissing you.' He dipped his head and kissed her lightly, the air burning with intent and purpose. 'I regret I'm not the man you need. The man who can give you all you deserve. I'm a security watchman, Cornelia. A man who may be asked to leave the police force permanently.'

'Why?' She cupped his jaw, sympathy shining in her eyes. 'What happened, Stephen?'

His pulse thudded in his ears, the glass around them seeming to crack and splinter to let in the cold, night air. How could he tell her about the murders? How could he bear to see the disappointment in her eyes?

He clenched his jaw. 'I'm not the right man for you, even if you were to ever come to want me. Believe that, please.'

'But—'

'My life is not the same as yours. The things I've seen. The things I've done...' He shook his head, sickness coiling in the pit of his stomach. To hold and kiss her and then let her go was agony, but he had to, lest he lose the fragile hold he had on any chance of making a new life. A life free from responsibility. Culpability. 'It's too much to expect—'

'Don't.'

The sharpness of her tone silenced him.

Her eyes blazed with determination, her cheeks aflame with irritation. 'Don't make choices for me. Don't tell me what I need or what I want. This is my life, Stephen. Mine. And I intend to live it just as I want from now on. No rules from anyone but my children.'

He closed his eyes. 'I apologise. The last thing I wanted was for you to think—'

'How will you be spending Christmas?'

Surprised by her question, he frowned and stepped back. 'Most likely alone. My mother has been invited to her closest friend's, which is good. I'd rather be on my own.'

'Why?'

'Because I am better off that way.'

'Is that so?'

'Yes.'

She crossed her arms. 'Well, I'm sorry, but I refuse to accept that and ask that you consider spending Christmas with me and my family. In Oxfordshire.'

Panic and claustrophobia rose on a wave inside him. 'But we barely know one another.'

'Which is exactly why I want you to come. It's just for a few days. Lawrence has invited Elizabeth and Joseph Carter to join us too. It will be the perfect opportunity for us to get to know each other, to get to know them. Wouldn't it help if you could gain Joseph and Elizabeth's trust so you could look for Lillian's killer in your own way? On your own terms?' Her eyes softened. 'Won't you at least think about it?'

Indecision wracked him. Was she really only asking because of Elizabeth Pennington and Carter? Was the memory of how their lips fused so easily, the fire that was so effortlessly ignited between them, not branded in her mind, as it was in his?

Of course it wasn't. She had been married, had children. He needed no further proof that her bastard of an ex-husband had made love to her. No doubt there was a time when she was admired and courted all over the city as a young and beautiful woman.

Everything was about the case. Anything else he'd seen in her eyes was his own imagining... his own hoping.

He turned away from her and paced a circle.

Yet he couldn't think of anyone he'd rather spend Christmas with. But he wouldn't be alone with Cornelia. He'd be with her family, her *extended* family, *and* his employers.

A dangerous energy slowly hummed deep inside him. What did he have to lose by spending Christmas with the Carters? He could study them, find out more about Lillian. If he was at Culford Manor, there was little chance of Joseph Carter escaping Stephen's notice to disappear and do something foolish.

She stared at him, eyebrows arched. 'Well?'

'It seems madness to even consider—'

'What did you discover when you went to Pulteney Bridge?' She lowered her voice and led him to a settee at the side of the glasshouse. 'Are you any closer to finding who might have been responsible for Lillian's death?'

Stephen sat and gripped his hands, staring at the patch of carpet between his feet. How much did he tell her? He was aware that she was a woman on a mission to prove herself. A mission inspired by an ex-husband who had no appreciation of just how strong a woman he had married.

He met her intense stare. All amiability and desire had vanished from her eyes, leaving only curiosity.

'My contact took me to where the possible suspect can often be found. He's sleeping rough by the river edge. I don't have a name or anything more than hearsay, but my informant told me that Lillian Carter wasn't the only woman killed around those parts.'

'There have been more murders? My God.'

'I was shocked too. I've decided to speak to my old inspector at Scotland Yard and ask if he'd be willing to do some digging for me. If we can find more links between Lillian's death and the others, then we may know more about the type of person we're looking for.' He rubbed his jaw. 'I hope to God it doesn't turn out to be someone who has killed multiple times. I'm worried about what we've got ourselves involved in, but it's too late for me to turn back now. Joseph Carter needs to know that I'll see this through to the end.'

'I agree. Do you still think it's fair for us to keep any progress from him and Elizabeth?' She looked towards the door as though the Carters might appear at any moment. 'I'm sure neither of them knows about the other murders. One of them would've given that information to you if they'd known. I'm convinced Esther invited the Carters to spend Christmas with us to keep Joseph away from Bath for a few days. Elizabeth is desperate for him to be happy. For them to try for a family.'

Stephen shook his head. 'If the look in his eyes when he talks about Lillian is anything to go by, I can't see that being a possibility anytime soon. It's clear how much he loves Elizabeth, but the man is suffering. Deeply.'

She entwined her fingers in his, holding them tight. 'Come to Culford Manor. Spend Christmas with me. With Elizabeth and Joseph.'

He scrambled for an excuse, any excuse, not to go, but... he wanted to be with her. Slowly, he nodded, lifted her hand to his mouth and pressed a kiss to her knuckles.

'Christmas at Culford it is.'

36

'Gower. It's good to hear from you.'

Stephen pressed the phone to his ear and leaned back in a chair in his mother's hallway, relieved by the easy tone in Inspector King's voice. 'It's good to speak to you too, sir. How are things at the Yard?'

'Going along. Obviously, it's not the same with you not being here. How is Bath's finest department store? Is it keeping you busy?'

'You could say that.' Stephen stared towards the front door, hating the sudden feeling of complete inadequacy that enveloped him. 'I can say the one thing a department store shares with Scotland Yard is that no two days are the same.'

'I imagine so. Albeit on very different scales.' King cleared his throat. 'So, to what do I owe this phone call? I'm assuming you telephoned for an update on the investigation?'

Stephen closed his eyes, a headache building in his temples. 'Only if there is anything you're willing to share, sir. I actually telephoned you for another reason entirely.'

'Oh?'

'Why don't you tell me about the Board's investigation first? If it's as bad as I'm anticipating, then I might keep quiet about my reasons for speaking to you today.'

'Sounds ominous.'

'It is. So, how is it looking for me?'

'Hold on a minute.'

Stephen frowned as he heard a scrape of a chair, a few muted footsteps and the closing of a door before King returned to the phone.

'Just making sure we've no listening ears. Right, well, what can I tell you?' He blew a breath. 'They are taking their damn time, I can tell you that, but I'm hopeful, Gower. Very hopeful. You have an exemplary record, both here and when you were in the Bath constabulary. Your promotions have been rapid, and entirely justified, with every kind of documentation to support your seniors' decisions. The only problem the Board are sticking with is that you sent Walker out alone, to one of the most poverty-stricken areas around here. A constable who they consider far too inexperienced to have dealt with a possible violent assault on not one but two women.'

Stephen dug his fingers into his forehead, his shoulders hunched. 'It's the same thing I've been beating myself up over for months and they're right to consider it. I should've gone myself or, at least, gone with Walker.'

'Hey, you made what you considered the right decision at the time. Hettie Brown and Fay Morris were prostitutes, who, according to your statement, were inebriated and hysterical. You neither sent them away nor ignored their claims. You had a child beating to deal with and sent Walker in your place to follow up on the women's allegations. You did not fail in your responsibilities, Gower. Any one of us might have done the same. How were you to know the killer had been harassing Miss Brown and Miss Morris for months? Had they visited any police station prior to coming here? No. Had they reported a fear of any kind to anyone? No. You made a decision on what was presented to you.'

Whether or not King had a point, Stephen shook his head. He should have gone. Not Walker. 'Well, the fact of the matter is—'

'You didn't rest until their killer was found and have done everything myself and the Board have asked of you since. Fact. Now, I am chasing this investigation up every couple of days and the Board knows I want you reinstated. They know the regard I have for you and that all of your fellow officers wish to continue working with you. It's going to take a little more time, but I'm confident we'll get there.'

'Maybe.'

'Not maybe. Definitely. Now, what is it you wanted to talk to me about?'

'I've been... helping someone out while I've been here.'

'In what way? This doesn't sound like you've been carrying an extra heavy box of ladies' frocks to womenswear.' King laughed.

Stephen smiled despite the gravity of what he was about to ask. 'No, not quite.'

'Well, what is it?'

'There was a recent murder in Bath where a young woman helping the poor was beaten and left for dead by the river.'

'I don't know anything about it.' King's voice sobered. 'How have you managed to get involved? You should be keeping a low profile.'

'I know, and I tried, but the request for help came from my

Pennington's employer, Joseph Carter. I did my best to put him off, but the more I learned about the case and how he was linked to it, the harder it was for me to walk away.'

'How is he involved in murder, for crying out loud?'

'The recent murder and that of his first wife's are similar, sir. Too similar for me to pretend Carter is under any sort of delusion. I had to at least listen to him and carry out a few preliminary enquiries.' Stephen clenched his jaw. 'I failed Hettie, Fay and Walker. I won't risk doing that again with someone else.'

The sounds of an active police station mixed with King's breathing as Stephen waited for the inspector's response.

At last, King spoke. 'And you want me to see what I can find out this end? Why?'

'Because there's a chance I've stumbled on a case of not two murders, sir, but several. I have an informant who thoroughly knows the slums and he's spoken to the vagrants around the area. There's a chance I might be able to find the killer if I can find a link between these murders. I'm not convinced they're random. How can they be, when two of the victims seem to be charitable women trying to help those less fortunate? That is not the sort of person to be targeted without prior motivation.'

'I understand what you're saying, but I can't see how I can help from here.'

'If you could just contact Bath police. See what they are doing about this most recent case and if they are treating Lillian Carter's death as cold. They won't speak to me when I'm suspended, but they might speak to a senior inspector of Scotland Yard. Anything you can uncover will help. Joseph Carter and his second wife, Elizabeth Pennington, are good people who do a lot for their staff and customers. I feel it's my duty to help them.'

There was another long pause before King sighed. 'All right,

Gower. I'll make some enquiries, but no promises. I'll be in touch again soon.'

'Thank you, sir.'

The line clicked and Stephen replaced the receiver. All he could do for now was wait.

37

A few days later, Cornelia stood in Pennington's atrium and clapped along with the rest of the staff as Elizabeth finished her motivational speech, which concluded with a small wrapped gift and a Christmas bonus for all.

The atmosphere inside the store crackled with seasonal festivity and Cornelia took a deep breath of satisfaction as she watched her employers leave their places on the grand staircase and head to the upper floors.

But, as the staff dispersed, concern shrouded Cornelia's brief happiness.

Despite the bravado in front of their staff, Elizabeth and Joseph suffered an ongoing pain that had hovered over them for the entirety of their romance. A lingering ghost of a murdered wife. The loss of a woman who had meant so much to Joseph and, it seemed, many others. Something that, until resolved, would never leave a young and in-love couple to pursue a potentially wonderful future.

She glanced at her watch. Her final shift before her break for the holidays had come to an end and it was time to head home to pack, in preparation for the family's departure to Culford Manor.

Unfortunately, the prospect failed to fill her with happy anticipation. The only positive aspect she looked forward to was that Stephen would be there. A man she had to be careful not to fall in love with. He seemed to be avoiding her since their kiss. If she were to rush headlong into matters of the heart, she would be hurt again, and she could not allow that to happen when Alfred and Francis seemed, at last, better settled.

She glanced around and spotted Stephen talking to a middle-aged couple, his expression serious, as it always was while at work. Her body burned with treacherous attraction as she studied the fall of his dark hair, his firm, chiselled jaw and imposing physique.

How was she to keep a hold of the emotions tumbling through her when she'd seen a different side of him? A side that hummed with sensuality, strength and excitement, and showed just how committed and passionate a man lurked beneath his professional surface. A side that drew her like a magnet and made her ache with wanting each night as she lay alone in bed.

He waved the customers farewell. Their gazes met.

She tentatively smiled and he winked.

Her smile widened, before she walked across the marble floor towards the corridor that led to the staff quarters. She should be ashamed that his brief acknowledgement gave her such a ridiculous amount of pleasure. It was important that she held on to her newly won independence.

Yet, when she looked at Stephen, it wasn't independence she desired, but unity. Partnership. Two people who understood one another's pain, hopes and dreams and would work together to achieve happiness.

A connection with a man of her own choosing. Not that of her parents.

A man she'd found and come to deeply care for, quickly and without negotiation, effort or cajoling.

Yet fear struck like ice in her heart.

If she were to make a second mistake and expose her children to a man who might one day walk away, they would never forgive her, and she would never forgive herself. What if she'd made a huge mistake inviting Stephen to Culford manor? What if she had allowed Elizabeth and Joseph's sufferings to fade into insignificance beside those of her own wretched heart?

No. She would not think that way.

Stephen was a good man. A man who cared about her and seemed to have her boys' welfare at heart. He was not David.

Taking her coat and hat from her locker, she quickly put them on before pulling out her purse. She hurried along the corridor and out of the staff exit at the side of Pennington's.

With just three days until Christmas, Bath's streets were filled with the smells, sights and sounds of the season. The day's earlier rain had stopped, leaving the paved streets glistening beneath the coloured lights spilling like glittering paint from lit shop windows.

'Mistletoe for sale!'

'Tuppence for a sprig of holly!'

'Buy your baubles at half the price!'

The stallholders shouted their wares with jovial voices, the evening air filled with the scents of roasting chestnuts and burning firewood.

She couldn't wait to wrap the gifts she'd hidden in her wardrobe and beneath the stairs at Lawrence's house. Gifts purchased with her own earnings and the generous staff discount that Elizabeth Pennington had put into place the

Christmas before. For Cornelia, this money had been a godsend. She wanted to do all she could not to rely on her inheritance. To live a life of her own making.

Turning into The Circus, she focused on the holly and ivy twisted around the railings in front of Lawrence's house. The decorations were all thanks to Helen. Her brother's trusted servant had been busier than ever with Esther bedridden, but not once had Helen lost her temper under pressure.

Everywhere Cornelia looked nowadays, she saw women who inspired her. That would not change when she returned to Culford. She would not allow Harriet or anyone else to undermine her ever again.

She entered the house and removed her hat and coat, hanging them on the stand in the hallway. Voices and laughter drifted downstairs from the nursery and her heart lifted as she realised that she wasn't too late to kiss the children goodnight. Once again, Helen had earned her gratitude.

Hurrying upstairs, Cornelia pushed open the nursery door and peered inside.

Francis sat on the floor, his pleading gaze tilted towards Helen. 'But Mama said we can go to bed half an hour later every night until Christmas Eve.'

Cornelia's eyes widened at Francis's impudence even as she bit back a smile. Slowly and silently, she pushed open the door, crossed her arms and feigned a glare. 'I don't remember saying any such thing, Francis George Parker.'

'Mama!'

'Aunt Cornelia!'

The children leapt to their feet, including a rather red-faced Francis, and buried their faces in her stomach. She clutched them tightly and smiled at Helen, who shook her head, pretty blue eyes gleaming with affectionate amusement.

'I think Francis will be quite the poker player when he's grown, Miss Culford.' Helen glanced at him. 'He really has the most unnerving knack of making me doubt myself.'

Cornelia laughed, ruffling Francis's hair as he gazed up at her with eyes as innocent as the day he was born. 'Oh, don't say that. The last thing I want for either of my sons is to frequent gambling halls. Now then, I think it's time for bed, children. Helen has more than earned an early night.'

'Oh, I'm quite happy to put them to bed.'

'No, I insist. Go. Make your escape before it's too late.'

Laughing, Helen nodded. 'Fine. Then on your head be it. The children are as excitable as a cartload of monkeys.'

Once she'd closed the door behind Helen, Cornelia sank to the floor and the children sat in a circle around her. She looked in turn at Alfred, Francis, Rose and Nathaniel. 'Now, in my purse, I have a small packet of liquorice for each of you.'

Their collective gasps filled the room and her heart.

'But...' She raised her eyebrows. 'You will only be given this special treat if you tidy the nursery, walk quietly to your bedrooms and get into your nightclothes.'

They nodded gravely, eyes glued to Cornelia and the purse on her lap.

'I don't want to hear a peep. I will come to your rooms in exactly fifteen minutes and I expect you to be sitting cross-legged on your bedroom carpet, backs straight and mouths open. Am I clear?'

Another round of nods. 'Good. Then off you go.'

The children scattered, whispering and giggling, and Cornelia walked along the landing to Lawrence and Esther's room.

She gently knocked on the door.

'Come in.'

Cornelia entered to find her sister-in-law dressed in a lace nightgown, folding clothes and putting them in an open suitcase on the bed.

She immediately rushed forward and gently took Lawrence's pullover from Esther's hands. 'What are you doing? You should be in bed.'

'I should be no such thing. Doctor Rubinstein came by today and confirmed I am fit and well enough for gentle exertion and the trip to Oxfordshire.' She took the garment from Cornelia, her eyes rimmed with fatigue but flashing with characteristic wilfulness. 'And I'll thank you to say as much to your brother, when he gets home.'

The look in Esther's eyes was one Cornelia had learned to heed. She slowly sat on the bed. 'I see. Lawrence is at the hotel?'

'He is. I don't expect him before I fall gratefully asleep, but...' She closed the suitcase and locked it. 'I am happy to have been of some use today, at least.'

The frustration in Esther's tone was obvious and Cornelia reached out to take her hand, urging her to sit down.

Esther seemed to hesitate before she sank onto the bed and sighed. 'Fine, I'm tired.' She flashed a cheeky grin, her eyes sparkling with humour. 'But not out. I am truly looking forward to spending Christmas at Culford. It's a chance for us to all be together. Including Harriet. I've barely got to know her, despite being married to Lawrence for months now. I'm sure he'll come to see the importance of being as close to her as he is to you.'

'Of course he will.' Cornelia forced a smile, not entirely convinced that Lawrence would see anything worthwhile in the forthcoming trip. Harriet or no Harriet. 'Has he voiced any more doubts?'

'No, which is actually more worrying.' Esther waved her hand. 'But let's not dwell on Lawrence right now. We will tackle him once we arrive at the manor.' She squeezed Cornelia's fingers. 'The good thing is Elizabeth came by this afternoon and Joseph is happy to spend Christmas with us.'

'He wasn't to begin with?'

'No, but once Elizabeth told him Mr Gower was joining us, Joseph perked up.'

Dread unfurled in Cornelia's stomach. 'He mustn't pressure Stephen too much. I suspect that would be the very worst thing Joseph could do. He must trust Stephen.'

'Oh, he does.' Esther gave a firm nod, her eyes determined. 'Elizabeth is not one to hold back and has laid down rules, which I suspect Joseph will be only too willing to obey, if it means he gets to talk to Mr Gower and spend time with the woman he loves. Now, how are you feeling about Christmas? Are you as unhappy as Lawrence about the manor house?'

'Lawrence suffered a great deal more than me during our childhood.' She drew a long breath. 'I'm more fearful of spending time with Mr Gower than in the house, if I'm honest.'

'Oh?'

'Yes, I...' She looked into Esther's concerned eyes, but confession of her feelings for Stephen stuck in Cornelia's throat. It was too soon. Too silly. Too dangerous to share such things. She shook her head and forced a smile. 'All will be well.'

'Of course it will. Mr Gower strikes Lawrence and me as a man of his word. Are we wrong?'

'No. No, you're not. Now...' Cornelia stood. 'I have four children who are waiting for sticks of liquorice.'

'Sorry?'

Cornelia laughed. 'Don't worry, I have everything in hand.'

She walked to the door, feeling as though she had just lied to Esther in the biggest way possible.

38

Stephen shook hands with another security watchman and relieved him of his place at the store's entrance. The December morning was bright, with barely-there wisps of clouds covering a hazy sun that seemed to cheer the moods of the suited men and women rushing in and out of Pennington's doors.

He tipped his hat to two young women as they emerged behind him, smiling and laughing, decoratively wrapped gifts cradled in their arms.

The moment they had walked away, Stephen's smile dissolved as his mind whirled, his head and heart not really at work at all.

As each day drew closer to Christmas, the more he worried about his decision to spend it at Culford Manor. Anything could go wrong. Between him and Cornelia, or even between himself and his employers. Then what?

'Penny for them, Gower.'

Stephen blinked and stared wide-eyed at Inspector King's beaming face, his grey eyes glinting with amusement as he climbed the steps.

'Sir. Whatever are you doing here?'

'A man's entitled to a bit of last-minute shopping two days before Christmas, isn't he?'

The inspector glanced at an elderly woman as she tutted her way past them where they stood blocking one of Pennington's double doors. Stephen held out his hand, urging King to the side, immensely pleased to see him despite knowing that, for the inspector to make a personal trip to Bath, he was here for a lot more than Christmas shopping.

The question was, was he here with news of Stephen's future or news about Lillian Carter and the other women?

Tension inched across Stephen's shoulders. Inspector King's impassive face as he studied the crowded street gave nothing away, but Stephen knew all too well how adept the inspector was at controlling his expression... whatever the circumstances.

Stephen tugged at his lapels and forced as much nonchalance into his voice as possible. 'Well, you're in the right place for shopping, sir. There's no doubt about that. Shall I take you inside?'

The inspector arched an eyebrow, his wily gaze locked on Stephen's. 'On the contrary, it might be better for us to speak out here. What I have to say shouldn't take long.'

Stephen glanced towards Pennington's doors. 'If this is about Joseph Carter, it might be for the best if I take my break. If Carter sees you—'

'As you wish. I'll wait here, shall I?'

King looked away and stared ahead, rolling back and forth on the balls of his feet. Trepidation knotted Stephen's stomach. Maybe the inspector wasn't as good at hiding bad news as he'd thought. He quickly entered the store.

He approached a fellow watchman. 'I need to get out of here

for fifteen minutes or so. Are you all right to cover for me? I'll be as quick as I can.'

The other man glanced left and right and winked. 'Sure. You owe me the same, though.'

'Of course. I won't be long.'

Stephen hurried back outside and, once he stood beside King, the inspector descended the steps. Lifting his chin, Stephen walked confidently along the street, refusing to give in to the negative thoughts nagging him.

Once they reached the bottom of Milsom Street, King nodded towards an empty spot at the side of the street. 'Let's talk here. We don't want to risk anyone overhearing what I'm about to say.'

King's brow furrowed as his gaze bored into Stephen's. 'You were right about the killings. Another woman was killed in much the same way as Lillian Carter and was also known for her beauty, charity and kindness. With this most recent killing, that makes three dead, Gower. God only knows the sort of man we're looking for, but, whoever he is, he's cold, callous and has a serious problem with goodwill.'

'Goddamn it.'

'Exactly. Now, here's what I suggest we do—'

'We?' Stephen shook his head. 'You can't be involved in this, sir. Bath is nowhere near London and way beyond your jurisdiction.'

'This man is dangerous. I'm not prepared to stand by and do nothing. I'm not that kind of a man, any more than you are. You came to me for help and you've got it.' The inspector pulled a folder from inside his coat and held it out. 'I did some research and in there you'll find some suspects I think you should start with. The first killing took place approximately two years before the murder of Lillian Carter.'

Stephen slowly flipped through the pages, his mind reeling at the idea that he was embroiled in the hunt for a man who'd killed multiple times.

'Bath constabulary needs to be made aware of this, Gower. This is bigger than us. *Much* bigger. I think we're looking for someone who has served time for other things in between these murders. Things that have made him disappear for no longer than two or three years.'

'Petty theft. Assault.' Stephen rubbed his hand along his jaw. 'Neither of those things would have meant incarceration for very long.'

'Exactly. So I started there, and a couple of names stand out because the theft and/or assault charges were made by women, or friends of women, who had been trying to do some good in this city. See what you can make of my notes and do what you will, but for God's sake, be careful. Call me if you need anything else and make sure you contact the Bath police.'

Stephen closed the folder. 'And you're all right with me doing this? Mixing myself with police work when I'm suspended?'

The inspector smiled, his gaze softening. 'Suspended? Whatever gave you that idea?'

'What?'

King gripped Stephen's shoulder. 'You've been exonerated, son. Found innocent of any wrongdoing, as I knew you would be. It's over, Gower. Your place remains at the Yard.'

Stephen stared at the inspector, unsure what to think or feel. 'I have my job back?'

'As I always knew you would.'

'But—'

'For the love of God, man. You're looking at me as though this is bad news. Is work really that good at Pennington's?' King laughed and looked around as though checking for listeners. 'You do what you have to do here, hand in your resignation and get yourself back to London. That's an order.' He moved to walk away and stopped, eyebrows raised. 'And don't do anything that's going to put yourself at risk in the meantime. Do you hear me?'

'I'll be all right, sir.'

'Aye, that's why I'm leaving this in your hands. For now.'

Once King had disappeared into the crowds, Stephen leaned against the shop wall beside him. He had his position at the Yard back, yet indecision battled inside of him. What now? He had unconsciously convinced himself he would be asked to leave the force. Have his reputation as a detective and a man smeared with his failings for the rest of his life.

But he'd been found innocent.

Cornelia came into his mind and he swallowed hard. Could he really go back to London and leave her behind as though his deepening feelings for her didn't matter? Her pretty eyes glinted in front of him, the taste of her lips tickled on his. Christ. Things had only become more complicated.

He flipped through the folder again.

Bath.

Women.

Murder.

He slapped the folder shut and closed his eyes.

And, of course, Cornelia. A woman there was every chance he could come to love. A woman involved with something that could lead to her being hurt... or worse.

He opened his eyes and pushed his hand into his hair.

God help me. What the hell do I do now?

39

Elizabeth glanced at Joseph as they travelled in his car towards Culford Manor. The mood between them over the last few days had been improved by a slight change with Joseph's confidence in Stephen Gower. At first, she'd been pleased that Joseph had seemed happy to step back and give Mr Gower some space, but now, as she observed Joseph's tight grip on the steering wheel, she worried that it was the chance to be at close proximity to Mr Gower that had buoyed her husband's mood.

She cleared her throat. 'You seem a lot happier, the closer we get to Christmas.'

'I am.' He glanced at her. 'I love the store as much as you, but it feels good to have a few days away together.' He squeezed her hand. 'We'll make the most of it, I promise.'

Rare uncertainty niggled inside her as Elizabeth stared ahead. 'Good, because I don't want anything to spoil this time. Cornelia and Lawrence were really kind to invite us and Christmas is about the children, not the adults. We must do all we can to ensure they enjoy it.'

His smile wavered. 'Why wouldn't we?'

Determined to be heard, Elizabeth ignored the coldness that had seeped into Joseph's tone and sat straighter in her seat. 'Esther and Lawrence are my friends, Joseph. They have a life that I want to be a part of.' She took a deep breath. 'A life that I want for us one day. Children matter. That's all I'm saying.'

His jaw tightened. 'I couldn't agree more. However, I suspect you're more concerned that I will harass Mr Gower from morning to night while we're here. Am I right?'

'Of course not,' she lied, clasping her hands in her lap.

'Good, because I want to enjoy this time as much as you.'

She studied him, regretful that she felt she had to say something to him before they arrived at the house, but not completely sorry. 'Anyway, there is no need for you to badger Mr Gower in any way. Cornelia has promised me he's doing everything he can.'

'As am I.'

The mysteriousness in his tone caused Elizabeth to look at him again. 'Meaning?'

'Meaning I saw Gower talking to someone outside the store. Someone who had constabulary written all over him. I'm sure Gower is extending the search and bringing in help.'

'But this man could have been anyone.'

He shook his head. 'He was a policeman. I'm certain of it. The more people Mr Gower has helping him, the better. I can feel a breakthrough on the horizon, my love. A breakthrough that means we can start to concentrate on the future, rather than the past. Regardless of the doubt I sometimes see in your eyes, I want that as much as you.'

Despite his words, worry continued to grip Elizabeth. This time away could just as easily end in a blazing row occurring between them rather than joyous celebration. 'Joseph—'

'Plus, you should be reassured that I've not said a word to Mr

Gower about my suspicions he's widening the net. Surely you can see that I'm not completely incapable of exercising some self-control?'

He glanced at her and the pride in his eyes softened a little of the hardness around her heart.

She smiled. 'I do.'

'Good.' He took her hand and placed it on his knee. 'I know how much you want a family, Elizabeth. I do, too. Once Lillian can finally rest in peace, I will be entirely yours for the rest of my life. I promise. I love you.'

Tears burned behind her eyes as Elizabeth settled back in her seat, relief washing through her, even as she hated the weakness her love for Joseph provoked in her. Ever since he'd walked into her life, he had been by her side in everything. From the store to the fights with her father to the triumphs and disappointments of her colleagues and friends.

She wasn't sure she still wanted to be the independent woman she'd once so ardently sought, and the reason was the man – so different than her father – sitting beside her.

'Thank you, Joseph.'

'For what?'

She smiled. 'Everything.'

He winked at her and, although reassured, only time would tell how the next couple of days would unfold, but now, with her feelings made clear, Elizabeth had no doubt Joseph would keep his word and not harangue Mr Gower.

Fingers crossed, a fabulous Christmas time would be had by all.

40

Cornelia gratefully accepted a glass of claret from Lawrence as he joined her and Esther in front of a roaring fire in Culford's opulent drawing room.

'Thank you, brother. This is just what I need after getting the boys to bed. They are beyond excited for Christmas Day.' She sipped the wine and turned to Esther. 'How on earth did you manage to settle Rose and Nathaniel so quickly?'

Esther laughed. 'I think they've been so worried while I've being confined to bed that, now, they're behaving like complete angels.'

'Hmm, maybe they are at the moment.' Lawrence sat in a wing-backed chair. 'That won't last long, what with tomorrow being Christmas Eve.'

'Alfred and Francis spent the whole of their bath and story time guessing what they are going to get.' Cornelia looked at the portrait of Harriet above the fireplace and sighed, suddenly and unexpectedly impatient to see her sister. She, Lawrence and Harriet had spent so much unnecessary time apart since their mother died. 'I know I shouldn't be upset by Harriet's not being here tonight, but she could easily have refused an offer of dinner at the Cambridges'. She knew of our coming over a week ago.'

Lawrence shook his head. 'My dear sister, I fear you've forgotten Harriet and her ways. I, for one, am grateful for the lack of drama tonight. From tomorrow morning, it will be one histrionic episode after another, if I know our sister at all.'

'True.' Cornelia smiled. 'But she's young, rich and single. I expect she has her pick of suitors and has been thoroughly enjoying tormenting them.'

Esther put her teacup on the small table beside her. 'Is there anyone in particular Harriet has in mind? The few times I've been with her, she's spoken of little else other than marriage.'

Lawrence gave an inelegant snort and sipped his wine. 'Harriet is certainly taking advantage of her new-found freedom. With mother dead, she can bide her time and wait for the man of her dreams. When she last wrote to me, she mentioned booking a suite on the *Titanic*. It wouldn't surprise me if she has that all in hand by now.'

Cornelia stiffened. 'The *Titanic*?'

'You've gone quite pale, my love.' Esther touched her hand to Cornelia's. 'Do you know something we don't?'

'She can't.' Cornelia put her wine on the low table in front of her, her hand trembling. 'David intends spending his honeymoon on the *Titanic*.'

'What?' Lawrence glared, his cheeks mottling. 'He told you that?'

'Yes.' Panic coursed through Cornelia. 'I don't want him anywhere near Harriet, whispering his poisonous lies about me. What if she listens to him and I lose her as well as everything else?'

'She won't listen to anything he has to say.' Esther squeezed Cornelia's fingers. 'Will she, Lawrence?'

He looked from Cornelia to Esther, his jaw tight. 'I can't say it's impossible. There's nothing Harriet enjoys more than gossip and scandal, but I really hope she'll see it's David who is at fault rather than you, Cornelia.' He drained his glass. 'I'll see what I can do to dissuade her from taking the trip. The last I heard, she was negotiating with her friend, Susannah Varson, about the voyage.'

'Negotiating?' Cornelia frowned. 'What do you mean?'

'Well, even Harriet wouldn't be so bold as to travel to America unchaperoned. She has asked Susannah to come along, too. All expenses paid by Harriet, of course.'

'Then why on earth would she refuse?' Cornelia stood up and paced about. 'According to the newspapers, the *Titanic* is the most luxurious ship the world has ever seen. Which is precisely why David will want to be on its maiden voyage.'

The drawing-room door opened and Harriet's butler, Lucas Adams, entered. No more than thirty years old, with dark blond hair, blue eyes and a tall physique, he was a handsome man, and Cornelia couldn't help but smile as she looked at Harriet's newest member of staff.

He dipped his head. 'Mr and Mrs Carter have arrived, sir.'

Lawrence stepped forward to greet Joseph and Elizabeth. 'Welcome. Both of you. Come in and have a seat by the fire. You must be cold after the journey.'

'We are. Even Joseph's motor car doesn't keep out these December winds.' Elizabeth approached Cornelia where she stood, waiting. 'Thank you so much for welcoming us here for Christmas.'

'Not at all.' Cornelia smiled, her thoughts immediately turning to Stephen and what would happen once he arrived tomorrow. 'Would you like some wine?'

'Lovely, thank you.'

Adams walked towards the drinks cabinet and Cornelia quickly intercepted him. 'I'm quite happy to see to our guests, Adams. Would you mind taking Mr and Mrs Carter's cases upstairs?'

'Yes, ma'am.'

As she filled two glasses with wine, Cornelia thought once again of Harriet. How was she to dissuade her from boarding the *Titanic*?

She stoppered the decanter.

'So, Cornelia...' Joseph Carter took the glass of claret she offered him. 'I was surprised, yet happy, when Elizabeth told me Mr Gower has also accepted your invitation to spend Christmas here. Are you' – he raised his eyebrows – 'romantically connected, by any chance? It would be wonderful if Pennington's brought more couples together.'

Heat leapt into her cheeks. 'Um, no...' She laughed. 'We're just friends and colleagues. Nothing more.'

Joseph lifted the glass to his lips, gaze glittering with amusement above the rim. 'Well, I think I'll keep an eye on you two, regardless.'

Cornelia picked up Elizabeth's glass.

'So, when is he arriving?' Joseph pressed.

'Tomorrow evening.'

'I see.'

'I'll just take Elizabeth her drink. If you'll excuse me.' Cornelia joined Elizabeth and Esther in front of the fire.

'Here you are.' She handed Elizabeth her wine before sitting in an armchair beside her. 'After we've eaten, I'll show you where you'll be sleeping.'

'Thank you.' Elizabeth sipped her drink. 'Did Joseph mention Mr Gower to you?'

Cornelia nodded as, once again, her worry rose that she'd

made a mistake asking Stephen to Culford. She could imagine him being cross-questioned to the point where he'd be forced to leave.

Annoyance passed over Elizabeth's face as she glanced at her husband before inching closer to Cornelia. 'And?'

She held her employer's shrewd gaze. 'And I told him Mr Gower is expected tomorrow evening.'

'He didn't ask about the investigation? Mention Lillian?'

'No,' Cornelia said, lowering her voice. 'And Mr Gower must not be made to feel he cannot relax while he's here. It's Christmas. He deserves a holiday as much as any of us.'

'Absolutely.' Elizabeth's brow furrowed. 'And Joseph has promised me as much. I just hope he doesn't go back on his word once Mr Gower arrives.'

Esther leaned closer. 'Is Joseph really becoming so entrenched in this investigation that he won't enjoy himself for a few days?'

Elizabeth stared at her husband's turned back. 'It's most likely my fears that are making me doubt him. I just want the investigation resolved. The whole ordeal is taking its toll and I love him so much.'

Esther took Elizabeth's hand. 'Everything will be all right. We must leave Mr Gower to do what he can.'

Cornelia frowned. What could she say or do to help the Carters? To help Stephen and protect him from their questions? Maybe a distraction was needed. Something that Elizabeth and Esther would find just as engaging as looking for a killer.

Romance was never far from any woman's mind. Not even the minds of her forward-thinking employer and sister-in-law.

She cleared her throat. 'I care for Mr Gower. Probably more than I should.' Their eyes instantly lit up, as Cornelia suspected they would.

'So...' She lifted her chin, nerves leaping in her stomach now that she'd admitted aloud what burned in her heart. 'I would very much appreciate you helping me to make Mr Gower's time here an enjoyable one.'

Esther grinned. 'Oh, we will.'

'Most definitely.' Elizabeth touched Cornelia's knee. 'I will do my utmost to divert Joseph. A potential romance is just what we need to brighten things up. Well, that and the children, of course. I can't wait to see them again. Are they well, Esther?'

Pleased the topic had turned to the children, Cornelia sipped her wine and leaned back on the sofa, only paying the smallest attention to Esther and Elizabeth's conversation. Instead, her mind was consumed with thoughts of Stephen.

The memory of his kisses tingled on her lips and her body warmed at the thought of being held in his arms again. Didn't she owe it to herself, and her boys, to seize life with both hands? Time was short, precious and, deep in her heart, Cornelia believed she and Stephen had come to Bath, to Pennington's, for one reason and one reason only... Each other.

41

The cab rambled along Culford's long, gravelled driveway and Stephen breathed deep. Light snow drifted lazily, occasionally whipping left and right on a wind that had turned bitter since he'd left home. A faint layer of white covered the edges of the roof tiles and terrace balustrades. Garlands of holly and ivy had been wrapped around the pillars of the impressive porch, and two decorated fir trees stood on either side of the double entrance doors.

From inside the house, lamps in a few of the windows added to what should have been a welcoming ambience. Yet the house felt like a huge, menacing phantom, rising black and imposing against a dark and cloudy sky. Stephen's gut told him being here was a bad idea. *Very* bad. Was it because of this house that Cornelia and her brother chose to live in Bath?

He opened his mouth to tell the driver he'd changed his mind, but the words stuck in his throat. He needed to speak to Cornelia, insist that she step back from the investigation now it was almost certain he sought a man who had killed more than once.

His jaw clenched and he turned away from the view.

He had been late getting away from Pennington's on what had been a manic Christmas Eve. Miss Pennington had released as many staff as she dared, and the remaining few had worked admirably on the condition that, in future, time off at Christmas would be on rota. When her father had been in charge, Christmas for the staff hadn't even been a consideration.

So, tired but washed and scrubbed as well as his work-worn suit would allow, Stephen was here at eight o'clock. He just hoped he hadn't delayed dinner.

The cab came to a stop in front of the stone steps leading to the front door, and Stephen gripped the bag that he'd held on his lap for the entire journey. As soon as his feet touched the ground, indecision swept over him once again. What in God's name was he doing here? Did he really think this visit would be a chance to convince Cornelia to step back from the investigations? From him? He still had no idea whether or not he'd be returning to London in the New Year, so how could he ask anything of her?

He studied the facade of the house. He didn't belong here. He didn't belong anywhere. Abruptly, he reopened the cab door. 'I've changed my mind. Can we go back to Bath?'

Just then, the huge oak front door creaked open behind him.

'Mr Gower. Leaving us so soon?'

Damnation.

Lawrence Culford had his hand outstretched. 'I hate this place as much as the next person, but I'm sure my sister would be disappointed if you didn't at least give it a chance.'

Knowing he now had no choice, Stephen accepted Culford's hand. 'Mr Culford, sir. It's good to see you again.'

'And you.' He glanced at the cab. 'I'll have the butler take care of the fare. Let's get you inside.' Culford picked up Stephen's case and walked towards the manor. 'So, what was it about the house that one look had you wanting to return to the city?' His eyes glinted with amusement. 'Not that I blame you. To me, the place is as ugly as they come. To Cornelia, too. To Harriet, though, our younger sister, Culford Manor represents everything she loves about life.'

'You have no intention of living here yourself then, sir?'

'No, never. This is Harriet's house now. It was left to me by my mother, but I have no need of it, so I ensured that ownership was split equally between myself, Cornelia and Harriet. Although I'm not sure Cornelia would ever want to live here either.'

Concern filled Stephen that Lawrence Culford was mistaken and Cornelia could one day choose to leave Bath and live here in the country. Of course, he had no right to feel anything about Cornelia's future decisions. She was finally free of a husband who had treated her like dirt. Why wouldn't she want her children to grow up in a place like this rather than the city?

'No,' Culford continued, with pride in his voice. 'Cornelia is my sister through and through. A survivor. Someone determined to live life on her own terms.' He flashed a smile as they entered the largest hallway Stephen had ever set eyes on. 'And I couldn't be more gratified. Ah, Adams, would you kindly take Mr Gower's hat and coat? I also need you to pay the cab outside. Here.' Culford handed the butler a cash note.

Stephen lifted his gaze up the grand staircase to the long landing stretching in both directions at the top. He imagined the place had twenty or more rooms upstairs and God only knew how many downstairs.

Culford slapped Stephen's shoulder, making him start. 'Let's go through to the dining room, shall we? We've just sat down at the table, so your timing is impeccable. I hope you're hungry.'

They passed the staircase and walked along a corridor. As they entered the dining room, Stephen was greeted by a chorus of welcome from the adults sitting around the table.

He nodded hello to everyone, steadfastly preventing his gaze from lingering on Carter's for any longer than necessary. He turned to Cornelia.

She looked phenomenal. Her red silk gown complemented her dark hair and bright blue eyes to perfection. Unwanted yearning stirred inside him.

Smiling, her eyes shining, she said, 'Mr Gower, I am so glad you made it. Here, come and sit next to me.' She laid her hand on the empty seat beside her. 'You can help me keep the children in line.'

He tipped a wink at the children, who all giggled and nudged one another, before he walked the length of the table. His seat was far away from Carter at the other end, for which he was grateful. There was no doubt the man would confront Stephen at some point over the next couple of days, but at the dinner table could not be where the inevitable conversation took place. The moment he sat down, a maid filled the glasses in front of him. One with wine, the other with water.

The talking resumed and he sat quietly while Cornelia conversed with Esther Culford.

As Cornelia talked, he studied the gentle slope of her nose, her full, tempting mouth and dark brown hair. His treacherous heart swelled with a longing that was infuriating and futile. It didn't matter how much her beauty affected him, or how deeply her soft scent infused his senses, her proximity made for as tormenting a situation as he'd ever been in.

But she would never be his.

His fingers itched to slide beneath the table and grip hers, to tilt her head towards him so that he might kiss her.

It was useless. A fantasy.

She was worthy of so much more than a detective who'd betrayed two civilians' trust and directed a promising detective to his death. Regardless of the Board's conclusion, Stephen could never imagine forgiving himself. Wasn't he, even now, a man who was no further forward in helping a good and loving couple to find the peace they needed?

He abruptly picked up his wine. As he brought the glass to his lips, his eyes met Carter's.

Carter nodded, his gaze intense.

Stephen drank. Maybe this time he wouldn't fail. Determination rose hot behind his chest as he took a second sip of wine. No, this time, he would triumph.

He would find Lillian Carter's murderer and lay Carter's ghosts to rest. But, as for Cornelia, her safety and happiness were paramount, and she would only find those things far away from the investigation.

Far away from him.

42

Cornelia couldn't believe it when Lawrence and Esther rose from the table, suggesting that they show Elizabeth and Joseph the new billiard room. It was profoundly amusing that her brother and sister-in-law felt the children would benefit from seeing it too.

As their voices faded along the corridor, she slowly turned to Stephen.

He softly smiled, mirth shining in his dark brown eyes. 'Well, that wasn't the subtlest exit I've ever seen.'

'No, it wasn't.' Cornelia smiled, delighted by the amusement in his eyes. She'd rarely seen him so relaxed and she was suddenly keen to be alone with him behind a locked door. 'Why don't you join me in my father's old study? Harriet's maid will soon come to clear the table. It would be better if we can talk alone and uninterrupted.'

A flash of uncertainty sparked in his gaze before he stood, easing her chair back to allow her to stand. When they stood face to face, her mouth barely inches from his, she fought the urge to lean in to him... to lean *on* him. The atmosphere burned with unspoken words.

She quickly turned away before she did something as idiotic as grab his hand and press it to her breast. Or kiss him hungrily, like her body, soul and mind pushed her to do.

When he raised his hand as if to touch her face, she hurriedly swept from the room. What was the point of succumbing to the need burning inside her? What was the advantage of pursuing a man like Stephen Gower when her children remained so confused and insecure? Her family as unsure of her intentions as she was herself. The stigma of her divorce continued to hover over her boys in the school playground and even drew occasional whispers at Pennington's.

Hopelessness pressed down on her as she walked ahead of Stephen into the entrance hall and along one of the three corridors. His footsteps followed her, sure and steady, as she walked along the wood-panelled walkway, the black wall sconces flickering, sending shadows rippling across portraits of horses and hunting prints.

As Cornelia reached the door of her father's former domain, her steps faltered as memories assaulted her. Verbal condemnation, her father's words like puncture wounds to his children's self-esteem, but Lawrence... dear, darling, Lawrence had sustained beatings, thrashings, isolation and hunger.

'Cornelia? Are you all right?'

She took a breath as she felt a sudden need to open up to Stephen. She fought back her fear and vulnerability and directly met his gaze. 'My father was a cruel man. His whims and the punishments he meted out were a mirror to his soul. A deep darkness that Lawrence, Harriet and I are only truly coming to understand as we grow older.'

He gently took her hand. 'He hurt you?'

She nodded. 'He hurt all his children. Come.'

The room was in darkness, the logs in the enormous grate unlit.

She shivered and crossed her arms. 'I think I may have made a mistake bringing you in here. I thought Harriet might use this room nowadays... but then maybe even she can't pretend the cruelties in here never happened.'

After he'd walked into the room, she slowly closed the door and locked it.

She forced a smile. 'We should speak quickly, before the others notice us missing.'

He came closer, the musky scent of him scattering her dark memories. When she was with Stephen, when she looked into his eyes, she felt entirely safe, entirely human. As though her parents and David had each lost their power to destroy her life.

Tears pricked her eyes.

An abandoned shawl lay on a sofa and she snatched it up, throwing it around her shoulders. Holding it tightly against her breasts, Cornelia tried hard not to shiver – from the cold, not from her need to be held by Stephen.

He held out his hand towards the sofa. 'Why don't we sit? I have something important to say to you.'

The tone of his voice did not speak of love or desire, but of solemnity and seriousness.

Determined to not give into her heart and have it broken a second time, Cornelia brushed past him.

They sat side by side and his gaze wandered over her hair and face before settling on her eyes. 'Cornelia...' His chest rose and he spoke quickly. 'I met my old inspector yesterday. He came to Pennington's.'

'About Lillian?'

'Yes. It's possible whoever attacked her has attacked before and was behind the recent killing. It's also highly probable this animal could strike again.'

She tightened her fingers on his. 'Then we need to find him urgently. More so than ever.'

'*I* do, not we. I don't want you near this any more.'

'But—'

'No, I mean it.'

He placed his hand on her thigh, his dark gaze boring into hers. Heat from his fingers seared through her clothes and, God help her, she wanted more of his skin on hers. More of his strength inside her.

She swallowed. 'I can't leave you to go after this man alone, now that you've told me he could kill again.'

'Neither can I have you exposed to danger. You have Alfred and Francis to think of. Your brother and sister. Even Mrs Culford and Miss Pennington. You have many, many people who love and care for you. Please, let me take this investigation from here. I intend to speak to the Bath constabulary and my inspector is doing all he can, using the resources he has at Scotland Yard.'

'I see.'

'You have to believe I won't forsake Carter and I won't forsake you. The biggest failure of my life led me to leave London and a job I loved. If I fail again, God only knows where I'll go or what I'll do. If I know—'

'What happened?' Her heart bled for the pain behind his eyes, the fervour in his voice. 'What made you leave London?'

He hesitated and then shook his head. 'You don't need to know.'

'Yes, I do. I *want* to know. I want to know *you*.'

The shawl slipped from her shoulders. His eyes roamed over

the neckline of her dress to the inch of décolletage she'd half-heartedly convinced herself wasn't for his benefit.

'Stephen, please.' She raised her hand to his jaw. 'Tell me.'

Voices sounded in the distance, but neither of them moved. Instead, he clasped her hand and pressed a firm, lingering kiss on her palm.

Slowly, he lifted his head. 'Cornelia. Beautiful, wonderful, amazing Cornelia. Why did you have to come into my life now? Why have you stirred a need in me I have neither felt nor wanted before now?'

A tear rolled down her cheek, but she smiled, her heart swollen with love for this man.

This policeman. This hero.

'Tell me.'

He lowered her hand and entwined her fingers in his. 'There were two women. Prostitutes. They came to the station, believing their lives were in danger, and I took their names but thought them drunk, deranged, maybe both. I went on another call instead. A young boy had rushed into the station saying his younger brother was being beaten by his father, and so I sent another officer to follow up the women's claims. I made that little boy my priority, not the women.'

Pain etched his face and her heart ached for him. 'A child must always come above an adult. You made the right choice.'

'You don't understand.' His jaw hardened. 'Those women were found killed, beaten to death, that very night. Left for dead in an alleyway, as though their lives were meaningless. The officer I sent after them? He was killed too. Stabbed through the heart.'

'Oh, Stephen.' She closed her eyes, only imagining the burden he must carry every day. It was no wonder he had left

London, come to Bath to be with his mother, his family. She opened her mouth to console him, when he spoke.

'The Board undertook an inspection into the part I played in the tragedy. I failed them, Cornelia. I failed my honour and I...' His eyes burned with self-hatred and anger. 'I failed my badge.'

Fear and hopelessness wound tight inside her. 'Their deaths were not your fault. You did what you had to do in the moment.' She shook her head, leaned closer to him, willing him to release his guilt. 'Their passing was no more your fault than Lillian's is Joseph's.'

Unable to bear the agony in his gaze, she clasped his face and kissed him, pouring her comfort and love onto his lips so that he might understand what he had become to her. What he meant to her.

His lips barely moved against hers and then, like a spark from a flint, he pulled her close and crushed her breasts against the hard planes of his chest. Arousal shot through her. The intensity of their kiss deepened, his hand on her breast as she wantonly moved her fingers across his knee towards his crotch.

His breath merged with hers as she pressed her hand to his erection. A low, guttural groan escaped him. They could be so much to one another. Could show each other a whole new way to live and love. Find solace, comfort and happiness in one another's arms.

It was as if the last few weeks they'd grown to know and care for each other culminated on an urgent wave, consuming them, urging them on in a way that was illicit, but impossible to stem.

He tugged at her bodice and she leaned back to loosen the ties. His eyes searched hers for permission, and she nodded.

Gently, he drew open the bodice and lowered his head, carefully lifting her breast from her chemise to take her nipple into his mouth. She closed her eyes and moaned, pushing her chest forward so that he might feast harder.

Arousal burned, her lust so fierce that she feared they might never have the opportunity to sate it. She pushed her hands into his hair, holding him against her bosom, relishing the soft strands in her fingers and the coarse roughness of his attentions.

She wanted this man in her bed and in her life. There could be no going back. Not any more.

43

Stephen lifted his head from Cornelia's breast, his heart thundering and his erection straining. He would have given anything to make love to her. To see her flushed and happy after their lovemaking, his own body comforted and replete from being with a woman who had somehow touched places inside him he had thought dead.

She watched him, her cheeks tinged pink, her breathing soft. 'What is it?'

'Your family. Us...' He shook his head, shameful tears pricking his eyes as he lifted a curl from her cheek. 'Our lives are so different. The investigation... Everything is just too dangerous, and if anything were to happen to you, happen to me, what then?'

'Isn't that a risk every person takes with someone at some time?' She pulled her rumpled chemise back over her bosom and focused on re-lacing her bodice. When she spoke, her voice was barely above a whisper. 'But it's not really the investigation worrying you, is it?'

He swallowed. 'It's *just* the investigation.'

She swept a trembling hand over her hair and straightened her shoulders. 'Tell me the truth. I deserve that if I am to walk away from you. Turn my back on a man I really believe I was meant to meet. Meant to know.'

Her honesty was shaming in the face of his cowardice. How, after everything she had been through in her marriage, did she manage to be so forthright? To wear her heart so openly on her sleeve? He would never possess half of her strength. Further proof he was not the man she needed.

He tugged at the lapels of his jacket before pushing the hair back from his brow. 'I can't allow it to come to mean something that we've met. That our feelings are deepening for one another. I have a job to do for Mr Carter, and I must make myself whole again before I can be anything to anyone. Anything to you.'

Her eyes clouded with sympathy that struck like a knife in his chest. She could now see how truly weak he was.

She took his hand and the sympathy in her eyes vanished, only to be replaced with fiery passion. 'You are not an island, Stephen. You can't grow, change or get better alone. Don't you understand? I am living with my brother, working at Pennington's after Esther recommended me to Elizabeth. Your advice, wisdom and encouragement were what secured my divorce. I would be nothing without the people around me. Can't you see that?'

His heart lurched painfully to hear her talk about herself in such a way. He clenched his jaw, passion burning inside him. 'Don't ever say you're nothing. Not ever.'

'Then why do you think *you* are?' Her gaze turned angry, her fingers tightening on his. 'Why can you not welcome the love and care of these new people you've met since you started working at Pennington's? Why should I stop helping and caring for you?'

A firm rap sounded at the door.

'Cornelia?' Lawrence asked. 'Is everything all right?'

With her eyes on Stephen's, Cornelia said, 'I'm fine. We'll be there in a minute.'

Lawrence Culford cleared his throat. 'We'll be in the drawing room. Ruth has prepared coffee.'

They both stood as her brother's footsteps retreated. Stephen stared at the beautiful woman in front of him. What could he say to Cornelia without further provoking her frustration? She was right in everything she'd said. Everything she'd accused him of. She deserved to know that after the honour he'd had of touching her – of loving her – he was not a cad, but a man afraid. How was he to resist her? How was he ever to close his eyes and not see the perfect blue of hers? How was he to breathe and not smell her scent?

'Please, Stephen. I will leave you to do as you will with the investigation if that's what you want, but...'

He stared deep into her eyes, longing to embrace her, to kiss her hair and tell her everything would be all right. But to do so would be foolish when space between them was imperative.

'But?' He feared whatever she said next would break down his feeble, self-imposed barriers.

'But...' She sighed. 'Unless you specifically demand it, or if I ever feel you are wrong for me, wrong for my boys, I won't walk away from us.'

Before he could respond, his heart damn near bursting from his chest, she swept to the door. With a final flash of fire from her eyes, she unlocked it and marched into the hallway, leaving him standing alone.

She'd said she wouldn't walk away... before she had even learned of his exoneration. Was it madness that he would not give them a chance?

He ran his hand over his face, innumerable emotions tumbling through him. He'd be a liar to say he didn't want to explore what might grow between them. Be a liar to deny how much he had enjoyed her family's – her sons' – company throughout dinner. He'd seen so much of their mother in Alfred and Francis's eyes. So much of Cornelia in their easy smiles and laughter.

He'd also seen her determination in Francis's assessing gaze. Seen the wary, protectiveness in Alfred's as he'd slid his arm around his brother's shoulders or cast a look at Cornelia as though checking she was happy. Stephen was thirty years old and had hardly any experience with children. Did Cornelia really think him kind enough, wise enough, to be a part of Alfred's and Francis's lives?

Another knock and Lawrence Culford strolled into the room, his hands relaxed in his pockets, as he surveyed the space. 'Well, well. Nothing's changed in here over the years.'

Stephen straightened his shoulders. 'Cornelia said this was once your father's study?'

'Indeed. His study and a place for things other than work.'

Stephen carefully gauged the man in front of him. A man who owned the prestigious Phoenix hotel. A man who'd thrown caution and society to the wind and married a woman who worked in a department store. A woman who now carried his child. Was Lawrence Culford not living, breathing proof of how convention could be tossed aside if a person was brave or determined enough?

Culford paced around the room, picked up and replaced a glass paperweight on the huge oak desk. 'My sister is very fond of you, Stephen. Fond and proud.'

He frowned. 'Proud?'

A small smile curved Culford's lips. 'Oh, yes. She hasn't said as much, but, with Cornelia, her actions speak louder than words about her feelings. You've struck her good and proper. So why don't we retire to the drawing room and finish this Christmas Eve on a note that will lead us splendidly into tomorrow?'

Uncertain, Stephen stared at his host. He should excuse himself and leave the house immediately. He should thank Culford for his hospitality and then exit with an excuse...

Instead, he smiled. 'What's life for if not for a little risk?'

'I couldn't have said it better myself.' Lawrence held his hand out towards the door. 'After you, my friend.'

44

With her stomach entirely stuffed from the huge Christmas lunch Harriet's staff had prepared, Cornelia collapsed back on the sofa in the drawing room, the remainder of a glass of wine in her hand. Her heart swelled as she watched Stephen laugh and play with the children and their new toys at the foot of the Christmas tree, warmth spreading through her to see Alfred and Francis so happy.

They had barely mentioned their father, but it pleased her that David had at least seen fit to telephone the boys on this special day, even if he'd spoken to them for barely more than ten minutes. It seemed that Stephen was providing at least a little relief from Alfred and Francis missing their father... not that David would have ever indulged in such boisterous carpet play.

A waft of floral perfume alerted her to Harriet's approach and Cornelia smiled as her sister sat beside her. 'Your staff have done you justice. Lunch was astounding,' Cornelia said.

Her sister gave a dismissive wave, her eyes narrowing as she studied Stephen. 'Oh, who cares about food when you have invited such a delicious distraction?'

Cornelia considered Harriet and the way her skin skimmed over her cheekbones, accentuating her thinness. Despite her too-slender frame, she was still beautiful. Her dark hair shining and perfectly styled, her subtle make-up bringing out the blueness of her eyes and pinkness of her bow lips.

Still so sophisticated.

Cornelia was assaulted by a stab of fear that Stephen might come to see that too and quickly pushed it away. 'There is no need for you to eye Stephen so hungrily. He'll be leaving first thing in the morning.'

Harriet turned, her smile almost lupine, her eyes glittering with mischief. 'Is he your lover?'

'Of course not.' Heat warmed Cornelia's cheeks as she drained her wine. 'Any man I have interest in will be so much more than a lover. I have the children to consider.'

'I see. So, you're behaving foolishly once again.' Harriet's laugh tinkled and she lifted her glass in a toast. 'Well, here's to one of the Culford daughters who will never learn.' She drank. 'Did Mama not teach you anything?'

'What is that supposed to mean?' Annoyed, Cornelia fought to keep her temper. 'Stephen and I work together, and he was alone this Christmas. Is it so wrong that I asked him here? The children are clearly enjoying his company and I suspect Lawrence likes him well enough, too.'

'Likes him?' Harriet patted Cornelia's knee. 'Our dear brother is merely sizing up the man who has clearly taken your heart. The man who will undoubtedly end up breaking it, just as David has.'

Cornelia glared. 'If you only joined me to provoke my temper, Harriet, I think it best I leave you alone.'

'I apologise. I just wanted to warn you, that's all. You are my beloved sister, after all.'

'Your tone implies the opposite.'

Harriet's gaze softened and, slowly, the spite left her eyes. Abruptly, she stood. 'Come with me.'

'Where are we—'

'Let's get our coats and take a stroll outside. Come on, the children will enjoy some fresh air.' She clapped her hands. 'Do you mind if we steal the children for a while, Mr Gower? Cornelia and I thought we'd take them outside for a spell.'

Stephen rose and brushed at his knees. 'Not at all, Miss Culford.'

Cornelia briefly met Stephen's quiet gaze before she rose, every nerve in her body on high alert. For all Harriet's wealth, status and influence in the local area, she was still the Culford child who had spent years being manipulated by their mother.

The children raced out of the room ahead of them as Cornelia's suspicion gathered strength. Her sister hadn't meant to start their conversation with such spite. There was something much deeper bothering her. Something was most definitely wrong.

Stepping forward, Cornelia forced a smile. 'Right, shall we go to the pond? If it's not too icy, maybe you children can walk along the wall, like we did in the summer. What do you say?'

Their shouts echoed around the hall until Adams opened the front door and Alfred, Francis, Rose and Nathaniel rushed outside into the cold afternoon.

Harriet walked confidently forward and offered Cornelia her elbow. Giving in to the inevitable, Cornelia slipped her hand beneath her sister's arm and they strolled outside into bright sunshine. The morning's frost had been melted by the mild temperature and, a blessing considering the time of year, the pathways were secure under Cornelia's boots.

She kept her counsel and waited for Harriet to speak. It was never very long before her sister had something to say. Whatever the circumstances.

'So.' Harriet smiled. 'For all your protestations, are you secretly keen on Mr Gower?'

Cornelia studied her. Would there really be any harm in confessing her feelings to Harriet? 'I am.'

'You would consider marrying him?'

Cornelia's smile dissolved. She'd considered making love with Stephen. Thought about how he played and interacted with the children. Had even considered the days out they might have, evenings in front of a blazing fire... but marriage?

'I doubt such a thing has entered his mind, any more than it has mine.'

The children ran in circles around each other on one of Culford's vast lawns and Cornelia drew Harriet to a slow stop. She released her arm and took her sister's hand.

'What's wrong?'

Harriet's eyes shone with what looked to be unshed tears before she looked towards the children. 'I want to marry.'

Cornelia frowned, concerned by the desolation in Harriet's tone. 'And you will. You're beautiful. Rich. Strong and decisive. How can you think there is the slightest chance you will not marry one day?'

'Not one day.' Harriet faced her. 'I want to marry as soon as possible.'

'But why?'

'Because I'm afraid.'

'Of what?'

Harriet slipped her hand from Cornelia's and gripped her gloved hands in front of her. 'Of the very real possibility Mama has ruined my life.'

Cornelia slumped her shoulders, hating that her sister bore

the same insecurities as a result of their upbringing as she and Lawrence. For all her bravado, Harriet hadn't escaped those years any less scarred than her siblings. She gently touched her arm. 'That will only happen if you allow it. Mama's gone. Your life is your own now.'

'Is it?' Harriet's eyes flashed with undisguised fury. 'I go to dances, balls, fancy dinners and soirées, but not once has a gentleman displayed any amorous intentions towards me. There's every possibility Mama has made me so forthright, so determined to succeed, that I'll never find a man I respect enough to spend my life with.'

'Mama was a bully, Harriet. A tyrant and a villain-in-arms alongside Papa. You are not her and, if you chose it, never will be. A man will come into your life when you least expect it.'

'Like Mr Gower has into yours?'

'We're talking about you, not me.'

'Fine.' Harriet whirled away, turning her back and covering her face in her hands before she abruptly dropped them and stepped close to Cornelia again. 'Lawrence has said he doesn't want me to travel on the *Titanic*. That David will be on board. I don't care, Cornelia. I have no interest in what David has to say. Please, you must persuade Lawrence that you don't mind me going. Susannah has persuaded her parents to accompany us. This is the perfect opportunity to get away from here and meet a man so much better travelled than any I might meet in Oxfordshire. A good man. A rich man. A man who can oversee the estate as only a gentleman could.'

'As only a *gentleman* could?' Cornelia stared, incredulous. 'God forbid Esther should hear you talk that way. Or me, in fact. Lawrence gave you a third of this house, Harriet. He knows you can look after the estate and its tenants as well as he ever could. Lord knows, you are more *au fait* with the running of this place than Lawrence or I would be nowadays. You don't need a man to oversee Culford, but you might want a man because your heart longs for it. Could that be true?'

'Maybe.' Harriet sighed and looked again at the children. 'You have to consider everything you do with the utmost care because you're a mother. I don't have that responsibility, but I want it.' She turned, her eyes glassy once more. 'I want a family of my own, a husband who loves me. Is that so much to ask? Can't you allow me to travel to America and let me have an adventure? You divorced David. You've taken control of your life. Let me do the same, please.'

'You have to consider everything you do with the utmost care because you're a mother.'

Harriet's words echoed in Cornelia's mind as her sister continued to talk. Yet, Cornelia could no longer hear Harriet over the thudding of her heart. Her sister was right. She had to think of Alfred and Francis, always.

Her boys ran screeching and laughing across the grass as they chased Rose and Nathaniel, their cheeks rosy-red and their smiles wide. Why shouldn't Harriet have an adventure? She deserved it after living alone with their mother for so long. As for Alfred and Francis, Cornelia couldn't deny how happy they were here. Just as they'd been in the summer.

Was she being selfish by remaining in Bath? Should she return to Culford and raise Alfred and Francis in a home that might one day be theirs? Yet, in Bath, she had thrived... come alive. Fear squeezed her heart. Could a parent ever truly guarantee their child's safety? Their happiness?

'Cornelia? Are you listening to me?'

She blinked and faced Harriet. 'Sorry?'

Harriet rolled her eyes. 'I asked if you will convince Lawrence I should board the *Titanic* in April? I will ensure all is taken care of here. Adams, Cook, Ruth and the other staff are more than capable—'

'Yes.'

'What?'

Cornelia drew in a long breath, realisation, truth and reality sweeping over her. 'Yes, you should go.'

'Really?' Harriet clutched Cornelia's hand in a hard grip. 'You mean it? You'll speak to Lawrence?'

'Yes. Yes, I will.'

'Oh, thank you.' Harriet pulled Cornelia into an embrace and squeezed her tightly. 'Thank you so much.'

With a parting squeal, Harriet took off across the grass to play with the children, leaving Cornelia staring blindly after her. Harriet had the right to a life of her own making. She was young and free, her entire future stretched out ahead of her.

Cornelia inhaled a shaky breath. *As for me? I have a decision to make and the guiding factor has to be the children.*

45

Inside the Manor, a quietness had fallen, and Stephen took the opportunity to escape into the drawing room. Despite it being Christmas Day, his thoughts about Cornelia and how he'd have to speak to Carter sooner or later continued to play havoc with his mind. He entered the room, relieved to find it empty, and walked to the tall sash window that gave an unobstructed view of the south-facing gardens.

Cornelia and her sister were playing with the children around the pond. Francis held his mother's hand and Nathaniel held his aunt's as they walked the boys around the low wall that surrounded the freezing water. Nerves rippled through him as he thought of one of the children slipping into the pond's depths. He'd been pleased and grateful that the children had so quickly warmed to him, even inviting him to join in their play.

It had also pleased him immeasurably to see the delight in Cornelia's eyes as she'd quietly watched them. How was he to deny the pleasure it had given him to be included in such normality even for a while?

Footsteps sounded behind him and Stephen inwardly sighed as Carter entered the room, his smile wide.

'Ah, there you are, Stephen. I was hoping to catch a moment alone with you. Shall we take this opportunity to talk?'

There was little point in putting off the inevitable. 'Of course.'

Carter sat in one of the wing-backed chairs in front of the stone fireplace, which was decorated with garlands of holly and tiny silver bells, a huge poinsettia shining resplendent in a silver bowl on the hearth.

The decor should have been cheering, but Stephen was far from cheerful as he took a seat. 'I assume you want to discuss my investigations into Lillian's death?'

Carter's eyes darkened with expectation. 'I do. I told Elizabeth I would do my utmost not to ruin our Christmas in any way, but you have to appreciate how hard it is for me not to speak of it while you're here.'

'I do appreciate that, and I'm prepared to share what I can. So let me tell you what I've uncovered.' Stephen leaned forwards. 'It could be that Lillian was targeted by this individual because of her charity work. It appears that—'

'Wait.' Carter frowned, his gaze angry. 'You think because Lillian was a kind woman, a generous woman, with a heart bigger than anyone I've ever known, those qualities were what got her killed?'

'Yes.' Stephen gripped his hands together. 'I believe the man we are looking for may have killed before. Could even be responsible for the recent killing you, astutely, recognised had similarities with Lillian's.'

'Why on earth would someone get killed because they were helping the poor and needy?' Carter shook his head. 'You're wrong. You have to be.'

'The why doesn't always make sense. Even if a perpetrator is brought to court and they are found guilty, their motivations can still be incomprehensible. But that doesn't make their crimes any less real.'

'For the love of God.' Carter collapsed back in his seat and ran his hand over his face. 'Giving and caring were more than duties to Lillian. They were her passions. She called charity her purpose. Her reason for being on this godforsaken earth. Now you're telling me she was killed for her strengths? Her calling?'

Stephen's heart twisted with sympathy. 'I'm sorry.'

Carter's eyes filled with a mix of anger and pleading. 'I need you to find this man. Get him locked up for the rest of his evil days.'

'And I have every intention of doing just that. My inspector at Scotland Yard is also doing what he can from London alongside my investigations here. He wants this killer caught as much as you do.'

'Your *previous* inspector, you mean?'

Stephen said nothing. Until he'd told Cornelia he was free to return to London, he wouldn't tell anyone else.

Carter seemed to calm down as his grip on his chair's arms relaxed a little. 'So, what do you plan to do next?'

'Well.' Stephen blew out a breath. 'The most pressing thing is to identify a viable link between the other killings and Lillian's. If my theory is right, then it was the women's work that particularly angered the killer. So far, all I know is that they delivered charity to the needy. Independently and from the kindness of their hearts. I need to find—'

'Not independently.'

'Sorry, I know you often accompanied—'

'No, you misunderstand.' Carter leaned forward again. 'Lillian was part of a group.'

Dread dropped like lead into Stephen's heart. Could this mean an entire organisation was on the murderer's radar? 'A group?'

'Yes. They weren't an official group, but just a circle of young, determined and generous women who came together to do some good in the city's slums. They would meet at each other's houses occasionally, to discuss strategies, but mostly they just called on one another for support.'

'Would Lillian have kept a list of names belonging to this group? Is it possible we could find out whether the two other women who were killed were a part of this organisation?'

Carter got to his feet, his face more animated than Stephen had seen it since he'd arrived at Pennington's. 'As far as I can remember, she kept a box with papers relating to her charity work. There could be something in there, but I can't remember coming across it when I sorted out her things after her funeral.'

'But that's not to say you couldn't find it now.' Excitement churned in Stephen's stomach. 'When you return home, I want you to find this box and let me have everything it contains. There could be something in there that will be helpful.'

'I can't leave here until tomorrow, at the earliest. If I suggest we leave tonight, Elizabeth will not be best pleased.'

'Tomorrow is soon enough. It's Christmas Day. There's little either of us can do until morning.'

'Yes, you're right.' Carter walked to a cabinet at the far end of the room. 'I think we deserve a drink, don't you?'

'Why not?'

As Carter poured them each a snifter of brandy, Stephen's spirits fell. If it came that Lillian Carter's charity organisation was the killer's target, the entire investigation had just burst wide open. How many women were in the group? How could he help the Bath constabulary to contact these women and ensure their safety until the killer was apprehended?

He stared at the hearth.

Things had just gone from bad to bloody hellish.

46

Elizabeth looked at Joseph where he was bent down in front of a bureau in their attic, his brow furrowed as he discarded document after document from inside a leather trunk. They had been searching for Lillian's papers relating to her charitable organisation for over an hour.

'Where in God's name can they be?' he grumbled. 'She kept anything of any importance in this trunk. I'm sure of it.'

Feeling helpless, Elizabeth gently laid her hand on his back. 'We'll find it. Try not to get so frustrated. It will be here somewhere.'

'But where? We've looked in every possible place.'

She looked around the disordered boxes, bags and paraphernalia that lay all over the wooden floor. Joseph was adamant that, after Lillian's funeral, he'd packed up her belongings and kept them in storage in the attic above Carter & Son's. Once they'd married, he'd meticulously gone through everything he wanted to keep, give to charity or throw away. A painful process that meant his memory was clear about what he'd kept.

'I am entirely certain the box relating to her charitable work came with me from the shop.' He stood and put his hands on his hips. 'It felt wrong to throw away something that was so important to her.'

A floral box in the far corner of the room caught Elizabeth's eye and a rush of certainty swept through her. 'What's this?'

She walked over and drew the box from beneath a bag of old clothes.

'That's it!' Joseph eagerly took the box from her and flipped open the lid. 'God, I remember now.'

They sat on the floor in the middle of a stream of sunshine which shone through the skylight making the dancing dust motes glint.

Joseph feverishly extracted the pages, his gaze passing over each piece of paper, his smile growing. 'She was definitely part of a group. Just as I told Gower. Here, look, the names of her associates. There are...' He tapped his finger down the page. 'Six in total.'

'Six?' Elizabeth swallowed, dread forming a knot in her stomach. 'And Mr Gower thinks there's a possibility the killer could target all of them?'

'Yes. We need to give this to him immediately.' Joseph looked at his watch. 'If I hurry, I should be able to catch him before he leaves the store.'

They stood and Joseph took her hand.

'Thank you for agreeing to not go in today so we could look for this. You mean the world to me, you do know that?'

Elizabeth smiled. 'As you do to me. Joseph...' She drew her gaze over his handsome face, worry for him rising once again. 'These papers do not mean Mr Gower will find Lillian's killer immediately.'

'I know.' His smile vanished as his eyes darkened. 'But they do mean he should be able to do all he can to warn and protect the others on this list. If these women are cautioned, they have a better chance of escaping this animal's clutches than Lillian ever did.'

Worry for him continued to nag Elizabeth as they descended the stairs and entered their bedroom. She sat on the bed as he changed his shirt and put on the black suit he always wore at Pennington's. Words battled inside her. She did not want to shower pessimism over his hopes, but more protect him from possible disappointment.

His face shone with renewed vitality, his smiles coming her way over and over again as he dressed and fixed on his cufflinks.

Elizabeth forced a smile and tried her utmost to bury her anxieties. She owed it to Joseph, to herself, to fully believe that the box contained the information Mr Gower needed to find the link between the murdered women.

'You mentioned that Mr Gower referred to his inspector in the present tense while we were at Culford Manor. Do you think there's a possibility he could leave us sooner than we thought? That he intends to return to London?'

'I don't know. He was never really clear on why he was in Bath in the first place, but it was his police experience that made me offer him the watchman position. I am still determined to eradicate the shoplifters at Pennington's, and having someone with his experience watching the goings-on can only be a good thing.'

'Absolutely.' Elizabeth frowned. 'It will be a shame if we lose him.'

Joseph walked to her dressing table and picked up Lillian's box before taking Elizabeth's hand and pulling her gently from the bed. He brushed his lips over hers, gaze happy. 'We won't. I'm sure it was a slip of the tongue when he spoke of his inspector. Why would he leave Pennington's after doing so much for us? He must have a want to stay.'

'True.' Elizabeth smiled. 'I also suspect some romance brewing between him and Cornelia.'

'As do I, my love. As do I.' He kissed her again and headed for the door. 'I must go. I'll see you later.'

Elizabeth walked to the window and stared into the street, waiting for Joseph to emerge. She crossed her arms and took a heavy breath, praying that whatever Lillian had written on those papers provided a breakthrough. What a victory it would be for Joseph's first wife to posthumously provide the very key to incarcerating her killer. Hope burned deep in Elizabeth's heart as a feeling of inevitability stole through her. If there was one thing she knew, without a shadow of a doubt, no one should ever underestimate the power of women. Whether they be alive or dead...

47

Cornelia looked up from the jewellery counter at the hundreds of customers milling around Pennington's ground floor on New Year's Eve. The time she'd spent at Culford Manor had given her the space she'd needed to ponder over her future.

Yet she was no closer to deciding whether to remain in Bath or return to the manor. How was she to be sure of what was best for Alfred and Francis?

Guilt whispered through her. Their smiles hadn't been quite as happy since returning home to The Circus, their eyes not shining with as much joy. But, once all the excitement and sparkle of Christmas had faded, would they really like living with Harriet? Surely it was the space and fresh air that had brought colour to the boys' cheeks rather than their aunt?

They had enjoyed being able to run free and play outside without the dangers of passing trams, horses and motor cars. The privilege of having a bedroom each rather than sharing. The excitement of the horses in the stables and the gardens that needed constant tending. Her boys had devoured every aspect of country life. Absorbed every facet of a life they could quite possibly have been destined for, if their parents' marriage hadn't failed.

The right thing to do – the *only* thing to do – was go to Culford, where they were happiest, but that didn't stop Cornelia's heart from sinking at the thought of leaving Bath and Pennington's.

Of never seeing Stephen again.

Lawrence had finally approved Harriet's plan to travel aboard the *Titanic* and their sister had been ecstatic, entirely convinced she would meet the love of her life during her trip. As for Cornelia? Her gaze followed Stephen's progress through the crowds. His hands were clasped behind his back and his brow furrowed.

He could never be hers.

She'd been a fool ever to imagine he would.

David had abandoned his children for wealth and status, wrapped up in the excuse of falling in love. If she were to act on her selfish love for Stephen, her children would think that adult love went hand-in-hand with abandonment.

She could not allow them to believe such a thing. It was part of her role as their mother to teach them the importance of commitment, tenacity and strength, whether that be to a relationship or a position.

If they were given the opportunity to learn about the workings of an estate, of the lives and hardships of Culford's tenants and staff, it would provide more insight into real life, compassion and understanding than they would ever learn living amongst the wealthy in Bath.

At Culford, she could expose her boys to those less fortunate without exposing them to the poor and needy in the city's much more perilous slum areas.

Culford was definitely calling her home.

'Might you be able to help me?'

Cornelia started. A woman was standing in front of her. 'Oh, I do apologise. How can I help you?'

'May I take a look at that tray of brooches, please?'

'Of course. These just came into the store this week.' Cornelia smiled at the customer as she picked up a diamond-encrusted brooch. 'As a New Year incentive, we are offering a ten per cent discount on any purchases made today. Do you see a piece in particular you like?'

The young woman smiled sheepishly. 'I do. In fact, I wish I could have them all. Dear Papa gave me some money for Christmas and told me to buy myself something pretty.'

Cornelia nodded. 'Well, in that case, looking at the lovely green of your eyes, maybe this beautiful emerald and diamond floral bouquet? As you can see, the cut and design are exquisite. A piece of jewellery that will last forever. It would be a wonderful heirloom to pass on to a daughter.'

The woman laughed and pressed her hand to her chest. 'A daughter? My husband and I *are* trying for a family.'

'How wonderful.' Cornelia looked up to find Stephen watching her. A jolt of attraction shot through her and she quickly faced her customer. 'Then who's to say you won't have a beautiful baby girl in these coming months? This is truly a most lovely piece.'

'I'll take it.' The woman beamed and unclasped her purse. 'Wrap it quickly before I change my mind.'

'Of course, madam.' Cornelia lifted the brooch and carefully laid it on a piece of black velvet before returning the tray to its drawer and locking it. 'I'll be right back.'

She picked up the brooch and walked to a counter which contained Pennington's signature black and white boxes and black tissue paper. Trying her hardest not to sneak another look in Stephen's direction, Cornelia was preparing to wrap the brooch when a shadow fell over her.

'Good afternoon, sister.'

Cornelia looked up and almost dropped the brooch. 'Esther! Whatever are you doing here? Is Lawrence with you?'

Esther's eyebrows lifted as merriment sparkled in her hazel eyes. 'Do you think that brother of yours is ever likely to let me go anywhere alone these days? He's upstairs in the toy department with the children. I insisted on a visit to Pennington's before all the happiness I felt at Christmas dissolves.'

'It *was* wonderful at Culford, I must admit.' Cornelia turned back to wrapping the brooch, carefully placing it in a velvet-lined box before pulling a sheet of tissue paper towards her. 'I couldn't have made a better decision. The boys had a wonderful time.'

'As did you.'

The playful tone in Esther's voice surprised Cornelia. 'What do you mean?'

'I mean...' Esther widened her eyes and tilted her head. 'The romantic possibility between you and Mr Gower was obvious.'

Cornelia dropped her gaze to the wrapping, drawing some ribbon from the reel beside her. 'We... Stephen and I are—'

'Nothing short of adorable. He's all moody and strong and in control and you're all of a fluster, confused and totally besotted.'

Cornelia knotted the ribbon with a sharp tug. 'I am none of those things. In fact... just wait right there. I'll be straight back.'

Pasting on a smile, Cornelia returned to her customer.

'There you go, madam.' She turned to one of her young colleagues. 'Martha? Would you mind escorting this lady and her beautiful brooch to the cash desk?'

'Of course, Miss Culford.'

Cornelia waited until the customer and Martha were swallowed by the throng before returning to Esther.

Her sister-in-law said, 'Well?'

Taking a long breath, Cornelia sighed. 'I've decided it would be best if the boys and I went back to Culford and live our lives as was planned all along.'

'All along? Cornelia...' Esther touched Cornelia's hand where it lay rigid on top of the counter. 'All along vanished when David abandoned you and the children for *that* woman.' Esther's eyes burned with passion, her jaw tight. 'You have to go forward with what *you* want now. Of course, the boys are your main priority, but not once have I heard you say you might want to live at Culford. If that's truly what you want, then, of course you must go, but I fear...' She lowered her voice. 'You would be running away from a man who could make you exceedingly happy. If it's the investigation making you—'

'It's not.' Cornelia took her hand away. 'Stephen and I might have come to feel something for one another, but I belong at Culford. I belong where my children are happiest. Wouldn't you go wherever Rose and Nathaniel were happy? Where your new baby will be happy?'

Esther's eyes filled with sadness. 'Yes. Yes, I would.'

'There you are, then.' Cornelia swallowed, more than a little disappointed Esther hadn't said Cornelia's logic was wrong. 'I'll be handing in my notice at the end of the week and then the boys and I will leave Bath. Now, I must get on before Mrs Hampton starts breathing down my neck.'

She walked along the counter and approached a waiting customer. 'Good afternoon, madam. How may I help?'

As the customer continued to browse the glass cabinets, Cornelia cast a furtive glance in Esther's direction, but she was nowhere to be seen. Releasing her held breath, Cornelia swallowed. No doubt Lawrence would be as dismayed as Esther about her decision to leave Bath, but if she was to remain, it would be for selfish reasons only.

Two very important, but very selfish reasons: Stephen and Pennington's.

The reasons for her to leave mattered so much more: Alfred and Francis. Always.

Her brother and Esther would come to understand that... as she hoped Stephen would, too.

48

Stephen put on the sorry-looking flat cap he'd picked up for a couple of pence at the market and examined his dirt-smeared face in the bedroom mirror.

This will either work or it won't.

He patted his hands over his jacket and trouser pockets. Some notes and loose change.

His trusty cudgel.

Some paper and a pencil.

The minimum he needed for tonight's excursion... Brute strength and quickness of mind could possibly be others.

Leaving his bedroom, he reached the hallway and glanced through the open parlour doorway. His mother sat in her favourite armchair, her knitting needles busy between her fingers.

A floorboard squeaked under his foot and he hissed a quiet curse.

'Stephen?'

He looked longingly at the closed front door. 'Just popping out for a quick pint, Ma. I won't be late.'

'Well, that's nice, but it wouldn't hurt for you to let me see your face while I'm talking to you.'

Muttering another curse, Stephen drew himself up to his full height and walked to the parlour door, braced for an onslaught.

She laid the knitting in her lap... and flinched. 'Good Lord above. Why on earth are you dressed like that? They'll not take kindly to you walking into the pub like that.'

Stephen touched his hand to the brim of his cap. 'There's a reason for it. That's all I can tell you, I'm afraid.'

She studied him, her mouth pinched into a tight line.

Trying his best not to fidget under her scrutiny, Stephen held her gaze.

Emitting a rather inelegant sniff, his mother picked up her knitting. 'Right. Then I'll leave you to your business.'

Surprised, and more than a little concerned by her lack of curiosity, Stephen said, 'That's it?'

She didn't look at him, her fingers busy at her needles once more. 'That's it. If you're daft enough to get yourself tangled up in the one thing you came here to avoid, that's your own doing. Good luck with it.' She lifted her head and met his eyes. 'Just be careful.'

Stephen winked. 'Always. I'll see you in the morning.'

He quickly left the house and hurried along the busy streets towards the centre of town. The night was cold, with sleet blowing in every direction on a rising wind. As he stepped up his pace, his mind once again went over the contents of the box Joseph Carter had given him.

The papers and log sheets inside had identified the six women who had worked closely to aid people from the slums, ensuring that charity was bestowed on needy children and adults up and down a huge stretch of the River Avon.

Stephen had sent an urgent telegram to Inspector King with

the names, knowing he ought to be able to make more headway with the officers at Bath constabulary than Stephen could.

But, for now, the next step was Stephen's.

Keeping his head purposefully low, with eyes shielded beneath the brim of his cap, he descended the worn steps into the darkness beneath the bridge's long-reaching shadow. The grunts, snorts and coughs of the destitute surrounded him as he walked, his gaze darting left and right as he headed for the clump of trees he'd previously been shown by Herman Angel.

He put his hand around the cudgel in his pocket and ducked into the foliage. He'd barely stepped a few feet inside before he knew he wasn't alone.

The movements were subtle – the stench of unwashed skin and acrid breath not so much.

Forks of moonlight illuminated two sets of eyes as they watched him from below the brims of their hats, the scarves pulled high over their noses.

Trepidation gripped him and Stephen tightened his fingers on the cudgel. 'I want no trouble. Just looking for a friend.'

'Piss off.'

The man who'd spoken remained seated on the ground, but his associate slowly rose to his feet, bent almost double, his bones seeming to creak in the enclosed space. He lifted his hand to his scarf.

Stephen's shoulders tensed as he planted his feet more firmly and slightly apart.

The man lowered his scarf and pushed up the brim of his hat, his eyes widening in warning.

Herman.

Stephen carefully kept his expression hostile and gave a slight nod, understanding.

'Who are you looking for?' Herman demanded. 'There isn't

anyone worth looking for down here. Why don't you do as my friend asks and piss off?'

Stephen squared his shoulders. 'I've been given a coin or two to help someone. A coin or two I'm willing to share if you can help me.'

The vagrant on the floor shifted, causing the stench from his clothes and breath to rise in an invisible cloud. 'And what's stopping us from picking you up and shaking the bloody coins out of you?' He flicked his head towards the entrance, his gaze on Herman. 'Get rid of him.'

'One question.' Stephen raised his hand. 'That's all I'll ask and, if your answer is good enough to send me on my way, I'll go.'

'I said, pis—'

'Why don't we take the offer of a laugh when it presents itself?' Herman stepped in front of Stephen and eyed him from head to toe, obscuring the other man's view. He winked. 'What's your question?'

Whatever happened next, they would watch each other's backs.

'The gentleman who gave me the coin has been asking questions about a murder.'

'What murder?'

'The murder of a young woman who used to come around these parts offering food, blankets and the like. Seems she got killed for her efforts. You hear about that?'

Herman shook his head. 'Not me.' He spoke over his shoulder. 'You know anything?'

The second man raised an earthenware jug to his lips and drank deeply before lowering it and swiping the back of his hand across his mouth. 'He's talking about that toff's wife. Why would anyone care about her, if her bloody husband don't?'

Stephen tensed, adrenaline raising the hairs on his arms. 'It could've been her husband asking about her.'

'Doubt it. He's married again, so clearly he can't give a fig about what happened to his first missus. Married himself a right nice piece, too. She owns Pennington's, of all places. How in God's name he managed to snag her, I don't know. Used to own a shop on the bridge. Now look at him. Seems to me he didn't deserve his first wife. I hope the way she went, what happened to her, haunts that toff day and night. Might as well have been his hand around the knife that stabbed her.' The man's voice was taunting, evil and laced with nauseating glee.

Herman's jaw was a hard line and Stephen's blood simmered hot beneath the surface of his skin. He hadn't mentioned a knife.

'So, you have no idea who killed her?' Stephen took a step forward, brushing past Herman. 'Seems wrong to me that any man should raise his hand to a woman, let alone stab her and leave her to die in a place where she was trying to do some good.'

The man's eyes narrowed. 'You're talking like you actually care about her. All women have motives. There was no more charity in Lillian Carter than the rest of the do-gooders who come around here, handing out bread and water as though they'll get themselves a better place in heaven than the rest of us. Shit-stirrers, the lot of them.'

It was all Stephen needed to hear.

His blood pumping, he lunged for the man, drew him up by his coat collar and slammed him against the slimy, wet wall. Once, twice, three times, until the man's breath rushed from him between cracked lips, his head swaying from side to side in his drunkenness.

Stephen clenched his teeth. 'Who killed her? Give me a

name. I mean it or, so help me God, I won't be responsible for what happens next.'

'Piss off.'

Before Stephen could do anything, a fist whistled past his face and smacked into the vagrant's cheek. His head snapped back, hitting the wall with a crack.

'Goddamn it.' Herman shook out his fingers. 'Just cough it up, man. Who killed her?'

Stephen shook the man again. 'A name. Now.'

'I don't know his bloody name, all right?' The man's bloodshot eyes burned with anger. 'He lives in Victoria Park, but you'll never get to him. He's got a gang. A whole load of them who watch his back. You're wasting your bloody time.'

'What does he look like?'

'Big, broad fella. Menacing. Hair as black as night and his eyes...' The vagrant shook his head. 'Are eyes no man or woman wants to look at. You'll know him when you see him, trust me. He's a bloody giant among thieves.'

Revulsion twisted Stephen's stomach. To think of a man of this described size preying on women was more than he could stand. How in God's name had he managed to get away with killing? Not once, but three times. Were people so afraid of him they would rather turn a blind eye than help take him off the streets?

Stephen loosened his grip and shoved the man again. He looked at Herman.

Before Stephen could so much as open his mouth, the other man's fist caught him on the jaw, the strength of the blow vibrating through his teeth. As he shook the pain from his head and the stars from his eyes, the man shoved past them, sending Herman stumbling backwards and Stephen lurching to the side.

He was out from the cover of the trees and away.

'Goddamn it.' Stephen rubbed his jaw. 'We've got no chance of catching up with him. He probably knows the shortcuts from here to oblivion better than we ever will.'

'Maybe, but at least you're another step closer in your investigation.' Herman smiled. 'Even if you've got a bruised jaw and ego to go with it.'

Stephen took off his cap and pushed his hair back from his forehead. 'Funny, Herman. Really bloody funny.'

49

The knock at Lawrence's front door startled Cornelia, who was reading a novel in the drawing room. Who on earth could be calling at this time in the evening? She'd insisted everyone, including the servants, go to the pantomime tonight because she'd wanted time alone to think. Time to contemplate how she would heal her broken heart again.

A second knock.

Unsure whether it was wise to answer the door, she slowly stood and walked downstairs. When she reached the front door, she took a walking cane from the stand beside her. Gripping it tightly, she straightened her shoulders. 'Who is it?'

'Cornelia? It's Stephen. I need to see you.'

'Stephen?' She hurriedly returned the cane to the stand and looked down at her body. She only wore a nightdress and robe. The tone of Stephen's voice had indicated something was wrong. She unlocked the door. 'Whatever are you— My God, what happened to your face? Why are you dressed like that?' She waved her hand, urging him inside. 'Come in. Quickly.'

He stepped inside, where the light in the hallway starkly illuminated his injuries. A bruise bloomed red at his jaw, his hair was dishevelled, and he bore a cut to his lower lip.

'Have you been involved in a fight? You have blood...' She gaped at him, her hand rising to her chest. 'Stephen, what have you done?'

'Disturbed your evening by the looks of it. I'm sorry. I'll go.'

She clasped his hand. 'You will do no such thing. What happened?'

'Don't worry. Everything is all right. Can we go into the kitchen? Maybe I shouldn't have come here, but I wanted to see you.' He grimaced. 'Plus, I was hoping you could clean me up enough to prevent my mother seeing me like this.'

'Oh, Stephen.' She pushed her arm through his. 'Come with me.'

Carefully, she led him along the hallway and down the short staircase to the kitchen. 'Have a seat at the table and I'll find Helen's box of bandages and ointment. You really look a frightful mess.'

'Are we alone?'

'Yes. Everyone is at the theatre.' She opened two cupboards before she located Helen's box of tricks and then dampened a cloth. When she turned, her eyes met his.

He frowned. 'I should go. I didn't think—'

'We're alone, Stephen.' *Please don't go.* 'They won't be back for a long while yet.'

'Well, I'm glad about that, considering the state of me, but as for you being alone in a house at night, that's a different matter.'

'I was armed with a walking cane. I am more than capable of looking after myself. Ask David.' The second she mentioned David, she regretted it. Stephen's eyes darkened, his jaw a hard line. 'Sorry. David's treatment towards me is not something to joke about.'

'No, it isn't.' His gaze softened and tenderly moved over her face. 'But I'm glad to know you didn't meekly accept his violence.'

She put a sponge to the opened bottle of ointment. 'No, I didn't. I can promise you that.' She dabbed the broken skin at his jaw. He winced. 'Sorry. So, are you going to tell me what happened?'

'Herman Angel and I got into a scuffle with a vagrant at the bridge.'

'Herman? The man who came to Pennington's?'

'Yes. I went to Pulteney Bridge tonight, in the hope of finding another lead for Lillian's killer. After speaking to Joseph at Christmas, I think it's highly likely Lillian was targeted as part of a larger group of charitable women. Herman told me he believed this man might return to the bridge and I'd hoped to get lucky.'

Sickness rolled through her imagining him skulking about in such a horrible place at the dead of night. 'So, you're dressed like that to go unnoticed amongst the vagrants?'

'Yes, but it was fortunate Herman was there. When push came to shove, we got this man to talk and now I know where I can find the killer. He's in the city.'

'In Bath? Then you must tell Joseph. He'll—'

'Telling Carter is the last thing I want to do. God only knows how he'll react. It won't help him, or Elizabeth, if he's arrested and imprisoned. I have to deal with this the correct way.'

'You're right. Of course, you're right.' She briefly closed her eyes. 'What will you do?'

'First thing tomorrow, I'll go to the police station. My inspector promised to speak to them today, so they should know the gravity and urgency of the case by now. Now I know where this man is likely to be, they can apprehend him.'

She gently wiped his face. 'Good. If this vile situation can be brought to an end, it's much more likely nineteen-twelve will be a wonderful, wholly freeing year for Elizabeth and Joseph. Finally. They deserve that.'

'They do, I was grateful that I had someone else with me tonight. The river is not a place to go alone. It only tells me more about the sort of woman Lillian Carter must have been. It makes me understand that Carter is as attracted to strong women as I am.' He stared into her eyes. 'Women like you.'

She dropped her gaze, fearful of the growing connection between them, fearful of the foolishness of falling in love with him. She had made her decision and was leaving. Doing what was best for her children. She purposefully changed the subject. 'Have you heard anything more about your case?'

'My case?'

She lifted her eyes. 'From the Board. Have they made a decision yet?'

He stared at her before slowly nodding. 'Yes. Yes, they have.'

A horrible insecurity pressed down on her. She was leaving and, if Stephen was acquitted, he would undoubtedly return to London. If found guilty…

'I've been exonerated. I can go back to my work at the Yard whenever I'm ready.'

'Oh, Stephen.' Tears pricked her eyes. From happiness for him or pity for herself, she couldn't be sure, even though she had no right to such feeling now that she'd no longer be here. 'That's wonderful. I'm so happy for—'

'I came to Bath to get away from my work, my life, only to meet you.' His pained gaze bored into hers. 'A woman I have come to care for deeply. A woman I could love.' He lifted his hand to her chin and brushed his thumb across her lips. 'And I have no idea what to do about it.'

He leaned towards her and although her brain screamed at her to move away, stand up, anything to open the space between them, Cornelia moved closer. To see him hurt, to know he had put himself in danger in order to bring Joseph Carter peace only made her want him more, love him more. He was an innocent man. A good man.

They kissed, moving closer to each other, kissing deeper, until she eased back to catch her breath. 'I have to think of the children.'

He softly stared at her. 'I know you do.'

She swallowed, her heart heavy. 'I've decided I must return to the manor house. Permanently. Alfred and Francis are so happy whenever they are there, and their happiness means everything—'

'Of course it does. You have to do what is best for them. I would never ask you to do anything that meant your children didn't come first.' He took her hand and lifted it to his mouth. He closed his eyes and pressed a firm, lingering kiss on her knuckles before looking into her eyes. 'The fact you're returning to Culford only makes it easier for me to tell you I'll be leaving Bath too. As soon as possible. When I was at the bridge, when that vagrant was sneering at me as though I was little more than dirt, I knew my work with the police is far from over. That I need to go back to London. To do something to stop criminals from getting away with violence, theft and murder. I've made mistakes, but those mistakes are lessons I'll never forget.' He touched his hand to her cheek. 'But I have to go back.'

Her heart thundered as understanding of their lost opportunity swept through her, but so did strength. They had to follow their different paths. Even if they took them in opposite directions.

But she loved him and wanted him... even if only for this one night. Slowly, she returned the ointment to the box and stood.

'Cornelia?'

'You're right.' She ran the cloth under the tap and laid it out on the drainer to dry. 'We have to do what is right for each of us.' Opening the cupboard beneath the sink, she replaced the box and smiled, tears burning her eyes. 'So, now, it feels right that we go upstairs, wouldn't you say?'

A muscle in his jaw twitched and a raw hunger shone in his eyes. They stood inches apart, their eyes locked and her body humming with the desire to touch him, pleasure him, have him deep inside her.

He lifted her into his arms. She gasped and put her arms around his neck. 'Tell me the way.'

His voice was a rough, arousing growl and she pressed her mouth to his. 'Upstairs. Second floor.'

Once they reached her bedroom, she leaned over to open the door and Stephen kicked it shut behind them.

She laughed at his self-satisfied expression as he carried her to bed. He laid her down and removed his jacket, his tie, boots and socks before joining her.

She pulled him close and roughly kissed him, her entire body simmering with need. It had been so long since she had made love, so long since she had felt desire like this. Now Stephen had set her body afire.

He fumbled with the ribbons at the edge of her nightgown.

Impatient for his touch, she moved away from him and, with a gentle nudge, pushed him back. He collapsed against the pillows, his gaze hungry on hers.

She shrugged her robe from her shoulders and tossed it to

the side. Without fear or embarrassment, she lifted the hem of her nightgown and pulled it over her head. The cool air made her nipples harden as she basked in Stephen's admiring gaze, his study moving over her body, lingering on her breasts, her stomach, her centre...

A new confidence swept through her as Cornelia unbuttoned his breeches and pulled them off his feet, absurdly pleased that he wore no underwear. With Stephen, she felt attractive; with Stephen, she felt powerful and strong. Her core tightened as she lay against his chest. They kissed, his hands slipping into her hair as she pushed her fingers into his hard shoulders, the muscle and tendons like rope.

He shifted his weight so they were side by side and ran his fingers over her breasts, inched lower with a featherlight touch to her stomach. She pulled back and closed her eyes, her body quivering.

At last, he reached the place she wanted him to explore and her breath caught. She writhed against his fingers as he teased and rubbed until heat washed through her, her yearning unbearable.

'Take me, Stephen. Please. I want this so much.'

He moved over and kissed her. She opened her legs wider, urging him, wanting him, and he entered her with a dominance that was thrillingly erotic. She groaned aloud. Never before had a man shown such passion towards her, such utter lust and desire. Her body responded, and she gripped his buttocks, urging him to take her harder, deeper, wanting him to fill her completely.

'Open your eyes, Cornelia.'

She did as he asked, and he thrust again. She gripped him tighter. He growled and kissed her, his teeth grazing her lip, igniting another rush of sensations.

Their bodies grew slick with perspiration, need and desire filling the room as their moans grew and then...

Stephen's groan mixed with her whimpers as her orgasm exploded, lighting her up and sending her spinning to a place of love she had wanted to believe existed but had never really known for certain.

Until now.

50

Early the following morning, Stephen strode along the street housing Bath's police station, his mind focused and his body sated. The condition of his heart was another matter entirely, but now was not the time to think about how he was supposed to leave Bath and Cornelia. They had joined together heart, body and soul. He didn't doubt the same sad thoughts had troubled her since he'd left the evening before.

As soon as they'd found the strength to move after their lovemaking, they had dressed in haste, Cornelia brushing and rearranging her hair with lightning speed, before ushering him downstairs and through the front door. Her beautiful blue eyes had filled with panic and guilt as she remembered Alfred and Francis.

If their separation hadn't been so bloody heartbreaking, their tripping, fumbling and racing back to normality would have been almost comical.

As it was, there was nothing funny about not being with her.

He reached the station steps and looked up at its facade. A large Georgian building, the age-blackened stone and smeared sash windows gave a gloomy welcome. Although not precisely imposing, the station certainly had a presence that went some way towards reassuring the city folk that, even if some criminals escaped capture, others wouldn't. One in particular, the man who'd taken Lillian Carter's life and the lives of two others, would not, Stephen promised himself now.

He purposefully climbed the steps and pushed open one of the station's double doors. The interior, with its dark wood-panelled walls and dusty electric lamps was depressingly dismal. A row of chairs lined one wall, where several members of the public sat looking tense or fearful.

He walked to the counter and the duty sergeant raised his head. 'Can I help you, sir?'

'Good morning.' Stephen glanced over the sergeant's shoulder towards the offices beyond. 'I'm here to speak with Sergeant Whitlock on the authority of Inspector King of Scotland Yard.'

Looking decidedly unimpressed, the duty sergeant asked, 'Might I ask about what, sir?'

Stephen cleared his throat. 'My name is Stephen Gower. I'm sure if you tell Sergeant Whitlock I am waiting to speak to him on the instructions of Inspector King, that will suffice.'

The sergeant cast his suspicious gaze over Stephen's face, before nodding towards the row of seats. 'Take a seat. I'll see if Sergeant Whitlock is available.'

Stephen flashed his most amiable smile. 'Appreciated.'

He walked to the chairs but didn't sit, his body tight with tension. As soon as he'd returned home after leaving Cornelia's, his mother had appeared at the top of the stairs, holding a hand-delivered message for him. Her eyes had been filled with concern, having decided that Stephen was involved in some form of espionage that explained why he'd left the house masquerading as a down-and-out.

Inspector King's instructions had been simple and to the point:

```
Be at Bath police station by 8 a.m. and
ask for Whitlock.
```

'Mr Gower?'

Stephen turned.

A stout man in his early fifties came forward, hand outstretched. 'Sergeant Whitlock. Won't you come through to the interview room?'

Stephen shook his hand. 'Of course.'

He followed Whitlock through some corridors to an empty interview room. They each took a seat either side of a steel grey table.

Whitlock leaned back and laced his hands over his slightly protruding stomach. 'So, your former inspector has told me the situation and is of the opinion that you are on the trail of a murderer. A man who has killed a number of times, if your findings are accurate.'

The sergeant's scepticism wasn't lost on Stephen and he fought to keep his temper under control. 'That's correct.'

Whitlock gave a wry smile, his eyes dancing with amusement. 'Sir, I have to be honest with you. These claims seem far-fetched, to say the least. Neither you nor Inspector King can expect me to—'

'What we expect, sir, is your complete co-operation.' Stephen leaned forward, his hand curled into a fist on top of the table. 'Trust me, Inspector King would not be pleased to find that you consider the women, whose names we've given you, of such little importance that you prefer to discuss the merits of my investigation rather than ensuring their safety.'

'Is that right? Well, let me tell you something, *Mr* Gower. I only have so many officers I can risk sending out on a fool's errand. My inspector has asked me to ensure—'

'These women are forewarned, thus forearmed? That it would be a good idea to find and arrest a suspected killer?'

Whitlock glanced at the paper he'd put on the table and cleared his throat. 'Do we even have a description of the suspect? A guarantee that he'll be where you think he should be? Otherwise—'

'I can't possibly provide a guarantee he'll be there when we decide to surprise—'

'We?' Whitlock huffed a laugh. 'There will be no *we*, Gower. You are not working for Scotland Yard, or any constabulary, come to that. I understand you are under investigation for you part in—'

'Now that's where you're wrong.' Stephen reached into his inside pocket and removed the second of the two telegrams he'd received from Inspector King. 'My inspector thought you might want to read this.'

He slid the telegram across the table and leaned back, crossing his arms. Seconds ticked by while Whitlock read.

Whitlock coughed. 'I see. So, as of today, you are reinstated to your former rank as detective sergeant at Scotland Yard.'

'I am.'

Whitlock pushed the telegram back across the desk and stood. 'Then I suppose you and I need to assemble a team.' He threw Stephen a pointed glare. 'Under my authority, of course.'

Stephen raised his eyebrows, prepared for another showdown. 'You'll act on the information you've been given?'

'Indeed I will.' Whitlock gave a firm nod. 'Never let it be said that I'm not a fair man. Let's go and get this bastard.'

* * *

It didn't take Stephen long to warm to the sergeant and gain respect for his work. In less than three hours, Whitlock had briefed his team and had officers in place, ready to apprehend their suspect in Victoria Park. One group had been sent ahead to scour the area, noting anything suspicious. News soon came back that the park appeared quiet, but one stretch in particular was known to the public as a no-go area.

They would start there.

The latest victim, and the previous victim before Lillian, had now been linked to the same group of charity workers Lillian was associated with. The remaining three had been contacted with strict instructions not to leave their homes until the suspect was caught. The killer had managed to take the lives of three of the group... he would not take any more.

Once the area was surrounded with uniformed and plain-clothes officers, Stephen and Whitlock took the lead. Although still doubtful that they'd be fortunate enough to find their suspect in the disused building, Stephen could do little else but act on the intelligence of Whitlock's colleagues.

If they didn't find who they were looking for today, the net was definitely closing in. He just hoped and prayed the son of a bitch hadn't been forewarned and was now halfway across the county.

Just as they were within a few feet of the door hanging lopsided on its hinges, four men, including one aptly described as a giant, rushed out. They charged straight for Stephen and Whitlock, clearly intent on battering them to the ground.

Stephen raised his cudgel, tensed and ready. If he died, so be it, but he would not go down without a fight.

The suspect punched him hard in the face. Pain exploded around Stephen's eyes even as adrenaline rushed through his body. With a roar, he raised the cudgel and swung it, smacking his assailant square in the jaw.

Blood spurted. 'You fucker!'

Stephen leapt on top of him, snatched a pair of handcuffs from his pocket and deftly secured the man's wrists behind his back.

Breathing heavily, Stephen looked around. What could have been chaos was more of a well-co-ordinated victory, and he tipped a nod of approval to where Whitlock was fastening handcuffs on a second man.

Police officers were everywhere. The suspects contained and secured. They'd never stood a chance.

51

Cornelia carried a box of Pennington's bags through the atrium towards the jewellery counter, her gaze automatically drawn to the double doors, where Stephen would never stand again. She could see his handsome face and slow smile in her mind's eye and sadness once more gripped her heart.

He'd come into the store two days ago, jubilant with the news Lillian's killer had been arrested and that Frank 'The Blade' Wilson now faced three charges of murder. Although disgusted that, after his brief jaunts in prison for lesser charges, Wilson had returned to Bath time and again to reoffend, Stephen was adamant the killer would never again see the light of day.

Wilson's loyal, misguided cronies had formed a protective circle around a man they respected and feared in equal measure. Wilson had carried an unsubstantiated grudge against Lillian for years, claiming he found it repulsive how she chose to distribute aid to the poor. That she, and her associates, were intent on luring the children into child labour or worse, or getting vagrant adults imprisoned or killed.

Entirely uncorroborated and ridiculous claims.

He'd told Whitlock he had been sent by God to rid the world of women pretending to be good when they were evil. Clearly mentally unwell, Wilson had hidden behind an erroneous shield that had speedily broken once the three men arrested alongside him realised they could negotiate a lesser prison sentence if they told the police what they knew.

Cornelia drew a shaky breath and continued through the atrium. She hesitated when she spotted Elizabeth and Joseph talking together at the foot of the grand staircase, their heads close together, Elizabeth's hand protectively curled around Joseph's arm. Stephen had told her Joseph had taken the news of Wilson's arrest with a mix of elation and profound frustration that he now had to leave the man's sentencing to the court. Cornelia had no doubt the ripples of the investigation, and Joseph's years-old trauma, would take a long time to fully dissipate from his mind or heart, whatever the judge might decide.

She continued forward, barely noticing the people, noises and sights around her. This morning, she had handed in her notice to Mrs Hampton, who, although disappointed, said she would speak to Elizabeth on Cornelia's behalf. As soon as her leaving date had been confirmed, she would start packing for Culford manor.

Alfred and Francis were ecstatic, and their delighted faces had been the final confirmation that returning to Oxfordshire was the right thing to do.

Not that Harriet had seemed best pleased when Cornelia telephoned to tell her of their imminent return. A nugget of suspicion began to form in her mind that Harriet had not been running the estate in a way Cornelia would approve.

'Cornelia? Might I have a word?'

Cornelia turned at the sound of Elizabeth's voice behind her. 'Good afternoon, Miss Pennington.'

Elizabeth smiled, but her eyes were shadowed with concern as her gaze searched Cornelia's face. 'I spoke to Mrs Hampton this morning. Is it true? You wish to leave Pennington's?'

Cornelia nodded. 'I do.' She frowned. 'How is Mr Carter?'

Elizabeth glanced around them before steering Cornelia to the side of the busy walkway. She nodded a hello to a trio of elderly women as they passed by before facing Cornelia. 'He'll be fine. In time.'

'If there is anything I can—'

'I'll look after him. Don't worry.' She smiled softly, but her green eyes reflected her concern. 'Apologies if I'm interfering, but can I ask if you are leaving because Mr Gower is returning to London? Only, Esther mentioned that feelings seemed to be deepening between you. I realise Oxfordshire is closer to London than Bath, but I thought you were happy here.'

Which will only make the temptation to not contact Stephen all the harder. Cornelia straightened her shoulders. 'I am. I was. But my children love the Culford estate and I owe it to them to return there.'

'Owe it to them?'

'Yes. The estate will one day belong to all of our parents' grandchildren, if they should want it, and I think it's my responsibility to make sure Alfred and Francis are given the opportunity to love it as Lawrence and I never did.'

'And that's it? Nothing else?'

Further words and explanations flailed on Cornelia's tongue. How much could she admit to Elizabeth of her feelings for Stephen? How could she ever confess to anyone they'd made love yet still he chose to leave, just as she had?

She drew on every ounce of her inner strength. 'I've concluded we belong at Culford. It's where my children should grow up and what is best for them.'

'And is Culford what's best for *you*?'

She held Elizabeth's gaze. 'It is. With my ex-husband living his own life now, Culford is where I belong.'

Elizabeth frowned. 'You've told Esther and Lawrence?'

'Yes. Esther wants me to do whatever I think best.'

'And Lawrence?'

Cornelia looked around the shop floor, turning away from Elizabeth's penetrating stare. 'He's fine.'

'Fine?'

'He doesn't exactly love Culford.' Cornelia paused, her brother's reservations and disappointment resounding in her head. 'He wasn't happy there as a child, but I can't allow the past to dictate my future. None of us can.'

Elizabeth studied her, the line deepening between her brows. 'Well, I can't stop you from leaving us if that's what you want, but...'

Cornelia waited for Elizabeth to continue. Her objections held no water; Cornelia was leaving. She might have come truly to care for Pennington's, for Elizabeth and Joseph – for all of the staff, in fact – but doing what was right and good for one's children demonstrated true commitment and love. Two things her boys deserved more than anything else.

Elizabeth cleared her throat, her expression defeated but businesslike. 'All right. If you want to leave, I'd like you to work two weeks' notice. After that, you are free to leave.'

'Thank you.'

Elizabeth turned away and then stopped, her gaze curious. 'Do you think you – *we* – will ever see Mr Gower again?'

The *we* held connotations of just how much Stephen had

come to mean, not just to Cornelia, but to Elizabeth and Joseph too. The admiration in Elizabeth's eyes was testament to how much Stephen had done for her and her husband.

Cornelia doubted whether Stephen either saw or understood just how wonderful a man he had become to so many people in the short amount of time he'd touched their lives.

She forced a smile. 'Who knows if I will see him again? But I'll never forget him or the time we spent together.'

'No, neither will we. He's a good man.'

'He is.'

'You and Mr Gower will always have a place at Pennington's if either of you ever want to return.' Elizabeth squeezed Cornelia's arm. 'You'll be missed.'

Tears pricked the back of Cornelia's eyes. It suddenly felt incredibly wrong to be leaving Pennington's. A place where she had grown to be happy, gained confidence… and found a man she truly loved. 'Thank you.'

With a final squeeze of Cornelia's arm, Elizabeth abruptly turned and walked into the crowds. Her red hair and confident poise shone among the customers. Wherever Elizabeth was in the store, she stood out. A woman who had done whatever she had to do in order to make Pennington's hers. Cornelia would try to embrace the lessons she had learned from Elizabeth and apply them to her own life.

But as she returned to the jewellery department, she felt that, by leaving, she showed none of Elizabeth's courage and tenacity. Was she not really running away from life? Wasn't she going backwards by returning to Culford?

Yet her heart told her that Harriet needed her home, whether she realised it or not. Plus, the boys needed to be where they were happiest. Was she not showing strength of a different kind by sacrificing her own needs for those of her beloved family?

She was strong and determined. Her personal happiness was not important right now. If that would ever change, she did not know, but she'd hold on – she'd fight on – until the world showed her it was time to step forward and become the woman she was supposed to be.

52

Stephen waved to his mother as she stood on her doorstep and flapped her handkerchief in farewell. Her kind gaze held his, before she gave a curt nod and walked inside, closing the door behind her.

He'd miss her.

When he'd given her an exclusive Pennington's food hamper and a bunch of flowers as a parting gift, his heart had lifted to see the delight her eyes. He would not leave it as long to come back for a visit next time.

He took a deep breath and started his walk into town. Would life ever be normal again now that he'd met Cornelia Culford? He very much doubted it.

Whether his decision to see her again today would be his undoing, he didn't know, but he refused to disappear like a thief in the night without telling her what she meant to him. What she and her family had done for him.

The January day was cold, the sky grey-white with the impending threat of snow, and Stephen's breath plumed in puffs ahead of him as he stepped up his pace. He adjusted his grip on his suitcase and pulled his scarf a little higher beneath his chin, his mind full of what to say to Cornelia.

He couldn't let today be the last time he saw her. No matter how much better it would be for his heart to sever all contact, he couldn't abide the idea of never seeing her again. He could only hope she felt the same.

Even though they'd seen each other and shared briefly snatched conversations at the store, their lovemaking had hardly been mentioned and, now he was leaving, he imagined she'd concluded he was a cad, a selfish, career-obsessed man who picked up and then dropped women at his pleasure. Nothing could be further from the truth. It didn't matter that he'd told her he was leaving before they ventured upstairs to her bedroom that night. His feelings had only deepened afterwards and, judging by the way she looked at him when he came to Pennington's to break the news of Wilson's arrest, their increased intimacy had mattered deeply to her, too.

Yet, despite his love for her, he couldn't stay in this city. He belonged in London. Belonged at the Yard. Being a good husband and partner to Cornelia, and a good stepfather to Alfred and Francis, was impossible when the pull of his service to the police was so strong.

If he stayed, he'd fail them. Whether it was the endless night shifts, inevitable trips away from home, or the emotional wear and tear as a police officer, he doubted he could ever be the husband Cornelia deserved. He wanted her happy. To find love with a man who had the time to spend with her and the children without the constant pressure of criminal activity vying for his attention. The thought of Cornelia being with someone else, as she'd been with him, caused a tight knot in Stephen's stomach and he marched purposefully forward, stomping away his pain with every step.

He began his descent along Milsom Street, Pennington's stretching towards the sky like a beacon summoning consumers everywhere. Unexpected pride swept through him that he'd played even a small part in a store that was like no other. Pennington's had a prestige, an incomparable atmosphere, that enveloped its staff and customers. Smiling faces, the ceaseless ping of cash registers and laughter that resounded from the atrium through to the Butterfly restaurant demonstrated just how special Pennington's was to so many. It was a place where he'd hoped he would find escape, but it wasn't to be.

And, if Cornelia intended to return to Culford manor, it seemed she hadn't found hers there either.

Reaching Pennington's, he took a deep breath and walked through its double doors.

The store still shone in all its seasonal brilliance, the twelve days of Christmas not quite over. Stephen immediately looked towards the jewellery section and quickly found Cornelia as she walked out from behind the counter. His heart jolted. She was everything he could ever want in a woman, yet still he could not sacrifice his work to be with her.

Walker's, Hettie's and Fay's deaths would forever haunt him, but his capture of Wilson had served to boost Stephen's confidence and reaffirm his duty. He had to go back.

He wove his way through the crowds and glanced at his watch. Lunchtime. Pleased to have caught her near her break, he quickened his pace.

'Cornelia?'

Her blue eyes widened as two spots of colour leapt into her cheeks. 'Stephen! What are you doing here?'

He smiled, pleased by the happiness in her eyes. 'I'm here to see you. I couldn't leave without saying goodbye.'

Her gaze dropped to his suitcase. 'You're leaving now?'

'Today, yes, but I'd hoped to treat you to lunch, as a way of thanking you for everything you and your family have done for me.'

'Thank me?' The light in her eyes dimmed a little. 'That's what you came here for?'

'That, and because I couldn't leave without seeing you. You're in my head, Cornelia. My heart, too, if I'm honest.'

Her eyes lit up once more. 'In that case, how can I refuse?'

She took his arm and they boarded the lift to the fourth floor and Pennington's Butterfly restaurant. He couldn't be sure what she felt upon seeing him again, but her reaction gave him hope that all was not lost between them.

Pennington's opulent cream and pale green restaurant was as busy as always, with its chandeliers glinting in the mirrored wall panelling.

At the table, Stephen pulled out Cornelia's chair before he sat beside her and placed his suitcase beneath the table. When he looked up, she was watching him, her gaze unreadable.

He itched to take her hand but refrained. 'Are you all right? What is it?'

'You. I wish you were happy in Bath, Stephen. I wish my children were happy here, too.'

The need to touch her was too much and he finally relented, taking her hand and gently squeezing her fingers. 'I wish it, too, but we'd end up hurting each other more if we were to stay in a city where deep down neither of us belongs. I have to go back, Cornelia. Scotland Yard is my calling, no matter how much I wish I could take you with me.'

She nodded, tears glinting in her eyes as she gently pulled her hand away from his. 'So, this is it. We say goodbye and never see one another again?'

'Not if you don't want that. Could I not visit you at Culford? Maybe you'd even want to venture to London one day.'

Doubt and worry clouded her eyes before she looked down at the table. 'Do you think that would be wise?'

Disappointment struck him hard. 'Don't you?'

She raised her head, her eyes dry and her colour a little paler. 'I don't. It would be foolish, painful even, for us to come in and out of each other's lives. We couldn't possibly be happy if—'

'Cornelia, please.' He gripped her hand again, his need to see her so raw he couldn't tamp it down or extinguish it. 'I don't want this to be the end for us.'

Her gaze travelled over his face and lingered for a long moment at his mouth. Slowly, she lifted her eyes to his and sighed. 'Neither do I. For all the heartbreak it might mean, I'll see you whenever, and however, I can.'

Relief flooded through him, and he leaned towards her, his gaze searching hers and his heart filling with joy from the love he saw in her eyes. 'I love you, Cornelia.'

She froze. 'Sorry?'

He couldn't move or speak. His confession had slipped from his tongue like water over a boulder. 'I mean...' He shook his head, dropped his shoulders. 'I love you.'

She grinned, leaned closer and firmly crushed his lips with hers, seemingly oblivious to the people around them.

53

At the Cavendish Club two weeks later, Cornelia looked around the table, where she sat with Elizabeth, Joseph and the staff from Pennington's jewellery department. The Carters had been generous in offering to send her off in such style.

She breathed deeply and picked up her glass of champagne. 'This place is marvellous.'

Elizabeth smiled. 'I'm glad you think so. Esther and I have had some truly fabulous times here over the past couple of years. The Cavendish was once viewed as indecent, the music too loud and the clientele too free and easy. Not so much any more.'

Joseph took a sip of his drink. 'That's not to say Elizabeth and Esther always behaved decorously, I'm sure.'

'Hey.' Elizabeth laughed and nudged him playfully. 'I'm the mistress of Pennington's. I'm decorum personified.'

Cornelia joined in with their laughter, pleased how Joseph's mood had slowly begun to lighten over the last few days, his eyes once more focused on Elizabeth or the store. The love between her employers seemed to be returning to how it had been before the murder that had reawakened, deepened, Joseph's anguish about Lillian.

Her thoughts were momentarily distracted from Stephen, for possibly the first time in two weeks. She looked towards the four-piece band playing on the stage, at couples and trios of women enjoying the music, problem free and enjoying their liberty. Would she ever be as happy?

She would return to the manor the day after tomorrow. Their bags were packed, the largest of her belongings already on their way to Oxfordshire by coach. All that was left to do was say goodbye to her Pennington's colleagues this evening, pack up any last things at Lawrence's house and she would be away from Bath and onto a new chapter in her life with Alfred and Francis, who were so much brighter and happier since she'd confirmed they would be returning to the manor house.

Maybe, in time, she'd feel differently about her childhood home too.

'Why the glum face, Cornelia?'

Elizabeth's voice broke through her thoughts and Cornelia said, 'I'm not glum. A little pensive, maybe, but definitely not glum.'

Joseph stood. 'How about another bottle of champagne?'

Cheers of approval sounded around the table.

Cornelia smiled. 'Joseph really is the most extraordinary man. You must love him very much.'

'Oh, I do.' Elizabeth said. 'I don't think I've ever been as happy as I am right now. With that monster Wilson being charged with Lillian's murder and that of the other poor women, Joseph has changed. The fire he had when he first came into the store has returned. The biggest thing I've learned about my husband over the past year is without a focus he isn't happy.'

'And what is his new focus?'

Elizabeth eyes lit up with mischievous joy. 'Me.'

Cornelia laughed. 'You? Haven't you always been his focus? He rarely takes his eyes off you.'

'Maybe, but now when he looks at me, it's for a particular reason. A reason with a goal.'

Cornelia grinned as comprehension struck. 'He's agreed to try for a baby?'

Elizabeth nodded.

'Oh, Elizabeth. That's wonderful news.' Cornelia put her glass on the table and pulled Elizabeth into an embrace. 'I am so happy for you both.'

'And what about you?' Elizabeth eased out of Cornelia's arms. 'Will you be happy, away from Pennington's? Away from Lawrence and Esther? She's so concerned about the reasons you're returning to Oxfordshire.'

'I know, but everything will work out how it's supposed to. The children...' She briefly closed her eyes. Her decision to leave always seemed to sound so centred around Alfred and Francis... which, of course, it was. 'This is what they want. What they need.' She sighed. 'I just hope I can give them everything they expect of me. The divorce hasn't been easy for them and David has no sympathy whatsoever. Neither Alfred nor Francis has particularly enjoyed school here either. I'm hoping that will change in Oxfordshire.'

'Of course, you can be all they need. I've seen you with your children.' Elizabeth squeezed Cornelia's hand. 'You are a wonderful mother and they love you.'

Cornelia looked towards the bar, where Joseph laughed with the barman. 'I just keep holding onto this idyllic picture of family life that I'm no longer sure exists.' She looked at Elizabeth. 'My childhood was far from perfect. My marriage too. Maybe that's why I've been looking for something, anything...'

Stephen came into her mind and her eyes burned with tears. 'Maybe even *someone* to make my life and the children's lives how I think they ought to be.' She shook her head. 'Such a notion is childish. Fantastical. Life is hard. Nothing worth fighting for is ever gained easily. I know all this, but still...'

'That doesn't mean the life you want is unattainable. You only have to look at Esther and me to know how hard the fight can be. How forcefully women have to sometimes defy convention and write their own rules.' Elizabeth frowned. 'You *can* be happy, Cornelia. Trust me. You may have to raise your children alone for a while, but who knows what, or *who*, is around the corner? My goodness, Joseph just walked straight into the store and into my life before I could blink. Now look at us. You have to trust and believe in yourself before anyone else can come into your life. Although, I wonder if that has not already happened.'

Cornelia frowned. 'What do you mean?'

'I mean, I think you're half in love with Mr Gower.' Elizabeth smiled. 'Am I right?'

Heat immediately leapt into Cornelia's cheeks and she reached for her champagne. 'Maybe, but that's neither here nor there.'

'How can you be so nonchalant? Don't you want to pursue whatever it is between you?'

Cornelia sighed. 'We've agreed to stay in touch. Maybe something could happen one day but, for now, Stephen's life is in London and mine is in Oxfordshire.'

'But who knows in the future? For now though, you must embrace all the blessings you have right now. Those beautiful boys of yours. The love Lawrence, Esther and I have for you. A wonderful house on a beautiful estate. Start from there.'

Cornelia looked into Elizabeth's eyes. The determination and confidence she saw in her gaze moved something inside her.

Elizabeth was right. She had to find her own path. Not look to Lawrence, Stephen or anyone else to show her the way, or have them to lean on. Loving a man who lived amid danger, murder and destruction was not only madness but entirely the opposite of what she wanted for Alfred and Francis.

Cornelia raised her glass. 'To women and all we can do. Alone.'

Elizabeth grinned and clinked her glass to Cornelia's. 'To women.'

54

Having finished typing up the last of his reports for the day, Stephen leaned back at his desk at Scotland Yard and stretched his arms above his head, releasing the knots in his shoulders. The one thing he hadn't missed when he'd been in Bath was paperwork. It seemed to be increasing with every case, actual policing becoming lower and lower in importance.

A month had passed since he'd returned to the Yard, and his instinct that the force was where he belonged hadn't waned. He loved the job. Loved making a difference.

After receiving a lengthy talking-to from Inspector King, Stephen had admitted he'd felt the deaths of Constable Walker, Hettie Brown and Fay Morris had been the final nails in the coffin of his career. Yet his mindset had slowly changed over the last few months, and he knew the reason was because he had found Lillian Carter's killer and brought peace to Joseph Carter.

That, and his newly thawed heart.

Each person he'd met in Bath had managed to slip beneath his carefully tended armour. The sights he'd seen, and the brutality he'd had to make sense of before leaving London, had made him a colder, more distant person, but now he'd changed.

His heart was open... and vulnerable.

Yet he was tired of protecting it. Tired of watching his colleagues being met by wives, children and lovers at the end of the day. Tired of only drinking with work colleagues and other men who had no one waiting for them at home.

He pushed up from his chair. It was nearly ten o'clock at night and the shifts had changed a couple of hours ago. There was only a skeleton staff in the offices, as well as Inspector King across the way in his private office, his door open.

Stephen took his suit jacket from the back of his chair and shrugged it on. He stared towards King's office, his mind reeling with an impossible idea.

He'd been in since eight that morning and had enough work to justify another hour at his desk. Yet, tonight, he didn't want to stay.

Tonight, he wanted to telephone Cornelia. Have her soft voice fill his ear and his heart.

Lifting his overcoat from the stand in the corner, he pulled it on and snatched his hat from the hook beside him.

Despite picking up the phone only to replace it in its cradle a hundred times over the last five long weeks, Stephen hadn't contacted Cornelia. He hadn't penned her a letter or dictated a telegram. Instead, he'd imposed a purposeful distance in an effort to cool his love and need for her.

His actions had failed dismally.

He couldn't avoid what was in his heart.

He'd finally accepted he was not to blame for Walker's, Hettie's and Fay's deaths. The man who'd beaten them was guilty of taking their lives, but Stephen could certainly be blamed for too hastily dismissing what the women had tried to tell him. He'd allowed another case to steal his attention and thought that he could only focus on one problem at a time. Cornelia had taught him that a cry for help from a stranger might be just as important as a cry for help from a loved one. A plea for sympathy might be as vital to a person's happiness as finding a killer and bringing a grieving family peace.

Life and humanity were constant. Who knew when anyone might have cause to reach out to someone else? And what if the person they begged to listen turned their back? What if a stranger needed saving? A young son or daughter so unhappy they would leave home and risk life on the streets?

Family. He wanted to be a part of Cornelia's family. To learn what it truly meant to open his heart and trust in God that his loved ones would come home safely every evening.

Life was not only made up of police files and cases. He'd been living with that belief for far too long.

He took a long breath, approached Inspector King's office and rapped on the open door. King had his back to Stephen and was gazing out of his window into the city's darkness.

He abruptly turned in his chair. 'Gower. What are you still doing here? You were in first thing.'

'I could say the same to you, sir.'

The inspector drew his hand over his face, exhaustion etched in the lines at the corners of his eyes. 'Close the door. Let's have a drink, shall we?'

Stephen slowly closed the door. A drink might go some way towards easing the inspector's nerves, once Stephen had finished what he had to say. 'How was your day? I thought I saw you dressing down McDonald earlier.'

'I was. He's all right. A bit wet behind the ears, but he'll learn the way of things soon enough.' King smiled as he poured a measure of brandy into two short tumblers. 'After all, you picked things up. Eventually.'

'I did.' Stephen took a seat at the desk and accepted the offered glass of brandy. 'I want to speak to you about something.'

'Oh?'

Stephen cleared his throat. 'Life.'

The inspector raised his eyebrows. 'Life?'

'Yes, and my lack of one.'

'I see. And might I ask what's brought on this soul-searching? Anything to do with your time in Bath?'

Stephen sipped his drink, unnerved by King's wily instinct. 'Yes, as a matter of fact. I met someone while I was there. Someone who's made a bigger impact on my thinking than I appreciated when I left.'

'Ah, a woman.' King smiled and shook his head. 'Yep, they have a way of doing that, I'm afraid. So, what are you telling me?' His expression sobered. 'God, man, don't tell me you're going to be father in a few months' time.'

'No, nothing like that.' Stephen laughed, the mention of fatherhood not altogether as unwelcome as he would have expected. 'She's left Bath and now lives at her family's estate in Oxfordshire. Or should I say *her* estate. Hers, her brother's and sister's.'

'Not short of a penny or two then?'

'No. Not that I could care less if she was as rich as a queen or as poor as a pauper.'

'I see. So, why are you telling me this?' King lifted his drink to his lips and stopped. 'Wait. Please don't say you want to be transferred to Oxford? For the love of God, Gower. Are you trying to send me to an early grave?'

'Is it possible? A straight transfer, I mean?'

'It's possible, but I've only just got you back and now you're asking me to release you for a second time in as many months.'

'This will be the last time. I promise you.'

'And if things don't work out with this woman as you'd like them to? Then what? You come back to me with your tail between your legs?'

'It will work. I know it will.' Stephen swirled the liquid in his glass. And he did know. He wanted to spend the rest of his life with Cornelia. The rest of his life with her children. 'She's all I want.'

King raised his eyebrows again. 'All you want? Well, she must be someone pretty special indeed.'

'She is.'

The inspector drained his glass. 'It's late. Get yourself home, get some sleep and if you still feel the same in the morning, I'll see what can be done. At least this time you're not saying you're giving up the job altogether.'

'No, sir. The job is what I do. What I *want* to do, but I love Cornelia. She's who I want to be with for the rest of my life.'

'All right, I understand. Get out of here before I start crying.'

Laughing, Stephen stood, picked up his hat and left King's office, his smile wide and his heart full.

55

'I have been here for three weeks, Harriet, and not once have I heard you thank a single member of this household for anything.' Cornelia snatched her sister's breakfast plate from the table and walked to the buffet. 'You're acting like a spoilt heiress. Someone who deserves privileges, without thought of the how or why.'

Harriet stood and threw down her napkin, her blue eyes enraged. 'Don't you dare say that to me. Who do you think has been managing the estate while you and Lawrence do whatever you want? Me. I know my staff and they know me. You are more of a visitor than a mistress.'

She marched from the room into the hallway and Cornelia trembled with suppressed anger as she followed. 'Culford is an estate with workers and tenants. I thought you were afraid of them looking on you in the same light as Mama! If you continue as you are, that's exactly what will happen.'

'So what if it does?' Harriet whirled around. 'I have my own way of doing things. If you don't like it, leave. Go back to Bath. Go back to Lawrence. I don't care.'

She mounted the stairs and Cornelia strode after her. 'I came here to be with you. To help you.'

'Is that so? Well, all I have heard from you is criticism. *"You can't go to that party alone, Harriet." "What time will you be home, Harriet?" "Would you like to play a game with me and the children, Harriet?"'* She stormed across the gallery landing before abruptly stopping. 'I don't want your life, Cornelia. I want *mine*. I want to do things how I want. I want a husband who understands me. Who loves me for all I am. Faults as well as strengths.'

Cornelia stared, her heart racing. 'And you think I don't?'

'Not in the same way. You are happy to live as a wife who cares for her children, cares for her husband and little else in between. I want more than that.'

'Such as?'

'Such as balls and parties. Jewels and fun. Travel and discovery.' Harriet glared. 'And that's exactly what I shall have.'

Harriet stormed towards her bedroom, flounced inside and slammed the door. Cornelia gripped the banister as frustration bubbled inside her. She stared below into the enormous entrance hall, where Ruth wandered to a side table and put down a large vase of flowers. She did not wear the expression of someone happy in her work. Instead, her hands flitted a little shakily around the blooms, her shoulders stiff with tension. Was this Harriet's doing? Did the staff fear her sister, just as the previous maids had feared their mother? Cornelia tightened her grip on the banister. How dare Harriet act so spitefully when she knew first-hand the misery their mother had caused her children and staff?

Ruth looked up, as though she'd sensed Cornelia watching her.

She immediately smiled. 'Good morning, Ruth. Those flowers look wonderful.'

The young maid dipped a semi-curtsey and gave a hesitant smile. 'Thank you, ma'am.'

'Miss Cornelia, please, Ruth. Why don't you take an hour or so for lunch today? It's a beautiful day. You could walk into the village.'

Ruth's smile vanished. 'But the mistress—'

'Will be absolutely fine. Please, take the hour and I'll speak with Harriet.'

'Thank you.' Ruth flashed another brief smile. 'Thank you very much.'

'You're welcome.'

Ruth hurried along the corridor towards the kitchen and Cornelia pushed away from the banister. She purposefully strode to Harriet's room and rapped on the door. Without waiting to be invited, she entered.

Her sister sat at her dressing table in her robe, rubbing cream onto her face and neck. 'For someone who holds manners so high in her priorities, you are sadly lacking, Cornelia.'

Biting her tongue, Cornelia sat on the bed and studied Harriet's reflection in the mirror. There was no denying being lady of the manor suited her sister, but it wasn't a life Cornelia wanted or felt she could adjust to. In the short time she'd been here, she'd had a glimpse of what it would mean for her and her boys to live at Culford. What would be expected of her children as they grew. Living here could lead them along a path Cornelia had worked hard to avoid. Self-centredness. Greed. Snobbery. Entitlement.

She was adamant that would not happen.

She crossed her arms. 'So, life at Culford is what you want? Along with its status and a husband who is willing to satisfy your every whim?'

'Exactly.' Harriet replaced the lid on her pot of cream and

stared into the mirror. 'I know exactly what I want. Maybe it's time you concentrated on the same.'

'Meaning?'

'Meaning...' Harriet stood and walked across the room to the wardrobe. 'It was plain to me and everyone else here at Christmas that you are in love with Mr Gower. Yet, instead of staying in Bath and entrapping him, you run home with the rather weak excuse that you are doing so for your children.'

Cornelia's anger simmered dangerously. 'Entrap him? Is that really what you consider the way to lasting love?'

'Men are a breed all of their own, dear sister. There is absolutely no harm in forcing their hand a little.'

'You really are the most—'

'Modern woman? Independent and intelligent thinking? I couldn't agree more.'

'A fool. If you think any man will stay faithful to you when he has been hoodwinked into—'

'Just because you lack the finesse and charm to keep a man faithful does not mean I'm the same.'

Hurt slashed at Cornelia's chest and she took a deep breath to calm herself. Why was she surprised by her sister's callousness? Harriet was as unaware of others' feelings as their mother had been. Yet how could she leave her to her own devices unless Harriet made it impossible for Cornelia to stay?

Forcing a calmness into her voice, she uncrossed her arms and dropped her hands to the bed. 'I'm here for Alfred and Francis, nothing else. Not counting the last few days, they have been happy here. As far as the disintegration of my marriage is concerned—'

'What do you mean *not counting the last few days*?' Harriet turned from the wardrobe and eyed her carefully. 'What happened to change their minds?'

Cornelia sighed. 'You.'

'Me?' Harriet's eyes widened. 'How on earth could I have affected their happiness? I spend as little time with them as possible.'

Cornelia shook her head. 'Exactly. You have neither made us welcome nor encouraged the boys in their learning or play. I fear the longer we stay here, the quicker their spirits will be broken. The house is cold, Harriet. As cold and unfeeling as it was when Mama was alive. Can you not see that? The boys were so excited to be here, to spend time roaming the estate, learning more about farming, the way the tenants live.'

'And? I haven't done anything to change that.'

'You have. You constantly tell them to be quiet. You ship them out of the kitchen when they are perfectly happy to spend time with Cook. You won't let them look in on the horses without your permission—'

'The house is the way I want it.' She pulled out a long, blue dress and tilted her head as she studied it. 'I want to be a society wife, Cornelia, not a mother. I want to be wined and dined. Dance and laugh. If you don't approve of that, then maybe you shouldn't have brought your children here.' She put down the dress and glared. 'Go. Your name will remain on the estate deeds as Lawrence wishes, but there will be no need for you to worry about me or this house once I am married.'

Cornelia shook her head, annoyed how Harriet only referred to the boys as Cornelia's children and never once as her own nephews. 'And I suppose you will meet your husband on the *Titanic*? That's still your grand plan?'

Harriet grinned, her eyes lighting up with glee. 'Precisely.'

Slowly, Cornelia rose from the bed. 'I have given Ruth permission to take an hour or so for lunch so that she can spend some time away from here.'

'That is quite all right with me. I will be joining Susannah for lunch elsewhere.'

'Good. Then I will leave you to dress.' Just as Cornelia reached the door, she turned, her hand on the knob. 'I can see I was far too hasty in thinking the boys belong here.'

'I couldn't agree more.'

Cornelia pulled back her shoulders as a wave of certainty swept through her. 'They belong with me, wherever that might be. I will ensure they are content. I will ensure they come to realise that happiness lies inside them regardless of where they might live or who they marry.'

'Oh, that is so sweet. Completely inaccurate, of course, but sweet.' Harriet smiled. 'You will return to your little house?'

'No, the house is sold.'

'Then where do you plan to live?'

Stephen's face burned brightly in Cornelia's mind. Could she try to reunite with him on a permanent basis? Ask him if the idea that they might be together wasn't entirely extinguished?

'Cornelia?'

She blinked and met Harriet's curious gaze.

'I asked where you plan to live.'

Cornelia smiled. 'Quite possibly London.'

Harriet's gaze filled with disbelief. 'London? You barely have an interest in socialising here, let alone in so grand a city.'

'Who said anything about socialising?'

'Why else would you live in London if not for the parties, the soirées, the theatre?'

'That's for me to know and for you to learn in due course.'

'But—'

Cornelia swept from the room and hurried along the landing, her heart swelling with certainty. It had taken coming back to Culford to make her accept she and the boys would never be any happier here than Lawrence and his family would have been. Culford was a monument to financial greed, selfishness and social-climbing. Things she wanted no part of for herself or her children.

She had been wrong to sacrifice Stephen. Wrong to sacrifice her new joy at Pennington's. She was not to blame for the failure of her marriage, and she was not to blame for having to move her children temporarily to Bath. She had done what she needed in order to survive, and she would do so again.

Hurrying downstairs, she entered her father's study and pulled some writing paper from one of the cubbyholes in his bureau. Taking a deep breath, she extracted a pen from a wooden pot, dipped it in ink and put it to the paper.

Dear Stephen…

56

Stephen got out of his car and stared once more at the facade of Culford Manor.

A mixture of excitement and apprehension swept over him as he closed the door. The mass of windows hid rooms of such a size and luxury that his confidence Cornelia would still want him faltered. The Culfords were rich beyond his imaginings and Cornelia deserved the life she was born to.

He had to keep at the forefront of his mind that this was a woman who'd chosen as independent a path as possible after her divorce. Living with her brother was a temporary solution only. Cornelia had sought work. Her own money. A life of her own making.

But maybe that life could include him, too.

He approached the front door, pushed away his residual nerves and lifted the big brass knocker.

'Good afternoon, sir.'

'Adams, good afternoon. I'm here to see Miss Culford. Is she in?'

The butler shook his head, his expression seemingly one of tired regret. 'I'm afraid not, sir. She's gone.'

Stephen stared. 'Cornelia's gone?'

'Left, sir. Early this morning.'

'This morning?'

'Adams? Who is it?' A female voice sounded behind the butler. 'Don't leave a visitor standing on the doorstep.' The door widened, and Cornelia's sister appeared. 'Oh, Mr Gower. This is a surprise.'

Stephen eyed her carefully. The annoyance in her eyes had quickly changed to what looked like glee. He dipped his head. 'Miss Culford.'

'Well, don't just stand there. Come in, please.'

'I'm here to see Cornelia. If she isn't—'

'Then I must tell you what I know about her whereabouts, mustn't I?' She gripped Stephen's wrist. 'Come in. Adams, please take Mr Gower's coat and hat.'

Seeing no alternative, Stephen allowed himself to be ushered into the house.

Once he'd been relieved of his outer garments, Harriet tucked her arm into his and led him along the dark corridor to the drawing room. 'So, you have come looking for my dear, dear sister. How romantic.'

'Romantic?' *What had Cornelia told her?* Harriet didn't strike him as the subtlest of people when it came to people's privacy. 'I am merely here to—'

'Sweep my sister off her feet? To take her to your humble home and leave her there to cook and clean, while you carry out important police business?' Harriet laughed. 'Oh, my dear man, I'm not sure I could allow such a thing.'

Stephen clenched his jaw and chose to keep his counsel. For now.

She led him to the settee in the drawing room. 'Take a seat and we'll have some tea.'

'Miss Culford—'

'Harriet, please.' Her smile didn't quite reach her eyes. 'After all, if Cornelia returns your feelings, we could soon be in-laws.'

Stephen leaned back on the sofa and pinned her with a stare. 'Where is she?'

'I couldn't possibly say.' Harriet waved her hand dismissively, her smile dissolving. 'She swept out of the house, full of pomp and purpose as though she knew exactly what she was doing. The poor boys had no choice but to trail after her like a pair of dutiful puppies.'

'I can't see Cornelia forcing her boys into anything.'

'And you think you know my sister better than I do, Mr Gower? I think not.'

The clinking of crockery heralded Ruth, carrying a tea tray with cups and saucers and a tiered plate filled with small sandwiches and slices of sponge cake. Stephen inwardly groaned. How was he to make the sharp exit he wanted now?

'Just put everything on the table, Ruth.' Harriet nodded towards the low table in front of the sofa. 'I will serve Mr Gower.'

'Yes, ma'am.'

Harriet poured the tea and, when they were both settled with a cup and saucer, she said, 'So, what can I tell you about Cornelia? Well, firstly, she has come to the conclusion she no longer wishes to live here. That Alfred and Francis will be happy wherever she decides to take them.'

Stephen stilled. Cornelia had left Oxfordshire permanently? As proud of her as he was for clearly standing her ground with her exceedingly stuck-up sister, he was also aware that he might be shortly having yet another request for

Inspector King. There was every chance the man's head might explode this time.

He cleared his throat. 'Which is where exactly? Has she returned to Bath?'

'I don't doubt it for a minute, no matter what she might have claimed as she left.'

Impatience hummed through him. 'Which means?'

She shook her head, her expression bored. 'She suggested she might drag the two boys and herself to London.'

'London?' Dread curled through Stephen. 'Cornelia has gone to London?'

'Oh, of course not.' She slid her cup and saucer onto the table, her head turned from him as she laid out two plates. 'Sandwich?'

'Harriet, did Cornelia specifically tell you she was going to London?' Hope and fear leapt into his heart. Had she gone to find him? Had she come to the conclusion that they needed to be together, too? That their love was too real, too important? 'Why?'

'Why?' She laughed. 'If you don't know that, then you are terribly ignorant about my sister. She is headstrong and full of inconsequential gestures. She might have said she was going to London, but whether she could actually bring herself to do it is another matter entirely.'

'You're wrong.'

She flinched and irritation seeped into her voice. 'I beg your pardon. You cannot come into my house, speak to me so dismissively and expect—'

'When have you ever known Cornelia to not do exactly as she intended?' He pushed his tea onto the table and stood. 'She left Oxfordshire and moved the children to Bath. She told her brother she would gain employment and she did. Why on earth do you think for a moment she would not travel to London with Alfred and Francis, once her mind was made up? I need to go.'

'Mr Gower, wait.' Harriet stood, her cheeks flushed and her eyes glinting with irritation. 'She would have gone to Lawrence in the first instance. There is absolutely no possibility she would go off to find you without—'

'To find me?' His heart beat a little faster. 'Is that what she said?'

'Yes, of course. Why else would Cornelia do such a nonsensical thing? Firstly, she follows mother's bidding and marries that ghastly David. Then she—'

'Enough.' Stephen spun away from her and headed for the door. 'I'm leaving.'

'Mr Gower. Please, wait.'

Harriet's hurried footsteps sounded behind him, but Stephen continued into the hallway to retrieve his coat and hat.

'Mr Gower, please listen to me.' Harriet gripped his arm. 'You must at least call my brother. If I am wrong in my assumption that Cornelia left for London, I will not be wrong in thinking that she won't leave without saying goodbye to Lawrence. She wouldn't do that to him.'

Indecision warred inside him as he studied her, his body rigid with tension at the thought of Cornelia being alone with her children in the city.

Harriet tugged his sleeve. 'Come, you can use the telephone in the parlour.'

His mind reeled. What had made Cornelia change her mind about Culford? He didn't doubt part of it was the woman who led him by the wrist right now. Could he really dare to believe Cornelia loved him enough to bring her children to London? To school them there? Share in his life as a sergeant at Scotland Yard?

Hope burned as they entered the cream and lemon parlour, the weak February sunshine gleaming through the floor-to-ceiling windows. Yet Stephen felt no comfort in the brightness of the afternoon. Instead, dark foreboding and worry coiled through him.

He spotted the telephone on a small side table and, pulling his arm from Harriet's grasp, he strode forward and lifted the receiver.

'What's the number?'

She gave it to him before theatrically flinging herself into a chair, her blue gaze steely. He dialled the number.

'Culford residence.'

'Good afternoon. Might I speak to Mr Culford, please?'

'He isn't here, I'm afraid, sir. Might I take a message?'

Stephen squeezed his eyes closed. 'Is Mrs Culford available?'

'Might I ask who's calling?'

'Stephen Gower. It's a matter of urgency.'

'Just one moment, sir.'

He glanced at Harriet. She studied her nails as she swung her crossed leg back and forth. Gritting his teeth, he turned away.

'Stephen? It's Esther. Is everything all right?'

'Esther, thank God. Is Cornelia at the house? Is she with you?'

'Cornelia? No, she's at the manor.'

He gripped the phone tighter. 'No, she's not.'

'But how do you know—'

'Because I'm at Culford now. She isn't here, Esther, and hasn't been since first thing this morning. She's gone to London.'

'London?'

'She's looking for me. It's my fault, but I'll find her. Tell

Lawrence I'm sorry, but he's not to worry. She'll be fine. I'll ensure it.'

'Oh, Stephen. What was she thinking? Why on earth didn't she come to us first? I know how she feels about you, but to take the children...' She sighed. 'No, she wouldn't do that without saying goodbye. Come to Bath. I will contact Lawrence and he'll be at the house by the time you arrive.'

Stephen stared at the wall ahead of him. Harriet had presumed the same thing, but what if she and Esther were wrong, and he wasted precious time in Bath when he could be in London?

'Are you certain she wouldn't go straight to London? If she hasn't come to you, then where else could she be?'

'Just come to the house. We'll sort out everything together. As a family.'

'As a family?'

'As a family, Stephen.'

'I'll see you shortly.' He replaced the receiver and gripped it, willing his heart to slow down. What did Esther mean? Was he included? Excluded? Dare he hope that he might come to be a part of Cornelia's family? A trusted part?

Harriet slowly stood up and clasped her hands in front of her, her eyes reflecting a confusing sorrow that he didn't have time to wonder about. Yet, for a split second, he felt as if he ought to comfort her.

He nodded. 'I'll see you again some time, I'm sure.'

She gave him a tight smile, her eyes shining in the sunny room. 'I do hope so, Mr Gower.'

57

Cornelia held Alfred's and Francis's hands as they stood in front of Scotland Yard.

The Victorian grey-stone building stretched towards a thick, cloudy sky, wisps of smog curling around its edges like long-reaching fingers. Cornelia shivered. Was she wrong to bring the boys to a place where criminals had come and gone, been incarcerated or released on bail?

She drew back her shoulders. Everything would be all right once they found Stephen. 'Right then.' She gripped Alfred's and Francis's hands tighter and forced a smile. 'Let's go and find Mr Gower, shall we?'

She led them up the stone steps and through the Yard's double doors. The vast lobby was busy with uniformed officers milling around. The space was surprisingly bright and welcoming, but she didn't doubt for a moment that this was little more than illusion.

She approached the front desk. 'Good afternoon. I wonder if I might speak to Sergeant Stephen Gower.'

The young officer nodded. 'Do you know which department he works in, or the name of his superior?'

'Oh.' The self-imposed confidence she'd adopted like a protective blanket started to unravel. 'I don't. I... Would you be able to look up his name?'

Alfred tugged on her hand. 'Mr Gower might be with Mr King.'

Cornelia threw an apologetic smile at the constable. 'Who?'

'Mr Gower told me at Christmastime that he works with the best inspector in the whole of London. I think he said his name was Mr King.'

'Are you sure?'

Alfred shrugged.

She faced the constable. 'Could you check?'

'If you'll just wait here, I'll ring upstairs. Do you have an appointment? Only...' He glanced at Alfred and Francis. 'This isn't normally a place we'd see children, Mrs...'

'Culford. Miss.'

He raised his eyebrows and glanced again at Alfred and Francis.

Heat warmed Cornelia's cheeks. 'I mean, I was Mrs Parker, but I'm divorced. These are my children. They—'

'I quite understand.'

Cornelia mentally admonished herself for faltering instead of standing tall. She had come to London convinced it was right to find Stephen, yet now a horrible, niggling doubt began to surface.

The duty officer looked past her and immediately straightened. 'Ah, he's just come through the door. Inspector King, sir. Do you have a moment? This lady wishes to speak with you if you can spare her a few minutes.'

Cornelia spun around as older gentleman with neatly combed, silvery hair and a matching, rather impressive, moustache came towards her. He frowned. 'Might I help you, madam?'

Cornelia swallowed her nerves and held out her hand. 'My name is Cornelia Culford. Are you Inspector King?'

'I am.' He shook her hand and glanced at Alfred and Francis, before bending over to speak to them. 'And who might you boys be?'

Pride swept through Cornelia as Alfred and Francis stood to attention.

'Alfred, sir.'

'Francis, sir.'

'Well, it's nice to meet you.' He shook the boys' hands. 'And is this lady your mother?'

'Yes, sir.'

'Well, in that case, why don't you give me and your mother a moment alone, eh? There are some seats over there.'

Cornelia held Inspector King's steely gaze.

He lowered his voice. 'Can I ask what you think you are doing by bringing your children into Scotland Yard? This is not a playground.'

'I understand. I am looking for—'

'Sergeant Gower, I know.'

'But how do you—'

'Because he mentioned your name once... or twice.' Disapproval emanated from every part of him. 'But, as fond as he seems of you, I can't think he'd like a mother, however desperate, to bring her children to a place that carries such risks. We cannot control who comes into this part of the building, Miss Culford. Did it not occur to you—'

'No, Inspector, it did not.' Irritated and tired, Cornelia glared.

'I came here from Oxfordshire. Alone and doing my best by my children. If you could kindly let Stephen, Sergeant Gower, know I am here, then—'

'He isn't here.'

She flinched. Icy cold fingers of fear touched her spine. 'Well, where is he?'

'I'd presumed with you, but as you're here, I have no idea.'

'I don't understand.'

Cornelia glanced at Alfred and Francis where they sat staring at her, hands clasped in their laps. What was she doing? The inspector was right. She must be out of her silly mind to bring the children here, to think that Stephen would welcome her surprising him this way.

She faced Inspector King. 'I have no idea what to do. Where to even start to look for him.'

The inspector cleared his throat, his gaze ever so slightly softening. 'Well, you could start by making your way back to Oxfordshire.'

'Sorry?'

He gently took her elbow, moving her away from a group of gentlemen who approached the desk behind them. 'Gower asked for a direct transfer to Oxfordshire, which I granted. He left the station yesterday and was to report for duty first thing Monday morning.'

'But...' She frowned. How could she and Stephen have missed one another? Did he ask for a transfer to be with her? Surely there could be no other reason. Tentative euphoria rose inside her. She had to get back to the manor house as soon as possible. 'I'd better go, Inspector. Thank you for your help.' She offered him her hand. 'I apologise for interrupting your work.'

He took her hand and nodded. 'Gower is a good man, Miss

Culford. If there's anyone worth having a wasted journey for, it's him. Good luck.'

'Thank you.' She hurried towards the children. 'Come along, boys. We need to get home.'

Francis grinned. 'To Uncle Lawrence's?'

'No, to Culford.' She took their hands and pulled them towards the entrance. 'It seems Mr Gower has gone to Oxfordshire.'

'But—'

'No buts, Francis. Come along, Mama never should have brought you here.'

She led them from the building and out onto the street, which heaved with people hurrying in every direction. Cornelia walked blindly forward. She should have waited for Stephen to respond to her letter, but her impatience to see him, to look into his eyes and confess the depth of her feelings had been too much.

'Mama, wait.'

Alfred's voice halted her. 'Darling? What is it?'

'We can't go back to Aunt Harriet.'

'We have to. I'm sorry, but—'

'Mr Gower wouldn't stay there, Mama. No one would stay with Aunt Harriet.'

She managed a small smile. 'She isn't a monster, Alfred.'

'No, but she isn't you, and Mr Gower loves you.'

Tears leapt into her eyes. 'Oh, Alfred.'

'We have to go back to Bath. Mr Gower will go to Uncle Lawrence for help. I know he will. He's a nice man, Mama. He makes you happy. He makes me and Francis happy.' He glanced at his brother, who grinned in obvious agreement. 'We go back to Uncle Lawrence's house and Mr Gower will be there, I promise.'

Cornelia looked at her sons' faces, their eyes pleading and so full of love. 'You two are—'

'We don't care about Papa and his new life any more. We want to be with you. You and Mr Gower, Uncle Lawrence, Aunt Esther, Rose and Nathaniel. Please.'

'Oh, my loves. So do I. More than anything.' She pulled them into a tight embrace. 'Let's go home. Let's go to Bath.'

58

Stephen gripped his hands between his knees as he sat on the sofa in Lawrence Culford's parlour, while the master of the house paced back and forth in front of him, his wife watching her husband with worried eyes.

The guilt and inadequacy Stephen had felt over Walker, Hettie and Fay had been more than he'd thought he could bear, but suspecting Cornelia, Alfred and Francis had travelled alone to London came a close second.

Lawrence suddenly stopped, his blue eyes full of accusation as he glared at Stephen. 'If anything has happened to her—'

'You can kill me.' Stephen wiped his hand over his face. 'It would be no less than I deserve.'

'You left her, Gower. Illustrated all too clearly that your work was more important than her. How the hell do you think that made her feel?'

'I understand that now. I had no idea she would think of following me—'

'Then you don't know my sister at all.'

Stephen's jaw clenched. He did know Cornelia. He knew her as well as he knew himself. 'But I should've considered the possibility. All that matters is I find her and tell her I love her. I want to be with her.'

'And your police work? What about that?'

'I've secured a transfer to Oxfordshire. I assumed she would want to live at Culford, but it seems I was wrong.'

'Of course you were wrong. She belongs here. In Bath.'

'And if that's what she wants, I will live here too. With her.'

'Just like that? You think your superiors are going to put up with you transferring here, there and everywhere while you get your life in order?' Lawrence's gaze blazed with fury. 'After everything Cornelia has been through, has survived, she deserves stability. Stability and to know where she belongs and be happy there.'

'And that's exactly what she will have.'

'You're a detective. You said yourself your work is in your blood. How am I supposed to believe—'

'Maybe I am, but I am neither like the perpetrators nor the victims I have dealt with.' Stephen pushed to his feet and stood in front of Culford, their similar heights meaning their eyes locked, Culford's gleaming with a combativeness that Stephen didn't doubt was reflected in his own. 'My future is in my hands, in Cornelia's and the children's. You have my word.'

'To hell with your word.'

'Will you both stop?' Esther glared at both of them, her hand protectively gripping her swollen stomach. 'Having the two men she loves fighting will neither cheer Cornelia nor sort out whatever it was that made her go to London without telling us. Both of you need to think of her and the children now, not yourselves.'

Stephen closed his eyes. She was right. Cornelia and the boys' absence – their safety – was all that mattered. As soon as he saw them again, *if* he saw them again, he would take all three in his arms and vow to be there for them for the rest of his damn life.

The faint sound of a telephone ringing sounded in the hallway and Lawrence Culford rushed from the room.

With his heart pounding, Stephen stared at Esther. Her hazel eyes were wide with anxiety, her face far too pale.

Hurried footsteps stomped along the hallway before Culford emerged in the doorway. 'It's an Inspector King. Cornelia came looking for you at Scotland Yard. She went to London alone, for crying out loud.'

Stephen curled his hand in a fist, tension rippling through him. 'Is she with King now?'

'I have no idea. He asked to speak to you.'

Stephen rushed past him and into the hallway. He picked up the receiver. 'Sir?'

'For the love of God, Gower, why are you in Bath? I sent that young lady of yours to Oxfordshire this afternoon and just called to make sure the pair of you were together. Her sister just told me that Miss Culford never arrived.'

Stephen gripped the phone. 'Her family was adamant she would not go to London without talking to them first. Damnation. I've lost so much time sitting around here doing nothing—'

'Then get yourself to Oxfordshire right away. She had two young lads with her. I know how you feel the woman, but I have to say, you are taking on a hell of a lot of responsibility when you've hardly known her five—'

'I've known her long enough, sir. Thank you.'

Stephen replaced the receiver and stood stock-still, his heart thundering and his jaw tight as he looked at Culford. The wall clock ticked in unison with each beat of Stephen's heart as he stared the other man down. 'This is my fault. I'll take care of it. Take care of them.'

'I'm coming to the manor with you.'

What use would it do to fight Cornelia's brother? She loved Lawrence and her loyalty to him was unshakeable. If Stephen were to make a wrong move now, he could lose her.

'Do not do or say anything silly when you see her.' Esther's voice was firm. 'She's sensible and she's strong. Cornelia will protect the boys with her life.'

'That's what worries me.' Culford growled as he put on his hat. 'We need to go.'

Esther pressed a firm kiss on his cheek before facing Stephen. 'Bring her home to us, Mr Gower.'

He nodded and headed for the door, Culford close behind him, calling for his butler and demanding that his motor car be brought around to the front of the house.

Stephen stared along the street, shifting from one foot to the other as a cold wind whipped at his hair and face. *Are you safe, Cornelia? Please God, let you and the boys be safe.*

A hackney carriage rumbled over the cobblestones towards him and Stephen stepped back from the kerb, his impatience close to breaking as he and Culford waited for Charles and the car.

The carriage slowed down as it neared, and Stephen narrowed his eyes as he slowly drew his hands from his coat pockets. 'It's her.'

The carriage drew to a halt and Francis waved from the window. Happiness mixed with relief, and Stephen smiled.

'Thank God.'

He barely heard Culford's whispered exhalation as he continued to stare at Cornelia through the window, her face in shadow.

Stepping forward, he opened the door, exercising every ounce of self-control so as not to frighten the children with his need to pull their mother into his arms. Alfred and Francis took his offered hands and leapt onto the pavement into their uncle's waiting arms.

Stephen put his hand inside the carriage again and Cornelia slipped her fingers into his. Slowly, she alighted. 'Well, what a nice welcoming committee.'

'You're back.' He brushed a curl from her cheek, stared into her tired blue eyes. 'I thought—'

'That I was so madly in love with you I might be daft enough to take the boys to London to look for you?' Her eyes glinted teasingly, her gaze gentle. 'That I might have finally found my true home, a place of safety and security for my boys and the courage to bid David good riddance? Yes, all of those things are true, but the question is...'

He smiled. 'Yes?'

'Are you mad enough to love me back?' Her eyes shone with what looked to be tears, a hint of insecurity lingering in her gaze. 'Mad enough to accept me and my impetuous whims?'

He lowered his lips to hers and kissed her firmly, pulling her into his arms until he felt the sweet crush of her breasts against his chest. 'I am,' he murmured. 'Will you marry me, Miss Culford?'

She pulled back and frowned, gazing at the sky in feigned contemplation. 'Hmm...' She met his gaze and laughed. 'Yes, I think I will.'

Stephen bent his head and kissed her again, knowing he'd

forever find peace in her arms and she would find security in his.

They were together and, by God, the future was bright.

**

MORE FROM RACHEL BRIMBLE

Another book from Rachel Brimble, *The Shop Girls' Farewell*, is available to order now here:

https://mybook.to/ShopGirls4BackAd

ABOUT THE AUTHOR

Rachel Brimble is the bestselling author of over thirty works of historical romance and saga fiction. The first book in her series, *The Home Front Nurses*, is set in Bath.

Sign up to Rachel Brimble's mailing list for news, competitions and updates on future books.

Visit Rachel's website: www.rachelbrimble.com

Follow Rachel on social media here:

- facebook.com/rachelbrimbleauthor
- x.com/RachelBrimble
- instagram.com/rachelbrimbleauthor
- bookbub.com/profile/rachel-brimble
- tiktok.com/@rachelbrimble

ALSO BY RACHEL BRIMBLE

The Home Front Nurses Series
The Home Front Nurses
Dangerous Days for the Home Front Nurses
Winter Wishes for the Home Front Nurses

The Pennington's Shop Girls Series
A New Start for the Shop Girls
The Shop Girls Get the Vote
A New Start for the Shop Girls
Christmas for the Shop Girls
The Shop Girls' Farewell

Sixpence Stories

Introducing Sixpence Stories!

Discover page-turning historical novels from your favourite authors, meet new friends and be transported back in time.

Join our book club
Facebook group

https://bit.ly/SixpenceGroup

Sign up to our newsletter

https://bit.ly/SixpenceNews

Boldwood

Boldwood Books is an award-winning fiction publishing company seeking out the best stories from around the world.

Find out more at www.boldwoodbooks.com

Join our reader community for brilliant books, competitions and offers!

Follow us
@BoldwoodBooks
@TheBoldBookClub

Sign up to our weekly deals newsletter

https://bit.ly/BoldwoodBNewsletter

Printed in Dunstable, United Kingdom